KU-708-662

Steve Martini, a former trial attorney, has worked as a journalist and capital correspondent in the California State House in Sacramento. He has been engaged in both public and private practice of law. He lives on the US West Coast with his wife and daughter. Steve Martini is an internationally bestselling author, whose highly acclaimed courtroom dramas, *The Judge*, *Undue Influence*, *Prime Witness*, *Compelling Evidence* and *The Simeon Chamber*, are also available from Headline.

Praise for Steve Martini's electrifying bestsellers:

'The best debut, in my opinion, is *Compelling Evidence*'
John Grisham
'Compelling indeed . . . a terrific debut' *Sunday Telegraph*
'Nice insider touches, and a hard-punching climax'
The Times
'Tense and gripping' *Books*
'Martini's plotting proves ingenious' *Publishers Weekly*
'Thoroughly absorbing' *Literary Review*
'The courtroom novel of the year' *Kirkus Reviews*
'A rousing climax . . . a brilliant series of trial scenes . . . the characters are sharply drawn . . . the courtroom psychology is laid out vividly . . . readers will find their fingers glued to the pages' *Publishers Weekly*

Also by Steve Martini

The List

Steve Martini

HEADLINE
FEATURE

First published in Great Britain in 1997
by HEADLINE BOOK PUBLISHING

First published in paperback in 1997
by HEADLINE BOOK PUBLISHING

A HEADLINE FEATURE paperback

20 19 18 -17 16 15 14 13

ISBN 0 7472 4996 2

Typeset by
Letterpart Limited, Reigate, Surrey

Printed in England by Clays Ltd, St Ives plc

HEADLINE BOOK PUBLISHING
A division of Hodder Headline PLC
338 Euston Road
London NW1 3BH

To Leah and Megan

PROLOGUE

He held it to his right eye and searched for the telltale signs of heat, a wavy thermal image of someone hiding in the shadows on deck.

The old starlight scope was a relic from the '60s. He wished he had his night-vision goggles, but he didn't.

Vapors of hot steam coming from a pipe at the side of the ship threw up a ghostly green haze, its own kind of fog. He lowered the scope from his eye to re-orient himself for a moment. Then he picked up the search, starting where he left off, under the hundred-and-eighty-ton derrick that thrust skyward from the fore-deck.

'Do you see her?' His companion hovered over his shoulder.

'Not yet.' He kept looking.

'Maybe she made it inside already?'

'No.' She would have had to cross the open deck, and he would have seen her. 'She's there somewhere.'

He kept looking, scanning along the deck. Occasionally he hit a bright light on the ship and the image through the scope flared out. He would have to squint, pick it up, and start scanning again.

'You think he's on board?'

'Why else would she come here?' The man with the scope didn't want to talk. It made the instrument move in his hands, turning his search into a maze of jittery phosphorous lines.

'Let's just get her and go.'

'It's not that easy.'

'You think he's armed?'

'I don't know.' He doubted if the man would be armed. He couldn't have been expecting them. Still, if he was armed, they would deal with it. 'What's that?'

'What?'

'There.' He stopped scanning and focused in on a sliver of luminous green, like a fingernail moon, sticking out from the edge of a canvas tarpaulin just aft of the derrick.

Abby Chandlis was exhausted. The instinct for survival was strong, but it was not boundless. She was tired, and tired people make mistakes. She had made one at the airport, and they had seen her. Abby was running for her life.

She was pressed against the cold steel plates on the main deck, soaked through from the moisture of the fog and her own perspiration, hiding in the shadows created by the ship's heavy equipment. Her eyes searched the dock for movement.

Out there, somewhere among the pallets and giant steel containers, she knew they were waiting, searching for movement, listening for sounds. It was no delusion, she had seen them. Worse, they had seen her.

She moved just a few feet, slowly, crouching, hands in front of her, feeling along the steel deck until she was behind a stack of webbed life rafts covered by a canvas tarp. To move beyond this point would put her out on the open deck in clear view where they couldn't miss her. Sooner or later she knew she would have to chance it. She had to reach mid-ship and the superstructure that led inside.

Morgan was here on this ship. She had to find him. She had to warn him. She knew that they would kill him, just as they'd tried to kill her. Only now without intending it, she had led them to him.

Her hope lay in the fact that Morgan knew ships. He would know his way around this one, perhaps a quick way off, some avenue of escape they wouldn't be able to observe. Abby was sure of it. Together they would lose the men on the dock. As soon as they delivered the documents, it would be over. The two men would have nothing to gain by killing them. Once the information in the documents was known, the contracts and the copyright, it would all be over. The documents were what they wanted, their entire purpose in killing Morgan. Without realizing it, Abby had made him a target.

'Got her.' He zeroed in with the scope.

'You sure?'

'Yeah.' He pointed to the gangway stairs that led from the dock up onto the forward deck. He looked up at the bridge to see if there was anyone in the wing. He checked it with the scope quickly. It was clear. 'Let's move.'

They scampered down the ladder. He put the scope in his pocket and followed the other man, behind a line of steel containers. He felt in the back of his pants, the checkered handle of a nine-millimeter Beretta.

There was a line of cargo carefully stacked, two containers high beneath the huge dock crane, waiting for the stevedores in the morning to be loaded on another ship. The cargo was conveniently between themselves and the *Cuesta Verde*. If they stayed behind it, Abby would never see them. They would be on her before she could make a sound. Surprise was critical.

Silently they moved to the corner of the last container. From there it was a hundred-foot dash to the base of the stairs, all of it in the open. For the first fifty he estimated she could see them from the deck, that is if she was looking in the right direction. After that they would be too close to the side of the ship to be seen. From there it would be easy; up the stairs and slip in behind her.

'You first,' the other man looked at him and whispered.

This was his job and he knew it, so he didn't argue. Instead, he slipped off his shoes. Even rubber soles made noise on asphalt. He looped the laces together in a single knot and hung them over his shoulder. His companion did the same. Then without hesitating, he darted out from behind the containers, his heart pounding. If she saw him or heard him, she would take off. There were a million places to hide on a ship.

He made it soundlessly to the stairs, then stopped and listened. He heard nothing except the monotonous internal rumblings of the ship at rest, a motor here, and a generator there, distant rhythmic sounds unbroken by the patter of feet on the deck overhead. He looked back, then signaled for his companion to follow.

Twelve seconds later they were huddled together at the base of the stairs. Now they didn't talk. He went first, two steps at a time up the metal staircase, gripping the railing as he went, carefully so as not to rattle the metal scaffolding supporting the stairs.

He was just ten steps from the top, the gate in the

ship's gunnel, when he heard the clatter behind him, turned and looked. It hit two more times on the metal stairs before it fell with a thud to the dock below. The knot on his companion's shoes had come loose. The man was juggling the other shoe and finally managed to catch it.

She had been lost somewhere in the past when the noise brought her back to reality. She whirled and looked at the stairs behind her.

It could have been nothing, the creaking of the ship against the dock, but Abby didn't wait to investigate. In her heightened state she bolted, instincts taking hold, running headlong toward the ship's looming superstructure, her shoes echoing on the iron deck. She raced into the open companionway along the side of the ship and tried the first door she came to. It was locked. She tried pulling on the metal latch handles. She couldn't move them, frozen solid.

Now she heard footsteps behind her, muted heavy heelfalls on the iron deck, and they were coming closer.

She ran on, down the companionway. The next door was open, a dim corridor illuminated only by a single overhead bulb, underpowered. She stepped over the threshold and reached behind her to pull the door closed. It didn't move.

The footfalls came closer. Abby stepped outside and looked behind the door; a large brass hook fitted through a welded eye held the door open against the steel wall. She unhooked it, and as she did, she turned and saw them, two silhouettes against the glare of lights from the dock coming toward her, running full speed into the companionway.

Abby stepped over the threshold pulling the door

closed behind her. She fumbled with the metal latch handles on the watertight door and finally managed to close one of them, then another until she had all four shut. The problem was they could open them just as easily from the outside.

She held two of them closed in the down position at the top of the door by hanging on them with the weight of her body, then watched in horror as they opened the bottom two and pulled on the door. Three hundred pounds of iron, it flexed only slightly as long as she held the two latches closed. She felt them pull and fight to turn the upper latches.

Her strength ebbing, running on adrenaline, her arms ached. She couldn't hold much longer and she knew it. She turned her head to the side and rested it against the cold steel. Looking through blood-shot eyes she wondered what it would feel like to die. With this thought in her mind, her eyes focused on an object in the corner, a push broom, its long metal handle propped against the wall. Her feet dangling off the floor as she hung on the latches, she tried to hook the broom with her foot but couldn't.

They fought with the door latches, lifting her halfway to an open position before gravity set in and they let go. She dropped with a jarring thud, all of her weight hanging on her arms. The latches settled back into a full locked position as they concentrated their energies pulling on the door.

This gave her an instant of reprieve. She released her grip on one of the latches and instantly they turned it. The door was held shut by a single latch, and that was beginning to turn now that the weight of her body had been removed. It was now her strength against theirs, a losing battle having given up the leverage of gravity.

She reached for the broom, grabbed it with her free hand. Then turning it, lifted the broom head toward the ceiling, wedging the handle between the steel latch and the door, jamming it until it stuck. The latch was now held closed by the broom handle.

They pulled from the outside and the handle flexed but held. Slowly, Abby stepped away, her gaze glued to the latch.

They fought with it. She could hear them swearing, a string of expletives on the other side of the steel door. But it held.

She turned and ran down the dark corridor not knowing where she was going.

He fought with the handle. Something had jammed it.

'Let's find another way in.' They headed down the companionway. Two more doors were locked, their latches bolted on the inside. They came to a lighted porthole and could hear voices on the other side. He peered through near the bottom of the thick glass ellipse and saw two men talking in a small cabin. The one with his back to him was wearing oil-spattered coveralls, a crew member from the engine room, he guessed.

They slid under the porthole and kept going.

Halfway down the superstructure there was an alley that traversed the center of the ship from starboard to port on the main deck: broadway. He knew the term from his time on shipboard in the Marines. He watched from outside for several seconds before entering. This would be a main thoroughfare on the ship. The crew would use it regularly to move from one side to the other. Tied to the dock, with a skeleton crew, this passage way was now dark and abandoned. They entered and ran quickly, emerging seconds later on the port side of the ship. They retraced their steps toward the bow and seconds later found an open door. The two men disappeared inside.

The first explosion sent Abby to her knees in the dark passage way. A bright flash of fire lit up the corridor, and smoke began to billow from somewhere below decks. Klaxons and alarms sounded. She got to her feet, just as the second blast bounced her off of one of the steel walls and sent a stabbing pain through her shoulder. The shock wave set her ears ringing and finally threw her to the floor like a rag doll. She lay there stunned, her senses paralyzed, mind numbed, as heat from the metal deck embraced her in the folds of its comforting warmth.

In Abby's mind, images danced like a time-lapsed film. She hovered in the dim shadows of consciousness, shaking and exhausted, wondering if this was death, and searching in her mind to remember when it was, the precise moment that this obsession to surrender her identity had taken hold, and what had possessed her to do it.

CHAPTER
ONE

A bby Chandlis was approaching her middle years
and suffered the anxiety of nearly every woman –
that she would not age gracefully.

This morning the image in the mirror did nothing to
diminish this fear. Her hair looked like something left in
the aftermath of a tornado, spikes in every direction.
Even with the fine features of her face, a few lines had
begun to creep under her eyes. She was a candle burning at both ends.

She stood five-six, slender, and approached mid-life
with the velocity of an earth-bound meteor, sharing a
sense of its common destiny. Abby was beginning to feel
like a burnt offering in a culture where youth is the state
religion.

On top of it all, this morning she was late for work. By
the muted light of the bedside lamp, Abby groped in her
dark closet for something to throw on. She grabbed the
first thing that felt warm and long. She had no court
calls today, just a pile of paper on her desk.

She flung the flowing peasant dress over her head
and slipped the Birkenstocks on over a thick pair of red
cotton socks. It wasn't stylish, but it kept out the chill of

9

the cold winter winds of western Washington – short days and long dark nights.

It took her nearly forty minutes to traverse the seven miles between home and work during rush hour. She huddled in her office on the seventeenth floor, a sky-scraper pitched on a hill over Elliot Bay. She had a partial view of the Seattle skyline to the south, and if she leaned with her face close to the glass she could see the edge of the Space Needle in the distance.

She was pushing papers on her desk when the com-line rang.

'Yes.'

'A woman out here to see you.'

'I left a message not to be disturbed.'

'She's very insistent. Something about a book.'

Suddenly Abby felt the blood drain from her head. Who would come to her here at her office?

'Who is it?'

'I didn't get a name. You want me to ask?'

Abby thought for a moment. 'No. Give me two minutes, then send her back.' Abby didn't need them talking about the book at the firm. She glanced down and realized that she wasn't dressed for this.

She grabbed the small mirror and lipstick from the second drawer of her desk.

A few seconds later there was a light rap on the door and it opened. Abby ditched the lipstick and mirror.

'Ms Chandlis?' The female voice that inquired was not familiar, but still it raised tiny hairs on the nape of Abby's neck.

'Yes.'

The woman was tall, well dressed, and carried an expensive leather briefcase. She made her way across the office and held out her hand. 'I'm Carla Owens. You spoke with my office last week.'

Abby's jaw went slack. She stood there staring at the woman with a vacant expression. It took her a moment before she collected herself.

'Oh yeah. Sure.' She smiled brightly as a wave of apprehension washed over her. Then absently she wiped her hands on the skirt of her long peasant dress and reached out to take the other woman's hand.

'Can we talk here or is there somewhere else?' said Owens.

'This is fine. Please. Sit down.' Abby pointed to one of the client chairs.

As Owens adjusted herself in the chair, Abby fidgeted with her appearance. The premature graying wisps at her temple, and the long shapeless dress over Birkenstocks, offered the picture of some earth mother off the prairie. Abby smoothed her hair in hopes that somehow this might improve the image. She wished that perhaps she'd had a court call so she'd dressed better.

'You probably think I'm foolish to have come all this way especially after the call from my office?'

Abby said nothing but gave a tilt of the head, an indication that the thought had crossed her mind.

In her most frenzied fantasies Abby had never imagined that Owens would show up here. Five days ago her office had called Abby's house looking for Gable Cooper. Abby had told them that he was out of town and that she would have him call as soon as he returned. She figured she had bought some time, at least enough to find Cooper. Now what she had set in motion was suddenly careening out of control, and for Abby there was no way back.

Carla Owens was one of the most powerful literary agents in New York. She performed marketing magic for the written word. The hottest book deals on earth passed through her fingers. She represented presidents, people who wrote romances, and more recently the pope, of whom it was said it was easier to obtain an audience with than with Carla herself.

Protruding from the top of Owens's briefcase was a package that Abby recognized, a large FedEx envelope that had traveled many miles and showed the wear.

'Actually I was traveling in the area. So I thought I'd stop in and say hello.'

'Where are you headed?' asked Abby.

'Oh, just up from L.A., on some business. On my way back to New York.'

The woman's idea of traveling in the area was a triangle that spanned the country. She was in hot pursuit of Cooper and Abby knew it.

'I just thought I'd take a chance and drop in,' said Owens. She looked around as if she was half expecting to see some sign of the man.

'I didn't know you were a lawyer,' said Owens.

'Hmm. I guess I forgot to mention it.'

'Is Mr Cooper a client?'

'Just a friend.'

This seemed to please her.

'Is he in town?'

'No.'

This did not.

'I told you on the phone he's traveling.'

'I took the chance that he might be back by now.'

'I'm sorry you went out of your way,' said Abby. 'I told your office he would call.'

Owens offered a deep sigh as if her trip was for naught, spread her elbows on the desk, and smiled at Abby.

'How about some coffee?' said Abby. 'The least I can offer you after coming all this way.'

'Sure.'

Abby went outside and got two cups of coffee. When she came back in Owens had removed the large package from her briefcase and had it on the desk in front of her, still in the bright red and blue envelope that Abby had used to send it off nearly two weeks before.

'It's magic,' said Owens. She looked up at Abby.

'There's something absolutely beguiling about a man who can write in such a seductive voice. And the way he gets inside the female mind,' said Owens. She rolled her eyes. 'It's very important that I talk to him. The sooner the better.'

Owens wasn't exactly sure how much to tell this woman. As little as possible was the general rule. The agent's credo.

'I take it Mr Cooper asked you to send the manuscript to me?'

Abby swallowed hard. In her mind this was the literary equivalent of war, and in every war truth was the first victim. 'Right,' said Abby.

'If you don't represent him, do you mind my asking what you do?'

'Some typing. A little editing. Sometimes we talk about ideas.'

Owens was fishing. She was trying to find out if Abby was someone important in Gable Cooper's life. If she wasn't his lawyer, where did she fit?

She measured the woman. Abby was to the late side of thirty, but not unattractive. There was a possibility for beauty, but she had obviously taken no pains with her appearance. Owens was forming a picture in her mind. A little editing, the occasional back rub, a long night of

13

work that might turn into an indolent morning of slumber. It was possible that they were lovers.

'Then you collaborate with him?'

'I don't know if I'd go so far as to say that.'

Owens offered a smile that made evident what she was thinking.

'Let's just say we're friends. We spend time together. When he leaves he tells me where he's going, and he usually comes back.'

'I see.' Suddenly Carla's face was a curling smile. Abby was someone to contend with. Perhaps the trip wasn't wasted after all. If she couldn't bend Cooper's ear, Abby was the next best thing.

The two women huddled over their cups taking stock of each other.

'Do you know where Mr Cooper is?' Maybe Owens could run him down herself.

'Last I heard Mexico.'

'Big area.'

'Somewhere down by Cancun.'

That was smaller. Should she try for the name of a town? Owens wasn't sure. 'Is he at a resort?'

'No. Gable hates those places. People around pools all baking on cement. He's into remote areas. He's out in the Yucatan someplace. Beating the weeds.' This clearly put him out of touch.

Owens took a sip of coffee and considered the next question.

'What's he doing down there?'

'Gathering color for the next book.'

'He has another in the works?'

Abby nodded.

'Like this one?' Owens touched the package on the table in front of her as if it possessed healing properties.

14

Abby nodded again.

'It's vital that I talk to him,' said Owens. 'Could we try to reach him? Maybe tonight? I'd be happy to hold over. Pay for the call.'

Abby shook her head. 'No. No. That would be a waste of time. It'll take a number of phone calls to run him down. If he's where I think he is, there's no phone in the area. Besides, when he's working, he doesn't like to be disturbed.'

'Believe me,' said Owens, 'when he hears what I have to say he'll want to be disturbed.'

Abby looked at the woman over her coffee mug.

'Is there a publisher interested in his manuscript?' The lawyer bearing down.

'You might say that. But the details I have to give to Mr Cooper directly.'

'I see.' Abby had blown it, deviated from her planned cover story. Owens had surprised her by showing up here in her office. If Abby represented Cooper as a lawyer, she could have demanded answers. Now Owens had smoked out of her that they had no legal relationship. It was as if Abby were being denied a key to her own safe deposit box. She would have to produce Gable Cooper before she could find out what was in it.

'Does he do this often?' asked Owens.

Abby gave her a questioning look.

'Mr Cooper. Does he disappear like this very often?'

'Sometimes.'

'How long is he usually gone?'

'Depends. Sometimes a month, sometimes more.'

Owens said something under her breath that sounded a lot like 'shit.'

'Somebody must be able to get in touch with him.' Owens should have been the lawyer. Every answer gave birth to another question. 'What if there was an emergency? Doesn't he have family?'

Abby raised her eyes in thought. Shrugged her shoulders. 'I think there's a sister somewhere down in California, but Gable never talks about her much.' If Abby had a special gift, it was the ability to create.

'Do you have her name or number?'

Abby shook her head.

'You think her name might be on his Rollodex.' She was now suggesting prying into Cooper's private places.

'Gable keeps all his notes, including phone numbers, on scraps of paper in his pockets. Organization is not his middle name.'

Owens seemed to accept this without question.

'Is *that* real?' she asked.

'What?'

'His name?'

Abby considered for a moment, then fessed up. 'It's a pen name.' She shrugged. 'He likes classic movies. The golden age. His two favorite actors.' She offered an expression that said, 'Childish, but what can I say?'

'I thought so. What's his real name?'

'Oh no.' Abby started to shake her head, first gently and then with more conviction. 'I can't tell you that. Not until after I talk to him. I know he would be very angry if I did.'

Owens had checked *Books in Print* and a number of other sources to see if the name Gable Cooper showed up as authoring other works. It didn't.

Abby's reluctance to tell her his name fed a theory that Owens had been nurturing, a reason why the author might not want his true name to be known. If the theory was correct, the manuscript was worth vastly more than any of them figured.

'Tell me a little about him?' Owens played for time and information, a slip of the tongue.

'What's to tell?'

'How old is he? Is he good-looking?'

Though Owens didn't notice, Abby's eyes for a fleeting instant drew a dark, cold bead. The agent had wandered onto dangerous ground. Abby now knew with certainty that she had done the right thing.

'Is that important?'

'Oh, don't get me wrong. The book is wonderful. I'm sure we can find an enthusiastic publisher.'

'But if Gable is good-looking it helps?' said Abby.

Owens's face was a million expressions, all of them adding up to the word 'yes.'

'For television, and protein ads, it's a consideration. It helps,' she said. 'Please don't misunderstand, we're interested in talent, and the book's a great read . . .'

'But a little beefcake doesn't hurt.' Abby said this in a frank fashion, smiling, woman-to-woman. She might dress like a peasant, but she wasn't one.

Owens gave her a face of concession, winked at her over the coffee mug, and they both laughed. The ridges in Abby's cheeks as she did this were hard as steel.

'You know I'm not exactly sure how old he is. It's not something he talks about. We've had a couple of birthday parties for him, but he'll never tell us how many candles.'

'Sounds like a state secret,' said Owens.

'Chalk it up to vanity,' said Abby.

'What do you think, fifty?' Owens dipped her toe in this pool of uncertainty hoping she wouldn't have to go deeper.

'No. No. Late thirties, early forties tops.'

Relief blossomed on the agent's face.

'Has he ever been married?' She was nibbling around the edges.

'Twice.' This would mean that at least two women thought he was enough of a catch to go after.

'Good-looking?' Finally she stepped in it.

'Very. In fact, he's done a little modeling, years ago,' said Abby.

Owens's eyes grew like two oval saucers. 'Any pictures?'

Without thinking, Abby had dug herself another hole.

'I'm sure there are some. Unfortunately, I don't have them. I'm sure as soon as he gets back he'll be happy to send them to you.'

Owens probed for a little more description.

'Dark. About six feet,' said Abby.

'Sounds like a Ken doll,' said Owens.

'Ken dolls don't look dangerous,' said Abby.

'Really?'

'And very well spoken. Articulate,' said Abby.

'Speaks as he writes?' says Owens.

'You could say that.'

A growing satisfaction spread across the agent's face. The trip was not in vain after all.

'I can't wait to see the real item,' said Owens.

'In the flesh, so to speak,' said Abby.

'So to speak.'

Both women laughed. Abby a little louder this time.

By now, Owens was running up a dead end. No Cooper, and no way to get in touch with him, except through this woman who wasn't telling her much.

'Abby. Can I call you Abby?' Owens suddenly had one hand across the desk on top of Abby's as if to impress upon her the significance of the moment.

'I assume that you know a little about my agency? I mean, being a lawyer and all, you checked us out?'

In fact, Abby knew a lot – everything she could find on the Internet. She knew, for example, that the agency had ties with one of the institutional talent shops in Hollywood, which in turn had under contract some of the largest box-office stars in film. Mass entertainment had become a vast communal meal served up in package deals by agencies that controlled every aspect of the business. If you could get your nose under that tent, you could draw up a chair and sit at the table. The manuscript had not landed at Owens and Associates by accident.

'I know a little,' she lied.

'We're very selective. We take only a very few clients. I usually have fewer than a dozen. All very big.' She dropped some names, authors who if they sneezed left the entire publishing industry with a cold.

'Ordinarily we don't take people unless they already have a proven track record. At least three or four major bestsellers to their credit.'

'That must be very nice for you,' said Abby.

Owens gave her a smile. The two women were talking the same language.

'Because of our contacts, the influence of my agency, we are usually able to take these authors to that next higher level.' What Owens meant was into the stratosphere where books sales and movie deals grew by geometric progression.

'What I'm saying is that based upon what I've read –' Owens tapped the package on the table – 'we might be able to leverage your friend into an extremely favorable position.' Owens arched an eyebrow, waiting for a reply.

'I see.' Abby sat sipping her coffee contemplating the

good fortune of her friend, leverage being what it is in life. Owens fished in her briefcase for something.

'I'm going to be back in my office tomorrow, in New York.' Then she reached across the table and pressed several business cards into Abby's hand as if she should paper the walls of her office with these lest she forget the agent's number.

'My phone number.' She pointed to it on one of the cards.

'Do you think you might be able to find Mr Cooper for me quickly? Time is of the essence. There are opportunities being offered, and if we don't act quickly they may be gone. Do you understand?'

What Owens was worried about were her opportunities, the stream of sharks, other agents, who would swim in if word got out that Cooper was unrepresented.

'I can try,' said Abby.

'Do better than that. You've got to find him. It's important. To his career. To his life. From this moment on we're a team, Abby. You and I. You find him, and I'll represent him.'

Rah, thought Abby. Am I in for a commission? If Owens had an article of Cooper's old clothing, she would have rubbed it under Abby's nose at this moment.

'Oh, he'll come back,' said Abby.

'Yes, but will it be in time?' said Owens.

'Maybe if you told me what this was about? How long do I have?'

'Every moment is important. I can't tell you any more than that. But believe me, it's the biggest deal of his life. I hope you understand.'

Having fanned anxiety, Owens buckled up her briefcase and slipped out of the chair. 'It is important. You know that much.' She shook Abby's hand and headed for the door. When she reached it she turned and waved, a big glossy smile.

'Your Mr Cooper sounds fascinating. I can't wait to meet him.' With that she was out the door, closing it behind her so that she didn't hear Abby's last comment.

'Sweetheart, that makes two of us.'

CHAPTER
TWO

Jack stood in front of the mirror in the bathroom off his study scratching the little cleft on his chin and looking at the dark stubble. Something in the image troubled him. A single wisp of gray hair had slipped out from the sea of dark brown at one temple. At his age he could have a mass of these. But Jack led a charmed life in all ways but one, the only one that seemed to matter to him at the moment.

He was bare to the waist, trim and athletic, with a tan that he'd added to on a five-day trip to the Bahamas, an excursion to kill the frustration and pain of continued failure. A hot beach and the warmth of the sun always gave Jack the lift he needed in low moments. And the young girls in thong bikinis with tans to match didn't hurt.

But now he was back at Coffin Point and the realities of life, which at this moment in his mind were dismal.

He plucked the gray hair from his temple and washed it down the sink, put his body on the scale and weighed it. Lost three pounds. He always did in the tropics. Life was not fair, and Jack was on the winning side more than he had a right to be. He had the wild consolation that if he went to hell, a prospect that given his diversions in life was not entirely improbable, even in that hot place he could debauch himself, attract all the best looking women, and still lose weight.

He checked the luminous dial of his diving watch. Seven-thirty. He shaved, combed his hair, pulled a white polo shirt on over his head, and wandered in front of the dormered windows of his study. Beyond the yard and the marshes, a twin-masted ketch plied its way through the winding channels using its engine to buck the tide as it motored in the direction of Hilton Head.

He looked at the yard and the peeling white picket fence that separated it from the marsh. The old plantation house had seen better days. Jack had the money for repairs but not the inclination.

He walked to the desk and for a long moment simply stared down at the surface. There in the center on top of the leather-edged blotter was the letter with its envelope, ragged edge torn open across the top. It had arrived yesterday morning, the fifth such letter in two months.

He picked it up and read the words one more time, only five lines long, then folded it neatly and slipped it back into the envelope, headed out the door and down the stairs.

In the hall he paused long enough to open the center drawer of an antique secretary, reached inside and removed the nine-millimeter Beretta. He fished in the back of the drawer and found the loaded clip heavy with fifteen rounds. He slammed the clip into the handle and tucked the pistol into the belt of his pants at the small of his back. Now he moved quickly without hesitation down the hall, through the kitchen, and out the back door to the yard.

Salt air and sea breezes hit his nostrils as he paced across the yard, a hundred feet, past the brick patio with its chairs and umbrella-covered table; another fifty feet to the picket fence where he stopped, nearly in a daze. A bead of sweat trickled from the hair at the nape of his neck down his shirt. He looked at the boat in the distance, and for several moments stood alone, still, his hands resting on the pickets of the fence, his mind absorbed in thought. Then almost absently he slipped the envelope with its letter into the crack formed by the fence's top railing and one of the pickets. Trapped in this crack, the envelope's loose left end in the gap between pickets fluttered in the breeze. Jack looked at it in a trance, and slowly moved away as if he were making one final attempt to distance himself from the letter's bad news.

At the patio, he reached behind his back, removed the pistol, and laid it on the table. Then he slumped into one of the chairs and stared off into nothingness. He sat there still and silent for more than five minutes.

Finally he reached for the gun, kicked off the safety with his thumb so that the red dots appeared at each side. He pulled the slide back and let it go, slamming a round into the firing chamber. Carefully he held the muzzle up close to his mouth, until he could easily reach out with the tip of his tongue to flick the white dot on the front site.

In a flash he leveled the muzzle and pulled off five quick rounds. The roar of gunfire sent birds billowing into the air from the trees. He realigned the sights and fired ten more shots, emptying the clip.

Fifty feet away, little punched-out pieces of paper fluttered to the ground where they joined a small but growing pile – the fractured trademarks and names of a dozen book publishers. With rejection letters Jack always concentrated his fire on the company logo in the left-hand corner.

CHAPTER
THREE

'You have a minute?' Abby poked her head inside his office door.

Morgan Spencer sat behind a large oak desk, its surface swept clean. He dropped the document he was reading, lifted his glasses, and smiled.

'Come on in and shut the door.' He reached into his desk drawer and pulled out a large bundle of paper held together by a rubber band.

'As they say in the trade, you owe me a night's sleep.'

'What did you think?'

'Good stuff.'

Spencer was one of Abby's few sounding boards. He couldn't write, but he had a good ear.

'Who is this guy Cooper, anyway?'

'That's what I wanted to talk to you about.'

Morgan had a sparkle in his eye and a quick word for every circumstance. He loved Irish limericks and any film featuring Peter O'Toole. In fact, there was something in the aspect of the man that reminded Abby of the actor in an earlier day. He was eight years older than Abby but a generation wiser. He was Abby's Father confessor, the uncle she never had.

They had worked together on several cases. In the increasingly competitive atmosphere of the office, he had taken her under his wing and offered her protection from the slings and arrows of the corporate climbers. The problem was that of late, Morgan's ability to protect anyone, including himself, was beginning to fade. The firm had been caught up in the disease of corporate downsizing.

She noticed that he was looking at a firm management document known as 'The Book.' In essence, it was a partnership agreement that governed the internal workings of the firm.

'What's up?'

'Just had a battle with Cutler.'

Lewis Cutler was African American, the firm's new managing partner installed by a group of young turks hell-bent on control and increasing their own profit margin. He had gotten the nod from the management consultants and in turn been elected by the partners in order to deal with the secretaries and clerks, many of whom were minority. It made it harder for these laid-off employees to argue they had been dealt the race card from the bottom of the deck. 'The twit wants to cut my bonus,' said Spencer. 'Can you believe it? Twenty years they wanna treat me like an associate. The policy's carved in stone. Right here.' He pointed to the place on the page. 'A pro rata share. That's what it says, in the Queen's English.'

'Actually it's Latin, Morgan.'

'What I hate about lawyers. Always want to get technical.'

The power group in their late thirties had all come out of a single law school in Washington State. In business they acted like a social fraternity, tight and exclusionary.

28

There was nothing benign about it.

Like Abby, Spencer had gone to school out of state. Though he had been in the firm for more than twenty years, the guys he'd practiced with had all retired or left the firm, and the economics of law practice had changed. His speciality, honed over two decades, was Admiralty, and it had fallen on hard times.

'I'll be damned if I'm gonna let 'em get away with it. I've got a surprise for that bastard.' He was talking about Cutler. 'He just doesn't know it yet.'

Spencer didn't have much of a temper, or if he did he concealed it well. This was as angry as she had seen him, a little red in the face and thumping the surface of the desk with a purposeful finger. He was the kind who was slick and quiet. Abby had never gotten cross-wise with him so she'd never felt his sting, though she'd seen it demonstrated in court on a few occasions. It wasn't until Morgan enveloped you with his affable smile that you felt the point of his sword.

'Maybe I should come back later?' said Abby.

'No. No. What is it?'

'You've got problems of your own.'

'Yeah, but yours are always smaller. God, you're looking good today. Why don't you move in with me and I'll make an honest woman out of you?' Morgan was kidding but only partly.

She smiled, and he twinkled. It was the one problem with their relationship. Morgan always hoped for more than friendship. Abby didn't.

Early on she had taken herself out of the running for a partnership in the firm. In college she had studied what she loved – literature – but everybody she knew told her that writing words didn't pay. In a job market racked by increasing uncertainty, Abby made a deal with the devil and went to law school. Now she was paying the price.

She had grown to hate the practice of law. The best lawyers loved a good fight. The constant rancor with opposing counsel, judges, and at times one's own clients was the stuff to spike adrenaline in a good trial lawyer. For Abby it only produced ulcers.

Her only reprieve came at night when she pursued her dream with a missionary's zeal. Toward that end she worked for more than eight years and penned three novels. They were good stories with a literary edge. She won an award with one of them. Published by a small company in New York, they garnered solid reviews and kudos from her editor. But without marketing or promotion they suffered the fate of the vast bulk of general fiction in this country. They died on the shelves.

When lawyers became hot in fiction, all her friends told her to pen a legal thriller. They were the same friends who told her to go to law school. Abby ignored them. Writing was her own way of running from the law.

'You took that seminar last year on intellectual property and entertainment law?' she asked.

'Down at USC,' he nodded. 'They give me the exotic locales. Cutler gets four days on Taxation in Belize, and comes back on the "S.S. Lust." I get two days in L.A.'

'Would you like a client?'

'Sure.' He looked at her over his shoulder, still searching for the materials. 'I have them here someplace.' He swung around in his chair and started pawing through the drawers of the credenza behind him. 'The syllabus and some books, if I can find 'em. What do you need?'

'A registration of copyright. I've never done one.'

'Oh hell, I can do that.'

'Have you done one before?'

'Simple form,' he said. 'I think I even have one in the materials. Who's it for?'

'Me.'

He swung around and looked at her from under arched eyebrows. 'Writing again?'

She nodded.

'Well, good for you.' He went back to the credenza. 'I wish I had the gift.' He was talking about writing. 'You write lies and they pay you. All of mine are in the courtroom, verbal, and they call it perjury.'

'They aren't lies. It's called fiction, Morgan.'

'Right.'

A year ago, Abby's publisher was bought out by a larger company. In the shuffle of reorganization, they fired her editor and rejected her next manuscript, offering a number of vague reasons, all of which added up to a single fact – in the publishing business Abby had become used merchandise, a name with a failed track record. In today's publishing world it was better to be a virgin author, someone who had never seen print, than to have committed the mortal sin: producing a book that didn't make its way onto the bestsellers list. The list was everything. It was all that mattered. The message was clear. What Abby needed was to reinvent herself.

Her former agent, a small-time operator who worked alone from a brownstone in Manhattan, took Abby's manuscript to two other publishers. One checked her record of sales and passed. The other came back with an astonishing request – before they decided whether to publish they wanted to see a photograph of the author.

Abby was dumbfounded. The agent explained that this was becoming increasingly common. Publishers, if they were going to put money behind a book, wanted to know if the author could carry their load on the television talk show circuit if the book caught on, whether their likeness could be used to advantage in print ads. Or, thought Abby, whether it might be a detriment on the dustcover.

Abby didn't like it. More than offended, however, she was scared.

Faced with no alternative, she finally submitted. A week later, after the photograph was sent, her manuscript was rejected. Of course she could not be certain of the reason, whether it was her work or her looks, but for a woman approaching middle years, personal insecurities weighed heavily, and in Abby's mind, she knew.

'At least one of us is doing something we enjoy,' said Morgan.

'You enjoy the practice. You complain a lot, but you enjoy it,' she told him.

'I'd enjoy it more if somebody would nudge a few of these supercilious pricks out of some windows.' He was talking about Cutler and his entourage.

While Morgan fumbled in the drawer, Abby looked about the office. In the corner stood a large object, a hunk of brass the size of a lectern with a handle and gage. It was an engine room telegraph. It had come off an old ship salvaged by one of Morgan's clients, now no longer in business. Even the position of the telegraph's handle said volumes about Morgan and his career. It was set at 'Stop.'

'I thought your publisher usually did the copyright?'

'I don't have one yet.'

'Why don't you wait until you sell it? Let them deal with it.'

'It's a little more complicated than that. I'm doing this one under a pseudonym, a pen name,' said Abby.

'Hmm?' Morgan swiveled around in his chair and looked at her.

'Gable Cooper,' she said.

'You wrote this?'

'Don't act so surprised. I *can* write.'

'No. No. That's not what I meant. It's just I would never have guessed. Your other books were so different.'

'You mean no action. Not much plot,' she said.

'Yeah. Well, that's part of it,' said Morgan. 'But this one. It grabs you by the gut and keeps you turning pages. I'm not kidding. I was up all night two nights running. Cutler owes you his life. If I wasn't so tired I'da killed the son of a bitch during our meeting this morning.'

She laughed.

Over time, Abby's agent had drifted away, no longer returning her calls. The process made a lasting impression. There had always been something secure about writing. She had the talent. Her age and how she looked didn't matter. There was a certain comfort in the knowledge that you could write until you were old and frail, and all that mattered was the quality of your thoughts strung together in words and sentences. Now all of that had been swept away.

But Abby was no quitter. She was angry and made no pretense. In the fickle business of fiction she was tenacious, and in her own way a risk taker. She had been all of her life. It was something that her father, now deceased, had instilled in her at a young age, a fierce independence, and a willingness to take a chance. It was what kept her writing, engaged in a long-shot venture on those cold dark nights – and what caused her to do the crazy thing she was now doing.

'Why not just do it under your name?' said Morgan.

'I have my reasons.'

'And they are . . .?' He looked at her.

'*My* reasons.'

He shook his head.

Abby was wondering if she'd come to the right place for help. A stranger might have asked fewer questions.

'The publisher will still do a copyright.'

'I know they will. But I want a separate one, in my own name.'

He studied her for a moment.

'I want you to do it off the books.' Abby meant that there would be no record of the services performed on the firm's billing records. 'I'll pay you.'

'Don't be silly.' He fumbled in the files for a second, looking for the materials again. Then he looked up at her. 'No, actually you can pay me, but not with money. I want to know why you're doing it? Using a pen name?'

'Because I don't want anyone to be able to find out that I wrote it.'

'It's a fine piece of work,' said Morgan.

'It's a shamelessly commercial manuscript, written in a shamelessly commercial fashion,' said Abby. 'I know what it is.'

'You talk like it's a bastard child,' said Morgan. 'It may not be fine art, but I couldn't put it down. You shouldn't be ashamed.'

'I'm not ashamed. I have my reasons. Can we leave it at that?'

'Only if you want to stiff me on the fee.'

Abby was a thousand pained expressions. 'Alright. I'll tell you. But it can't go any further than this room. Do you promise?'

'Lawyer-client,' said Morgan. 'All the privileges.'

'Fine. I don't intend to identify myself as the author to

anyone. To the agent, the publisher, or anyone else. I'm convinced the book will do better without me.'

'Being pretty hard on yourself,' said Morgan.

'I'm not. They are.' The *they* in this sentence were the giant publishers in New York. 'If my name's on it they won't buy it. They certainly won't push it. And I want the book to have a chance.'

'At some point you're gonna have to meet with them. Don't they get a picture for the cover?'

'Yes.'

'What are you gonna do then?'

'I'm gonna give them someone else's. A man's photograph,' said Abby.

Morgan sat there shaking his head. He couldn't believe what he was hearing. 'You're a good-looking woman.'

'I'm almost forty. Besides a man, a good-looking man, is more likely to catch their attention.'

'Who?' said Morgan.

'I haven't found him yet.'

'You're out of your mind. Please tell me you haven't done anything about this yet? I mean, you haven't talked to a publisher?'

'Just an agent. But I think she has a publisher lined up.'

'What did you tell him?'

'It's a her. And I told her that Gable Cooper was out of town. On business. I'm busy locating him now.'

'And she believed you?'

'I told her he has dangerous looks. She wants the book. She wants Gable Cooper. She wants the whole package. And I'm going to deliver it.'

Spencer sat with his head in his hands, shaking it.

'There's nothing illegal, Morgan. There isn't.'

'Just a little friendly fraud,' said Spencer.

'People do it all the time. Pen names.'

'Oh yeah. People use pen names. But this. You're gonna trot this guy out?'

'They want beefcake. I'll cut 'em a slice. Young and juicy. And they'll pay through the nose.'

'You actually think they're gonna pay a man more than they would a woman?'

'A young man. Good-looking. You bet your ass.'

'Why?'

'Ask them. Besides, it's not just the gender. I've got a blemished track record. Books that never came close to the list. They don't make a star out of somebody like that. It isn't done. In this business, you get one shot at being discovered. They want a fresh face so they can tell the world it's their discovery.'

'But this?'

'So I'm giving them tight buns to go along with it,' said Abby.

'They'll sue you nine ways from Sunday,' said Morgan.

'For what?'

'For fraud. Try that on for starters.'

'No they won't.

'Why not?'

'Because to prove fraud you have to prove damages. And to prove damages they would have to prove that they would have paid less to me, a woman, than they would have to the hunk I put in front of them.'

Like a riddle, Morgan thought about this for a moment, then smiled. 'Title Seven.'

Abby nodded. 'They'd have to admit to discrimination.'

'They'd be on the horns of a dilemma,' said Morgan.

'With a prong in each cheek,' said Abby. 'Besides, if the book is successful, why would they want to sue? If the book isn't successful, who cares? There'll be nothing to fight over.'

Morgan admired the ingenuity. She had thought it all through. She was not all writer after all. There was more lawyer there than he had credited.

'Doesn't it bother you that somebody else is gonna take the credit for your work?'

'Only until the paperback publication,' said Abby.

'What then?'

'Then I intend to go public.'

'You think they'll let you?'

'How can they stop me? If we put it together the right way, with a copyright to prove that I wrote the work. Maybe a contract with whoever I get to do Gable Cooper. They won't have a choice.'

Morgan had to admit it sounded like fun. More fun than he was having practicing law. 'Maybe I could do it. Be Gable Cooper, I mean.'

Abby didn't know how to tell him. Morgan could read it in her eyes. She didn't have to.

'I know. Things are sagging in all the wrong places,' said Morgan. 'And the hair's starting to get a little thin.' He reached up and mussed the shaggy top knot.

'Now who's being hard on who?' said Abby. 'But I don't want to get you involved.'

'I see. You just want me to help you plot this fraud, not perpetrate it.'

'Can it be done? Can you copyright it in my name and can you keep them from finding it?'

Morgan paused, thought about it. 'I think so. Does anybody else know what you're doing?'

Abby thought for a moment. 'Just three people.'

'Who?'

'You and I, and Terry. She's staying at my house for a while, so she knows.' Abby and Theresa Jenrico had been tight since grade school.

'Is he hitting on her again?'

Abby nodded.

'What an asshole.' Spencer was talking about Joey Jenrico, Terry's estranged husband. The two women and Morgan had socialized after work a few times at a bar around the corner.

'What Joey deserves is a shot in the head,' said Morgan.

'Are you offering your services?'

'I know some people.' He pushed his nose off to one side with a finger like some busted prize-fighter. 'Could be done very discreetly. Drive over him in his bed with their Mack truck. I mean, what's a little mayhem when we're already doin' fraud?' He winked at her.

She looked at him and laughed.

He made a few notes. 'You haven't told anybody else about what you're doing on the book?'

'There will have to be one other person.'

'Who's that?' said Morgan.

'Gable Cooper.'

He was not bad-looking, dark with a shadow of a beard. But then it was late afternoon. The clerk eyed him sort of sheepishly, a young girl at an older man, good-looking at that.

'Can I help you?' she asked.

'I'm lookin' for Abigail Chandlis.'

'I don't know if she's in. What's your name?'

'Joey Jenrico.'

'And what does this regard?'

'That's what I wanna talk to Chandlis about.'

'No, I mean does this regard a case in the office?'

'Yeah. My divorce.'

'Are you a client?'

'No. You guys represented my wife.'

'Oh. Just a moment.' By now red lights and alarms were going off in the brain of the receptionist. There had been enough shootings in law firms by irate husbands in the last few years that clerks in the big firms had undergone more training in emergencies than the National Guard. She hit the button under the desk that signaled security on the first floor, the yellow button that told them to come up without guns drawn. She looked for bulges in the man's coat but didn't see anything, all the while smiling.

'They'll be right out.'

Then she hit the com-line. But it wasn't Abby that she called. The security pros had told them that the lawyer involved in the case was the last person you wanted. If Abby came out, she might as well be wearing a big bull's-eye.

A second later, a young guy, suit and tie and about seven feet tall, came into the reception area from an office in the back.

'Can I help you?'

Dan London was a former cop turned lawyer. Before that he was a tight end for the University of Washington team that went twice to the Rose Bowl and kicked ass each time. He was the firm's pick for internal security.

'Yeah . . .' The guy's dimensions alone were enough to slow Joey down. 'I'm lookin' for one of your lawyers.'

'I'm a lawyer,' said London.

Joey didn't realize they made them in that size.

'Yeah, but I'm lookin' for Chandlis.'

'I'm afraid Ms Chandlis isn't in right now.'

'Right.' Joey wondered if this was the one Theresa was seeing. He'd been told by a friend that some lawyer was seen partying with Theresa at a restaurant downtown. He was intent on kicking somebody's ass. But if this was the guy, Joey was gonna have to come back with a fork lift.

'Maybe I could wait.'

'I don't think so,' said London. 'She's not coming back today.'

'Where is she?'

'Out.'

'Oh.'

By now there were two guys in blue caps and white shirts wearing forty pounds of hardware around their waists outside the door. Joey turned and saw them through the glass.

'Maybe I could come back.'

'I don't think that would be a good idea.'

Joey gave him arched eyebrows as a question mark.

'Are you represented by counsel?' asked the lawyer.

'Why? Am I under arrest?' Joey thought maybe this was a form of Miranda. He was a loser. He'd spent a lifetime passing 'Go' and he hadn't collected two hundred bucks yet.

'No. I mean, did a lawyer represent you in your divorce?'

'Oh yeah.' Joey was relieved.

The lawyer was laughing. Joey didn't like it. Still it was better to be laughed at than arrested. So he laughed, too.

'If you want to talk to Ms Chandlis, have your lawyer call her.' He stuck a business card in Joey's hand. 'She can't talk to you, anyway.'

'Why not?'

'Professional rules. If you're represented by a lawyer, she's not supposed to talk to you.'

'I didn't know that.'

'Well, you do now.'

Just like a cop, thought Joey. If he had a hammer and got behind the guy, he'd show him.

'Nice to have met you,' said the lawyer.

'Yeah.'

The two guards collected Joey outside the door and escorted him to the elevator. Downstairs they put his name in a book; the equivalent of Wyatt Earp posting you out of town. Joey would never get through security and upstairs again. If he wanted to see Chandlis, he would have to do it someplace else.

As he passed through the big glass revolving door, he felt the chill wind off the Sound hit his face. It turned his cold sweat icy. Joey knew he'd dodged a bullet. He felt his stomach at the belt line and rejoiced that the two guards hadn't done the same. Because he had a record, he couldn't get a permit. But whenever he went looking for his wife, Joey Jenrico always carried a gun.

He answered on the second ring and before he could say hello, Abby was on him.

'Where in the hell is the check?' It seemed like she was always exasperated when she talked to Charlie.

'Abby?'

'I'm flattered,' she said, 'that you could recognize my voice from among the throngs you must owe money to.'

'They haven't paid me in two months,' he said.

'And you haven't paid me in five.'

'Listen, I'm having a hard time.' It was the story of Charlie's life.

Charlie Chandlis was Abby's ex. They had been married for eight torturous years during which Abby saw him mostly on weekends, and then only between legal briefs and trips to Walla, where the state's maximum security prison was located. Charlie was a criminal appellate lawyer in Seattle who lived on the edge along with most of his clients, several of whom were on death row.

He owed her a total of nine thousand dollars, half of their credit-card obligations at the time of the divorce. The cards had been in Abby's name, but Charlie had racked up most of the debt. The court had ordered him to pay it in installments over twelve months. He was now four installments behind.

'What's the story this time?' she asked him.

'Indigent defense panel. What else?'

None of Charlie's clients could pay the freight, and so the taxpayers did it for them. They hired Charlie to tie the system up in knots, or at least that was Charlie's self-avowed mission in life – endless appeals. The money for fees was never enough to go around. There was always more crime than public dollars to pay for lawyers.

'They cut my fees. They hold my money. What am I supposed to do?'

'Tell them you have bills.'

'Right. Only welfare recipients get their checks on time from the state. You know that,' said Charlie. 'Mine they hold for at least ninety days. Sorta like the aging of good meat on a hook so that when it arrives it'll be ripe, and properly appreciated.'

It was a good story, but it didn't solve Abby's problem. She had taken sixty days off of work to finish the book once she was in striking distance. She had also taken a loan and factored Charlie's payoff into her budget. Now the bank was calling and the piper had to be paid.

'Charlie, I've got my own problems.'

'They took my car last week,' he told her. 'Repossessed it. Right out of the lot behind my office. Now I'm hoofing it, and taking the bus,' he said.

Charlie was his own kind of loser, well educated but hell-bent for poverty.

'Charlie, you've got a law degree, you passed the bar, why don't you . . .'

'Let's not get into that again.'

It was a good part of the reason their marriage had broken up. Charlie was a true believer, part of the pony-tail set from the sixties who believed that feeding the root of every crime was some social injustice. It was Charlie's sacred mission to get things right. Somewhere in the quest for ultimate justice, Abby and what was left of their marriage had gotten lost.

'It's five months since I've seen a check,' she told him.

'Can't pay if I don't have it,' said Charlie. He said something about blood out of a turnip and then she heard his hand over the mouthpiece and part of another conversation.

'. . . it should be hand carried. Have it messengered,' said Charlie.

'What? My check?' said Abby.

'No. No. It's some documents we need to file with the court before five.'

Always on the edge, Charlie's life was one big statute of limitations.

'You could go to jail, you know.' Abby was no fool, so she'd hired a lawyer in the divorce. She reminded him that her lawyer had threatened to get an order to show cause why Charlie should be held in contempt when he missed the first payment. The lawyer also told Abby that it probably wouldn't work. Charlie lived in the courthouse. He was on a first-name basis with all the judges. He would blame the system and they would buy it, giving him only a stern warning. In the meantime, Abby would be stuck with a bill from her own lawyer. So she spent her time and money on long-distance calls, jerking him around on the phone, with virtually the same result.

'You got ten days,' she said.

'Then what?'

It was a good thing he couldn't see the vacant expression on her face over the phone, though he could read it in the crackling silence on the line. It was an idle threat and they both knew it.

'Listen, I'll get you the check as soon as I can. Really.' His voice dropped an octave like he was about to impart some state secret. 'I haven't told her yet, but I'm not even gonna to be able to pay my secretary this month.'

'Why don't you put her on the phone so I can tell her,' said Abby.

'Gotta go,' said Charlie.

'How do I pay my rent?'

'Tell 'em to wait.'

'Right. I guess I don't eat this month,' she said.

'I'll come over and take you out to dinner,' he told her.

'You have enough money to take me out to dinner, but you can't pay your bills?'

'New credit card,' said Charlie. 'They keep sending these applications in the mail.' He laughed. Good-time Charlie.

It was another sore point. Abby couldn't get a credit card if her life depended on it. Charlie had ruined her credit rating. Now he had a new card in his own name.

'Why can't you borrow against it?' she asked him.

'Can't do that. They'd take it away faster than I could flash it. The secret of credit is not to need it,' said Charlie. 'Listen, why don't I come over?' He changed the subject on her.

'Don't bother.'

'Why can't we get together? For old times' sake.'

'Old times weren't all that good,' she told him.

'They weren't all that bad, either. Not as I remember.'

'I guess it all depends where you were sitting,' said Abby.

There was some pained silence on the phone that was quickly filled by Charlie. He always seemed to be the first to rebound after a fight.

'Listen, I gotta run,' he said.

'Charlie?'

'I'll get the check to you. I will,' said Charlie.

'Sure,' in the next life, thought Abby. As Charlie hung up, she wondered if she would be eating cat food by the end of the month, or if the bank was into restructuring personal loans, and if so, at what level of usurious interest rates.

CHAPTER
FOUR

It was one of the jagged teeth in the Manhattan skyline, a mammoth tombstone facing the East River – a hundred and twenty stories of steel and glass known to those who inhabited it simply as 'The Towers.'

It was home to one of the three networks, along with a publishing consortium that had euphemistically and otherwise become known over the years as Big-F. Together the package made up an entertainment and news conglomerate that along with the building that housed them was now owned by an Australian tycoon.

In the lobby there was security as tight as anything in the White House. No one got past the armed guards to the elevators without a call upstairs, a visitor's pass, and an escort who came down to collect them.

Today that honor was performed by Alexander Bertoli's secretary, who greeted Owens on a first name basis.

'Carla. Nice to see you. How was your trip to the coast?'

'Just fine, Janice. Wonderful.'

'Alex is waiting for you upstairs.'

Owens would give the details to Bertoli himself.

In the past two years, Big-F had fallen on hard times.

47

It had suffered restructuring, downsizing, and layoffs after a leveraged buyout, and had slipped from second place in annual profits among the giant publishers to fifth. There had been three changes at the helm in the last decade, and Alexander Bertoli, C.E.O. and publisher of Big-F, was worried that a fourth might now be in the works.

He was pacing the carpet of his palatial office on the hundred and fifth floor when the door opened and the secretary admitted Carla.

'Sweetheart. How was your trip?' Bertoli traversed twenty yards of deep wool, to touch cheeks. 'Let me take your coat.

'Harold, get Carla a drink. She's frozen.' Bertoli snapped his fingers at his man, who took Carla's order and disappeared behind the large bar next to the fireplace.

'Are you asking about the trip or the business?' said Carla.

'Both. You know me, darling. I'm always concerned for your welfare.'

'Of course. Well, in a word, the trip was hell. What can I say?' said Owens.

This was not the part Bertoli was itching to hear, but he put up with it.

'Air travel is not what it used to be,' said Carla. 'Even in first class, it's a lottery to see if you get a seat. Overbooked every flight. And the service.' She rolled her eyes. 'Your bags get better treatment. A thirty-five-hundred-dollar ticket and they give you corn flakes for breakfast and a stewardess with an attitude.'

Bertoli laughed. 'I told you. You should have accepted my offer. I could have had the Gulfstream pick you up at Santa Monica, take you north, a little business, and then home. I offered,' said Bertoli.

'I know you did, and you're a sweetheart for it.' Carla had her own reasons for not wanting the intrusion of Bertoli's corporate jet. The thirty-million-dollar ego container had been leased for him two years before as part of the compensation package to lure him from another house. She suspected that if he sent the plane it would come with strings – in a word, Bertoli on board with contracts ready. Ever since he read Gable Cooper's manuscript, Bertoli was hot for the property. Carla had plans, and while they might include Alexander, she wanted other options. Business was business.

Twenty tongues of blue-tipped flame licked the air from a large gas log in the fireplace, and Carla moved to warm herself in front of them.

'Well, tell me what happened? Did you meet him? Talk to him? What's he like?'

Bertoli was a bundle, every nerve poised for good news. God knows he'd had enough of the other kind lately. His predecessors had made the classic mistake in publishing; one big egg in a single basket. Another publisher had stolen it.

For the last four years Big-F had spent millions on a high-risk gambit building a single author. His first book rocketed into the stratosphere and stayed at the top of the bestsellers list for over a year. Each successive book followed. There were motion pictures and mammoth book sales until the author's name was a household word.

For three years money flowed into the coffers of Big-F like water over Niagara, and during this time the company did little to balance its publishing list. They had a few other mid-bestselling writers, but no one approaching the stature of The Author. This was the lopsided fountain of prosperity that Bertoli inherited when he took over – a leaning Tower of Pisa pouring out money.

What The Author didn't know is that his own agent had been seduced in a sweetheart deal by Big-F. They were paying him more than a million dollars a year under the table to shackle The Author to the wall at Big-F, to prevent him from shopping his wares to other publishers.

A few lesser authors in the agent's stable were thrown into the pot for seasoning and treated as hors d'oeuvres; their contracts picked up for a fraction of their value, they became tasty morsels for Big-F. These were the halcyon days of deception.

Then six months ago it happened. The earth shook. The Author's agent died. If timing is everything in life, the agent couldn't have picked a worse time for his to end. Bertoli and Big-F were involved in intense contract negotiations with The Author, contracts that were not yet signed.

Cut adrift in corporate seas at a critical time, swimming with the sharks, The Author was getting nibbles like monkey bites from half the agents in North America. In this chaos he turned to the only person he felt he could trust – his lawyer.

Bertoli considered his options. Maybe the lawyer would take the same deal as the agent. There was a problem. Lawyers had a written code of ethics, not that Bertoli thought it meant much to most of them. But they also had state bars and courts to enforce them. That was a problem. In a fit of morality, the lawyer might set him up. Big-F could end up in a monumental law suit. Worse, Bertoli could end up in jail.

He negotiated as best he could. He made a huge offer, an offer he thought The Author couldn't refuse. He tried to ingratiate himself, extending the prestige of his office and his own services as word meister to edit The Author's books. But the lawyer had a point. If Big-F was willing to offer thirty million for three books, maybe somebody else was willing to offer forty. The company had created its own version of Kong, an eight-ton literary gorilla – and his lawyer was about to manipulate one of the giant's fingers in an obscene gesture of farewell. Bertoli hated lawyers.

When they didn't come to terms over dollars, the lawyer found the door and The Author followed him. In a single blow, Bertoli lost the top of his list, and about fifty-five percent of Big-F's annual profits. It was a move likely to put Alexander Bertoli on the shelf with other moguls of business – right next to the Ford Division Chief who signed off on the Edsel. The departure left a huge hole on Big-F's Summer list. It was something that Bertoli was back-pedalling fast, trying to fill. Carla's new client looked like the answer to a prayer. If he could only get him signed and move the manuscript toward publication fast enough. The book had all the signs of a blockbuster.

'What did he say? Did he know about the film stuff?'

'I didn't see him.' Carla had uttered only four little words. But given the look on Bertoli's face, one might have thought she'd injected hot lead into his veins.

'What do you mean you didn't see him? Why the hell not?' His courtly manor evaporated like steam. Carla looked at him as if perhaps he wanted to take back his kiss. 'Is he represented by somebody else?' The first thought that entered Bertoli's mind, somebody had out-hustled her. Though in the pit of his heart Bertoli knew that it would be easier to reverse the laws of physics than to beat Carla to a hot client. Still, if this was the case, Carla wouldn't be staying for supper even though her place was already set at the small table in front of the window. Alex was not one to squander a business meal. He would be working his Rolodex for a quick substitution.

'He's not represented by anyone as yet. But you're looking at his future agent. I have a lock,' said Carla. When she wanted, Carla could drip confidence, and at this moment it was staining the carpet of Bertoli's office.

'You said you didn't see him?'

Carla dropped into one of the large club chairs facing the fire.

'Yes, but I saw the next best thing. The woman he lives with.'

'Ah.' Bertoli moved closer.

'And we have an arrangement,' said Carla. 'He's as good as signed.'

'I knew you could do it.' Bertoli was back in her camp.

'When are you gonna sign him? Is he coming to New York?' For the moment, everything waited for the agent. Until Carla could get her leash on him, Gable Cooper would not be doing tricks for anyone.

'As soon as he gets back in town. Now from your side,' said Carla. 'Any word on how the manuscript got out to Hollywood?' This had been a mystery since the book had gone nowhere except Carla's office and Bertoli's shop. It had to be a leak in one of these two places.

'No. But if it works, I'll kiss 'em,' said Bertoli.

Carla wasn't telling him the other part of her plan. Not until she had Gable Cooper signed on the dotted line. Then Bertoli could piss and scream all he wanted.

'Do we know anything about him – this guy Cooper?'

'We know it's not his real name,' said Carla.

'What's his name?'

'I don't know. She wouldn't tell me.'

'Why not?'

'I'm not sure.'

'What's her name? This woman?'

'Abby Chandlis.'

Bertoli took a pen from his pocket and made a note.

'What's she like?'

'She's a lawyer.'

Bertoli looked at her like this was a clock-stopper.

'Don't worry. I don't think it's exactly lawyer-client that we're talking here.' Carla looked at him and smiled.

'Ah. He's into fucking lawyers,' said Bertoli. 'A man after my own heart. What does he look like?'

'According to her, if she's telling the truth, he's done some modeling. He's supposed to be very good looking.'

Bertoli's eyes perked up. A movie deal and good looks to boot.

'Why wouldn't she tell you his name?'

'That wasn't real clear. She said he wouldn't like it.'

'But you have a theory?'

Carla gave him a whimsical look, and an equivocal bob of the head that could pass for a nod. For reasons known only in the demented minds of artists, bestselling authors had been known to craft novels under a pseudonym and sell them to publishers, attempting to conceal their true identity. It was crazy. In many cases their names would have propelled a book on the *New York Times* list before it was even published. But their egos had taken hold and they actually started to believe that it was the art of their words rather than marketing that sold their books. They were looking for confirmation. It rarely worked.

'It's possible he has a track record under his real name,' said Carla. 'Doesn't want us to know.'

'Maybe the man has a contract with another publisher and he would rather be free?' Bertoli had a more devious mind. 'You think he might be a big name?'

'It's a possibility.'

This appealed to Bertoli's mercenary side, the opportunity to raid talent from another house. Then it hit him. What if it was The Author? It was just the kind of game his lawyer might play. Chinese water torture. String him along and pull the book from Bertoli's reach at the last moment. He uttered this concern to Carla.

'Give it a break. You worry too much,' she told him.

'I get paid to worry,' said Bertoli.

'Then they aren't paying you enough. Besides, think about the upside, the fun we'll have if this guy's hot property. Gee, how did his name leak to the press two weeks before pub? And why is this mystery man hiding?' This was Carla's kind of game.

'He might not like it,' said Bertoli.

'Oops,' she laughed.

'You're awful,' he told her. In their minds they were both counting the money such a move might bring in.

'Are you ready to have dinner served, sir?' Harold nosed in.

'I think we'll wait awhile.'

'Yes, sir. Is there anything else I can get you?'

'No.'

Harold returned to his status as a potted plant in the corner.

'When's Cooper due back?' asked Bertoli.

'In a few days,' Carla lied, but she was hoping that in that time Abby could reach him. 'Gimme a week, I should have him signed.'

'Wonderful. Great.' Bertoli was up off the couch, rubbing his hands together. He didn't need the flames of the fire to warm him. The thought of another hot book, somebody to replace The Author, was enough to stoke the coals of his particular furnace.

Bertoli was looking at something more than the vague hope of success. There were many formulae to break out an author. Most of them involved risk, and each one could produce success in varying degrees, none of them guaranteed to work.

Most authors made it the old-fashioned way, one book at a time, slow incremental growth over a period of years. In the course of a dozen books, with modest investments for marketing and promotion, very limited risks on the part of the publisher, you could buy an audience. But to Bertoli's thinking, Big-F didn't have time for this. The company might still be around when it began to pay dividends, but Bertoli would not.

Then there was the way The Author did it; pure luck – a strong commercial story and great timing. Gable Cooper, though he couldn't know it yet, was on the same course. The fuel firing this particular engine was a movie deal brewing in Hollywood. Ordinarily it would have taken Big-F at least a year to plan and promote the debut of a big new author. But Bertoli didn't have that kind of time, not with a hole the size The Author left in his Summer list. With a film sporting a box-office star, Gable Cooper and his book were now on a fast track.

Success, fame, and fortune appeared to be right around the corner for this budding writer, and like The Author before him, he had backed into it.

'So what did they say out there?' Bertoli was talking about the first part of Carla's trek, to Hollywood, or more accurately Wilshire Boulevard in Beverly Hills. 'Is it true? Is he cast in the role?'

'Like concrete,' said Owens. 'He's read the manuscript and wants the part. Subject, of course, to script approval and somewhere in the neighborhood of twenty million in payment from the producers. But if they can buy the book for him, my people are telling me it's a go. Green light all the way to production.'

'Oh my God. Then it's true.' Bertoli rubbed his hands together in glee. 'I'm his biggest fan,' said Bertoli.

'No, his biggest fan is his banker. You come second,' said Carla.

Bertoli looked at her, wondering if he should argue the point, then laughed. 'Fine. I can live with that.'

'What you can live with is the fact that he's gonna save your ass,' said Carla.

'That too.' Bertoli made no bones about it, and instead lifted his glass and drank to Carla's words as if they were a toast.

Carla guessed that Alex was already doing some money changing in his head. If the movie brought in two hundred million, the initial book rights could be worth anywhere from a third to half of that, maybe more, and that was being conservative. The paperback tie-in when the film came out would start the money flowing all over again.

'He opens this thing, and word gets out, the hardback's gonna fly off the shelves.' Bertoli did his own little dance, a pirouette in place in front of the sofa. 'You know time is tight, but we could do something at ABA.' Bertoli was talking about the American Booksellers Association convention held in late spring. Usually it was reserved for books being promoted on the Fall-Winter list, but in this case you could kiss the rules good-bye. 'A beach book at the ABA,' said Bertoli. 'The presses will be smoking. We won't be able to keep this thing stocked. And the book, it's good. It'd sell itself. But with this . . .'

What Bertoli meant is that the film deal removed all the risk. It came as close to a guaranteed result as you would find this side of the pearly gates. Alex and his company wouldn't be flying alone. They'd be in the embrace of one of the major studios where marketing with smoke and mirrors was an art form. With a box-office star cast in the lead role, given the sums of money they would have to pay to get him, the studio couldn't afford to let Cooper's book fail. More than a year before the movie's release they would be bankrolling the marketing of Gable Cooper's hardcover book. It was what every publisher dreamed of, an unlimited budget using somebody else's money.

CHAPTER
FIVE

A month had passed since her meeting with Owens at the law office and Abby was now getting desperate. Owens was calling her daily. She needed to find Gable Cooper. To keep the agent off her back and buy time, Abby agreed to Owens's representation. She told Carla she was authorized as Gable Cooper's lawyer to do this. Carla didn't ask any questions.

This morning she used a pair of scissors to rip open the top of the large envelope and then removed the catalogue-sized loose-leaf binder. It contained at least two hundred pages with the name of a talent agency stenciled on the cover. It had taken several weeks and all of Morgan's efforts, but he had finally done it. A contact he had met during the entertainment law seminar had loaned him a copy of the directory, and Morgan had it sent directly to Abby.

Theresa hovered over her as she set up at the card table in the living room. It was cluttered with papers, the remnants of notes from the last manuscript. In the center was the old Underwood manual, built in the fifties and now nearly an antique. It wasn't that Abby shunned computers. She used one at work. But the manual typewriter was her forty-pound lucky charm when it came to fiction. She had written four novels on it including Gable Cooper's. There was a certain therapy in beating on the heavy keys. Abby was afflicted by the disease of over-writing. The old typewriter exacted a cost for revisions in the form of retyping, and so it served as a restraint.

'You know,' said Theresa, 'people go to jail for this kind of stuff.'

.'You worry too much,' said Abby.

'No, I mean it. Remember the guy who wrote the book about Howard Hughes? The unauthorized biography?'

'Where did you ever hear about that?'

'Hey, I read.'

'But that was years ago.'

'Don't change the subject. He did prison time,' said Theresa.

'Stop worrying. Gable Cooper isn't Howard Hughes.'

'My God, woman. He's a figment of your imagination. How do you know he isn't Howard Hughes? You haven't found him yet.'

Theresa Jenrico liked to laugh at her own jokes even with a bruised cheek. Theresa's husband Joey had used her for a punching bag for the umpteenth time just before their divorce five weeks earlier and, according to Theresa, she was now residing permanently with Abby, though how long this would last was not certain.

Joey was manipulative and chronically violent. Theresa had him arrested four times, and to date he had a perfect record; four busts – no convictions. She dropped charges each time, after Joey professed his love and vowed he would never hurt her again.

It was Abby who'd finally convinced her to go for the

divorce and then represented her in the ordeal. She also tried to talk her into a restraining order to keep Joey away, but Theresa told her it would only make matters worse.

'You're telling me that I'm being stupid,' said Abby. 'Look at yourself in the mirror.'

'Hey. I left him, didn't I?'

'Yeah. For the fourth time. What was it last time – two broken ribs? And the time before that a detached retina?'

'They only thought it was detached,' said Theresa.

'Well, lucky you.'

'I'm only telling you this cuz I don't want to see you get in trouble,' said Theresa.

'I'm not going to get in trouble. I talked with Morgan and he agrees.'

'Did you tell him everything?'

'What he needed to know,' said Abby.

'I'll bet. And the agent?'

'So far I'm managing to hold her off. I've told her he's on a junket, a trip into the jungles of southern Mexico for more color.'

'Sooner or later that's gonna wear thin,' said Theresa. 'What then? Hmm?'

'By then I'll find somebody.'

'Right.'

'You should have heard her,' said Abby. She was talking about Owens.

' "What does he look like?" "Does he have big baby blues?" "How tall?" "How thin?" "How young?" "Does he have hair halfway to his ass and cleavage of the chin?" Listen. If she wants a dimple on his pecker I'll find one – and if I can't, I'll make one,' said Abby.

Theresa looked at her, bright eyes. 'I got it.'

'What's that?'

'We can use Joey. You can hold him down and I'll do the honors. On his pecker, I mean.' The thought of circumcising Joey with a meat cleaver offered a certain sense of comic justice.

'He's too stupid,' said Abby. 'Besides, if he wrote the book, all the characters would speak with a slur.'

'Hey, I will say, Joey did kick the bottle.'

Abby wondered if it wasn't in Theresa's teeth at the time.

'Good for him,' said Abby. 'Call me when he kicks the bucket.'

'No, I mean it. He stopped drinking.'

'And the pope's gone over to Scientology,' said Abby.

They'd had this discussion before. Abby had warned her that if she didn't leave Joey, he would eventually kill her. The relationship had all the classic signs. Joey was a drunk out of control, a paranoid fueled by alcohol, with a raging temper that knew no bounds. If he killed and dismembered her, he would no doubt be too drunk to remember where he put the parts. He would beat the charges on a plea of diminished capacity.

'Don't change the subject. We're talkin' about you and this stupid thing you're gonna do.'

'It isn't stupid.' Abby centered the binder in front of her on the card table so that it was upside down to Theresa.

'Look at it this way. How often have you had a chance to play Pygmalion?'

'Pig who?' said Theresa.

'Greek Mythology. Pygmalion was a sculptor who hated women until he carved a statue of a gorgeous woman and promptly fell in love with his own work.'

'Sounds like some of the men I've known.'

'He called the statue Galatea and when he got tired hugging cold stone Pygmalion went crying to the gods, in this case Aphrodite, and asked that she supply him with a woman as beautiful as what he'd created. Aphrodite took pity and brought the stone to life.'

'So what are you telling me, that this Gable Cooper, this dream boat with a dimple on his dick, is your statue?'

Abby laughed. 'Not a statue, but he is my creation.'

'All I can say is I hope to hell you're praying to the gods. Cuz you're gonna need all the help you can get.'

Abby opened the cover and popped open the rings of the binder, removing the first page and holding it up for Theresa to see.

'The gods help those who help themselves.'

There, pasted to the page, was an eight-by-ten color glossy of some male hunk, blond, blue-eyed, pearly whites smiling at Theresa across the table.

'Who's that?' Suddenly she was all interest.

'Somebody from a talent agency in L.A.' Abby pointed to the binder in front of her. 'This is full of the same.' She fanned some of the pages with her fingers. It was an endless array of photos, all great-looking men.

'Spencer got it from somebody he met at a seminar in L.A. This guy was dating a woman who works at the agency. I'm going shopping,' said Abby.

If anyone found out she had a copy of the directory, the woman who palmed it from the talent agency would lose her job. So Abby had to be discreet.

Each entry contained a photo with the name of the actor, followed by a résumé including acting credits, address, and telephone numbers for their day job and home. Abby thumbed through the binder quickly. Most appeared to be waiters or sales clerks by day, all of them with looks to stop time.

Theresa moved around the table for a better look. 'Lemme see.' She picked up the photo.

'Oooo. He's nice. Michael Chapen. Redondo Beach. Do you know him?'

'Nope. But he's not my type.'

'I knew it,' said Theresa. 'You're sick. Lemme take your temperature.'

'I told the agent that Gable Cooper was dark. Mr Chapen doesn't fit the bill.'

'Ah.' Theresa pulled up a chair and sat down for a closer look. She was convinced Abby was nuts, but as long as she was going to do this thing there was no harm in indulging fantasy.

'So tell me. What are you gonna do?'

'I'm going to go through this and find the ones who come sufficiently close to the description I gave to the agent. Then I intend to call and set up auditions.'

'You're kidding me?'

'No.'

'You're gonna meet these guys?'

'Until I find the one I want.' Abby made it sound like buying salami in a store.

'You actually think they'll do this? What you're asking?'

'It's acting, isn't it? They're actors. Listen, for most of these people it's the opportunity of a lifetime. The chance to play a real live author. Who knows, they might even become famous.'

'Yeah, right. Their picture in every post office in America. Listen, the only possible silver lining in this cloud is if you both get convicted and they put you in the same cell with him.'

'What's wrong? I'm gonna pay the guy.'

'With what?' asked Theresa.

'A percentage of the advance and royalties on the book. Whatever I can negotiate.' Abby turned the page and suddenly Theresa swallowed her protests.

'Now he's tall and dark,' said Theresa.

'He might do very nicely.'

'Listen,' said Theresa. 'You need help? I could carry your luggage. Take notes.'

Abby thought she was joking, looked at her for a moment, and realized she was not. Suddenly they both started laughing.

Ron Sidner took the call directly. It came in on his back line, somebody he knew.

'Ron here.' He was typing a memo to the front office, coverage on a movie script sent to him by an agent.

'More news from Big-F,' said the voice on the phone. It was clear and precise, the words clipped with a certain air of formality and very businesslike.

'I have been told that the author's operating under a pseudonym,' it said.

'We figured that much,' said Sidner. He was cool, good-looking, and twenty-two. Good looks were a must in the industry, where deals were increasingly driven by kids in their twenties. Sidner had originally aspired to become an actor but had come to his senses when he realized there were better odds for success in the lottery. Since then he'd worked as a tour guide for one of the major film studios in L.A. before graduating to its story department. He was now bitten by the film bug and craved a spot in the executive suites.

'Yes,' said the voice, 'but did you figure the reason for the pen name?'

Sidner was all ears.

'Word has it, he's a bestselling author. A major name.'

Sidner suddenly stopped pecking away at the computer keyboard. 'Are you sure?'

'My information is from well-placed sources.'

'Gimme a name?' said Sidner. 'The author?'

'That I don't have, at least not yet. Give me awhile and I can probably find out.'

'How long?'

'I don't know.'

Silence from Sidner as he thought. 'There's an extra thousand in it for you, if the information is accurate and we get it before anybody else.'

'I'll see what I can do.' The voice was on retainer, part of a stable of film scouts maintained by studios in New York to keep an eye for potential hot properties in the book world. Most of these operated above-board, out of offices in the publishing district of Manhattan. They routinely combed the files of literary agents and publishing houses on the make for stories that might be scripted for film. A few of them, like the voice on the phone, were moles, secretaries and office assistants, who could be used when the need arose for inside information. This could run the gamut, from the price a publisher was paying for a book, to the scope of their advertising budget, and, most important, whether another studio might be interested in the property for film rights. People heard things in offices and passed them as gospel. Film was an industry fueled by rumors. Nothing was hot unless someone else wanted it, in which case the sky was the limit. It was an industry that operated on the premise that perception was reality, or if it wasn't, it soon would be.

'There's more,' said the voice. 'Owens hasn't signed him yet.'

'What are you talking about? She's had a month. She went out to Seattle.' This did surprise Sidner.

'She never saw him. He was out of town. And he hasn't come back. Off someplace doing research – on another book. From what I am told, it picks up where the first one left off.'

They didn't own the property, hadn't cast the star, weren't in production yet, and a sequel was already looming. Sidner buffered out of the coverage he was writing on the screen and quickly started a new memo while he talked.

'You mean after her visit here Owens struck out?'

'Not entirely. She made contact with a woman who supposedly lives with the author. The woman knows where he is, and according to my information is now working with Owens to contact him.'

'Got a name?'

'Abby Chandlis.' He spelled the last name and gave Sidner the address of her place of employment and what details were known about Gable Cooper and his whereabouts.

Ten minutes later Ron Sidner was centered in front of the huge oak desk, hand-carved in deep relief, a quarter-inch of plate glass protecting its surface. It was rumored that the desk once belonged to David O. Selznick, and that on one of its corners Clark Gable inked his name to the contract to play Rhett Butler.

Behind it, in a tufted wing-back maroon leather chair, sat Mel Weig, cool and detached, impeccably attired, the Armani suit coat buttoned even as he sat.

In another chair across the desk from Weig sat Stanley Salzman, head of production and Weig's number two at the studio. One never moved without the other.

Weig read Sidner's memo as he toyed with the twelve-thousand-dollar gold-braceleted watch on his wrist.

'Anybody else seen this?'

'No, sir,' said Sidner.

'Let's keep it that way.' He passed it to Salzman, who did a quick reading. Weig knew that just as his mole had penetrated Big-F it was possible that other studios had eyes and ears in his own. The fewer people who knew the contents of the memo the better. Weig had been responsible for hooking the actor interested in Gable Cooper's book. But if some other studio bagged the film rights, the deal would be gone, like a moveable feast. Box-office stars were no longer in bondage to the studios. They were free agents, signing contracts on a film-by-film basis. Studio execs had to crawl on their knees to get the hot ones, as Weig had on this deal. In the end, the actor came only because he longed to play the character created by Gable Cooper, and Weig knew it.

The com-line on his phone rang and he picked it up.

'Sir, I have Carla Owens for you on the other line.' It was Weig's secretary who had placed the call at her boss's directive moments before. He punched the line.

'Carla, darling. Mel here. How are you?' Some silence while she chatted.

'Oh good. Listen, do you mind if I put you on the speaker phone. Stanley Salzman, you know Stan, head of production? He's here with me, and I think he'd like to hear what's happening.'

An instant later Weig hit the speaker button and laid the receiver down.

'Carla, can you hear me?'

'Oh yes.'

'Hi, Carla, it's Stanley.'

'Stan, how are you. It's been a long time.'

'Too long.'

'Listen,' said Weig. 'We're very interested in what's going on with your man Cooper.'

'Oh, it's going great. Just fine.'

'Then you have him signed?'

'Done deal,' said Carla.

Weig looked over at Salzman whose dark eyes revealed the deception.

'Listen, what's he like?'

'I think your gonna love him.' She avoided direct answers. 'He's very good looking. I'm told that, in fact, he did some modeling. He's a marketer's dream.'

'That's good. That's great. When can we talk about numbers for the film rights?'

'Oh well, give me a few days. He's just getting back from a tiring trip to Mexico, so we should be on the phone in the next few days. I'd like to talk to him in more detail before we get down to specifics. Is that O.K. with you?'

'As long as you aren't talking to anybody else,' said Weig. 'Another studio or a producer?'

'Mel.' She made his name sound like a cat in pain. 'How could you think such a thing? No. No. As soon as he gets his feet back on the ground and we have a chance to talk, I'll be back to you.'

'Right,' said Weig. 'Take care, Carla, and I'll wait to hear.'

'Ta ta, be in touch,' said Carla and the phone went dead.

Weig said it all with his expression. 'We obviously can't rely on Carla. When will your source have more information?' he asked Sidner.

'We're not sure. He thinks maybe a few days.'

'What do you think, Stan?' Weig looked at Salzman.

'It looks like Carla's having difficulty lining him up,' said Salzman.

'Or playing games,' said Weig. He had a more sinister agenda in mind. 'She could be trying to buy time, to jack the price up. Get us into a bidding war with another studio.'

Though Gable Cooper couldn't know it, Weig's studio was already prepared to offer a million dollars for the film rights to the book. The hint that he might be a bestseller, and their inability to reach him to talk dollars that might bring a smile to the author's face, left them in doubt as to whether it would be enough. Anxiety in Hollywood always had a predictable and singular effect – a higher price.

'Where are we on the budget?' asked Weig. 'Can we go higher for the rights?'

'Looks like we may have to,' said Salzman. 'We could take a little off casting, some of the minor characters. That could take us up to three million for the rights.'

'Do it,' said Weig. 'If somebody else gets the book, it won't matter how much we reserved for casting.'

Sidner marveled at the exercise of power; two million more just like that – 'do it' – a million dollars a word.

'What else?' said Salzman.

'We can't wait,' said Weig. 'There's too many wagging tongues in this town. Get Ackerman and his agency to find the woman.' He looked at the memo. 'This Abby Chandlis. Have them contact her.' Weig thought for a second. 'No. No. On second thought, you better make the contact.' He looked at Salzman. 'And take Zitter here with you.'

'Sidner,' said the kid.

'What?'

'The name's Sidner, sir.'

'Whatever,' said Weig.

'So what do you want? Ackerman or us?' said Salzman.

'Both. Have the Ackerman Agency trail the woman. If Cooper, whoever he is, comes back to town, I want to be the first to know it. But I only want them to surveil.'

Salzman nodded.

'Then I want you to put yourself on a plane to Seattle. Get your ass up there and talk to this Chandlis woman. Romance her. Wine and dine her. Do whatever you have to do, but tell her we're interested in the film rights and we'd like to deal directly. Not through an agent. I'm tired waiting for Carla. She wants to bullshit us, she's gonna learn there's a price.'

'Is that smart?' said Salzman. 'I mean, Owens has already talked to her.'

'Tell her whatever you want, that an agent's gonna slow things down. That we don't like to do business with this one. Whatever gets us to Cooper. But get us there.'

'What if we get halfway through and they think they can find a better deal someplace else?' said Salzman. It was the concern in every agentless deal: people who fancied themselves artists could be notorious flakes – agree to a deal today and renege tomorrow. To the studios, agents weren't professionals representing talent. They were animal trainers with a leash and a whip. Their principal value was client control.

'Owens hasn't signed him. If we can get to him before she does, maybe we can limit this to one player, ourselves. If not,' said Weig, 'I'm afraid the price is gonna get very steep, in a hurry.'

CHAPTER
SIX

Jack had learned the art of origami from a woman he'd lived with in Thailand during the war – from his days in the Corps. She was young, as he was at the time, and sweet and had taught him many things from the Asian art of love to the construction of ornate Buddhist temples in miniature from folded pieces of paper.

The one in front of him at the moment stood more than two feet tall on top of the table. Terraced and decorated like a wedding cake, it had taken him more than two weeks to build. Soaking the paper in the solvent and letting it dry is what consumed most of the time. Still the fact that the temple progressed faster than his writing may have said something about his creative aptitudes, though if it did it was lost on Jack.

The upper six levels were constructed of plain paper, the early discards of his current work in progress, the fourth in a series of now unpublished manuscripts for novels. Maybe he had lost the touch. His last published work was a piece of non-fiction, a technical work for a small publisher in the southern states: *The Ragged Renegades Resource Book*. It was more of a pamphlet than a book, an epistle with a little humor added by an editor, on how to home brew your own explosives and incendiary devices. Jack was slipping and he knew it.

The base of the paper temple, the first two levels, were braced on the outside by heavier paper, light card stock with printing and handwritten words evident only on close inspection. The writing gave a unique appearance to the structure, as if the surface had been carved by the midgets who made it in some exotic script. These cards Jack had collected over a period of months.

Sometimes editors didn't even take the time to type a letter. Instead they hastily scrawled a note, often illegible, on stock printed with their name at the top, each one a variation on the same word: 'NO.' They would send these like postcards in the open mails. This practice in particular pissed Jack off, because the postman and anyone else who happened to touch his mail saw them.

He lifted the piece of plywood on which he'd constructed his masterpiece and carried it out the back door to the yard, Jack's place of special mischief.

He placed the sheet of plywood with the temple on top of an old tree stump sixty feet from the house.

Attached to the straw fuse, which disappeared under one edge of the little temple, he used a twenty-two caliber rimfire cartridge emptied of its powder as a detonator. Jack replaced the smokeless gunpowder with a carefully prepared solution, chemicals from a hobby shop, and a little black powder packed in around a single filament of fine steel wire. This in turn was connected by a tiny clamp to a length of lead wire that ran to a small battery near the rear of the house.

Years ago he'd been told about this. A common solution for soaking paper. It was said that a newspaper properly prepared and left to dry was virtually undetectable, except by sophisticated Neutron Vapor Analysis not used at most security checkpoints including airports. Carried under the arm with an outer covering of today's front page, it would look like any other newspaper. Tightly compacted it would also carry the explosive force of three sticks of dynamite.

He marveled at the things his own government had taught him, survival techniques and ways to wreak havoc, and wondered if this one would work.

There were no neighbors within a quarter-mile. The fact that the little paper pagoda had a lot of space for air inside meant the force would be muffled, more of a whoosh than a bang – so that when Jack touched the wire to the battery lead and the force of the explosion threw him against the side of the house and shattered a window over his head, he was for a moment at least stunned. A million tiny shards of paper, many of them singed, some still on fire, floated to the ground like golden leaves of autumn.

'Damn. It works.' Jack now knew how he would destroy the airliner, at least on the mythic pages of the manuscript he had not yet started.

CHAPTER
SEVEN

Abby rattled along I-5 in the slow lane at fifty miles an hour. She had to stop once to put oil in the old Plymouth. The odometer had quit working at a hundred and sixty-seven thousand miles, but the car still ran. Abby, ever frugal, babied it along. Theresa kept complaining that the springs were poking her in the ass. There was no doubt the car needed work, but Abby's resources were stretched to the breaking point. And at the moment she had more pressing matters on her mind. It took them a half hour to get downtown in the mid-day traffic, and she was worried that she would be late.

Abby was in the middle ranks of the baby boom. The leading edge of this demographic wave was now inching toward fifty. The boomers were being pushed along by the twenty- and thirty-somethings. Most of the men in her own age group who weren't married hung out in restaurants and bars that catered to younger women. The message to the woman over forty was 'get lost.'

It was an attitude that plagued the business world as well. For a woman involved in any form of entertainment, even at the fringes, in commercial literature, life beyond forty seemed a wasteland of lost opportunities.

Abby had no intention of accepting this, gracefully or otherwise. She covered the few wisps of gray in her hair with a rinse.

She was attractive and when dressed she could still turn male eyes as she did today, walking west on James Street, toward Pioneer Square. In three-inch heels she offered the illusion of height with a sassy walk, and a skirt that ended three inches above her knees. She was bare on the shoulders except for a light shawl, and freezing to death. But it all had a purpose; to keep Charlie's mind off the reason for her visit.

Gritting her teeth and coming up with new excuses for Gable Cooper's long absence, Abby had given Carla the run-around while she cleared her calendar at the law firm and narrowed down the list of possible candidates from the talent agency directory. Carla was now calling twice a day, and Abby was worried that the whole thing might fall apart. Somebody named Bertoli, a publisher, was pounding the agent. Carla gave her a deadline. Three more days and if she couldn't find Cooper the whole thing was off. Abby was desperate. Now all she needed was some money, a small stake to carry out her plan.

She called and accepted Charlie's earlier offer for lunch. He gave her directions to a small restaurant not too far from his office. He was surprised by the call but anxious to see her.

She hoped that he still had a penchant for the use of initials. Everything Charlie owned was always labeled 'C.W.,' 'Charles William Chandlis,' from printed stationery and business cards to his monogrammed handkerchiefs. She prayed that this habit hadn't changed. Somehow, knowing Charlie, she knew it hadn't. He was a creature of habit.

When he saw her a half block off, the way she was dressed, his face lit up like a Japanese lantern. He nearly sprinted the distance.

'Babe. Good to see you.' Charlie was all hands, first on her shoulders, then around her back. He aimed a big kiss at her lips, but Abby managed to turn her head enough so that it landed awkwardly on one cheek.

Since their divorce, on the few occasions when she saw him, Abby wondered increasingly how she could have ever loved this man. It was not that he was vile or evil, but they had nothing in common. Even now she sensed that to Charlie she was nothing but an object of gratification; something to wear on his arm for the world to see, and if he was lucky, to maneuver back to his apartment when they were done.

'It's good to see you, Charlie,' she lied.

'Yeah. Yeah.' He looked her up and down, like some kid on a first date. 'You look great! Really great! Lost some weight.'

Cat food will do that for you, thought Abby.

'You're looking good yourself, Charlie.' He always dressed well, though he'd aged since she'd seen him last. No doubt the result of a faster single life.

She managed to untangle herself from his embrace and they walked the few feet to the restaurant, where Charlie held the door and then followed her inside.

'Mr Chandlis. Good to see you again.'

'Oscar, how are you?' Charlie might not be rolling in it, but he had enough money to be on a first-name basis with the maître d'.

'I have your table in the back.' Oscar turned and led the way, menus in hand, threading his way between tables until they came to a booth in the rear of the restaurant, almost to the kitchen. Charlie was looking for something cozy.

Abby surveyed the terrain, a quick glance down the corridor where there was a sign overhead that read RESTROOMS. The phone she assumed would be in that direction. She couldn't see it. That was good.

'This O.K.?' asked Charlie.

'Fine.' She smiled and scooted in behind the table.

There was a chair on the other side, but Charlie didn't take it. Instead he slipped into the booth next to her so that their bodies were now touching. Abby felt uncomfortable.

A waitress showed up and Charlie ordered scotch and soda. Abby passed.

'I'm freezing. I should have brought something heavier to wear.'

'I was wondering about that.' Ever the chivalrous Charlie.

'It's really cold in here, don't you think?'

'No. Not especially.'

'Well, you're wearing a jacket, no wonder.' She looked at him and finally he got it.

'Oh. Here.' Charlie took off his suit coat and draped it over her shoulders.

Finally.

'Thanks.' She shivered as he wrapped it around her shoulders. It was no act. Oblivious as he was, the first part of her plan had worked, little thanks to Charlie.

'They have a great menu. I thought we could do lunch and then maybe head out.'

'Where to?'

'Oh, I don't know. Maybe over by Seattle Center. Take a walk. Then I thought maybe over to my place for a visit.'

'Oh, did you?'

'Why not?' Charlie was all innocence. No doubt he had a bottle of wine already chilled and two glasses back at his apartment somewhere close to the bed – ever the conniver.

'We'll see,' she said.

'Good.' Charlie took this for 'yes.' He picked up his menu and started to peruse. 'I can recommend the rack of lamb, it's very good. And, let's see. The lobster.'

'That's market price,' said Abby. 'Are you sure you can afford it?'

'Don't worry about it.' He laughed.

Abby felt better about what she was doing.

'Sir?'

Charlie looked up from his menu. It was Oscar, the maître d'.

'Telephone call for you.'

Charlie gave him a quizzical glance, then looked at Abby, a question mark. 'I didn't tell anybody at the office I was coming here.'

She shrugged her shoulders.

This was not a first for Abby. Through their marriage, on the few occasions when they went out to dinner, Charlie always spent his time on the phone while she amused herself and dined, for all intents, by herself.

'Just take me a minute,' he said.

'Sure. Take your time.' She turned back to the menu.

He slid out of the booth, and as expected Oscar pointed down the corridor toward the area by the restrooms.

She watched him go, hugging the jacket of his suit coat to her bare shoulders. A few seconds later she heard his voice, faint but still audible.

'Hello.'

Abby now worked quickly.

'Have we met? I mean in the office? I don't recognize the name. Could you speak up? I'm having trouble hearing you.'

She didn't have much time. But then it didn't take long. A second later she dropped her napkin on the table, and carefully laid Charlie's jacket on the bench seat, everything back in place. Then she slid out of the booth and took a quick glance down the hall. He was buried in a little corridor off to the side, leading to the restrooms, and couldn't see out.

She wound her way through the tables, and out the front door of the restaurant, and merged with the heavy noonday foot traffic on the sidewalk. A half block down she turned the corner. There at the payphone she saw Theresa still talking into the receiver. Abby gave her the high sign that all was well.

'Jeez. I think I got the wrong party,' said Theresa. 'You're not the Charlie Chandlis who does windows and rain gutters?'

'Who the hell is this?'

Abby could hear Charlie's voice over the phone from where she stood.

'Wrong number. Sorry.' Theresa hung up. She turned to Abby. 'Did you get it?'

Abby held it by the edges like a photograph for Theresa to see; Charlie's shiny new credit card, lifted from the wallet in his suit coat pocket.

She hoped he had enough cash to pay for his drink, or maybe Oscar would just put it on the tab.

After eight years of marriage, Abby knew Charlie like some people know the flu. Whenever he was around her bones ached. As she suspected, he still used initials on everything from luggage to stationery – including his new credit card. At the airport she signed the credit card slip for the two tickets to Los Angeles in the name of 'C. W. Chandlis.'

The ticket agents wouldn't check picture I.D.s until they got to the gate the next morning and then only to see if the last name on the ticket matched the passenger's driver's license.

Abby knew that Charlie would never call and report his card lost or stolen, at least not for awhile. He might do a lot of things, but he would never have her arrested. As a criminal defense lawyer it was against his religion.

Still she didn't abuse the privilege. She used the card to book a cheap room for herself and Theresa, clean but cut-rate, in one of the single story motels on Route 99 across from the airport. She decided to stay there because she knew Charlie would be looking for her at the house once he missed his credit card.

She got Theresa to come along by telling her she valued her judgment. Abby liked Terry, but this was a lie. Abby was afraid that in her current state Theresa, in a weak moment, might go back to Joey if only to try to talk things out. Joey seemed to have a hold on her that was messianic, like voodoo. He would beat on her, but in the end she would always come running back. Whether it was Joey's manipulation, or Theresa's insecurity, he always had the ability to make her think it was her fault.

At the motel, Abby brushed her teeth and got ready for a shower while Theresa lay on the bed and continued to fondle the photos in the talent agency directory.

'Come to Mama, blue eyes.' Terry rolled over on her back on the bed and hugged the picture to her breast, nearly bending the hard covers of the binder.

'Be careful. I may have to return that thing,' said Abby.

'Can I have the ones you throw back?' said Theresa.

'This is business,' said Abby.

'Just give me Conan the Barbarian here. He's blond. You can't use him anyway. You already said your guy's gotta have dark hair and big baby browns.'

'I didn't say anything about eyes. I told her Gable was dark, that's all.'

'Fine. I'll take all the blonds,' said Theresa. 'Line 'em up, turn out the lights, and tell 'em we're auditioning for a nude scene.'

'Why don't you just take a cold shower?' said Abby.

'What's wrong with a quick roll in the hay? I say if we're gonna check 'em out, we oughta do it right. Why go halfway? Besides, before you turn your guy over to this Carla, you might want to make sure all the equipment works. I mean, what if she gets him in a compromising position and he goes limp?'

Abby laughed.

'No, I mean it. You don't think it happens?' said Terry. 'I'll bet it happens all the time. I'll bet those literary types hump like bunnies. I mean, if your guy doesn't put out, that could blow the whole deal,' she said.

'Contrary to what you might think, we're not buying a male hooker,' said Abby.

'Right,' said Theresa. She turned another page in the directory. 'God. Look at the pecs on this one.'

Abby sighed and shook her head, but she didn't look.

'The way he stretches that shirt. I've seen more wrinkles on Roman body armor. You think there's any hair under there?' asked Theresa.

'I wouldn't know.'

'You like 'em with hair, or bare breasted?' Theresa

made it sound like white meat or dark, thigh or breast.

'Never really thought about it,' said Abby.

'Listen, sweetheart, every woman thinks about it. Now it's true you may never have thought about it up front. Maybe it was –' she rolled her hand at the wrist searching – 'what's the word I'm looking for?'

'Subliminal,' said Abby.

'What's that?'

'Means subconscious.'

'Yeah, that's it. Subconscious. I'll give you that, subconscious. But you've noticed,' said Theresa. 'It's like a tight rush. It never goes unnoticed. Now you may either be a fan or you're not. Me I'm a bona fide pec and bun lady. Into cheeks and chests. Give me something hard I can put my head against and sink my fingers into and I'm a happy camper.'

Abby said, 'You're awful.' With a mouth full of tooth paste this sounded like 'You owl.'

Theresa surveyed the picture again. 'I'm board certified in cheeks and chests. I can tell just by looking at this guy's pecs – the distance, the broad expanse like Montana, between his tits – that he probably has a prong the size of a titan missile.'

Abby looked wide-eyed at her friend through the open door, a mouth full of toothpaste. 'What?' But Abby couldn't hold a serious expression. She broke up laughing and spat toothpaste all over the sink and choked between laughs.

'You think I'm kidding?'

'No. I think you're sick,' said Abby.

'Listen. Studies have proven there's a direct correlation. Distance between tits divided by the surface area of the tush squared, equals length of the dingle dangle. Unless of course it's a full moon in which case gravity is neutralized, and the sky's the limit.' As she said this Terry's big brown eyes rolled in their sockets. Abby started laughing and finally dropped her toothbrush in the sink which was filled with water.

'Now look what you made me do.'

'Look for yourself.' Terry held up the picture. 'He's built like a pile driver,' said Theresa. 'In case you hadn't guessed, I like men and I'm not afraid to admit it.'

'I hadn't guessed,' said Abby.

'You know these're good pictures but next time you oughta tell 'em to put in a rear view. Sorta round out the whole picture as they say, so we don't have to waste our time.'

'Yeah, our time's so valuable,' said Abby.

'Yeah, but cheeks are important. I'll bet Carla's into buns. It's a power thing,' said Theresa.

Abby reached behind her with a hand and swung the door to the bathroom closed before she got another lecture on the attributes of the male body. Still, she could hear the voice outside in the other room as Theresa took it up another octave to account for the closed door. Now the people next door could probably hear as well.

'Here. Here we go. This one's really got a *tight* ass,' she hollered. 'Come take a peek. He's lookin' over his shoulder.'

'Hold it down,' said Abby.

'I'd like to hold him down. *Come out here and take a gander at this guy's ass.*' Terry was now shouting, for the world to hear. '*What's a matter, you afraid to look at titanium glutes?*' Theresa was now giving her a bad time and Abby knew it. She enjoyed her ability to embarrass Abby, to take it up a notch in a crowded situation.

Abby turned on the shower. The sound of water hitting hollow fiberglass was too much even for Terry to

86

overcome. She finally gave up, drowned out by the noise. A few seconds later, Abby adjusted the water temperature and climbed into the tub, pulling the curtain closed behind her.

She took a long hot shower, shampooed her hair, and stood for several minutes with the warm water running against the nape of her neck and down her body. She wondered what Charlie was doing at that moment; whether he might have a way of checking the credit-card charges so that he would be waiting for them when they got to the airport in the morning. This she quickly dismissed. Charlie would have to tell them the card was lost or stolen to get any information. They would cancel it. He couldn't be sure they would reissue the card. No. Charlie would be camped at her doorstep when she got home demanding his card back. This was as predictable as his initials on the plastic.

She went over in her mind the handful of candidates from the directory. She winnowed it down to the best three. She would start there.

Abby had to be careful in terms of what she said. She couldn't just go barging in and ask them if they would be willing to pull the wool over some New York publishing house. They would think she was out of her mind. She would have to feel them out. Theresa would love the sound of that.

She finally reached around and turned off the water. As the sound died, Abby could hear a male voice in the other room. Terry had finally tired of the book and turned on the television. That was good news, though it was louder than Abby would have liked.

She grabbed a towel and started to dry herself. The speakers on the set were really good. Must be stereo, she thought.

Then there was a loud vibration, something heavy and hard bouncing off a wall.

'Where is he? Is this the one? In the fucking book here? Open your mouth, sweetheart. Eat some more paper.' There was a loud smack, the sound of flesh and bone hitting the same.

'That's it. Now I know you can eat and talk at the same time. Tell me.' Another smack. 'Hungry? Have some more. Take your time. I'm enjoyin' myself. Ain't had this much fun since last time.'

It wasn't television. It was Joey Jenrico, his voice a little slurred – liquid fury.

Abby reached for her jeans, had one leg in, was bent over with the other foot up searching for the pant leg, when the thin wooden panel of the bathroom door splinted in her face. The only thing she saw were shreds of wood and Joey's foot. Fortunately for Abby it got caught in the splintered opening as he tried to pull it out, and Joey went down on his ass.

'Who the fuck?' He had a look of fright in his eye. Joey, in his current state, couldn't be sure if there was some brute on the other side of the door who had done this to him. Visions of Goliath at the law firm had caused Joey to leave the door ajar when he entered; just in case a quick exit was needed. It was the thing about taking courage from a bottle. If Theresa lived long enough and got lucky, some lover he stumbled in on might one day beat the crap out of Joey. That's if there was any justice in the world.

He pulled his leg out through the opening and saw Abby, and all that God had given her on the naked half of her upper body. There was a quizzical look in his eye as if at first it didn't register. Then he collected himself through the alcohol haze.

'Goddamn. My lucky day. The lawyer bitch. Kick the door and hit the fuckin' bull's eye.'

He was looking at Terry on the bed, her mouth full of paper, the torn and folded remnants of one of the photographs from the book.

'Two for the price of one,' said Joey. 'Well. They told me you was datin' a lawyer. But I figured it was a guy. Stupid me.' He looked over at Theresa, who was bleeding from the corner of her lip.

'Son of a bitch. I shoulda' known. Away for awhile and you go dyke on me.' He grabbed a heavy metal lamp off the dresser, a base the size of a bowling ball, and with both hands he flung it at Theresa on the bed. It sailed over her, hitting the headboard. The shade twisted and the bulb shattered, but the bulk of the massive lamp bounced harmlessly to the end of the bed.

'Goddamn we're gonna party tonight. Come here, bitch.' Abby was trapped in the bathroom, so Joey turned on Theresa again. She was paralyzed with fear.

With one arm in the sleeve of her blouse, Abby opened the bathroom door. By now Joey was on top of Theresa, slapping her face with both hands.

'Here, want some more to eat?' He grabbed the book and tore out another picture, poked his finger into the image's midsection so that if the photo was double-sided, the rear-end would have stuck out on the other side. 'You like asses so much. Eat this one.' He stuffed the picture whole into her mouth, then grabbed the electric cord from the broken lamp and looped it around her neck. He was beginning to take up the slack and pull when Theresa went for his eyes. She managed only to reach one cheek with her fingernails.

'Damn you.' He punched her full force with his left fist on the side of face, blood spattered from her nose onto the pillow. She was out cold.

By now Abby was through the door. She flung herself onto Joey's back, both arms around his neck pulling hard.

Joey rose up on his knees, throwing a shoulder toward the top of the bed. Abby went headlong over the top, landing on the pillows, the small of her back across the broken lamp, her feet up against the head of the bed and the wall. It knocked the wind out of her.

He grabbed the blouse and tore it off her arm, then pulled her down onto the bed like a rag doll. He tried to force his tongue into her mouth. Abby could smell alcohol like a distillery. He threw his body across her until he was straddling her on his knees at the edge of the bed. For a drunk he was amazingly agile.

He groped her breasts roughly. He put his hand on the waist band of her pants and ripped. The button shot off like a bullet. He tore the zipper open. As he raised up to reach inside, Abby thrust her hips high, as hard as she could. His knees went over the edge of the bed and gravity did the rest. His hands came out of her pants and Joey tumbled to the floor.

By now he was raging, though for a moment he was lost under the curtains from the window, looking like the headless horseman. He rose from his knees to his feet, still draped in the curtains.

With one hand he pulled down his zipper, with the other he fought to get the curtain off of his head. His pants went down around his ankles, underpants and all, fully exposing his bottom half, the curtain still over his head.

'Come here, bitch. Lemme show ya my cruise missile.'

Abby reached down and grabbed the lamp Joey had thrown at Theresa. It made a sound like a Chinese gong as hollow metal struck his head on the side. Joey's face had just cleared the cloth of the curtain so that his eyes looked like two glass marbles that had been scratched on concrete.

Abby wondered whether she should hit him one more time just for good measure. She was winding up as his bony knees buckled and he went down, dick first. Joey hit the floor with a thud.

She kicked him and pushed with her foot to make sure he was out. He went belly-up like a beached whale.

'Cruise missile, hell,' said Abby. 'More like a rain-soaked fire-cracker to me.'

CHAPTER
EIGHT

The evening air hung heavy with the odor of the tropics, in this case rotting bananas on the dock and the buzzing things that feasted on them.

He looked across at the *Cella Largo*, powdered his body with talcum, and donned the blue-black wet suit. Then he checked his equipment one last time: regulator and tanks. He checked his wrist compass for headings. Once in the water he would be blind.

Stripped to its essentials, a large ship is nothing but a floating power plant. The one he was looking at at the moment was an old oil burner, a stick ship with its cargo booms jutting to the sky, lit like a tree at Yuletide.

He possessed every piece of information available on this particular ship, courtesy of the voice on the phone, no doubt some drone. The people at the top always operated the same way using underlings and middlemen to distance themselves from the deed and any risk of incrimination.

According to the information, there were only two men on board, an officer and an engineer below decks to operate essential equipment.

He checked the pressure gauge on his tanks. They

were full. The device itself was not sophisticated or large. Its genius was simplicity. The object was to inflict just enough damage, and to leave nothing behind. It contained just enough explosives to do the job, an accelerant that would dissolve completely in salt water. The firing mechanism was a wooden clothes pin on a pull string. At the other end of the line was a small open parachute designed to be caught in a current of water. It was a variation on a car bomb he had once seen devised in Columbia to deal with a recalcitrant drug dealer who did not want to share territory. It blew the man's wife through the moon roof of her Mercedes.

The magic of the device was that the ship itself would detonate it the moment the engine started, like clockwork. The stirring of the giant diesel would muffle the blast. Anyone looking, after the fact, would think only one thing: a massive failure of the condenser head. Sea water streaming in and no way to stop it. The schedule was fixed. At precisely twenty-one hundred hours, the *Cella Largo* would fire up her engines to charge a bank of batteries used to power the inverter, which in turn provided electric power to certain circuits when the ship was in port. They would allow the engine to run for exactly forty minutes. Only this time they would not have nearly that long.

He checked his watch and realized that he was already four minutes behind schedule. He entered the water through a thick bank of reeds, and a minute later was engulfed in black murky waters.

The wheels touched the runway at LAX. Twenty minutes later the plane connected to the jet-way and they off-loaded like livestock down a shoot, everything but the mooing and cattle prods.

After being jumped by Joey at the motel, Abby and Theresa changed their plan and went stand-by on an evening flight to L.A. Joey was crazy, and the two women wanted to distance themselves as quickly as possible.

The departure lounge was already overflowing with the progeny of a canceled flight and another one delayed. People were standing in the aisles while others slept on chairs. The two women had to shoulder their way through the gathering crowd, hauling their luggage. Abby, swinging a nine-ton piece of Samsonite, nailed some guy in the leg. The man winced noticeably and groaned.

'Sorry. You O.K.?'

The guy rubbed his leg and gave her a dirty look.

'I'm really sorry.'

'It's alright.' He waved her off as if any effort on her part to minister to his wounds would only make it worse. She might drop the thing on his foot.

'Hold up,' Abby called to Theresa, and tried to catch her as she got lost in the crowd.

'Jeez, whadda they carry in their suitcases?' Stanley Salzman rubbed his leg while he held the fishing pole and trout net in his other hand. He wondered how he would explain the bruise to his wife when he and Sidner got back. Salzman was not much of a traveler. In fact, he hated it.

'What are those for?' Sidner pointed to the pole and the net.

'I got clothes to go with 'em,' said Salzman. 'For both of us, from wardrobe.'

'What for?'

'Let's hope we find this guy Cooper first thing. Maybe we get back tonight.' Salzman ignored the question.

'At least the woman Chandlis,' said Sidner. 'There's a chance we can cut a deal with her.'

'Carla didn't have much luck,' said Salzman.

'Carla didn't have a three-million-dollar budget.'

'I wish you'd quit saying that.' Salzman looked around as if somebody might hear. 'Three mil is tops. We don't start there. And we have to be careful. They get a whiff of that kinda money and suddenly they're gonna start thinking there's more where that came from, that we got pockets down to our ankles. Especially the woman, the lawyer. They're trained to think that way. There's only one way to buy rights, kid. Make 'em think you don't need it. Carla's first mistake.'

'Oh yeah. That's going to work. Two guys from Hollywood traveling to the back of beyond in search of an author nobody's ever heard of, and they're supposed to think we're only casually interested.'

'That's what this is for.' Salzman held up the pole. 'The Great Northwest. The home of the Sockeye. We're goin' fishin'. We just happened to be in the neighborhood. Thought you might be interested in selling your book to a major studio. Mixing a little business with pleasure. But we can take it or leave it.'

Salzman figured he was dealing with hicks. Open for a few thousand and grudgingly move toward six figures. Somewhere along the way Gable Cooper would cave like a card table, and give them an option on future works that would make slavery look charitable.

'You heard Mr Weig. Get the book at all costs.'

'Believe me, Mel Weig will understand if we erase a few zeros off of the check he has to write.'

It took him more than twenty minutes to cross the channel before his eyes glimpsed the ominous presence looming above. Forty feet up was a massive dark outline, a ceiling of steel plates curving at one edge toward the surface.

He came up slowly underneath the center of the ship near the keel. Using his flippers, he glided along the chine of the ship's curved bottom. Bubbles from the regulator's exhaust rolled off the barnacled plates and expanded as they floated toward the surface like shimmering silver balls.

He had only twenty minutes left by the time he found it; the entrance to the raw water intake. Here cold sea water was taken in and washed through the condenser to cool the engine. On most small trawlers a man could fit his hand into this opening. On the *Cella Largo* it was the size of a small cave, large enough to maneuver his entire body inside. But there was a problem. The opening was blocked by grillework. With all of the planning he'd never been told about this. He had not brought tools nor had he built time into his schedule to deal with it.

Quickly he pulled his diving knife from the sheath strapped to his ankle and poked at the rusting metal. He tried the screws that held the grille to the hull. They were frozen with rust. He pried at one of them and the head of the screw snapped off. A corner came loose. He checked his watch: nineteen minutes.

He slid the stainless-steel blade of the knife under the edge of the grille and lifted. Part of it, a sizable section, ripped free from around the screws, leaving a jagged edge of rusted metal like the rotting teeth of some sea denizen to guard the opening. Pulling and straining, he clawed his way inside. There was no time to waste. Seventeen minutes. Rusted metal ripped a gash in his wet suit and tore into the flesh of his thigh. He didn't even feel it, such was the rush of adrenaline.

He pushed himself free and swam deeper into the pipe. Using his arms he clawed his way along the water-filled duct until he was ten feet inside the ship's hull. He flipped on the flash light. The massive pipe took a turn. He followed it, careful not to bump the metal sides, something that might alert the watch in the engine room. Ahead he could see the fanlike blades attached to the impeller motor.

Gingerly he flipped around so that his head was now facing the opening in the pipe, the avenue of escape. Sixteen minutes to go. Now he worked frantically.

He removed the device from the bag and checked it under the light. The plastic covering was intact. It was taped to a small magnetized piece of metal. Carefully he lifted and placed it against the inside metal of the pipe until the magnet snapped and clung. With tremulous fingers he uncoiled the cord leading to the detonator. In his sojourn across the channel, part of it had knotted. It took some time to work these out. All the while checking his watch, time ticking away. He stretched out the line. With the small white nylon parachute open at the end floating free in the still waters of the pipe, the device took on a curious aspect. It looked like nothing so much as a dreaded Portuguese-man-o-war trailing a single deadly tentacle.

Inside the engine room Henry Handle looked at the clock pinioned on the pipe overhead. The second hand twitched, but it didn't move. It was frozen at eight forty-three. Henry wondered how long it had been stopped. He crossed the companionway and tapped the clock overhead with the back of his knuckle. It didn't move. He reached up and lifted the clock off of its hook. Suddenly it came to life. The sweep hand began to move. Henry looked at it. He couldn't be certain how long it had been stopped. He hung it back on the bolt and instantly it quit. He took it off, it started, put it back and it quit. Henry wasn't a whiz with machinery, but he knew what stopped clocks. He lifted it off again and instantly it started. He took a small metal pen knife from his pocket and raised it up toward the pipe, near the bolt. A half an inch away it jumped out of his hand and stuck fast to the metal of the conduit overhead.

'Son of a bitch.' Henry'd heard about salt water doing strange things to metal, oxidation in the form of rust, and worse, electrolysis that eats through it. But this was a first. He wasn't sure what was going on, but his principal concern at the moment was that he was late with the engines. He had no way of knowing how much time had passed since the clock quit. He walked back to the control panel and reached for the switches.

He was done. Using the flat of his palms against the smooth inner surface of the pipe, slowly, an inch at a time, he pulled his body toward the exit. He was careful not to kick with his fins. This might create a current in the pipe. He wasn't certain exactly how much force it would take to dislodge the firing pin and detonate the device. Given his present circumstance, he wasn't anxious to find out. He rounded the bend in the pipe and maneuvered his head out and past the grillework and into open water when the strap on one of his tanks hooked on a jagged piece of metal. He turned his head but couldn't see it. He gave a jerk with his body. Nothing. Somehow one of the straps to his tank had looped over an exposed edge of the grille. He reached around, tried his knife, but couldn't get it. He checked his watch. He had less than eight minutes to put distance between himself and the doomed ship. He offered up a lunging breaststroke with his arms in an effort to break free. The flippers on his feet hung like dead weight on a paralyzed man. He couldn't use them without stirring a current inside the pipe.

The upper part of his body protruded through the opening to the raw water intake like a man in the jaws of a giant whale. He was struggling to free himself when he heard it; an electrifying high-pitched hum magnified by the density of the water. It was an alarm transmitted through the steel hull overhead. Instinctively he knew what it was. Somewhere inside the bowels of the engine room someone had turned on the blowers, the fans that expelled diesel vapors. It was a prelude to the start of the engines. They were six minutes early.

It started as a deep rumble in the water, vibrations at the wide band of the sound spectrum, like some giant's phlegm-driven cough. The engine turned over but didn't start.

Frantically he tore at the strap. He tried to free the buckle on the belt to swim out of the tanks. The buckle caught. His hands fumbled with it.

Another cough of the engine. This time it kicked over twice and died. He owed his life to the cold-blooded diesel, notoriously hard to start. Finally the belt came free. He shrugged his shoulders out of the harness and swam. Just as the rumble began once more he hooked his foot. The strap of his fin caught on the metal and suddenly he stopped dead in the water. He looked back, his eyes bulging behind the glass of his mask. He reached down and freed his foot from the swim fin just as the blast hit.

The tempered steel of the pipe fractured like glass. Chunks of iron the size of a car door fell on top of Henry along with a shelf covered with heavy machine parts. It was strange, almost surreal, as if time had stopped. Henry lay on the iron bulkhead dazed, staring at the gaping hole over his head and wondering why nothing came out of it. There was only a thin spray and a few drops of salt water. His ears popped, and a second later the bubble from the blast dissipated out the end of the tube and rose along the hull of the ship toward the surface.

Then he heard it. Henry's eyes widened. Like the rush of Niagara, the water hit him with the force of a hydraulic cannon. He struggled with the weight across his lower body but couldn't budge it. Henry's legs were trapped. He called for help but his cries were drowned in the briny rush. Diesel fuel floated on the surface. Within seconds, the level had risen over his stomach to his shoulders. An instant later only his head remained above the water. He stretched and craned his neck to borrow a few seconds of life, when something hard and black hit his face in the rush of water. Henry looked in dazed wonderment as water rose above the level of his mouth and overtook his nostrils. His eyes bulged. He reached out a dying hand and with his last breath grasped the dark object that had slapped his face.

Like a bullet shot from the barrel of a gun he was expelled through the dark, soundless void like a body through rapids. Somewhere in the distance behind was a vague rumble. The resistance of the water finally stopped his headlong tumble, and he lay dazed, floating listless near the bottom. His first sensation was of choking. Hands reflexively to his mouth, he kicked hard for the surface. Swimming hand over hand, his frantic eyes probing the darkness, wondering if he was heading in the wrong direction. The senses of the inner ear were scrambled by the blast. He was out of breath, his lungs bursting as if on fire, as his outstretched hand met humid air. His head burst through the surface. He coughed and sputtered, grabbed his stomach with both hands, and retched up bubbles of sea water. He reached down and felt for his legs, uncertain whether both limbs would be there. Sculling the surface with his hands, he did a lazy circle with his body in the water. Behind him, perhaps two hundred feet away, there was an eerie incandescent glow from beneath the water at the side of the ship, a dozen points of shimmering light spanning the length of her hull. The *Cella Largo* settled into the water, the glimmering lights from its submerged port-holes streaming to the surface like a murder victim giving up its soul.

CHAPTER
NINE

The first two were dead ends. One of them had moved to Las Vegas a week before where he was doing stand-up comedy while he doubled as an aerobics instructor in a resort hotel.

They were down to the man Abby thought was the best-looking, but too young. His name was Jess Jermaine. He was twenty-six, dark hair, square jaw, a face chiseled from stone, and sparkling green eyes. When he opened the door to his apartment, Abby knew she was on the right track. If looks can be said to be magnetic, Jess Jermaine was the north pole, almost too good-looking. She guessed he stood just under six feet, with broad shoulders and a tan like a bronze god.

Standing in the open doorway to his apartment she explained that she was getting ready to audition several candidates for a role and that someone had given her Jess's name.

'It's a little unusual,' he said. 'Normally I get casting calls by phone from my agent.'

'It's an unusual situation,' she told him. 'A bit of a rush. But we're willing to pay for it.'

He opened the door and invited them in. Jermaine

studied Theresa, who was still wearing the oversized dark glasses.

The place was one big room, a studio with a fold-out bed in the couch.

He moved an old pizza box from a chair and offered Abby a place to sit. Theresa without asking flopped onto a large bean bag in the corner. It was the only thing left besides the bed, which Theresa considered for a moment, but it was covered with clothes waiting to be folded.

'You caught me doing laundry. I'd offer you something to drink, but I haven't done the weekly shopping.' He offered them a glass of water instead.

'We're fine,' said Abby.

'Looks like you could use a woman around here,' said Theresa.

'That's what my girlfriend keeps saying.' He pointed to her picture in the frame sitting on top of the television.

'Beautiful child,' said Theresa.

Abby shot her a dark look.

'Don't mind me. You guys talk. I'll just amuse myself,' said Theresa. She looked at the arm of the couch a foot away, some skimpy article in fake leopard skin that the hunk had not gotten around to. 'I'll just make myself useful.'

'What's the part?' Jermaine was ignoring her, talking to Abby. He was curious though he didn't give the impression that he was hungry.

'It might require some travel.'

'Film, television, or live stage?' he asked.

None of the above, thought Abby, but she would have to tread carefully or risk scaring him off. She was down to her last best shot for a Cooper stand-in. 'I think you'd have to characterize it as a live performance.'

'At least until they catch you,' said Theresa.

Jermaine looked at her, a little confused. 'I've done a little off Broadway,' he told Abby. 'A couple of years ago, before I came out to the coast.' He dropped onto the bed and draped a long leg in tight jeans over the arm of the sofa while he folded some socks. The T-shirt he was wearing was cut short, in the style of a college football jock. It showed a midriff, tanned, with abs rippled like a washboard.

'What we have in mind is not exactly Broadway,' said Abby.

'Yeah. Right town, wrong street.' Theresa was examining the leopard G-string she'd plucked off the arm of the couch. 'Do these things bind?' She smelled it like a connoisseur might a fine cigar, then pulled the pouch back and let it snap like a slingshot while holding onto the thong.

Abby gave her a look to kill.

'Can we cut to the chase?' said Jermaine. 'I've got an appointment in Studio City in an hour. An audition for a part in a commercial, and I don't wanna be late.'

'Then I take it you've done commercial photo shoots?' said Abby.

'I thought it was a part you guys were talking about. You're looking for a model?'

'Not exactly.'

'Well, what is it, a part or a shoot?'

'Your picture would be required, but there would be some acting as well,' said Abby.

'Where is it, how many days, and how much?' Just like that he was down to the dollars.

'The job's mostly in New York, I'm not precisely sure how long it will take, and the money – well the money is somewhat negotiable.'

Jermaine smiled as if perhaps he liked the sound of that. 'For photo shoots I get twenty-five hundred dollars a day, all expenses paid, accommodations in a four-star hotel or better, first-class air fare both ways, and I don't do anything in the buff.'

Theresa whistled low and long.

In fact, he never got any of these things, but he figured he might as well ask. He got up from the couch and crossed the room to where a calendar hung on the side of the refrigerator in the tiny kitchen.

'Let's see. I gotta be back in L.A. in a week, cuz I have another audition.' He had his back to them as he checked the calendar.

Abby looked over to see Theresa with the G-string over her head, the pouch arranged so that it covered her nose and mouth like an oxygen mask while she inhaled through the fabric, deep breathing. Then she laughed at Abby, who offered her an expression of fury.

Before Jermaine could turn around Theresa pulled the item from her head. 'What exactly defines the buff?' she said, dangling the G-string by its thong on a single finger.

'Underwear ads I do, as long as they're discreet, no cheeks.'

'Hey. Absolutely,' said Theresa. 'Do we look like ladies who'd come here and ask you to do something cheap, tawdry?'

'You'd be surprised at the things some people will ask you to do.'

'I'll bet I wouldn't,' said Theresa.

'I could tell you some stories,' said Jermaine.

'I'm all ears,' said Theresa.

'The man doesn't have time, *Terry*. Remember he has an audition.' Theresa had seen gargoyles with a more kindly expression than Abby's at this moment.

'I think we need to get to business,' said Abby. 'Cut to the chase as you say.'

She pulled one of her business cards from her pocket and handed it to Jermaine. 'I'm a lawyer. I have a client who shall remain nameless. This client is an author of some talent. For reasons that you don't need to know, the author has opted to write a major book, a novel, perhaps a bestseller, under a pen name. He does not want to be identified either to the public or the publisher. He's looking for someone to act as a stand-in.'

'Is that legal?' asked Jess.

'Yes. You can take my word. It's been thoroughly checked out. The job would include still photographs for the book's dustcover and if successful, public appearances. Perhaps television, and book autographing around the country if it comes to that.'

Jermaine made a face like he was impressed by the possibilities.

Theresa sat dumbstruck watching Abby and the ease with which she pulled it off, this final piece of subtlety, the ultimate lie: 'I have a client.' She didn't intend to tell Jermaine the truth until she thought she could trust him.

Jermaine's eyes lit up. 'You're kidding?'

'No.'

'Who pays for all this?'

'If there's any travel, the publisher.'

'I imagine there could be some good publicity,' he said.

'Yep.'

'And I get paid too?'

'A percentage of the advance.'

'How much?'

'We'll talk about that after I know whether you're interested.'

'I don't get it. What's the downside?'

Abby shrugged her shoulders as if there were none. 'Are you interested?'

'I don't know. Sounds good. I don't know anything about writing or publishing.'

'I need a decision.'

'What I don't understand is what's the point?' he asked. 'I mean, why is the author doing this?'

'From what we understand, the publisher's prepared to pay a lot of money to a man who wrote a novel that caught their attention. If he's good-looking and comes across well in the media, it feeds their confidence that they can market him. That makes the book more valuable.'

'You're kidding?'

'I wish I were,' said Abby. 'Are you interested?'

Jermaine started thinking. 'How much more valuable?'

'What do you mean?'

'You said if the author's good-looking, the book's more valuable. How much more?'

'We haven't entered negotiations yet. But you can forget any value-added formula. The author spilled his blood on this one.'

'Well, at least give me some guess as to what the book is worth?' he said.

'If I had to . . .' Abby considered for a moment. Owens didn't take clients unless they were worth multiples of six figures on a book. She wouldn't cross the country on a lark unless some publisher, maybe more than one, had an interest. It was always possible that the book could end up in an auction which would drive the price even higher.

'If I had to venture a guess, I would say maybe two hundred thousand by way of an advance, perhaps more.' She was being conservative. But it was better to be on the low side than to disappoint him later and have him walk out in the middle, after Owens had met him.

'And my portion?'

'Five percent?' said Abby. It was more of a question than a statement. She was desperate and Jermaine could smell it.

'Ten.'

'You'd have to sign a contract.'

He nodded.

'Done.'

They had to ring the bell twice and wait for more than a minute before the door opened. It had taken them two hours to find Abby's house in the University District.

A guy with a grizzled growth on his face who looked about six feet tall peeked out through the crack in the door left by the security chain.

'Whadda ya want?'

The glance exchanged between the two men on the stoop outside was one of amazement. Perhaps there was a God in heaven after all.

'Am I speaking to Gable Cooper?' Stanley Salzman already had a business card in his hand.

'Depends who's asking.'

'Someone with a business deal for you if you're Mr Cooper.'

The eyes that had looked out from under sleepy-hooded lids suddenly lifted.

'You are Mr Cooper?' Salzman slipped the business card through the crack in the door. In blue raised letters was the name of the studio and the logo that anybody who wasn't from Mars would recognize in an instant from the wide screen of a thousand movie theaters.

'Can we come in?'

They were wearing strange clothes. One of them had a tan cap with a bill that must have been a foot long. The thing had ear flaps. The other was dressed in some kind of canvas pants that looked like mildew had gotten to them in places. He had a canvas strap across his shoulder holding a straw basket on his hip. The entire affair looked like some kind of an antique fishing rig.

'Just a second.' Joey Jenrico closed the door, then walked down the hallway where he closed another. The second door led to a back room that Joey'd been trashing when the door bell rang. He'd already smashed all the dishes on the kitchen floor and emptied the contents of the refrigerator on top of them. Then he moved on to what he assumed was Theresa's room where he broke up most of the furniture and was working on Theresa's clothes with a knife when he was interrupted.

Joey would have told the two guys to get lost, except for the business card, and the mention of a deal; that and his mean curiosity. Joey was wondering if this guy Cooper was the one who was seeing Theresa. If so, he'd find the son of a bitch and either kill or cripple him, but not before seeing if there was a dollar in it. He wondered what the guys at the door were talking about. He could smell money, but how much?

He hustled back to the front door and opened it. Salzman came in first followed by Sidner, who asked where Abby Chandlis was.

'She's out,' said Joey.

'Then this is her house? We've got the right place?'

'Yeah. You were talking about a deal?' said Joey. First things first.

Salzman looked about and then suggested maybe they could sit in the living room to discuss business.

'Whatever.' Joey hesitated to give directions. He wasn't precisely sure where it was. Fortunately he hadn't had a chance to tear up the living room yet.

Salzman nodded toward what appeared to be the front room.

'Make yourself at home,' said Joey. 'I'd offer you drinks, but right now the kitchen's a mess.'

'We understand. We were just passing through,' said Salzman. 'On our way north for a fishing trip. You just get in yourself?'

Joey misunderstood the question and looked at them with a blank gaze. For a moment he thought maybe they'd been parked outside and had seen him breaking the screen and climbing through the side window.

'We heard you were down in Mexico,' said Salzman.

'Oh. Yeah.'

'A good trip, I hope?'

'Yeah. Had fun.'

'I thought you were working?'

'That too. What's this all about?'

'One of our colleagues at the studio heard we were taking a trip up here to do a little fishing, so he asked us if we could stop in and talk to you for a few minutes.'

Joey peeked through the blinds in the front window. He'd heard about cops gaining entry with some bullshit story when they suspected a crime in progress. Maybe a neighbor had called them. But he could see a fishing pole in the back window of the car parked out front.

'Talk about what?' said Joey.

'Your book of course.'

'Oh.' Joey thought for a moment. 'That,' he said. Joey gave them a lazy nod as if he knew what they were talking about.

'He thinks your book is pretty good. This friend of ours.'

'Then he already has it?' Joey was hoping he wouldn't have to find it. Given the state of the house, it was probably under the rest of the shit he'd already dumped in the back room.

'Oh yeah. I guess you're wondering how we got it?'

Joey shook his head like he could care less.

'Well. We have our sources. I hope you don't mind?'

'Why should I mind?'

'Precisely,' said Salzman. 'We were thinking maybe there's some film possibilities in the story. Nothing certain, mind you, but it has potential. We option a lot of things. Very few of them go into production, actually get made, you understand. But we like to keep the pipeline full of ideas.'

Joey raised his eyebrows in thoughtful contemplation. 'This pipeline, it must cost a lot to fill up? How much you willing to pay?'

Salzman smiled. Direct. He liked that. 'The kind of author I like. A bottom-line man,' said Salzman. 'A few thousand maybe. We understand that you're at work on a second book at the present time. A sequel?'

'I suppose,' said Joey. He didn't know what a sequel was, but it sounded like the movie man did so he went along.

'If we could package the whole thing, both books, tie them up at the same time, get a solid option on future works,' said Salzman. He sized Joey up in his mind and the picture came to pocket change. 'We might be willing to go as high as twenty, maybe twenty-five thousand.'

It was more money than Joey had ever seen at one time in his life. Dead or alive, this guy Cooper was valuable. Maybe he wouldn't kill him right away even if he was bonking Theresa, at least not before he did whatever this sequel thing was.

'You have to understand,' said Salzman, 'we only do this, go this high, because the studio likes to encourage a promising new writer. Feeding new talent so to speak.'

'Right. And when would this happen? This feeding of talent.' Joey was no writer but he knew bullshit when he heard it.

'As soon as our lawyers can put the contract together.' Salzman couldn't believe how smoothly this was going.

'How long would that take?'

Usually it took weeks, but under the circumstances they could use the standard form, the one they used with screen writers that gave them nothing but the money. They would grab off character rights and plant an option in the agreement that would guarantee that they owned all screen rights to Cooper's next three books. Before he knew it, he'd be on the studio plantation picking cotton out of his navel.

'I could make a phone call and have it back to you overnight express, three days tops,' said Salzman.

'Twenty-five thousand,' said Joey.

'I said twenty, maybe twenty-five.'

Sidner almost jumped on Salzman when he heard this.

'But since you've been so reasonable, twenty-five it is.' Salzman looked at his partner and winked.

Joey would have sold them whatever they wanted for a tenth of that, particularly if he could have it now, in cash.

'When do I get the money?'

'As soon as you sign the contract, we'll send the check.'

'No check,' said Joey. 'I want cash.'

'The studio doesn't deal in cash. What are you worried about, you saw the card. We're good for the money. Just give us the name for the check.'

'The name?' said Joey.

'We were led to believe that Gable Cooper was a pen name. You give us your real name, and we'll make the contract out and the check as well.'

Sometimes you live right, and the sun shines on you, thought Joey.

'I want it to go to a P.O. box. That alright?'

'That's fine. Anything you want.'

'The name's Joey Jenrico.' He spelled it for them while Sidner took notes.

'You wrote a wonderful book, Mr Jenrico. You keep it up,' said Salzman, 'and you'll have a big future in front of you.' It's what publishers, studios, and agents told every writer in order to keep their nose to the stone and their eyes off of business.

Sidner wrote down the name and mailing information along with Joey's social security number for reporting the payment to the IRS. Mel Weig was gonna love the price, though he would be disappointed by the fact that Jenrico was clearly no bestselling author. But then, what did he expect for twenty-five thousand – the fucking moon?

CHAPTER
TEN

Bertoli looked up the unlisted number and punched the buttons on the phone. It rang once before she answered.

'Carla. Alex here. You got problems.'

'What's the matter?' Carla Owens was sprawled on her bed with a pile of manuscripts, stuff culled by her staff that showed promise for new clients. Unfortunately none of it came up to the commercial quality of Gable Cooper's book. She saw one of those every ten years, if she was lucky.

'I'm hearing some troubling stories out of L.A.,' said Bertoli. 'Information that your friend Mel Weig has picked up the film rights on Cooper's book for peanuts.'

'What are you talking about?' Owens dropped the manuscript she was reading and lost her page.

'I'm talking about a screw job, that's what I'm talking about.'

'No film rights have been sold,' said Owens.

'Then somebody's dealing behind your back. I thought we had a deal, Carla.'

'I don't know what you're talking about. Slow down and tell me what's going on.'

'Somebody from the studio – I don't know who yet – got hold of Cooper.'

'Where did this happen?'

'I don't know.'

'When?'

'Yesterday. Maybe the day before. It wasn't clear.'

'What happened?'

'What do you mean what happened? They cut a deal directly.'

'They wouldn't do that,' she told him. 'I talked to Weig the other day. He gave me his word. I was getting ready to negotiate a deal. Just waiting for the right moment.'

'Well, they aren't waiting any more. And it gets worse. From what I'm hearing they tied the thing up for pocket change. Stole it,' said Bertoli. 'Not only the current book, but the new one he's working on.'

'What do you mean?' asked Carla.

'I'm hearing twenty-five thousand.'

'You're out of your mind,' said Owens. 'Weig knows it's worth more than that.'

'Yes, but the question is, does Cooper?'

'Who told you this?'

'You think we're the only ones with a leak in the pipeline? I've got my sources.'

'Who?'

'*My* sources,' said Bertoli. He no longer trusted her. He couldn't be sure whether she had been duped, or if maybe there was some devilish plan here and Carla was part of it.

In fact, she hadn't told him everything, including the fact that Abby had called her that afternoon to tell her that Cooper was on his way home and would be in New York in two days. The timing of Abby's call and now

Bertoli's information set off alarms in Carla's head.

'It's probably garbage,' she told him.

'No. I don't think so. It comes from somebody in a position to know. And if it's true, I'm not sure we'd still be interested in publication rights, certainly not for anything approaching the dollars we've been talking about.'

'Listen, Alex, don't panic. If something's going on I'll find out what it is.'

'It's a little late to find out, don't you think?'

'Are you telling me Cooper's already signed a contract?' There was actually cold sweat forming on her upper lip as she asked the question. If Cooper had signed away film rights for twenty-five thousand, they could all fold their tents and go home. Mega-bucks bestsellers and blockbusting films were not made in the bargain basement. The studio could recoup this kind of investment with something shot over a weekend in somebody's garage. Cooper's career would be over before it started.

'He hasn't signed yet. But I'm told that the terms are already agreed to verbally.'

'Any money change hands?'

'That I don't know. But I don't think so.'

'Then you know what they say about verbal agreements,' said Carla.

'What's that?'

'Not worth the paper they're written on. Let me look into it. I'll get back to you.'

The dial tone barely had time to stutter and Carla was punching buttons. It rang once, twice, three times and the taped message came on. She waited. The message beep lasted for several seconds. Abby hadn't cleared the earlier messages. Carla tried to piece it together. Abby must have called her from somewhere else – the studio in L.A.; Carla's devious mind.

'Abby. This is Carla Owens. If you're there, please pick up.' She waited for a moment. No answer.

'There's something that's come up that we have to discuss.' She waited again. Still no answer.

'Listen, it's urgent. If you haven't left already or if you clear this message, please call me. I repeat, it's urgent. It doesn't matter what time it is, just call.' She left phone numbers for her home, cell phone, and office on the tape.

She waited several more seconds hoping someone would pick it up. All she heard was the hiss of the tape as it turned inside the answering machine. What she couldn't have known was that it lay buried under broken glass and the rotting remnants of food from Abby's refrigerator. Still the message wasn't without an audience. Sitting in the corner killing time, playing mumblety-peg with a pocket knife into one of the kitchen cabinet doors, Joey Jenrico was waiting for Theresa.

A bby stayed in L.A. the next day and worked with Jess, briefing him on the book. She would take the red-eye from L.A. to New York.

Theresa was staying with friends in southern California. She would be there for at least a week. Terry was treating it as a vacation with Abby's encouragement and blessing, especially after their row with Joey at the motel. For a few days at least, Abby wouldn't have to worry about her friend.

The plan was that Abby would meet Carla alone in New York and that together the two women would pick up Jess at the airport the following day, presumably coming in from Mexico. Jess would transfer planes in Dallas so there would be no way for Carla to trace his point of origin.

Abby was the advance team. Meeting Carla alone would give her time to find out if Owens had any surprises in store. She and Jess had set up a signal; she would get sick if there was something he should know. They could regroup at the hotel for strategy and meet with Owens again once they'd made adjustments to their story.

He seemed to have it down pat, all the answers on how he wrote the book, how the story line came to him, how he selected the pen name and the title, what he was doing down in Mexico and where. For this Abby had brought some maps and travel brochures. Jess was even prepared to offer a few titillating details about the sequel, the follow-up book that Abby was now working on.

Jess was a quick study and by the time she left for the airport Abby was confident that he could pull it off. On the way to LAX she took care of a little business. She made a telephone call to Charlie's answering service and dropped an envelope in the mail. In the phone message she told Charlie that his credit card was in the mail. What she didn't tell him was that before she mailed it, she booked two round-trip tickets to New York as well as rooms in a modest hotel not far from Carla Owens's office using Charlie's card. Then she took a cash advance against the card to pay for the rooms and meals. In terms of expenses, she was not yet even with Charlie for the marital debts, but it was a good down payment. She told him this in a note that she sent along with the card. He would be wasting his time if he tried to file charges. There were some things the criminal law did not handle well, among them ex-spouses fighting over money. Prosecutors usually wouldn't get involved, and Charlie would know civil court was a loser. She'd clean his clock. After all, while the method of collection may have been unusual, the debt was valid.

Abby slept for most of the flight. She didn't arrive at the hotel in Manhattan until after two in the morning. She paid cash for the room, followed the bellman with her bags upstairs to her room, and was asleep within twenty minutes.

The wake-up call came at seven the next morning. Abby rose and showered. She didn't see it until she passed the closed door to her room the second time on her way from the bathroom to dress; a small white envelope on the floor. Someone had slipped it under the door in the middle of the night.

She opened it. Inside was a note on a hotel message slip scrawled in the hand of what she assumed was the clerk.

'Ms Chandlis: Sorry to do this to you at the last minute, but I won't be able to make it to New York. Something has come up. I've made arrangements. Trust me. Everything will work out.

Jess.'

The adrenaline raced through her body like molten lead. If he had been there at that moment, she would have killed him. 'Trust me. Everything will work out.' He had the brains of a banana.

Abby had been warned by Morgan and Theresa, and even that little voice inside her conservative lawyer's mind, not to trust a piece of beefcake with the dreams of her life. Now she was paying the price.

She had told Carla that he would be there the next day. If he didn't show up, Owens would start to suspect that something was going on. If Abby came clean and told her that she had in fact written the book, Owens would never believe her. It's the problem with coming clean after a lie, even the truth takes on the tinge of deceit.

Abby made a beeline for the phone. She called Jess's number in Los Angeles. It rang four times and was cut off by the mechanical voice of an operator: 'Your party is not answering. If you wish to leave a message, press the pound sign.'

Abby hit it so hard she broke a fingernail.

'Leave your message at the sound of the tone.'

'Listen, you son of a bitch. You made a deal. If you don't get your ass back here I'll wrap a law suit around your head like an iron mask. You won't live long enough to pay off the judgment. Do you understand me? And don't give me any excuses, just get your ass on a plane and get back here.'

Then she wondered whether by scaring him he might simply avoid her. It was something Charlie had told her in dealing with his special breed of clients. The first instinct of every flake is to run. She softened her tone a little. 'Wait, Jess. I'm sorry. I'm upset. I just want you to call me. I mean it. If there's a problem, we can work it out, but call me.' She left the phone number at the hotel and hung up, then sat by the phone and waited.

An hour went by. There was no response. She rubbed sleep from her eyes and looked at the red light on the phone. She cupped it with her hand to make sure. Maybe he'd called and left a message and they hadn't put it through. But the light was not on.

She called the front desk. No messages.

By now his plane would have left L.A. Jess was not coming, and Abby knew it. She saw her life going up in flames. She had spent two years writing a novel to die for, and now all of her work as well as her dreams were being undone by some Hollywood jock. She had visions of Jess lying in bed with some starlet bimbo, figuring ways to convert Abby's plane ticket into a trip to Vegas for two.

There was nothing she could do. She looked at her watch.

It was now eight o'clock. She was scheduled to meet Owens downstairs in half an hour for breakfast to talk, before they went to pick up Gable Cooper at the airport. Gable who was not coming.

There was no sense in prolonging the pain. She picked up the receiver and punched Carla's office number. If she couldn't get her perhaps her staff could head her off before she got to the hotel. Abby had no desire to meet with her, or to talk.

The phone was answered almost before it had a chance to even ring. The voice was exuberant, high-pitched.

'Hello.'

'Who is this?' Abby thought she'd dialed the wrong number.

'Who are you trying to reach?'

'I was calling Owens and Associates.'

'Abby, is that you?' It was Carla herself. 'I'm glad you got in. Did you get any sleep?'

'Not much.'

'Listen, if you're tired we can push everything back a few hours.'

'That's what I wanted to call you about. There's been a problem. It's Gable . . .'

'Oh, listen, darling. He's everything you'd said he would be, and more. We've been having a wonderful time here in the office talking.'

'What?'

'We've been visiting for the past hour. I guess you guys must have messed up on the flight arrivals. He came in by taxi early this morning and my service called me. We've had breakfast and have been talking ever since. Oh. And by the way, disregard that message I left on your answering machine. Somebody got their wires crossed. We'll get to the bottom of it when you come in. How long are you going to be?'

Abby was dazed, confused. Maybe the note was a mistake. It felt like a reprieve from the hangman. She looked at her watch, and then at the mirror. She was a mess.

'Give me forty minutes.'

'Good. See you then, darling.' With that, Owens hung up in her ear. It seemed Carla had what she wanted.

CHAPTER
ELEVEN

In New York it had been the winter from hell, and it looked as if it would never end. It was officially spring, and several inches of snow blanketed the sidewalks of Manhattan. People huddled in doorways emitting vaporous breath.

In the congestion and snow, it took Abby nearly an hour to reach Owens's office. It was on the fortieth floor of a skyscraper, a suite that took up most of the corner of the building. For a literary agent it was flashy. Abby had seen agent's offices before. The ones she had known were usually in brownstones or office buildings in the lower rent districts.

Carla's was on Madison Avenue, nestled among law offices and the executive suite of a major insurance company. Her name was emblazoned in silver script, letters a foot high across the black glass double doors.

OWENS & ASSOCIATES
LITERARY AGENTS

Abby counted nine names underneath Carla's stenciled on the sidelight.

When she pulled the brass handle, the door gave way like a bank vault opening, slow and hushed. A receptionist in a sky blue silk dress sat behind a sweeping black lacquer counter taking phone calls. The outer office looked like the flight bridge from a star ship, all curved symmetry and geodesic forms. She sank into the maroon carpet as she crossed the room, a cushion of plush to her ankles. There were walls of smoked mirrors so that she couldn't tell where room ended and the private corridors began. The reception area was cloaked in muted light from overhead canisters.

As soon as Abby reached the counter, the woman behind it looked up and smiled. 'Can I help you?'

'I'm here to see Carla Owens. My name is Abby Chandlis.'

'Oh yes, Ms Chandlis. They're waiting for you in Ms Owens's office. Just a moment. I'll ring.'

Abby looked about as the receptionist punched buttons and talked on the phone. A moment later she heard a voice, 'Ms Chandlis,' and turned. Standing in front of her was an African-American woman, tall and slender, with cheekbones like chiseled onyx and striking oval eyes. She was wearing a soft wool dress that clung to her flowing contours. Abby figured the dress must have cost at least a thousand dollars.

'I'm Jadra, Ms Owens's secretary. I'm pleased to meet you. I've heard so much about you,' said the secretary. 'If you could follow me this way. They're waiting for you.'

Abby walked behind Jadra down a long corridor, a labyrinthine affair of smoked glass walls through which Abby could see the dark outline of minions laboring inside, some on the phones, others hunched over documents and piles of manuscripts.

In the reflection of the walls, Abby self-consciously straightened her dress, anxiously aware of the fact that it was the best thing she owned. She hoped and prayed that Jess had kept to the details they had gone over in their briefing session in Los Angeles, and not adlibbed. She was still troubled by the note that had been pushed under her door and what had led him to change his mind, first not to come at all, and then to come early.

The corridor ended in a massive double door of striking contrast to the rest of the office, a swirling bird's-eye maple with modern brass handles.

As Jadra reached for the door, Abby took a deep breath and tried to compose herself. It swung open and she could see Carla facing her, seated behind a shimmering glass desk with transparent curved legs. It sat on a pedestal a foot above the rest of the office. On the same level were two client chairs facing away from Abby and the door. Jess sat in one of these with his back to her.

'Well, here she is now.' Carla rose from her chair, her arms extended like some high priestess about to slay a sacrifice upon an altar of crystal.

'Abby, darling, it's wonderful to see you again. How was your flight? You look wonderful. Doesn't she look wonderful? Come in. Come in. Would you like a cup of coffee?'

Before Abby could answer, Carla said, 'Jadra, get her a cup of coffee. Cream and sugar?'

Abby didn't feel like it, but it was easier to go along. 'Just black,' she said.

'Just black.' Carla repeated it as if Jadra was deaf to all but her own voice.

Abby took four steps and was halfway to the desk when suddenly Jess rose, turned and in two strides, came off the platform, and covered the distance between them. It was not until she glanced away from Carla and focused for an instant on the form moving toward her that she realized; the man coming at her like a loco-motive was not Jess Jermaine.

'So what have we got?' Morgan Spencer sat behind his desk looking at the contents of a small paper sack spread out before him on the desk.

Alvin Cummings stood at one corner and pointed with a ruler. Cummings was an investigator, retired from the military, and a specialist in naval ordinance. He had been brought in by Morgan's client, a maritime insurance company.

'Looks like a scrap of wood,' said Morgan. He moved it around on the blotter with the point of his pen.

'That's what it is,' said Cummings. It was less than an inch long and appeared to be charred at one end.

'The lab believes it's part of a clothes pin. You can see right there it has a tiny hole drilled in one end. If they're correct, this was where the string was attached that ran to whatever was used to detonate it. They found traces of nylon fiber, probably parts of the string.'

'Yeah, and maybe it's something they used to hang a clipboard down in that engine room. Pretty thin basis to deny a claim,' said Morgan. 'Anything else?'

'Some chemicals in the wood. They're not precisely sure what yet. But it appears to contain nitrates. Most of it would have dissolved in the sea water.'

'So final analysis is they don't have squat, but they don't wanna pay off. Is that it?'

Cummings looked at him and nodded.

'I'm gonna have to tell the client it's a no go,' said Spencer. 'They try to stonewall this one, they could be looking at bad faith, the boundless world of punitive damages,' said the lawyer. 'You want to tell them or should I?'

'I think we shouldn't be hasty,' said Cummings.

'There's something more?'

Cummings nodded. 'I think there was a bomb.'

'Fine. Even if there was, they can't avoid payment. Act of war clause wouldn't apply to terrorism or sabotage,' said Spencer. 'The ship didn't go down in a war zone. There's no exclusion for coverage.'

'I'm not talking terrorism or sabotage.'

'What then?' said Spencer. 'The boat's sitting in a harbor in some banana republic, a country with revolutions on alternate Tuesdays. It's what I'd be looking at. Crude bomb with household chemicals. Some guerilla group.'

'I don't think so,' said Cummings. 'Somebody went to a lot of trouble to make it look like an accident.'

'How so?'

'Ordinarily, if you want to send a ship to the bottom, you'd use shaped charges. It's easy enough to get on the open market. Or you just steal the commercial stuff from some construction company. This would be something you mold like putty. C-4 is the military version. You make a rope, as long as you want. Form it in a circle and attach it to the hull, and it'll cut a ring any size you want right out of the steel plates. You want a five-foot hole, make a five-foot circle. But they didn't do that here. You gotta ask yourself why?'

'I was hoping you'd know,' said Morgan. 'All that intuition working overtime.'

'Instead of a hole in the hull, we get massive failure in the condenser.'

'So?'

'So it's made to look like a maintenance problem.'

'Probably what it was,' said Spencer. It was easy for the carrier to say 'no – we won't pay' and for the investigator to feed them theories to match their fantasies, but in the end Spencer would have to feed those same theories to a jury. And what he had to work with here didn't look good.

'Except for one thing,' said Cummings. He lifted a black plastic bag from the floor, opened it, and reached inside. What he pulled out he tossed across the desk to Spencer, who caught it almost in self-defense. It was a large black rubber fin, a skin diver's flipper, the expensive kind that a pro would wear with adjustable heel straps to accommodate a diver's wet suit or dry suit. It had a pivoting plane on the front edge for more power in the water.

'We found that in the drowned crewman's hand. Regular death grip,' said Cummings. 'As well as traces of neoprene caught on the screen leading into the raw water intake. You can take my word for it. The *Cella Largo* went to the bottom because of a bomb.'

Morgan looked at the heavy hunk of rubber in his hand. The case had suddenly grown major complications. The file would be with him for years. Authorities would soon be discussing theories of murder.

Abby would have spoken but for the shock of it as the man's arms embraced her, his mouth covering hers. He was powerful and forced the breath from her lungs like bellows. For an instant, she thought his tongue was trying to invade her mouth, and she began to recoil. Then she realized that as he kissed her unresponsive lips, he was in fact trying to say something.

Under his breath and impaired by the crush of their lips it sounded a lot like: 'Hess's mother.'

Abby might have resisted, but at the moment she was in shock. His tongue grazed her closed lips, and he finally gave up the kiss and pulled his head away to the side for a long follow-up hug that nearly broke her ribs. It was an effort to keep her from speaking as he whispered into her right ear.

'The name is Jack. I'm Jess's brother. Keep your cool. We'll work through this. Don't blow it, sweetheart. Now give me a hug like you mean it.'

Abby didn't realize it, but her arms on his back, the only part of her that Carla could see, were limp as a rag doll. Thank God that at the moment her face was lost in his shoulder.

Reluctantly she flattened her hands against the breadth of his shoulders and squeezed. He was several inches taller than Abby and hard as a rock, and while she recoiled at the thought of enjoying the experience she couldn't claim that it was unpleasant, either.

'Good,' he whispered. 'Now smile.'

When he turned to face Carla again, this time holding Abby's hand, he was flashing a mischievous, broad grin. Abby's expression was one of smiling bewilderment. She felt sick and nearly looked the part. They walked hand in hand back to the client chairs, and he held one as Abby sat down. Jack then dropped into the one next to her.

'Abby are you O.K.?' Carla was suddenly focused on her. 'You look a little flushed.'

'Probably the trip,' Jack spoke before Abby could answer. 'She doesn't like to fly.' He pointed to the side of his head and smiled.

For a moment Abby thought he was giving the signal that she was mentally touched. Then he said, 'Inner ear thing.'

'Aw.'

Then he turned to Abby. 'Ms Owens has been telling me that the book is likely to draw a crowd in an auction for rights. She thinks it's quite possible we could get to *seven* figures.' He said the word 'seven' slowly so it would sink in, as if he was telling her to count the zeros before she spoke.

All the while Abby's eyes were on Carla seated across the desk. She heard his words, but what sent the chill down Abby's spine was the fact that Owens was not denying or qualifying them in any way. Instead she was nodding with a confident smile.

For the first time, Abby realized that the book she had written over two years of her life, sweat and toil, could be worth a million dollars. It made the hair on the nape of her neck stand out, and fired the blood in her veins. She smiled and shook, her hands trembling. A million-dollar novel. It was the stuff of dreams.

'I think she's overcome,' said Jack.

Abby nodded, but her voice had left her. As much as she tried, she couldn't speak.

'I think I should get her back to the hotel,' he said. 'I think the trip's affected her a little more than I thought.'

'Of course,' said Carla. 'We can talk again tonight over dinner, sign the contract in the morning. In the meantime, I'll straighten out the mess with this Joey Jenrico guy.'

With the mention of the name Abby's eyes darted. She wanted to ask, but didn't dare.

'I don't know where the studio got the idea that he wrote the book,' said Carla. 'Some interloper. But now I know what happened. Who he is. We'll take care of it. Get to the bottom of it.'

'What studio?' asked Abby.

132

'Oh, that's the rest of it,' he said. 'I'll have to bring her current back at the hotel. Carla says there's major film interest in the book out in Hollywood. We'll be talking about that tomorrow.'

As the three of them moved toward the door, Abby's knees were actually going weak. He held her hand and finally had to put an arm around her shoulder to steady her.

'It's just great, isn't it, darling?' He was talking to Abby, holding her up like some drunk. 'Ms Owens . . .'

'Carla. Please.' She corrected him.

He smiled, pearly whites that seemed to melt the agent in place. 'Carla thinks my book could be a major bestseller by summer.'

'Trust me,' said Carla. 'It'll be in the hands of passengers on every plane in the world, and around the pools of luxury resorts from Barbados to Bar Harbor, Trinidad to Tahiti. We have a unique opportunity with a publisher on the Summer list.'

'Don't you think it's great?' He was looking at Abby.

She gazed back at him, this stranger, tanned and tall. He looked like Jess, only older, with blue eyes, piercing, and deep as two tropical pools. He was nodding encouragement, a gesture for her to say something. But she was speechless. All she could do was to issue an inane smile.

Though she had planned all of this meticulously for months, the use of the possessive 'my book' by a man she had never seen before was like a sucker-punch in the gut for Abby. It carried her back to sober reality, to the realization that she had written a major bestselling novel, and she could not tell a soul. Abby had buried herself in a sea of anonymity.

'Who the hell are you?' Abby found her voice the instant the cab door closed behind the two of them and the driver pulled away from the curb.

'The name's Jack Jermaine.' He held out his hand for a shake. She ignored it.

'I forgot. We already kissed.' He smiled at her. There was something devilish and infuriating in the curl of his lips and the twinkle of those blue eyes.

Abby shot him a look that might have been something out of a spear gun with multiple barbs. 'Who invited you into my life?'

'I thought you'd be pleased.'

'You're Jess's brother?'

He nodded. 'Older and wiser,' he said.

'Where the hell is Jess?'

'If I had to guess, somewhere in a studio out in West L.A.'

'He made a deal to be here,' she said. 'I gave him tickets and told him I'd pay him.'

'Well, now you can pay me.'

'That's not the deal.'

'O.K. We'll go to Carla tonight and tell her I'm not really Gable Cooper. He's really my brother out in Hollywood, but he had a conflict, and couldn't . . .'

'Shut up,' she said. 'Let me think.' She thought for a moment, picking at the words out of his mouth.

'What conflict?' She was talking about Jess again. She wanted to know the details, the crisis that had led him to back out in order to measure it. Maybe it was true, in which case she might trust Jack a little more. Maybe the man was in the hospital half dead.

'He calls me in the middle of the night,' said Jack, 'and gets me outta bed. "Hey bro, is that you?" Who else would it be at that hour? That's Jess,' said Jack.

'Listen, he says, I got something for you. Now mind you, Jess's voice on the other end is sounding frantic at this point. I ask him what time it is. He tells me ten-thirty. I look at my clock, it's after one in the morning. Jess says it's only ten-thirty out there. I tell him, Yeah well, that's the funny thing about the sun and the rotation of the earth.'

'Has all of this got a point?' said Abby.

'I'm getting to it. He tells me he has got a phone call from an advertising firm late last night, I guess after you guys talked and you'd left. He didn't know what to do, so he calls me. He says this guy, this producer, is putting together a major campaign for a coffee company. One of those continuing soaps. You know the kind. Will she take it straight up or with cream, and will he do her doggie-style while she's loading the Mr Coffee.'

Abby looked at him with disapproval.

'Jess's words. I swear. That's what he said to me on the phone.' He held up two fingers like the Cub Scout salute. 'He's a little crude sometimes.'

'Yeah and you think it's cute.'

Jack gave her a sheepish grin that said she was probably right.

'So what about this thing? This ad?'

'Anyway, he tells me they've offered him the part. He says these kind of ads win awards, make careers. I say, yeah, right, Golden Globe. He says, no, no. The last two, the girl and guy who did these, are now doing appearances on *Good Morning America*.'

'That's why he's not here?' said Abby.

'Yeah. He said they were gonna start shooting in the morning. He had to be there. Then he tells me about your problem. And here I am.'

'My problem?' Abby looked at him like Vesuvius

about to erupt. 'My problem is that I trusted that flake of a brother of yours, some jock who uses fake leopard skin to floss the crack of his butt. I should have known better.'

Jack looked at her. 'Flossed the what?'

'Nevermind.'

'Hey listen. If you guys got it on, it's none of my business.' He gave her that look, a devilish grin, and then stared up at the cab's ceiling. 'That slippery brother of mine.'

'We didn't get it on.'

'Whatever you say.' Jack was still smiling, the devil in his eyes.

'If you must know, he was doing his laundry and on the couch was this thing, this . . .' She searched for the right word and then realized what she was doing. 'Why am I explaining this to you?'

'I don't know. Do you feel guilty?' Jack could take irritation to the level of an art form.

'Listen, asshole.' She said it with emphasis.

'This from the woman who was offended by the mention of doggie-style?'

'Shut up.'

He was still smiling, though he did stop talking.

'And what's this about Joey Jenrico?' she said.

'Who is he, anyway?'

'An acquaintance,' said Abby.

'Yeah, well, with friends like that you don't need any enemies.'

'Why. What did he do?'

'Seems the film people somehow ran into this guy in Seattle. They were looking for you. From there it gets a little hazy. All Carla knows is that somehow they came away with the impression that he was the author, this

Gable Cooper. And it seems he did nothing to set them straight. Now the folks in Hollywood think they have a deal with him for film rights.'

It was Abby's worse nightmare.

'Not to worry. I took care of it.'

'What did you do? What did you tell her?'

'I told her he was some guy I used to run around with years ago who is now off his nut. That he did drugs in another life and had a bad trip. It's a sad story, but the man now has trouble remembering the number of toes on his feet.'

'Wonderful. So now you've got Gable consorting with drug users.'

'Hey, listen, to these folks that would be a major marketing angle. I could have told her this Joey and I were former lovers and she would have smiled, scheduled us for Oprah, and calculated the audience share.'

She shot him a quick glance.

'I didn't,' he said. He held up a hand. 'So where do we go from here?' he asked.

'For the moment I figure some way to get you out of my life.'

'Well, you can think about it, but for right now, unless you want to throw away a good deal, I think we're joined at the hip as they say.'

'You have a high opinion of yourself. Maybe I don't see you as such a good deal.'

'Oh, I have my qualities. But that's not what I was talking about. That's right. I forget. You didn't hear the rest of it.'

'The rest of what?'

'You never told me who he was. This Jenrico guy.'

'Later. The rest of what?'

'You must have written one hell of a book. Someday

you'll have to tell me how you did it.'

'The rest of what?' She was getting angry again.

'Don't bang your head jumping up in the car, but Carla thinks the whole package, the book rights and film stuff . . .'

'Yes?'

'She thinks it's possible the whole thing, the author's take, could be worth as much as two million dollars.'

CHAPTER
TWELVE

A bby had not yet come down from the psychic buzz, the figures laid on her by Jack in the cab, as she was dialing a number in Seattle on the phone from her hotel room.

Abby had put Jack up in a room down the hall in the hotel for a night until she could think of what to do. While he was waiting for his room to be cleaned, Jack sat sprawled in a chair in the corner munching peanuts from a bag he'd taken out of the snack bar near the television set.

The phone rang twice. 'Starl, Hobbs and Carlton, law offices.'

'Katie. This is Abby. Is Morgan around?' Abby looked at her watch. It was early on the West Coast and she was hoping that Morgan would be there.

'Let me check.' The phone went dead while she was put on hold.

'You never told me who this guy Jenrico was?' said Jack.

'He was married to a friend of mine. He beat the crap out of her and she divorced him. I handled the case.'

'So now he has it in for the two of you.'

'You could say that.'

'How much does he know about the book?'

'Nothing.'

'Well, he must know something if he got the film people to buy into the fact that he wrote it.'

'I don't think he knows anything.'

'What about your friend? His wife. What's her name?'

'Theresa.'

'What does she know?'

'She wouldn't tell him.'

'So she knows you wrote it.'

'Yes, but she wouldn't tell Joey.'

'If she did, or if she does, you're gonna have a problem,' said Jack.

'What's that?'

'He has something to hold over your head that could be worth two million dollars, the truth about the book. If it came out at the wrong time. In the wrong way. That could do some real damage.'

He was right, and if he got to Theresa, it wouldn't take Joey long to figure it out. She was worried about something else, too, but she kept it to herself.

'I guess you think I could do the same thing,' he said.

She looked at him and wondered for a moment if he could read her mind. Before she could speak, the receiver came alive at her ear. It was Morgan's voice, the sound of someone rational whom she knew and trusted. She was beginning to wish she had taken his advice and abandoned the charade with the pen name, or used Morgan, regardless of his age. She was beginning to wonder if age was really an issue. Jack was forty-three. She'd demanded a look at his driver's license in the cab. There was only two years difference between him and Morgan. But there was something else. Like Redford, Connery, and Newman, Jack had something special.

'Good to hear your voice,' he said. 'How's it going back there?'

'As they say, there's good news and bad news,' said Abby. 'The good news first. The book is worth a lot of money.'

'How much?'

'Are you sitting down?' she asked him.

'Yes.'

'I'm hearing millions.'

'A million dollars?'

'With an "s" on the end,' said Abby.

There was stone silence from Morgan's end of the line, followed by a long low whistle. 'You're kidding?'

'Not unless the agent is blowing smoke.'

'Well, that's wonderful. Hey, when you're famous, can I tell people that I once knew you when?'

'You can tell them you still know me.'

'Can I borrow money?'

'That we'll have to talk about.'

He laughed and so did she.

'Now for the bad news. Some flake has bulldozed his way into my life and now has Owens believing he is Gable Cooper.'

Jack looked at her from under arched eyebrows. A hurt expression.

'Who?' asked Spencer.

'His name's Jack. The brother of another flake. The guy I talked to down in L.A.'

'The Flake Brothers. I like that,' said Jack. 'It has a kinda ring to it. We could take it on the road. Maybe do a little leopard skin butt flossing.'

Abby turned her back to him. He thought she was

pissed. She was having a hard time keeping from laughing.

'Do you want me to deal with him?' said Morgan.

'No. No. Besides, what can you do from there?'

'I could fly out.'

'No. There's no point. I'm just gonna have to work it out somehow. Did you get the copyright done yet?'

'I'm working on it.'

'When will it be filed?'

'I'll get it finished tonight and file it overnight express in the morning. I'll call the registry at the Library of Congress and see if we can get it expedited. We should have the registration back in a week, maybe ten days.' Ordinarily it wouldn't be a problem. A common law copyright would be in effect the moment Abby typed the manuscript and put her name on it. The problem here was that her name was not on it.

'Good. The publisher won't have time to file in Gable Cooper's name before then. They don't even have a contract yet.'

Given what was happening, the copyright was Abby's life line. Without it, plus dealing with the enormous sums that were now being discussed and with a man she didn't know and might not be able to control, she would have no evidence of ownership. At least she had Morgan.

'Listen, I'm worried about you.' Morgan sounded concerned. 'I shouldn't have let you go back there alone.'

'I'm a big girl.'

'I know. But if anything happens to you . . .'

'What's going to happen? It's fine. It's just that I'm tired.' Things hadn't worked out the way she thought they would. Abby didn't like surprises, and Jack was a big one.

'There's one other thing,' said Abby. 'Do you remember Theresa?'

'Sure.'

'You remember Joey, her former husband?'

'Never met him. But how could I forget?'

'Somehow he managed to get his nose under this particular tent.'

'What do you mean?'

'I mean the book. Somehow he found out about it and managed to hook up with some people interested in film rights.'

'There's a film?'

'There's serious interest. It's part of the millions,' she told him.

'Jesus. This thing really is exploding. Watch yourself with this guy. What's his name?'

'Jack Jermaine,' said Abby. 'But right now I need help with Joey. I've got to get him out of the middle of this and put the fear of God into him. Any ideas?'

'I can put an investigator on him. Have him talk to the guy and tell him if he doesn't stay out of it we'll sue him for interference with contractual relations. Maybe threaten to have him arrested for fraud.'

'The first one won't mean anything to Joey. He doesn't have a pot to piss in. But jail. That's something Joey understands. Your investigator, do you have somebody who's large?' said Abby.

'I can find somebody. Why? Is the guy dangerous?'

'Usually just to women. But you never know.'

'I'll make sure our man has a firearm permit. That he's packing,' said Morgan.

'It's probably unnecessary, but just to be safe,' said

Abby. 'I'll call you tomorrow.'

'Take care of yourself. And Abby. Be careful with this guy.'

Abby looked at Jack, lounging in the arm chair, his leg thrown lazily over the arm, tossing peanuts into the air and catching them in his mouth like a trained seal.

'I will,' she said. 'Good-bye,' and hung up.

'You have a choice,' she told him.

Abby and Jack sat in a coffee shop in the lobby of an office building a block from Carla Owens's office. It was eight o'clock in the morning. They had an hour before she and Jack were to appear in Carla's office and Jack was supposed to sign the agency agreement. Abby had made a decision.

'You can either do as I say, or I'm prepared to come clean with Owens now, tell her everything, that I wrote the book, that I own the rights, and have her throw your ass down the back stairs.'

Before he could speak, she added, 'I know the book may not be worth as much if she finds out. But I'm prepared to take that risk.'

'Are you?'

'Yes.' Abby was going to set the rules now. She had no intention of allowing Jack to call the shots. He had already pushed his way too far into the deal by talking to Owens without Abby being present the day before. She was not going to have it happen again.

'Are you in or out?' she asked. Moment of truth.

He took her measure with a calculating look. 'What's my cut?'

'I thought you talked to your brother?'

'I did. But we didn't discuss money.'

'You came all this way and you didn't discuss money?

You're not interested in how much you're going to be paid?'

'Part of me is,' he said. 'The mercenary part.'

'And the other part?'

He thought for a moment. 'I suppose you'd have to call that curiosity, mixed with a little envy.'

She looked at him, a question mark.

'I wanted to see exactly how they publish a big book.'

'How did you know it was going to be big?'

'As soon as Jess told me the story line, read me the opening on the phone, I had a hunch.'

'And where did you gain this remarkable sense for commercial fiction?'

'Maybe I was born with it.'

'Maybe you ought to be a writer.'

'I am. I've got a chest full of finished manuscripts.'

'You'll have to show them to me sometime.'

'I've got a drawer filled with tattered rejection letters that go along with them.' He didn't tell her how the letters came to be tattered.

Abby could have lied to him. She could have told him that his compensation would be five percent of whatever she got; her original offer to Jess. But it was not the figure Jess had finally negotiated. She looked into Jack's blue eyes, the tanned face. If anything, he was better-looking than Jess, rugged and more mature. And there was something else. It wasn't so much an air of mystery as it was a look of danger. Jess was an Adonis, good-looking, but a child. Jack had some wear on him, a sort of lived-in look that you didn't get with a model. It showed in the craggy lines of his face, and the steely gaze with which he held her eyes at this moment. You had to wonder what other things these eyes had seen. Peering out from a television screen, or from the back of a novel's dustcover, it was the look to launch a million-dollar book, and Abby knew it.

'If you do everything I say. Do a good job. Play the role. Become Gable Cooper.' She looked into his eyes. 'I'll pay you ten percent of everything I get.'

'That's very generous,' said Jack. 'And I want you to know that I appreciate your honesty.'

'What do you mean?'

'That you didn't try to cheat me. To pay me less that you offered Jess, cuz maybe you're pissed or something.'

'I thought you didn't talk to him about money.'

'I lied,' he laughed. 'But I really do appreciate your own sense of ethics. That's really special.'

'Give me a break.' She got up and started to walk away from the table.

'Where are you going?'

'To tell Carla that I wrote the book.'

'Wait a minute. I didn't say I wouldn't do it.'

'Well I just did,' said Abby.

'Listen, I'm sorry. It was a joke. I give up.' He held both hands in the air like she had a gun. 'Don't throw this away. You'd be out of your mind.'

'You think you're that valuable?'

'Well . . .' He thought about it for a second. 'Yeah.'

'No one will ever accuse you of modesty.' She was still walking at a good clip. Abby reached the counter of the coffee shop, handed the girl the check and three dollars, and didn't wait for the change. She was out the door with Jack on her heels.

'Listen. You're making a big mistake.'

'No, I made a big mistake when I got involved with your brother and ended up with you.' She stopped and turned and faced him on the cold sidewalk near an intersection. 'Listen. I don't know when you're lying and when you're telling the truth. And when I have to trust somebody in a situation like this, that's a real problem. You may consider it funny. I don't.'

'I was only testing you.'

'Well, I don't like to be tested. I thought maybe we had something in common. That you were a writer. Unpublished, but still a writer.'

'That part was true. Scout's honor. I can show you the manuscripts. In fact I'd love you to read them.'

'In my spare time,' said Abby.

'I mean it. Listen. You can pay me five percent. That's what you wanted to pay Jess.'

She looked at him, wondering where the hook was.

'I don't want to see you lose this,' he said. 'How often does a deal like this come along? You've written an incredible novel. All the ducks lined up. How often do you think that happens?'

Abby had thought about it a lot in the last two days. 'Not very often,' she said.

'Once in a lifetime, if you're lucky,' said Jack. 'Do you think it will happen to you again?'

She looked at him but didn't answer.

'Don't count on it,' he told her. He sounded like the voice of experience. 'Do you think you'll ever be able to produce a book like this again?'

Before she could speak, he put his hand to her mouth. 'Don't answer that. Anybody who's ever put a word on paper would say no.'

He was right. It was the insecurity of the writer.

'Commercial or literary, it doesn't matter,' he told her. 'Whenever you've written something good, that you think is really good, your mind says, "I will never be able to do that again." Now maybe you will. But at that moment of completion, your mind says "no." Until you actually do it again, you will believe it is impossible. And if your mind says no I can't do it, too often and for too long, you never will.

'The good news is that for the moment you don't have to worry about it. What you have to worry about is not allowing these people to squander what you've written. Because that's what they'll do if you walk away from this thing now. Like abandoning a child,' said Jack. 'They will leave it to die.'

'What do you mean?'

'You might have been able to do it before, to come clean, to tell them the truth. But believe me, if you tell them now, they'll be offended that they were taken in, and embarrassed to let the world know it. They will take your confession as a sign of weakness, that you had 'em by the throat and lacked the courage to finish the kill. The law of the corporate jungle,' said Jack. 'They will tell you not to worry. They're gonna blow it out, take it to the top. All the while they'll be movin' on to the next project, somebody else's big book.'

He understood much more than she thought.

'You've been published before,' said Jack. 'How did it feel?'

She gaze him a quizzical laugh. 'Five thousand copies,' she said. 'There were heads of lettuce that had a longer shelf life than my books.'

'Right,' said Jack. 'And they'll do it to you again if you let them. They'll tell you they're doing a two-hundred-and-fifty-thousand-dollar ad campaign, and they'll do ten. They'll put your book on the street and if it doesn't grow legs and walk on its own in three days they'll pull the plug and watch it die. Even if the book starts to take off, they'll cap your press runs to avoid taking returns.'

Returns were the curse of the industry, stores sending back unsold books to the publisher for a refund, an age-old industry practice. Publishers, the smart ones, protected themselves by capping the numbers that they shipped. A store would order twenty and receive five and the author was never told.

'And they're going to do all of this to me because your face is not on the cover?' said Abby.

'No, because you blinked. Because they'll know you didn't have the courage to reel them into the boat when you had your book in their gill. If you pull out now and tell them the truth, oh, they'll publish your book. But they won't back it. You've passed the point of no return, Abby. You've taken a chance. If you don't finish it, they'll finish you.'

He was right, and Abby knew it. The first battle of publishing, the only one that really mattered, was with your own publisher. Win that, and the war could be over.

They stood in silence, the winds whistling through the canyons of Madison Avenue, people milling past them on the sidewalk. Jack held Abby's gaze for a long moment, their eyes locked. She couldn't be sure if she could trust this man, a stranger she didn't even know. But there was an ultimate truth to his words that sad experience had taught her she could not deny.

Jack left New York that day. Before he did, there was a tussel in Owens's office, hard-core dealing between Abby and Owens over the terms of the agency contract.

Carla had given Jack her standard form; in effect a personal services contract for life. Carla would have a piece of all of his future works even if he left her at some point and hired another agent to sell them. It wasn't until they were headed for the door, refusing to sign, that Owens opened another drawer on her desk and pulled out the real thing. It was what lawyers call an 'at will' contract. She was free to leave them and they were free to fire her at any time. It was the only thing Abby would let Jack sign. Beyond this, Carla got ten percent of everything she sold, except for foreign rights where she would take ten, and the foreign agents she employed would get ten. It was standard fare. In the end, Carla learned one thing: Abby knew more than she let on about the business of publishing.

After signing at Owens's office, Jack begged off. He'd had enough of business, told them he had things to take care of from his trip to Mexico, and asked Abby if she would stay behind to work out details with Carla for the sale of book rights. After all, she was the lawyer.

It was their plan. He told Carla he was going back to Seattle to write. Then he flew to Coffin Point. Inside the old plantation house he unpacked his luggage and repacked it with clean underwear and clothing, checked his mail, and dialed a phone number in California.

'Skytell pager. Please leave your message.'

He punched in his phone number and hung up. Then he grabbed his bags and went downstairs. In his study, he gathered a brightly colored box from one of the express overnight carriers. Jack had an account. It was red and blue, about the size of a shirt box. Jack had used them to send manuscripts to publishers and agents in the past, as well as a few other things. He assembled the box, and filled out the packing slip addressing it to himself at a hotel in Seattle for morning delivery the next day. He had made the reservations the night before from New York. As he was finishing the slip, the phone rang.

'Hello.'

'Jack. How'd it go?' It was Jess in Los Angeles. He'd gotten the message from his pager.

'Hey, you know when you called I was a little pissed off,' said Jack.

'Yeah, I know. Interfered with your beauty sleep. You gotta get a life, brother. Come out here and party. We don't hit the sheets 'til the sun's peaking over the mountains. And California girls *are* sweeter.'

'Pop was right. You never would have made it in the military,' said Jack.

'Hey, let me sleep 'til noon with a blonde in my bunk. I don't think that's unreasonable.'

'You're soft, Jess.'

'Well, Semper Fi to you, too, but let's stick to the subject at hand. What'd you think of her, this Abby chick?'

'Not bad. Fix her hair a little and get some decent clothes.'

'That's not what I meant. This stuff with her book?'

'That's why I called. I'm headed out to Seattle. There's a loose end out there I have to take care of.'

'Geez, you're really into this stuff. I hope she's paying you for all this.'

'Some things you do as a labor of love. Someday you'll learn that.'

Jess laughed.

'She went weak on me yesterday. Got scared and wanted to pull the plug on her plan. But I saved her from herself.'

'I'll bet,' said Jess. 'Oh please, Jack. Take me. Ravage me.' His voice played a high falsetto and then he laughed. 'And I thought you were just doing this as a favor to me? You dog. So is she good in the sack?'

'I thought maybe you could tell me.'

'What are you talkin' about?'

'Leopard skin butt flossing,' said Jack.

'What? Aw no. What did she tell?'

'She doesn't kiss and tell.'

'Whatever it was it's bullshit. I never touched her.'

'Don't bother, Jess. She told me all about it.'

'Hey, listen.'

'She even told me about that little birthmark. The one on your thigh.'

'Hey, now I know you're lying.'

'If she's with child, we'll know who to call,' said Jack.

'Right. Well it sounds like you had your chance to pull out . . .'

'You should really watch your choice of words, brother.'

'Cut it out. You know what I'm sayin'. If she wanted to pull the plug on the book, you coulda gotten out. Why didn't you?'

'Don't want to.'

'Why not?'

'Jess. Let me give a little advice. The next time you hand something like this off to somebody else, you might check to see what it's worth.'

CHAPTER
THIRTEEN

'How were we supposed to know?' said Salzman. 'We went to the woman's house and this guy answers the door. You tell me?'

'You get some identification?' said Weig.

'What, you think he's gonna be packing a driver's license in his pen name? He told us he was Gable . . .'

'That's not exactly how it happened,' said Sidner.

Salzman shot him a look, but it didn't deter the kid. Sidner figured he was the fall guy if Weig decided he wanted a head to roll. Salzman and Weig went way back.

The two of them were in front of Mel Weig's desk trying to explain how they'd cut a deal for twenty-five grand with Joey Jenrico who'd never read a book, much less written one.

'As I recall,' said Sidner, 'you asked him if he was Gable Cooper . . .'

'And he said yes,' said Salzman.

'No. He said, "It depends on who's asking." '

'Well, that's as good as saying yes.'

'Stop! Enough!' Weig slammed the desk with his open palm. 'For your information. This Jenrico is a high-school dropout with a criminal record and three misdemeanor convictions. He probably has the I.Q. of a brick. What that says about the two of you I'm not exactly sure.'

'Listen, Mel. No money changed hands. No harm done,' said Salzman.

'Not exactly,' said Weig. 'The harm is that Carla now has the real author signed, and she's on the war path. His name is Jack Jermaine.'

Salzman and Sidner looked at each other.

'I thought you said he was a bestseller.' Salzman tried to deflect a little of Weig's heat toward Sidner.

'It's what I was told,' said the kid.

'Well, that piece of misinformation could have cost us a bundle,' said Salzman.

'It still may. Carla knows we tried to go around her,' said Weig.

'Is she angry?' asked Salzman.

'A hornet with its stinger up your ass is angry. Carla's dripping malice like acid, and looking for some way to get it into my eyes.'

'You don't think she'd try to take the book to another studio?' said Salzman.

'She's making noises about some independent producers. She wants blood, and we may have to pay her the big bucks just to soothe her.'

'Why, if nobody ever heard of this guy Jermaine?' said Salzman.

'It's not gonna matter,' said Weig. 'Word is the buzz is on. Carla's already got the network morning shows,' said Weig. 'They're already lining up for this guy Jermaine.'

Her name was Sandra or Sally, or something else that started with an 'S.' Joey couldn't remember. He didn't much care. All that mattered for the moment was that she was down to a pair of leather bikini panties lined with jade colored beads, standing bare-breasted at the foot of his bed. Joey stood in the doorway to the kitchen watching her from behind.

When she turned and saw him she stuck her finger inside the beaded fringe at the front of her panties and studied him with wistful eyes. 'How do you like them? They've glove leather,' she said. 'Made by Indians in Arizona.'

'Them Indians do some fine work,' said Joey. 'Real crafty, if you know what I mean.' He smiled at her. Joey'd found her at a bar that was a hangout for the Western set, doing line dancing in a skirt that showed her cheeks whenever she stomped to the rhythm. Indian panties or no, in Joey's mind he was about to hang another beaver pelt on his own lodge pole. But before he did he wanted one more beer.

He turned into the dark kitchen and opened the refrigerator door. He was concentrating on the last bottle of Bud at the back of the shelf, his head lost inside the ice box, when suddenly it slammed closed, catching his head like a vice at the ears. If it hadn't been for the rubber insulation on the old door, it might have cracked Joey's head like a nut. As it was, he was on his knees, his head locked inside with the light on, dazed and wondering what he was doing on the shelf next to the mayonnaise.

With his knee still wedged against the door for leverage, Jack reached around inside of Joey's belt and grabbed the revolver. Joey'd worn it in the open for the girl's benefit once they'd gotten home.

Jack looked at it with an appraising eye. Thirty-eight Smith & Wesson.

'Nice piece, but you gotta be able to get it out of your

pants,' said Jack. He tossed it onto the kitchen table. It landed with a thud. Then he pulled his own, the nine-millimeter Beretta, eased up on the refrigerator door, and grabbed Joey by the collar of his shirt.

Before he knew what was happening, Joey was almost standing on his feet, with his ass pushed into the open refrigerator, looking at the cleft in Jack's chin.

'Now this is real smooth. No cylinder to get caught on your belt. And this part fits real nicely up your nose.' Jack pushed so that the half inch of barrel that protruded out from the end of the Beretta's slide was actually stretching one of Joey's nostrils.

'Now shall we talk?'

'Gnu na fuck are gnu?' It sounded like Joey had a truck parked up his sinuses.

'No, I don't think we'll start with that.' Jack turned and saw the girl standing in the doorway wearing Indian craft work and not much else.

'Could you give us a minute, sweetheart?' Jack smiled at her.

Looking into his eyes lighted only by the glow of the open refrigerator door, Joey's ass pushed halfway into it, it was as if she didn't even notice the gun. She offered a lustful look and melted her body against the frame of the door as if she wasn't going anywhere.

'Fine, you can stay if you like, but don't interrupt.' Jack turned his attention back to Joey. 'Now where were we? Oh yeah. We were about to discuss you. Why you like to beat on women, and a certain game you decided to play with my book.'

Joey's eyes got big.

'Oh. I forget to introduce myself. I'm Gable Cooper. I understand you were trying to steal my book?'

Joey started to shake his head and suddenly found it

caught between hard steel, the door of the freezer compartment in back, and Jack's gun up his nose in the front.

'Maybe we should try the other side.' With Joey's head pressed back, Jack had a clear line of sight. 'Looks like you've had some shit up there before. Maybe we should clean it out.' Jack clicked off the safety and cocked the pistol.

'Anyway, where were we? Oh yeah. My book. They were gonna have an investigator talk to you about a law suit or a criminal thing, you know, bring in the lawyers. All that kinda stuff. But you know Joey . . . Can I call you Joey?'

Jenrico nodded, as much as he could with a gun up his nose.

'Joey, it's my view that we're already too heavily lawyered. We live in a society that's far too litigious. What do you think?'

Joey looked at him, wondering what the word meant, and when he didn't nod in agreement, Jack did it for him with the muzzle of the gun.

'I mean look at O.J. A year watching strutting lawyers diddle around on television, and thump their dicks on the table. They put all the afternoon soaps in the toilet, ratings a cat wouldn't shit on, and when it's all over, what do we have? A bunch of unemployed actors, and books out our ass telling us what went wrong with the criminal justice system. Now I ask you, is that any way to run a society?'

Joey looked at him down the business end of the pistol and found himself shaking his head.

'Yeah. That's what I thought. Oh boy. I see you got chocolate-covered macadamias, the kind in the little jar. You know those are my favourites. Do you mind?'

Joey shook his head, the barrel of the gun still up his nose. With his free hand Jack took the jar off the top shelf of the refrigerator. Then not bothering to set the safety on the Beretta, he held the jar of nuts in one hand and fought with the lid, using three fingers of the other while the fourth slid around on the trigger of the pistol. The gun went sideways at a cocked angle and pushed hard so that Joey now looked like some pug-nosed boxer. He winced in anticipation, his eyes glued to the hammer at the rear of gun. Joey's life was at the mercy of a metal spring.

The girl in the doorway was in a trance, watching like it was some drama on the wide screen.

'You know you really shouldn't keep these things in the ice. Tends to make the nuts go soft.'

The only nuts Joey was worried about at the moment were not in that jar, but they *were* shriveling up.

'Oh and you got peppers. The kind in that vinegar stuff. Are they hot?'

Joey nodded.

Jack picked up the jar and was back at it with his fingers. Even with the cold air from the fridge, Joey had pimples of sweat forming on his forehead.

'Anyway, to make a long story short. I thought if we just took the time and talked we'd come to some common understanding here. You know they all told me you were an asshole, but somehow I knew you'd be a reasonable guy. There's something about getting to know someone up close and personal that makes even the biggest shit in the world seem human. What do you think?'

Joey's eyes wandered for a moment to the Smith & Wesson on the table, and then to the girl standing nearly naked in the doorway. Neither offered much comfort at the moment. Sue or Sharon or whatever her name was was actually giggling. Joey would kick the crap out of her when this asshole left. He felt the muzzle press hard against the septum of his nose, bringing his eyes off his dreams and back to Jack.

'You're letting your mind wander.'

Jack held up a pepper from the jar, dripping its juice down the front of Joey's shirt. 'Want one?'

Joey shook his head. Jack stuck it between his lips anyway, and pushed with his finger until it slid all the way inside. 'Chew. That's it. Taste good? Here, have another.' He stuffed two more in.

'I don't like the hot ones,' said Jack. 'They make my eyes water.'

Joey chewed carefully so as not to upset the cannon up his nose. He was getting cross-eyed looking at it.

'You know these nuts aren't very good,' said Jack. 'Maybe next time I come over you could have a fresh jar? Keep 'em in the cupboard,' said Jack.

Joey nodded.

'Oh Jeez, where's my manners? You could probably use something to wash that down.' He put the peppers jar down on the shelf and took the bottle of beer, popped the cap, and stuck the neck of the bottle halfway down Joey's throat, watching the bubbles come up in the bottle as Joey gagged. 'That's it. Close the mouth. Keep it in there.'

Joey inhaled some beer and a little pepper juice and started to cough. Jack pulled the bottle out of his mouth, sticking it upside down in Joey's belt so that the rest of the ice-cold beer ran down in the inside of Joey's pants.

'There, how's that? Cool you down there, too. Now where were we? Oh yeah. I assume we're not going to have any more trouble over this film stuff, are we?'

Joey shook his head quickly. He was getting the hang of it now, like one of those applause signs on a T.V. show. His nose was running and his eyes were beginning to water from the acid in the pepper.

'Want another?'

Joey shook his head.

'No, I wouldn't want to get rust all over my gun,' said Jack. 'And the girls, Ms Chandlis and the former Mrs Joey. What do you think I should tell them?'

Joey gave him a shrug with his shoulders.

'Maybe I should tell them not to worry cuz they're never gonna see you again?'

Joey gave him a look, not exactly certain what that meant.

'Or maybe I could tell them that nobody's ever going to see you again?'

He knew what that meant and shook his head vigorously.

'You know it has been delightful,' said Jack 'but I think we're gonna have to continue this at a later time.' He looked over at the girl and then whispered up close in Joey's ear. 'Joey. I think you must live right. I mean, with the audience and all.' Jack nodded toward the girl. 'Otherwise no telling what could have happened. Good night.'

Lowering the gun from Joey's nose, Jack took him by the lapel of his shirt and pulled him forward hard. At the same time, Jack threw his shoulder with all of his weight into the refrigerator door. The corner of the door caught Joey just above the bridge of the nose and with a thud Jenrico went to the floor, out cold.

Jack turned to the girl. 'You oughtta get some clothes on, sweetheart, you're gonna catch cold. I'd go if I were you. Something tells me he's not gonna be good company tonight.'

'Carla, what are you telling me?' They were on the phone, Bertoli and Owens.

'Alex, it's not like you didn't expect this. Now be honest. Did you really think I would bring you a book this hot for an outright purchase without testing the market?'

'I thought we had a deal?' Bertoli was using his hurt voice, the one he employed to spawn guilt in others. With Carla it didn't work.

'But how do I know what he's worth?' said Carla. 'Unless I test the market.' What she was talking about was an auction for Gable Cooper's book done by telephone after copies of the manuscript were sent to every large publishing house in New York. Bertoli knew that this could drive the price substantially higher. Bertoli had a problem, a gaping hole in his Summer list. The ABA convention was looming. If he was going to move, he had to do it now. Time was running out.

To this point he had been banking that as soon as Cooper signed with Owens, she would deliver him on a platter to Big-F. Though she was right, knowing Carla as he did, Alex figured there would be some expensive detour along the way.

'I told you we would pay a million dollars for the story, advance against royalties,' said Bertoli. 'What do you want? He's not a bestseller. He's untried. It's a big gamble. The book may fall flat on its face.'

'You don't believe that any more than I do,' said Carla.

'You know as well as I do that even the hottest story requires a hundred things to go right in order to reach the top of the list. Most bestsellers get thirty of them, if they are lucky,' said Alex.

'I'm sorry you have such a pessimistic view of things.' She reminded him that of the hundred things, this one already had the big one: the prospect of a hot movie deal with a blockbusting star to open it. Mel Weig had been on the phone all morning pleading for the rights and begging her not to take the book to another producer. He was at three million and counting. It was already a record for an unknown writer.

'I've already told you, Alex. You can set the floor. A million dollars.' What she meant was that if nobody came in above a million, Alex and Big-F would get the book for that price. Carla was busy turning his top-dollar offer into a minimum bid. She would then release the news on the movie millions and the land rush would be on. Bertoli and Big-F would be killed in the stampede and he knew it.

'Never,' he told her. 'Won't go for a floor,' he said.

'Fine, you don't want the floor, we'll go elsewhere.'

'I didn't say that. What do you want, Carla? You want a million and a half, fine I'll go a million and a half.'

'No, Alex. You know I think you truly believe I'm trying to gouge you.'

'Carla, how could I believe that?' His voice dripped with sarcasm.

'I just think I owe it to my client to find out the market value of his book.'

'And your ten percent wouldn't have anything to do with it?'

'Business is business,' said Carla. It was true that agents and publishers were there every day. The authors came and went. Usually in the tussle of business, the thought of future deals on other books and the requirements of good will would bring an agent to their senses, cause them to stop before they pushed for absolute top dollar. But it wasn't often that an agent saw a manuscript as hot as this one – perhaps once, twice if you were lucky, in a lifetime.

'Fine. Two million,' said Alex.

'Alex, you make me feel awful, but I told you. I can't.' It was going better than she'd expected. But then Bertoli knew as well as she did that the Cooper manuscript had one other thing going for it. If it worked, it would establish a new genre. If there was a way to reach the big time, that was it. Ludlum did it in the '70s with the international thriller; Stephen King in the '80s with horror; and Grisham later with legal thrillers. Each in their own day had put a new twist on an old genre and ridden the wave of their invention to the top. Now it was Gable Cooper's turn. The irony was that the mania of female revenge, the new genre, should be coined by a man. Carla had thought about this and whether it was a problem. She dismissed it when she saw Gable Cooper in the flesh.

'What do you want, Carla, my blood?'

What is it worth? she thought.

'It's against my better judgment,' she said, 'but four and it's yours.'

'Four million! You're out of your mind.'

'I guess we'll have to see.'

'That's crazy.'

'Fine, we'll see what it brings on the open market.'

'Three,' said Bertoli. 'And we get a solid option on his next book.'

Like a game of chess, it was the price Carla already had in mind. 'We keep foreign rights.' She spoke before Bertoli could collect the rest of the pieces. She would sell these, translations rights around the world, for another cool million.

'You really want to cut the heart out of me,' he said.

'Do we have a deal, Alex?'

'Deal.'

'Then smile.' Even though she couldn't see him through the phone line, she knew his face was a grimace at this moment. The acid would be churning in Bertoli's stomach for the next year until he earned back his three-million-dollar nut. The two-million-dollar package for book and film rights that she'd told Jack and Abby about was suddenly looking like six. Carla had learned the art of the deal. First rule: never oversell your own client.

Abby hadn't heard from Theresa since arriving in New York, and there was a lot of news. She wanted to tell her about the sale of the book rights. She was burning up inside. She had to tell somebody. Theresa and Morgan Spencer were the only ones who knew the truth, the only ones she felt she could share it with. Morgan wasn't home.

She dialed the number of Orange County, the friends Terry was staying with somewhere out near Anaheim. A woman answered the phone.

'Hello.' It wasn't Terry's voice.

'Hello. I'm looking for Theresa Jenrico.'

'Oh, Terry's not here.'

'Is she out?'

'No. She left this morning.'

Abby was surprised.

'Where did she go?'

'Home, I think. Said she had some things to take care of back in Seattle.'

Now Abby was worried. Theresa was supposed to be there for two more days when they would both return to Seattle and hook up at the airport before returning home.

'Is there a problem?' said the woman.

'No.' Abby thanked the woman and hung up. With Theresa back in town and Joey on the prowl, Abby was worried. She punched in the phone number to her house in Seattle. It rang and rang. There was no answer. She wondered why the answering machine didn't pick up.

CHAPTER
FOURTEEN

It was dark and drizzling by the time the cab driver dropped Theresa and her luggage at the curb in front of Abby's house. The driver slammed the trunk closed, pocketed his fare, and before she knew it she was standing there alone staring at the shimmering red of his taillights as they turned the corner. One of her suitcases was resting in a puddle.

'Thanks, dickhead.' She got a grip and started lugging toward the front door. If she was twenty with big tits and a skirt to her crotch, the driver would have hauled them up the steps with his tongue hanging out. To Theresa, men were all the same: interchangeable assholes. It was just that she couldn't live without them.

She trudged across the wet grass toward the small dark house with its shuttered windows and overgrown lawn. There was something not quite right with the scene she was seeing. It took her a moment, then it dawned; the front porch light was out. She remembered that Abby had made a point of mentioning it. She'd flipped it on when they left for Seattle to get Charlie's credit card. Abby never liked to come home to a dark house. The bulb must have burned out.

She was soaked by the time she reached the porch, her coat flapping in the wind. Once under the cover of the small portico, she took the time to stop and look. There were a few cars parked on the street, but she didn't see Joey's truck. She figured it was safe.

She fumbled with her key in the front door. In the dark it was hard to find the right one and get it in the keyhole. When she finally did, it turned, and the door swung open.

It was pitch black inside. Terry hesitated. For an instant, she thought she saw something move at the far end of the hall. She strained her eyes and tried to cut through the dense blackness. Nothing. Must have been her imagination. Ever since the motel at the airport her nerves were frayed. There was something wild in Joey's eyes that night, something even in his most violent moments she had never seen before, and it scared her. Theresa sensed that if Abby had not been there to stop him that night, Joey would have killed her.

She moved inside the door, lugging the two heavy suitcases. She tried to get beyond the entry in order to close the door behind her. With both hands full she had no chance when her feet hit an immovable object. She went down hard on the wooden floor. Something sharp cut deeply into her knee. She felt a searing pain and lay there shaking as the cold wind from the open door blew up her skirt. Crumpled on the floor she bent to examine her knee, her feet toward the open door. It was then that she saw it; the motion of a shadow on the porch behind her.

It was a late-night session on the speaker phones juggling the numbers, Bertoli at his end, Salzman for the studio in L.A.

Bertoli had made a name for himself not because the books he picked were all successful but because he had a knack for making people remember his successes and forget his failures.

Bertoli already had his people brainstorming. 'The thing with the booksellers convention,' he told Salzman. 'We got an angle. If you can get your network to do a piece on one of their magazine shows to include a segment on books and how they're sold.' The studio was part of a conglomerate that owned a television network.

'Not bad,' said Salzman. 'Maybe we do something like *Forty-eight Hours* with cameras following our author. We could get it to air the week the book hits the stores,' said Salzman. It was a glimpse of the corporate octopus scratching its own back. Both Bertoli and the studio were heavily invested in the book, but Bertoli wanted to control the early publicity to the greater glory of the book. The studio could worry about their film later. The question was how much Bertoli could get them to pony up.

'We do television,' said Bertoli. 'Fifteen- and thirty-second spots in major markets.' The ads would not be long, but they would saturate the airwaves in an opening blitz to drive the book onto the bestsellers list. Then they would pace themselves, clustering ads when the book started to slip to keep it in the public eye and on the list.

'National print ads in New York and L.A., *P.W.*, *Entertainment Weekly*, *People*, maybe *Time* and *Newsweek*,' said Bertoli. 'Not once, but maybe eight or ten times. We'll do teasers in some of the smaller papers. We hit the two coasts hard, and we do a T.V. satellite tour. On the day of publication we do insertions, the first two chapters into selected home editions of the *New York* and

L.A. Times.' What he was talking about was hitting the opinion makers where they lived to create buzz. It didn't matter if they read it, only that they talked about it falling out of their morning papers.

It was a pie-in-the-sky campaign. Why not? As far as Bertoli was concerned, L.A. was paying.

Salzman whistled. 'That's gonna cost a fortune.'

'I figured you guys for a million,' said Bertoli.

'A million!' Salzman was screaming on the other end.

Bertoli reminded him what would happen if the book fell flat. There would be no film. Besides, the studio was getting by cheap. It was going to cost the studio twenty million just to get the star to put his big toe on the set. By Hollywood standards, the book promotion was chump change.

'That reminds me,' said Bertoli. 'Can we use his name? "A major motion picture starring . . ." '

'I don't know.'

'What do you mean you don't know? I thought he was committed?'

'To these people, commitment is an endless courtship. He's a star.'

'So?'

'So they want to be perpetually wooed. The minute they sign on, all the noses in the Western Hemisphere pull out of their assholes. So why sign?'

They thought for a moment, then Salzman spoke. 'Whadda you want to do?'

'We'll use his name, but you don't know about it.'

'He'll sue the shit out of you.'

'Not if it works.'

'And if it doesn't?' said Salzman.

'If it doesn't, you and I are gonna be looking for work. What fool sues the unemployed?'

Theresa exploded in a string of expletives when she saw the cat center itself in the doorway out on the porch. Its long moving shadow cast by the street lights took five years off her life.

It mewed in the open doorway, begging, a plaintive cry about the foul weather.

Theresa let go a huge sigh and started to scratch. She looked at the mangy thing. 'Go. Scat.'

The cat took one look, then moved before she could, slipped through the door, and into the darkness down the hall.

'Shit.'

She reached down with her hand and touched what felt like broken glass. Her knee was bleeding, a jagged edge embedded in it.

She rubbed her fingertips gently over the area and the piece of glass came out. She thought she got most of it. In the dark, she couldn't tell, but there was a warm trickle down her leg to her ankle. She didn't dare crawl. Carefully she got to her feet, one knee bent a little in pain. Then an inch at a time, sliding her shoes on the floor, first one foot then the other, she made it to the wall. Using her hands, she felt around until she found the light switch, flipped it on. Nothing.

She shuffled with her feet down the dark hallway, the cat meowing ahead of her, a feline procession. At one point, it rubbed up against her leg and Theresa kicked at it hard. It wailed and slid halfway down the hall on the hardwood floor like a fluffy hockey puck.

Theresa left the front door open. She could feel the steady breeze down the hall. For some reason it was a source of strength, the open door, an avenue of retreat if she needed it.

Every few steps she was interrupted by objects on the

floor until her feet felt like two ice-breakers moving through a heavy flow. Someone had trashed the place, and Theresa knew who. She was wondering how she would tell Abby.

A few more steps and she was in the kitchen. There was a strong foul odor here and in the dark it took Theresa a moment to place it; rotting produce like a garbage dump. To the cat it was the smell of opportunity. It disappeared.

Theresa found a broom. 'Here kitty.'

A light from the house next door filtered through a window over the sink, and as her eyes adjusted Theresa could see the extent of the damage. There wasn't a dish or glass left that was not in pieces on the floor. Cabinet doors were pulled off their hinges and scattered. The drawers were all pulled out and dumped on the floor. The refrigerator was open, its light either smashed or out, and the contents spilled in a gooey mess. She stepped in what must have been juice. Her shoes clung to the floor like suction cups.

She felt inside the cupboard for the flashlight that wasn't there, then looked on the floor but didn't see it. Theresa tried the light switch on the wall. She knew it was no use. She was right. In the light from next door, she could see that the overhead fixture was still in one piece. It was the only thing in the room Joey had missed. He must have pulled the fuses or damaged the service box. But he'd also screwed up.

There on the floor on top of a pile of refuse was the box of spares, screw-in fuses for the ancient system. She picked it up and carefully stepped over the trash, around the overturned kitchen table. The place had a look of rage about it, like some crazed animal had gone on a rampage.

She kicked a few things out of the way, and the cat scurried out in front of her again. She almost threw the box of fuses at it but stopped herself.

She made her way across the kitchen, and opened the door to the basement. The stairs down were pitch black. She flipped the switch on at the head of the stairs. Sure enough, Joey got them all. She looked back one more time toward the kitchen in hopes that maybe she would see the flashlight or at least a box of matches, anything to light her way down the staircase. There was nothing. She stepped down into the black void, a few more steps, clinging onto the hand railing. She was halfway to the bottom when she looked back and saw the silhouette of the cat staring down at her from the top step.

She felt with her feet as she went, counting the steps. At twelve she hit the landing. She felt her way around the turn and it hit her. There, she could see something, a glow like a red beacon. Theresa froze. At first she thought it was a cigarette. She stared in stark silence for a moment. But it didn't move, and the glow was steady. She couldn't tell how far away it was. She reached out to touch it. In the pitch darkness, with nothing else but the beam of red light. There was no sense of depth.

Then she realized, took a deep breath. It was the tiny light on the lid to the old chest freezer. Joey hadn't gotten all the fuses after all. It didn't illuminate the basement, but still it was a comforting glow.

She felt her way along the concrete wall, and then down again, another smaller flight of stairs. Finally she reached the cement floor of the basement.

Now that she was around the turn in the stairs she couldn't even see the scant light from the open door to the kitchen up top. The electrical service box was mounted somewhere on the wall of the basement near a small wooden work bench. She'd helped Abby change a fuse during a lightning storm a few months earlier.

She felt with her hands, iron tools, a saw hanging on a nail over the bench. She was close. She moved along the bench, ran into the vice bolted to the edge and it drove into her side. Theresa groaned.

She rubbed her ribs, then suddenly felt something press against her leg. She jumped to one side, threw herself against the edge of the work bench, and felt it again. The cat meowed.

'Son of a bitch.' Her heart was pounding. She lashed out with her foot but missed the cat. They could see in the dark. Or was that a wives' tale?

She worked her way to the center of the work bench one more time, leaned over and felt a sharp metal edge with her fingers, a corner. Maybe it was just another tool. Then she felt the small hinged door. She'd found it. It was open.

Blind in the darkness she was afraid to feel inside the box with her hands. She couldn't quite reach. If Joey had removed fuses, her fingers might find an empty socket. Knowing Joey, it was probably what he had in mind.

She felt along the top of the bench. It was clear. Carefully she put one knee onto it and boosted herself up. She opened the box of fuses and removed one. Then, using it like a probe, she found an empty hole and screwed it in. A solid stream of light flickered on somewhere above. It wasn't much, but now she could see the gray outline of the box.

She grabbed another fuse and threaded it in.

The phone rang. She could hear it up in the kitchen. She had just found another empty socket.

Second ring. Third ring. Theresa wondered why the

answering machine didn't pick up. Then she realized its fuse must still be out.

The door above at the head of the stairs suddenly slammed closed.

Plunged into darkness, the noise of the slamming door echoed through the empty basement, the ringing phone upstairs. She nearly fell off the bench. Theresa was shaking, terrified. For an instant, before all light vanished, she actually thought she saw Joey. Tricks the mind will play.

She knelt stone still on top of the bench for several seconds, her hand glued to the fuse already one full turn into the socket. She listened but heard nothing.

It was the wind. It had to be. She should have closed the front door. She could go back up now and do it, but she was so close. The phone stopped ringing. A few fuses and the lights in the basement would come on.

She turned and it seated out, but nothing. She tried another, still no light in the basement. She picked one more fuse. Now she had to reach to the top of the box on the wall. It was awkward from the wooden work bench. Abby could have done it standing on the floor, but Theresa was several inches shorter. She sprawled with her stomach at the edge of the bench, legs dangling, her feet a few inches off the floor. She seated the fuse in the socket. The cat was at her again, rubbing against her feet.

She lashed out kicking, slipped on the wooden bench. The electric flash lit up the basement with an eerie blue glow, the smell of ozone, and the odor of burning flesh.

CHAPTER
FIFTEEN

Salzman was in his office pushing paper and picking sleep from the corner of one eye when the com-line rang.

'Yeah.'

'A Mr Jenrico on one for you.'

'Who?'

'Says his name's Jenrico.'

Salzman thought for a moment. 'I don't know any . . . Wait a second.' The idiot was looking for the contract. Salzman couldn't believe it. What balls.

'Do you want me to tell him you're out?'

'No. No I'll take it.' He sat for a second, then punched the button for line one. 'Hello.'

'This Mr Salzman?'

'Mr Jenrico, how are you?'

'I thought maybe you forgot.'

'How could I forget.' Salzman was smiling so the phone would catch the proper tone, beefing it up.

'Where are you?' He was hoping that Joey was at the studio's front gate where he could let him in, arrest his ass, and charge him with fraud.

'The airport. L.A.,' said Joey. 'I was wondering where

the contract was? Thought maybe we could have a meeting.'

'That's what I figured. There's been a little problem.'

'What's that?'

'Just a slight technical matter,' said Salzman.

'Tell me,' said Joey.

'Seems someone else claims they wrote the book.'

There was a long silence on the other end.

'You there?' said Salzman.

'Yeah. Yeah, I'm here.'

'We don't know what to do about this.'

'They're lying,' said Joey.

'That's what they're saying about you. Lemme ask you a question. We know you've never written a book, but have you ever read one?'

'What are you talkin' about?'

'You can read?'

'Yeah, I can read.'

'Then read my lips,' said Salzman. 'Go fuck yourself,' and he hung up.

'Stupid son of a bitch.' Salzman went back to his papers. Thirty seconds later the com-line rang again.

'Yeah.'

'He's back,' said the receptionist.

Salzman punched the button on line one. 'What part of the message didn't you understand? Lemme explain. You take your dick. You can find that?'

'*You* don't understand. I got somethin' I think you might wanna see.'

'No, you don't understand. I'm not interested in seeing you or anything you have. Whadda you think, we're stupid?'

There was some silence while Joey considered the matter.

'That mean you ain't gonna pay me?'

Salzman couldn't believe it. 'That means if you bother me again I'm gonna take personal pleasure in hunting your ass down and having it committed.'

'That would be a mistake.'

'And why's that?'

'Because you don't know who wrote the book.'

'Oh, we know. You don't have to worry about that.'

'No, you don't,' said Joey.

'The author's name is Jack Jermaine, alias Gable Cooper.' Salzman knew because Weig'd put Jack's picture under the clear acetate cover on his desk blotter as a reminder of how he'd screwed up.

'You're wrong,' said Joey.

'Listen, I'm sorry, but I don't have time for more bullshit.'

'No. It's the truth. He didn't write the book and I can prove it.'

'And how would you know that?'

'Because I have the original copy,' said Joey. 'The thing. The manuscript. At the house after you guys left. I looked and I found it. Somebody else wrote it.'

Salzman had visions of Joey typing, hunt-and-peck. 'Now lemme guess. You want to sell us this piece of shit manuscript?'

'I was figuring if you didn't mind.'

'Blow it out your ass,' said Salzman.

'Guess I'll have to take it to the magazine,' said Joey.

'What are you talking about?'

'He was real interested. Just as soon as I told him your studio was involved. I sent 'em your card.'

'What magazine?'

'*The Intruder.*'

The mention of the name raised bumps on the back of Salzman's neck.

'They're interested. They want to meet with me,' said Joey. 'That's why I'm down here.'

The Intruder was the kind of magazine that hung on the fringes of entertainment, pissed off stars by reporting that they gave birth to cosmic aliens. To call it a tabloid was an insult to yellow journalism.

'They pay pretty good,' said Joey.

'What did you tell 'em?'

'Nothing. Yet.' It was Joey's turn to smile.

Salzman was already in the dog house with Weig. He was responsible for Jenrico getting in the middle. Maybe it was bullshit. But what if he was telling the truth? What if he did have information and they were being scammed? It was the kind of story *The Intruder* would love, and not the kind of buzz the studio wanted. If there was substance, other papers might pick it up. The star would get cold feet. Three million bucks for film rights down the tubes. And Weig would blame it all on Salzman.

'How do I know you're telling the truth?'

'Show me the color of your money,' said Joey. 'We can meet and I'll show you what I got.'

Shit. Salzman thought it but didn't say it. Another meeting with the idiot.

'How much?'

Joey thought for a second. 'Same as the last time. Twenty-five thousand.'

'That's when you were writing the book,' said Salzman.

'How much you willing to pay?' said Joey.

'Two thousand, if your information is good and what you have is real.' Salzman was going to have to dig into his personal savings. He had no intention of telling Mel

Weig anything, not until he had a chance to look at whatever it was Jenrico was peddling.

'O.K., I'll come to the studio.'

'No.' Salzman thought for a moment. 'I want to meet with you, but only in Seattle.' He had no intention of letting Joey anywhere near the studio.

'Why do that? I'm already down here,' said Joey.

'I'll wire you some money. A couple hundred. Show of good faith,' said Salzman. Anything to keep Joey at arm's length. 'The Red Lion by SeaTac airport. You know where it is?'

'Yeah.'

Salzman looked at his calendar. He was booked solid with meetings. He would have to juggle. 'Next Thursday afternoon. Two o'clock. Come to the white courtesy phone in the lobby and ask for me by name. They'll put you through to my room. And bring the stuff. The manuscript. And don't even think about copying it.'

'You bring the money,' said Joey. 'And wire me something.'

He never got an answer because Salzman hung up.

Abby went stand-by on a late night flight, New York to Seattle with a stop in St Paul.

She tried to snooze, propped her head against the window on one of those little pillows, and covered herself with a blanket. The rumble of the engines would ordinarily put her to sleep, but tonight she was immune. She closed her eyes and saw only one thing, Jack Jermaine's face in Owens's office. He might have had the looks to stop time, but there was something else, something in the eyes that caused her to be cautious. The way he'd forced himself into her life was unsettling. She wondered where he was at that moment, and what he was doing.

With her head against the plane's inner curve, her nose pressed to the Plexiglas counting clouds out the window, she tried to sleep, but it wasn't working. Abby's mind was in overdrive. She tried to regroup. Things had gone dangerously out of control since leaving Los Angeles. She took some solace in the fact that the basic elements of her plan were still in place, though she wondered if she was deluding herself. How much control did she really have? How long before Owens tried to go around her directly to Jack, to get more books or some other concession?

There were serious legal questions here. Jermaine was for all intents and in the eyes of the law, her agent-in-fact. She had cloaked him with apparent authority by pushing him up front as the author. In their ignorance, Owens and Bertoli had a right to rely on this. If Jack signed further contracts without her knowledge, Abby would be bound by his actions. Jack had all the signs of a loose cannon. Abby would have to lash him to the deck and do it quickly.

She thought about Morgan. At the moment he was her psychic safety net, the only one she could run to with problems. She had confided in Theresa, but Theresa was useless when it came to business.

Morgan was a lawyer with a good mind. He was cool under pressure. She would sit with him in the morning in his office and go over the events of the last several days, Jack's insertion into her life, and work out her next move. Morgan would have answers. In his own way he had a calculating mind. She was unwilling to allow a stranger to control her. If need be, if Jack pushed her, she would come clean with Owens, tell her the truth about the book.

Six million dollars. How much of it would vanish with Jack if she told the truth? Would they still want the book without his face on the dustcover? It was a good story. It had driven intense interest in Hollywood. By now Abby had created certain expectations. Would they accept it with a woman as author? It was a strong male part, written in a male voice. Part of her wanted to know. Part of her didn't. How many novels got this far – unless you had a gimmick, a celebrity? It was a sad commentary. She consoled herself with the thought that she was not playing by any rules she had made. It was a deal with the devil and he had made all the rules.

It cost Abby nearly eighty dollars to get her car out of hock at the airport, almost more than the vehicle was worth. She was caught in the early rush hour and labored up I-5 in the slow lane stop-and-go until she passed the business district. Then traffic thinned and she moved at a break-neck forty miles an hour to her turnoff just beyond the bridge and the University. She was in a daze, half asleep, car on autopilot as she rolled through the stop signs and took the curves leading to her house. Her sleepless night was catching up.

As she turned onto her block all the anxieties that had been lapping at her subconscious suddenly crested and crashed. There in the middle of the street were flickering blue and red lights, a fire truck, and police cars. Abby wanted to think a dozen things, a kitchen grease fire, a car crash, a neighbor's heart attack, but in her mind she knew what it was. The only question was how badly he'd beaten her this time. And from the lights on the street, it didn't look good.

A lone cop in uniform was stringing yellow tape from the trunks of trees in front of her house.

Abby parked haphazardly at the curb. Left her purse and her luggage in the car, the door half open, and ran the distance toward the house. She was stopped at the tape.

'I live here. It's my house.' She tried to push her way through, but the cop stopped her and called another.

'Wait here.' The young cop held her at the line while a sergeant talked to somebody in plainclothes. The young cop went back to his tape but kept an eye on Abby.

'Can you tell me what happened?' she asked.

He shook his head. 'Lieutenant will be here in a minute.'

When the older cop returned he was with a taller man in a gray suit, slender with dark silky hair and looks that reminded her of a film star she couldn't place. There were wisps of silver at his temples, and a devious smile on his lips. *Kiss of the Spider Woman*.

'I'm Lieutenant Luther Sanfillipo.' He spoke with a Latin tilt to his voice. 'You are?' he looked at Abby.

'Abby Chandlis. I live here.'

'Of course.' He lifted the tape and Abby slipped underneath. By now a camera crew for one of the local television stations had found the action. Seeing the cops and Abby headed for the house, they trained their camera, the reporter shouting something barely audible from a distance as a uniformed cop held them back. It was the same question Abby had: 'Can you tell us what happened?'

The detective ignored them. 'Get those people off the grass,' he told the young cop. 'I'm sure Ms Chandlis here does not need to have her garden trampled.' He smiled at her and they walked on a few more steps.

'Tell me what's happened,' said Abby.

They walked far enough to be out of earshot of the

camera crew and stopped on the path that bisected the lawn at the front of the house.

'Do you live here alone?' he asked.

'I have a friend staying with me.'

Knowing looks passed between the cops.

'What's happened? Is Theresa alright?'

'Theresa?' said Sanfillipo.

'Theresa Jenrico.'

'She is the friend who lives with you?'

'Tell me what's happened?'

'Can you describe Ms Jenrico for us?'

'Are you going to tell me what's going on?'

'A description. It's a simple request,' he said.

'Five-five. Dark hair, shoulder length.'

The detective's eyes grew a pained expression. He turned around to one of his subordinates. 'Do we have a Polaroid?'

They looked at one another, a lot of shrugging shoulders; the cop's universal reply to the unknown.

'Well get one.' Sanfillipo snapped his fingers a couple of times, and in that gesture Abby placed his looks, the cutting image of the late Raul Julia. Tall, dark, with Latin good looks and the perpetual enigma of a half-smile.

They stood awkwardly for several moments, Abby, Sanfillipo, and his entourage.

'May I ask you where you've been?'

'Traveling,' said Abby.

'I can see from the state of your house that you have not been here. Pleasure or business?' he asked.

'What do you mean, the state of my house?'

'Please just answer my questions.'

'Business.' She handed him a card, the last one from her coat pocket.

His brows arched as he read the card.

'What type of law do you practice?'

'Mostly business, some bankruptcy and domestic relations. What has this got to do . . .?'

'Nothing criminal?'

'No.'

'No clients you have ever represented who might want to vandalize your house?'

'Is that what's happened?'

He gave her a look that was something just short of confirmation.

'May I ask you the nature of your business trip?'

'No, you can't.'

'Then perhaps you can tell me where this business took you?'

'Los Angeles and New York.'

'And how long were you there?'

Before she could answer, Sanfillipo was interrupted by one of the uniforms coming toward him holding two wet Polaroid prints out to dry.

'It's about time. Let me see.' He looked at the pictures, then shook his head grimly trying to decide which one.

'This is difficult.' Sanfillipo made his pick. 'It is not pleasant. You might want to prepare yourself.' He held the two photographs like a poker player, close to his vest.

Abby steeled herself.

'Do you recognize this woman?' He finally handed her the one in his right hand.

For a moment her eyes refused to focus on the picture and instead looked over the top at the detective and the cops hovering at his shoulder.

'Please,' said Sanfillipo.

When she finally looked it didn't appear real; skin the pallor of blue-gray and bulging eyes. The face was swollen, tongue protruding, bitten through in one place. There was no word for it. Grotesque was too mild. There was something about one of the eyes, Theresa's beautiful eyes. The lens was fractured like a piece of glass.

'Oh God!' Abby slumped and one of the cops caught her. She was gasping, trying to fill her lungs with air, uttering the only question she could think of. 'What happened?'

'Perhaps an accident,' said Sanfillipo. 'Get a chair.'

Abby's knees went weak. She stumbled a little but didn't fall. Sanfillipo grabbed her by one arm.

Abby stiffened. 'I'm O.K.'

He gave the order for a piece of lawn furniture on the porch, a light wicker chair, to be brought down.

'No. I want to see her,' said Abby.

'Now is not the time,' said the detective. 'For identification I must know. Is that your friend?'

Abby looked one more time. She nodded but couldn't speak, evaporating denial mode.

'The woman in the picture is Theresa Jenrico?' He pressed for unequivocal identification.

'Yes.

'How did it happen?' She wanted answers.

'Electrocution,' said the cop. 'For now we are investigating. Do you know anyone who would want to vandalize your house?'

Abby shot him a look. 'One person.'

'Who?'

'His name is Joey Jenrico. They were divorced.'

Sanfillipo had one of the other cops now taking notes.

'He'd beaten her several times. He wouldn't let go. Check your computer, you'll find a record. He was arrested and charged. More than once,' said Abby. 'No convictions.'

Sanfillipo raised an eyebrow.

'Theresa wouldn't prosecute,' said Abby.

He nodded like he understood. 'Do you have an address for Mr Jenrico?'

'She has a little book in her purse. It's in there.'

'That may be a problem,' said the detective.

Abby looked at him.

'We are having some trouble finding things inside.'

'I don't understand?'

'You have not yet seen your house,' said the cop.

They couldn't find the directory, Theresa's purse, or much of anything else. Everything was in pieces.

The coroner had removed Theresa's body in a black bag, but not before Abby had insisted on one last look. In her mind she prayed that perhaps she had leapt to conclusions with the photograph. Lying on her back on the gurney, as deformed as death had left her, the features of Theresa's face were now burnished in Abby's mind. It was an image she would carry to her grave.

Morgan Spencer had arrived. Abby had called the office.

Spencer took charge while Abby slumped in a chair on the front porch. Forensics was still picking through the belongings in her house. Abby could see some of the damage through the windows, though they wouldn't allow her inside. Morgan confirmed for Sanfillipo and the coroner the identification of the body.

'Then you knew her as well?' asked the cop.

Morgan nodded. 'Socially,' he said. 'We'd met a few times.'

'You will have to find other accommodations for

tonight,' the detective told Abby.

'She can stay with me.' Morgan spoke before Abby could answer.

'Are you sure?' She looked at him.

'I insist.' Morgan was halfway to having Abby move in. What he'd always wanted, even if it was separate rooms. He'd work on that later.

'Any sign of the purse or the victim's phone book?' Sanfillipo had stuck his head in the front door and directed this to one of the officers. They were now pawing through the carnage in the living room. There were a lot of stooped backs and shaking heads. The detective stepped back out.

'How are you feeling?' Luther asked Abby if she was up to a little walk.

'Where to?'

'Around back.'

Abby and Morgan followed the detective through the side yard to the back of the house.

'Mr Spencer, if you would wait here.' Sanfillipo took Abby by one elbow and ushered her through the door, down into the basement.

'Where are we going?'

'Show you in a minute,' said the detective.

There were two forensic technicians dusting for prints near the work bench. The surface of the bench was scorched, an arc of charred wood.

'Is this where it happened?'

Sanfillipo nodded.

'When is the last time you changed a fuse in the service box?'

Abby thought for a moment. 'Maybe a month ago. It didn't work very well. An old system,' said Abby.

'Yes. Do you remember this?' he pointed down to a

heavy piece of wire that ran out from under the work bench several feet.

Abby shook her head. 'What is it?'

'It's attached to the back of the fuse box. There was water in a puddle under the bench. When she turned the fuse in the right socket, it completed the circuit, pressed the wire to make contact. Two hundred and twenty volts,' said the detective. 'She must have been standing in the water. Touch the box and you're dead.' He turned to Abby. 'You've never seen this wire before?'

'No,' said Abby. 'It wasn't there.'

'It appears someone was arranging an accident,' said the cop.

'Joey,' said Abby.

He looked perplexed. 'How would he know that his wife would replace the fuses?'

'He wouldn't,' said Abby. 'He wouldn't care. I represented Theresa in her divorce.'

Suddenly Sanfillipo got big eyes. Things were starting to make sense.

CHAPTER
SIXTEEN

Twenty-four hours turned into seventy-two before the cops let Abby back in her house. When she got there, she remembered Sanfillipo's words about its condition. Still she was not prepared for what she saw. From first impressions it was beyond repair. She wandered with Morgan aimlessly for nearly an hour, from room to room, trying to figure where to start.

The police were still looking for Joey. Abby knew he was on the run. When he sobered and realized what he'd done, no doubt panic set in and he took off.

The police had left their yellow tape up outside around the trees as a courtesy, a barrier against the curious. Still, a few neighbors, people Abby recognized, could be seen jaywalking in front of her house, purposeless strolls, looking as they passed at the place where the woman had been killed. Within an hour, Abby knew she could no longer stay there.

In the afternoon, a man she'd hired came by to board up two windows at the back of the house. Joey had smashed them out of their frame. The police might not have found his prints, but to Abby, Joey's fingers were on every article in her house. His odor fouled the place.

She had never been an advocate of the death penalty, but in Joey's case she would make an exception. Lethal injection was too humane.

She could hear the workman pounding nails into plywood, sealing out the weather from her bedroom. It was raining again, somber light to add to her melancholy mood.

Late in the morning, Morgan had to return to the office. Now she was alone in the house. The workman finished. Abby busied herself straightening up, packing her possessions into cardboard boxes, whatever she could salvage. The rest went into large plastic trash bags, which Abby stacked at the curb until she had a sizable pile.

Morgan found her phone. The cops had taken her message machine to copy its tape and returned it. Morgan put the phone back on the kitchen countertop and hooked the machine up so that it worked again.

Abby hadn't been near the office since returning from New York, though she had called once to collect messages. There were none. This troubled her. She was told that one of the younger associates had been assigned to handle her workload for the time being. Abby saw Morgan's hand in this, easing her load while she dealt with Theresa's death. It was like him.

She was just about finished straightening in the kitchen when she noticed that the message light was flashing on her machine. She stopped and pushed the button. The first two were hang-ups. There was a message from Carla. It was more than a week old. She assumed it had been left on her machine before her house was vandalized. The final message was left by Lewis Cutler's secretary. The firm's managing partner wanted to talk to her. Abby called the office. Cutler's secretary answered.

'Hello, Marcia.'

'Abby.' The woman sounded startled when she recognized the voice. 'How are you?'

'You sound surprised,' said Abby.

'It's just that I didn't expect to be hearing from you. With all that's happened, I mean. How are you doing?'

'Cleaning up.'

'I heard about it. Your friend,' she said. 'Terrible. Terrible. If there's anything I can do?'

'There's not much anyone can do at this point,' she said.

'I suppose not.'

'Reason I was calling, I was going through my messages and found yours from Mr Cutler.'

There was silence at the other end. Abby thought Marcia was having trouble remembering.

'Something about his wanting to see me.'

'Oh, that.' There was another long pause. 'Let me see if he's in. What he wants to do,' she said. Then the line went dead while Abby was put on hold. She listened to elevator music piped over the phone while she tapped her fingers on the wall next to it and looked at her watch. It was taking longer than Marcia needed to find her boss, unless he'd disappeared. There were no chairs left to sit on in the kitchen so Abby stood, looking down the hall into the bedroom over the top of her mattress cut to its springs by a knife. Idle thoughts for an idle mind. Why, if Joey had a knife, had he taken the time to fashion an accident in the basement? She thought for a moment, then dismissed it. Who in their right mind would try to analyze Joey? On his best day he was psychotic. It was something for the police to consider. They probably already had.

Her gaze down the long hall wandered toward the

corner of her bedroom, now looking nearly normal. The small folding table that was her altar of work, the place where she wrote, rested upright again under the window covered by plywood. Abby had even managed to salvage a few of her reference books, a dictionary and thesaurus. But she still hadn't found her typewriter, the old manual. Morgan had scoured the basement looking for it. She wondered why Joey would take a typewriter.

'What are you doing this afternoon?' Marcia was back on the line.

'Cleaning up,' said Abby.

'Were you planning on coming by the office?'

'I wasn't, but I can. What's it about?'

'Mr Cutler would like to talk to you.'

'What time?'

'About two o'clock.'

'I'll be there.'

The offices of Starl, Hobbs and Carlton were subdued, a mirror image of Abby's own mood at the moment. She was the author of a book worth millions, but Theresa's murder had thrown a cloud over her life. New York and the meeting with Carla Owens seemed like something from another age.

In the confusion after the murder she had never had time to talk with Morgan about Jack and her problems with the book. It would have to wait until things calmed. She wondered if things would ever be the same again. Abby was beginning to regret that she had ever written the book. Most of all she rued the day she'd hatched the scheme to use a male pen name and supply it with a human face.

Today Abby had dressed the part for her meeting with Cutler. She wore the same gray wool business suit she had taken with her on her trip to New York and matching heels. It was the extent of her work wardrobe after Joey had dumped all of her clothes on the closet floor and poured bleach and vinegar on them.

She wandered down the long corridor toward her office. A few heads came up, eyes of sympathy acknowledging her presence. Still no one came out to say a word. It was like she had the plague. Violent death does strange things to people.

She didn't realize until she'd already passed the little cubicle outside her office that Marla, the paralegal who doubled as her secretary, was not at her desk. She was hoping she could pick up the loose ends of her business life starting with the messages and notes from her assistant.

She flipped on the overhead light and walked into her office. She had left papers and files on her desk when she went to New York. Her in-basket was full. Now it was empty, and the top to the desk dusted and clean.

She wandered out to Marla's station expecting to find everything there. She didn't. Marla's desk was cleaner than her own. The carousel with phone messages rested on the counter of Marla's desk. There was only a single small white envelope in Abby's slot on the carousel, marked personal. She opened it. Inside was a pink telephone slip: 'Call me at this number. It's important.'

It was from Jack Jermaine, dated two days earlier. More troubling was the fact that the return telephone number bore a 206 area code. Jack was in Seattle. Now he was shadowing her, intruding further into her life. She would call him alright, and give him a piece of her mind. She looked at her watch. One forty-five. No time like the present. She went into her office, closed the door, and dialed.

What she got was the operator at the Four Seasons, one of the swank downtown hotels. One thing was clear: Jack didn't stint when it came to money. She wondered if it was her own he was spending, perhaps part of an advance wheedled out of Carla.

'I'm looking for a Mr Jack Jermaine. I believe he's a guest.'

'One moment, please. I'll put you through.'

Jack picked it up halfway through the second ring.

'Hello.'

'What are you doing here?' Abby didn't bother with preliminaries.

'I read about your friend. Saw it in the paper, your name in the story. Are you alright?'

'I'm fine.' Abby didn't want to talk about Theresa's death. Not with Jack. She was angry. He'd followed her to the coast. 'I asked you what you're doing here.'

'This is probably a bad time, but we gotta talk,' said Jack.

'What's so pressing that you had to come out?'

'Things have changed,' he told her.

'How's that?'

'We have work to do.'

'What are you talking about?'

'I'm talking about the sequel. Carla called me the night you left New York. Put on the full court press. She wanted to talk about the next book in the series.'

'What series?'

'Seems they're assuming I'm going to write a series, using the same characters.'

'Who led them to that assumption?'

'I thought you did,' said Jack.

'It wasn't me.'

'Well, it wasn't me. Anyway, they're looking at a replay,' said Jack.

Carla and Bertoli were at it. Abby had smelled it in the first meeting. One or both were control freaks. If she had to guess, it was Owens. Before they were finished, they would be rejecting story lines and dictating their own plots, turning her into a ghost writer, using Jack's name and face.

'Well, call her back and tell her you won't do it.'

'What reason do I give?'

'I don't know. Artistic. Tell her you never intended to do a series. It cheapens the message.'

'This book contains a message? I must have missed it,' said Jack.

'Nevermind. Just tell her you won't do it.'

'Before I do, you better listen to the rest of it.'

'Rest of what?'

'Got your calculator?'

'Why?'

'They're talking doubling the deal on the second book.'

'What do you mean?'

'As in six million just for book rights.'

'You're kidding?'

'No, I'm not. We would still hold the film stuff and all the foreign rights. Maybe get another six for those.'

'*We*?' said Abby.

'Fine. You. But they want to hear from *me* with an answer as soon as possible. Carla won't let me sleep. She's called me three times in the last twenty-four hours. Once in the middle of the night. The woman's manic. Gotta give Alex an answer, she says. He won't wait forever. She says we need to do this in order to set the hook.'

'Bertoli's a eunuch,' said Abby. 'The only hook we have to worry about is the one Carla's trying to put through your nose. He'll do whatever she tells him.'

'My take, too,' said Jack. 'Why I didn't worry too much about getting back to her.'

'We haven't even published a book and they want more of the same, with the same characters. They call it publishing. They're creating swill,' said Abby.

'Question is do we want to belly up to the trough?' said Jack. It was an open line. He was waiting for an answer.

'Tell them to wait.' Abby thought for a moment. Where was Morgan when she needed him?

'Why don't I come down there and we'll talk.' Jack wanted to go for the deal. Abby could smell it. But he didn't have to write the book.

'No. Just stay where you are.'

'We need to talk,' he said. 'I'll come by there.'

'No.' Abby couldn't tell if he'd heard her or not, because Jack had already hung up.

It was a strange feeling, like winning the lottery. Suddenly, if Carla was right, there was a six-million-dollar payday just waiting to be collected, and another one in the offing. For the first time since traveling to New York, the thought actually settled on Abby: she did not have to practice law any longer. She could do whatever she wanted. There was no question she hated her job, but it was an anchor to the normal world, where real people lived. Abby didn't like to think of herself as rich. She had never been there, done those things. She came from working-class parents. Her father was a warehouse foreman. Somehow the thought of being rich ripped her from her roots.

In every way commercial publishing was a game of chance; the right book at the right time with the right publisher and the right budget. Writing a novel was like pulling the handle on a slot machine. If you were lucky enough to line everything up at one time, you won. If not, you went to work on the next book.

Abby had seen them on T.V., winners being handed checks the size of bill boards, all uttering the same mantra – 'It won't change our lives. We'll continue to work, cuz we love our jobs.' A week later they would disappear like dust, off to the south of France. No one would hear from them again. The insidious thing that memory did.

Lewis Cutler's office was a show place, the kind of digs designed to make a statement. In Cutler's case, the message was 'I got the power.'

When Abby arrived at the secretary's station outside, there was no small talk. Instead she was ushered in immediately. It was the first time she didn't have to wait.

Cutler sat behind the desk in a cushioned high-back leather chair, hunched over a pile of papers.

'Come in. Sit down.' He motioned Abby toward one of the client chairs without looking up. 'With you in a minute.' Still not looking at her.

He ignored her for several more seconds while he issued instructions to Marcia, handing her some papers he had finished. She turned to go.

'Take the stuff in the basket, too.'

Marcia came back, and as she reached over to grab the stuff in the out-basket her eyes drifted toward Abby sitting in the chair. It was Abby's first glimmer that something was wrong; a look that you would give only to the terminally ill.

Marcia left the room, and Cutler put his pen down.

'You've been away for several days.'

'Personal leave,' said Abby.

'Personal business as I understand it.' He made it sound like an accusation, like anyone in the firm with a personal life had to apologize.

'I heard about your friend. I'm sorry. Have they figured out what happened?'

'Not yet.' It was not something Abby wanted to discuss with Cutler. 'They're still investigating.' She left it at that. She guessed that if Cutler had concerns about this it was limited to the possible fallout on the firm. Two women living together, one of them found dead, could be a matter of cruel speculation among the small-minded in Cutler's circle.

'It makes what I have to do particularly painful,' he said.

Abby raised an eyebrow.

'As you know, there have been a lot of changes in the firm over the past several months. What you might call a restructuring.' The use of the code word was abrupt, just like that, no preliminaries. It caught Abby flat-footed and sent her into an adrenaline rush.

'We've had to do some downsizing,' said Cutler.

'I hadn't heard.'

'That's because you've been away. Much of it was announced last week.'

'Announced?'

'Layoffs,' said Cutler. 'Fourteen positions.'

'I didn't know. Am I . . . ?'

He nodded.

It wasn't that she cared about the job as much as the message that it seemed to convey; that she wasn't good enough for them.

'You're not alone.' This was supposed to make it easier.

'I understand,' she caught herself saying it even though she didn't know why.

'I know what you're thinking,' he said.

In fact he didn't have a clue. Abby sat in the chair with a smile on her face. Cutler figured shock. Abby was thinking that if he'd waited two more days he probably could have had her resignation without asking.

'You're thinking why you?' said Cutler. 'There's nothing personal in it. It's just that you hold one of the positions affected by the restructuring.'

He was prepared to respond to questions she didn't even ask. Cutler no doubt had taken a course on how to do this.

'I want you to know that before we made the decision we looked at all the possible alternatives. I'm sorry to say that there's no possibility of part-time work in the firm. We've already considered that and it just doesn't fit into our plans. Nor is there a chance for some form of reduction.'

She looked at him quizzically.

'Reduced pay,' he said.

Abby started to open her mouth to tell him that she wouldn't consider it. Cutler anticipated. 'Nor can we delay the decision,' he said.

She hadn't asked for a thing. In fact, she was enjoying his discomfort, wondering why he was running off at the mouth.

'May I ask how the firm is restructuring?' said Abby.

'That's confidential, at least at the moment. It would be easier,' he said, 'if you were to tender your resignation.'

Now she raised an eyebrow. 'Easier on who?' She

knew where he was headed, cutting her off from unemployment benefits. If she quit, she wouldn't get them. This would help the firm's bottom line.

'It would look better on a résumé,' he said. 'We'd be prepared to offer you a letter of recommendation.'

'Are you saying that if I don't resign you don't give me one?'

'That's not what I said.'

Abby felt a rush, thought for a second. He was talking to the six-million-dollar woman and the prick didn't have a clue. She wasn't about to tell him. She thought for a moment, looked at him, and said: 'Why not?' Just like that she'd quit.

Cutler looked up from his desk, an expression like he'd missed something. No one went this easily.

She wondered what the partners would do with her pay. No doubt divvy it up into bonuses for themselves.

'I'd like to say good-bye to Marla.'

Ah, finally there was something he could deny her. 'That's not possible.' Now he felt more in charge.

'Why not?'

'Ms Evans resigned last week.' He said it almost with a smile.

Marla Evans had two kids and a mortgage. Without notice, without any warning, they'd waited until Abby was out of town and fired her. She wondered why Morgan hadn't told her. Then it hit her. Maybe he was on the hit list as well. But how could they fire a partner?

'I'd like to say good-bye to Mr Spencer.'

'Not on the premises,' said Cutler. 'Now that the decision has been made, we'd prefer that you clean out your desk and be out of the office quickly. Say an hour,' said Cutler. It was one of the rules fashioned by the canning consultants. You didn't want the canee hanging around the water cooler poisoning the labor pool.

'We can provide assistance if you need it,' he said.

Abby looked at him.

'To clean out your desk.' It was almost as if he was trying to provoke an argument, searching for a normal reaction, some anger. She wasn't going to give him the satisfaction.

'That won't be necessary.' Instead she offered a smile. 'And I want to thank you.'

He hesitated but couldn't resist. 'What for?'

'For being such an asshole. It always makes it easier.' She got up and headed for the door. There was no apology. No 'sorry this had to happen,' no justification or cause. Just 'clean out your desk and disappear in an hour.' Modern American business etiquette.

He had done this three times in the last two days, and in each instance Cutler had returned to the papers on his desk before the person he sacked made it to the door. With Abby he watched her go, until the door closed behind her, wondering if perhaps she might have gone around the bend, and whether she might be coming back with a gun.

On the way out she passed Marcia's desk.

'Oh.' The secretary looked up. 'I have to ask you for your keys to the office.'

Abby reached in her purse and pulled out her keys. She broke a nail sliding them off the ring. She was angrier than she looked. She dropped the two keys on the secretary's desk.

'And your parking pass?'

'That I paid for through the end of the month,' said Abby. 'I think I'll keep it until then.'

Marcia looked at Cutler's door as if she didn't quite know how she would break this to him.

'Tell him to sue me,' said Abby. When she turned,

there was a uniformed security guard standing in front of her.

'What do you want?'

'He's supposed to stay with you until you're finished. Then escort you from the building,' said Marcia.

'Is that really necessary?'

'It's the procedure,' said Marcia.

Now she knew why no one would make eye contact when she showed up in the office. It had nothing to do with Theresa's murder. It had to do with another killing, the one Cutler had just performed in his office.

It was like a parade of humiliation down the hall, Abby and the security guard, the hardware on his belt squeaking and jingling like some jailer. Every eye in the office came up for a glance as she passed by the phalanx of open doors down the long corridor. She wanted to scream 'I'm worth six million dollars' but couldn't even whisper it. By the time she reached her own office, Abby felt like the scarlet woman. She had difficulty restraining herself when she saw him sitting behind her desk with his feet propped up.

'Are you comfortable?'

Jack looked at her and immediately removed his feet. 'You look awful.'

'Thanks.'

He uncoupled his hands from behind the back of his neck and got out of the chair. 'Who's he?' he pointed to the security guard.

'Didn't get your name,' said Abby.

'Harold,' said the guard.

'Harold, meet Jack. The two men in my life.'

'How you doin'?' said Jack.

The guard actually waved, not exactly certain what he should be doing.

Abby could not remember a moment when she'd felt so low.

'Your timing, as always, is impeccable,' she told Jack.

'Why's that?'

'I really don't feel like company right now.'

'I understand. But I thought we could talk.'

'Not just now.' Abby started going through the drawers of her credenza, taking things out and stacking them on top of her desk. She was exhausted, emotionally and physically, at the end of her string. Jack sensed it, rolled the chair her way, and Abby slumped, almost falling into it.

'Are you alright?'

'Fine,' she told him.

'You want some water?' Jack looked at the guard. 'Get her some water.'

Harold hesitated but only for a second.

'Now.' It was the thing about dominance. Harold disappeared down the hall.

'What's wrong?'

'What isn't,' said Abby. 'My best friend's been killed. I've just been fired. A security guard is standing over my desk while I clean it out. And when I come back to my office you're sitting in my chair with your feet on the desk.'

'One out of four ain't bad,' said Jack.

Even in her present mood, Jack got a smile. 'Don't you ever take no for an answer?'

'No.'

'Maybe I should have Harold throw you out.'

'Let's see if he can find the water cooler first.' He fanned her with some paper from one of the drawers.

'Do the cops know what happened to your friend?'

'Theresa?'

Jack nodded.

'They're not sure. Still looking into it. You never told me what you're doing here,' she said.

'What I said on the phone. They want another book.'

'No. I mean what are you doing in Seattle?'

'Bringing you the news.'

'You could have done that on the phone. In fact, you did.'

'I thought it would be better if we worked out the details in person. Don't want to mess anything up,' said Jack.

'God forbid,' said Abby.

He eased her back in the chair until she was reclining, then spun it around so that her back was to him. Then he began to slowly rub her shoulders and the nape of her neck.

'What are you doing?' she asked.

'Keeping up appearances. You never know when Carla might have somebody watching,' said Jack.

It wasn't lost on Abby that he'd never answered her question; what he was doing in Seattle.

'Right. And who would be watching us?'

'How the hell do I know. Want me to stop?'

'No.' His hands on the back of her neck melted the tension in her spine like snow on a hot day.

'By the way, how did you get in here?' Abby looked up at him, an inverted image overhead.

'Nobody out front. I let myself in.'

'Just like that?'

He nodded.

'But there's an electronic lock on the door.'

'And a button on the secretary's desk,' said Jack. 'Laid a book on it. Does the trick.'

'You really don't take no for an answer, do you?'

Harold was back with the water. Jack used a little on Abby's forehead. She sipped the rest from a paper cup.

'Got any boxes?' He turned to Harold.

'Some out by the stairs,' said the guard.

'Well what are you waiting for? Get 'em.'

The guard was wondering if this was in his job description. Jack shot him a look and Harold disappeared down the hall one more time. He was back a minute later with two boxes.

It took Jack ten minutes to empty the drawers of Abby's desk and credenza, and a couple more to load her books and a sweater off the coat tree in the corner. He taped the tops of the boxes closed and handed one to Harold. 'Here, make yourself useful.'

The guard found himself stooped over with the weight of the box. The bottom rested on his can of pepper spray in its holster on Harold's two-hundred-dollar webbed belt. Just when he figured Jack was going to carry the other box, Jermaine picked it up and slid it on top of the first one, wedging it under Harold's chin. Then he turned to Abby. 'Ready to go?'

'That's mine, too.' She pointed to the coat tree.

'No problem.' Jack picked it up, slipped it under the crook of Harold's arm, pushing the guard's elbow down like a clamp to hold it in place. 'There. How's that?'

Harold couldn't talk. His chin was jammed with boxes and if he moved his arm the coat tree would fall out.

'Gotta be careful of that,' said Jack. He tapped the can of pepper spray hanging on Harold's belt. 'Move too quickly, it could go off. That stuff'll burn the pupils right out of your eyes.'

Jack took Abby by the arm and they headed out the

door, followed by Harold the thirty-eight-caliber bellboy.

Out front, Jack opened the door from the inside. The two women were back at reception. They looked at the strange entourage. Harold in uniform with boxes. Jack opened the outer door for him.

'It's the white Ford, up front. Third floor parking garage.' He would have stuck his keys in Harold's mouth, but the guy would have broken a tooth, he was that angry.

'Ladies,' Jack gave them a casual salute.

They looked at Abby as if they'd never seen her in quite this same light before.

They couldn't take their eyes off of Jack, his steely blue gaze and bullshit grin, like where in the world did she get him?

CHAPTER
SEVENTEEN

It was like central command, the war room, Jack and Spencer seated at the dining room table at Morgan's house. Jack had already signed contracts put in front of him by the lawyer. He wasn't happy about it. The documents were intended as insurance, proof to the world that Abby wrote the book and that Jack was a stand-in. Morgan at work. Jack didn't read them and Morgan kept all the copies. It wouldn't do to have them floating around.

'Is that everything?' said Jack.

'No. We have a problem,' said Abby. With her departure from the firm and the annihilation of her house, Morgan's was the only place they could meet.

It was a spacious Georgian on Queen Anne Hill, a sweeping staircase, Tara on a movie set. The kind of place a middle-aged lawyer owned when he wanted to make a statement. In this case, it was a message Spencer could no longer afford. Property taxes were breaking his back. He was fighting for his life at the firm. Cutler was withholding his annual bonus, telling Morgan to sue him. And on top of everything else Spencer owed alimony to his wife. He and Anne had divorced after twenty years. She was claiming a part of his practice as community property. The man was being steamed, rolled, and pressed.

'What's the problem?' said Jack.

Abby flung her coat over the back of the chair. It fell on the floor and she didn't bother to pick it up. Her hair looked like smoke in a wind storm. She was wearing jeans and a soiled work shirt from packing the last boxes at the house. She felt around inside her briefcase and pulled out a yellow legal pad with some notes on it.

'The guy's name is Robert Thompson. He called this morning about nine-thirty. I'm only guessing as to how he got my number. Said he works for *The Intruder* and he's doing a feature piece on novels and the people who write them. Immediately bells started going off,' said Abby.

'Why is he calling you?' said Jack.

'I have been published.'

'Don't take offense,' said Jack, 'but not that anyone would notice.'

'At least she's in print. Not like some people I could mention.' Morgan had picked Jack's brain. Found out he was a frustrated writer, unpublished, and now he was using it. It was one of Morgan's less endearing qualities, the talent to find a flaw and exploit it. He had taken an instant dislike to Jack. Abby knew what it was. He was jealous.

Privately Morgan told her that it burned him that Jermaine was about to be crowned king of pulp fiction on a book he had no part of. But Abby knew it was more than that. He didn't want Jack working with her, on the book, or anything else. It was awkward. Abby didn't know how to tell Morgan that she was only a friend.

'Cool it, guys.' She didn't need a fight at the moment.

'The thought had entered my mind. I mean, I'm not exactly at the top of anyone's list.

'Anyway he gets into it. Wants to know if I'll answer a few questions. I ask him how he got my number. He says he has his sources. I tell him I'm busy. He says it won't take but a minute. Then he tells me I don't have to answer any of this. That I can hang up anytime I want.'

'Journalism's answer to Miranda,' said Morgan.

'Exactly,' said Abby. 'By now the adrenaline is leaking out of my ears. Why would I want to hang up? I ask him. It's killing me. I'm wondering what he knows. Seems this feature piece is about manipulation of the market place. The games authors and publishers play to push books. How they use the media.'

'But why is he calling you?' said Jack.

'I'm getting to that. It seems someone has told him that I have a client who is posing as the author of a soon-to-be big novel.'

'Oh shit,' said Jack.

'My thoughts exactly,' said Abby.

'How much does he know?'

'I don't know. I stonewalled him. Told him I didn't know what he was talking about.'

'And?'

'And he folded. He didn't have any names. Didn't seem to know the title of the book or the publisher. If I had to guess, all he knows is what he's been told, which was just enough to get to me.'

'You think he believed you when you told him you didn't know anything?' said Morgan.

'If incredulous tones on the phone are any measure, he didn't buy it. He starts asking me what I'm afraid of. Tries to give me legal advice. Consoles me by telling me that whatever it is I'm doing, it can't be a violation of any law. So why not just tell him the truth?'

'Right. So he can stick the hot poker of journalism up our ass,' said Jack. 'The ultimate cleansing experience. Every reporter's form of absolution.'

'So what do we do?' said Spencer.

'I got a better question for you,' said Jack. 'What if he finds Carla or Bertoli and starts asking them questions?'

'I've thought about that,' said Abby.

'If they start thinking about the money they're paying, and wondering if they've been had, it's all over,' said Jack. 'They'll flush the book. To say nothing of six million.'

'Which brings us back to what do we do?' said Abby.

There was a long silence around the table.

'He may not call back,' said Spencer.

'He may show up at her front door tomorrow,' said Jack.

'That would seem to depend on how much information he has, and how big a story it is.'

'Do I have a vote?' said Jack.

'Let's hear it.' Abby looked at him.

'You should leave Seattle. The booksellers convention is next week. Go to Chicago. See what Bertoli is doing on the book.'

'I was planning on going anyway,' said Abby.

'Good. Then don't come back.'

'What are you talking about?'

'Disappear somewhere. We'll find a place. That way you can write undisturbed,' said Jack.

Abby considered it.

'Make yourselves scarce. I mean, if this guy doesn't have anybody to talk to, he has no story. We cut down his sources.'

'Still, somebody's been talking to him,' said Morgan.

'Who?' said Jack.

'Only one person we can think of,' said Abby. She was looking at Spencer. 'Joey.'

'Why would he?'

'I wasn't sure,' said Abby. 'Not until this morning when I finished packing. There was something missing from the house. I haven't found it and I've looked everywhere. There was an early copy of the manuscript. It was typed on the back of some old letterheads, reams of paper they were throwing out at the firm. I figured the back side was perfectly good. I could do a draft. I knew I was going to have to retype anyway. Nobody would ever see it. I threw it in a box under the table in the bedroom. It's not there. I've turned the house upside down.'

'That and the typewriter,' said Morgan.

'Your typewriter's missing?' said Jack.

Abby nodded.

'What the hell's Joey gonna do with a typewriter?' said Morgan.

'Probably write ransom notes,' said Abby. 'You want your papers back, it's gonna cost. If I know Joey, he's looking for the highest bidder. Wait long enough and he'll come to us.' She reminded them that he'd already tried to mess with the film stuff.

'He wouldn't do it again,' said Jack.

'You don't even know him,' said Abby.

'Call it intuition,' said Jack. 'I think he can be persuaded.'

'I think he smells money,' said Morgan.

'We could pay him off,' said Abby.

Both Morgan and Jack gave her the same look. 'That would be a huge mistake,' said Spencer.

'I agree,' said Jack. 'Lemme talk to him.'

'Why you?' said Morgan.

'Because I think I can be more persuasive.'

'This is business. It should be handled in a business-like way.'

'I know the kind of business he's in,' said Jack.

'Maybe he found the copyright,' said Abby.

Morgan shook his head and gave her a dirty look as if to say, what was she thinking about?

'What copyright?' said Jack.

'Nothing.' Abby realized she'd blown it. Jack didn't need to know about the copyright. Morgan had taken care of it, with a registered copy now tucked away neatly somewhere in his files. Abby was wondering if maybe the reporter would be looking for it.

'So how much does he really know?' Spencer changed the subject. 'Joey, I mean.'

'We have to assume he has the manuscript,' said Abby. 'It doesn't take a mental giant to figure if it's on the back of law office stationary that Jack didn't write it. It's got my handwritten notes all over the margins. He could hold it over our heads.'

'He's running from the cops,' said Morgan.

'Yeah and he probably needs money,' said Abby.

'But the only players he's aware of for the moment are the film guys,' said Jack.

'That we know of,' said Spencer.

'Let's assume his access is limited,' said Jack. 'Besides, Joey would be dazzled by thoughts of dealing with Hollywood. Let's assume for the moment that's his play.'

'Let's assume,' said Spencer. 'How do we stop him?'

'We reason with him,' said Jack.

'You don't know Joey,' said Abby.

'It's all a matter of persuasion,' said Jack. 'Or there is

another possibility. You could come clean.'

They looked at him.

'Why not? Tell them the truth, that you wrote the book. What? Don't look at me like that. I think the problem is you don't have enough confidence in yourself.'

'It's not just that,' said Abby. 'There are forces here that you can't fight. Mindless rules of marketing that govern every book that is printed. I've been published three times. They don't break people out who have been published three times, no matter what they write.

'They won't break you out unless you're a fresh new discovery. Haven't you noticed? They're publishing bilious piles of commercial shit, but all of the authors are prodigies. I give you Gable Cooper.' Abby motioned toward Jack, who wasn't sure if he should take a bow.

'You can see the headlines,' she said. 'Record money paid to first-time novelist. That's the hook,' she told them. 'Why do you think Bertoli stepped up to the dollar mark so easily?'

'It's a good book,' said Morgan.

'There's a lot of good books,' said Abby. 'I checked. To this point the largest sum paid for a first novel was two million dollars. He now owns the record at three. He's gonna ride it like a horse all the way to the winner's circle if he can. He'll flog it 'til it dies in every press release and feature piece they can muscle. It'll be what Jack's introduced with on every television talk show. "We have with us the author whose first novel earned him a record six-million-dollar payday." The IRS will be waiting outside in your limo,' said Abby. 'I can read Bertoli like a book, and follow his spin like a gyroscope.'

Spencer'd never fully understood her cunning mind.

Abby knew the game they were playing. She bore the scars to prove it.

'If I'd written only one book before, maybe they could bury it, treat this as number one and hope nobody found out. But three. No chance. So we're going to do it my way. Let them blow Jack through the roof. Then we'll step up and tell the world what really happened. Who did what. They can lick the egg off their face when we're finished,' said Abby.

'So that's it?' said Spencer.

'That's it.' She offered no apologies and didn't tell them the rest of it. There was a risk involved in the one big book path to stardom that Abby hadn't mentioned. If it didn't work, the author's career was over. It had happened before, more than once. No one would ever push such a writer again. They had marketing leprosy. It was the genius of Abby's plan that she had hedged this bet. If it didn't work with Gable Cooper, there was always another story, another pen name, and another face to put behind it. Sooner or later she would seduce the publishers at their own game. She had confidence in her ability to write and to invent high concept stories. It was where every blockbusting book had to start; with a good idea. All she needed was a pencil and a mailbox, and she was in business. In a way, Abby was her own form of the literary terrorist – a force they couldn't stop.

CHAPTER
EIGHTEEN

The phone rang once and Salzman grabbed it. He was sitting on the edge of the bed, his overnight bag still packed, ready to go. He had no intention of staying in Seattle if he didn't have to.

'Hello.'

'Is that you?' It was Jenrico's voice.

'It's me.'

'What room are you in?'

'Nevermind. We'll meet down there. In the bar. Five minutes.' Salzman didn't trust Joey beyond the line of sight. He'd brought the two grand, but he wanted to keep it in his room until he saw what it was Joey had.

He took the elevator down. Jenrico was standing at the bar. He was wearing a tank top and a dirty pair of jeans with a hole in the ass. The corner of a worn leather wallet was sticking out of this from the back pocket. Hooked to his belt was a ring of keys hung on a cheesy chrome chain. Joey might have passed for a biker, except he was too sleazy.

'Hey, Mr Salzman!'

'Keep your voice down,' said Salzman. He looked for

a box or a large envelope, something big enough to hold the manuscript.

'Where is it?'

'What?'

'The manuscript. What do you think, I flew up here to have drinks?'

'I got it. You brought the money?'

'Don't worry about the money. Where is it?'

Joey reached into one of the tight pockets at the front of his jeans, pulled out a folded piece of paper, and handed it to Salzman. It was moist with sweat.

'What the fuck is this?'

'A piece of it,' said Joey.

Salzman looked for a place, somewhere away from the lights and the bar. He saw an empty table and made for it, Joey right behind him. They sat down and Salzman opened the paper, flattening it out on the table with his hands.

'So what the hell is this?'

'First page,' said Joey.

'I can see that. Where's the rest of it?'

'Outside.'

What he'd given him was the title page to the novel with Gable Cooper's name typed underneath it.

'Look at the other side,' said Joey.

Salzman turned it over. There at the top was the letterhead:

STARL, HOBBS & CARLTON
ATTORNEYS AT LAW

The names of associates and partners was in small print running down the left-hand margin like snot off a kid's nose.

'So?' said Salzman.

'It's what I was telling you,' said Joey. 'Your guy didn't write the book. Otherwise it wouldn't be printed on the back of that.'

'Anybody could have typed this. One page. Doesn't mean a thing. Why didn't you bring the rest of it?'

Before Joey could answer the bar maid came over. 'Can I get you gentlemen something to drink?'

'A beer,' said Joey.

'No. We're not gonna be here that long.' Salzman started to get up. The waitress drifted off.

'I got six hundred pages, all typed on the back of that stuff,' said Joey. 'Some of it's got hand-written notes all over it. And like I say, if you don't want to look at it, I can take it to the magazine.'

That stopped Salzman. He'd come this far.

'Why the fuck didn't you bring it?'

'Where's the money?' said Joey.

'You'll get paid.'

'Yeah, right. The check's in the mail,' said Joey. 'We already did that one, remember? Cash or you don't see any more.'

Salzman reached in his pocket, took out two hundred dollars, chump change, and slid it across the table. 'The rest is here in the hotel. But I wanna see what you got before I pay anything more.'

Joey got up, pushed the two bills down into his pocket, and headed for the door. Salzman followed him. When they got outside the hotel's front entrance Joey turned. 'Wait here.'

Jenrico crossed the parking lot to a point about two hundred feet away, to an old rusted-out Chevy pickup. Salzman watched as Joey slid between two vehicles, his truck and the car parked next to him, a tight squeeze.

Joey couldn't get the door to the trunk open. The other guy had him jammed in. The driver was still there stooped over in his trunk. Salzman guessed he was busting his hump with some luggage that Salzman couldn't see from where he was standing.

Joey said something to him. From where Salzman was it sounded a lot like 'hey shithead.' He couldn't hear the rest of it. Still the guy didn't pull his head out of the trunk.

A second later an airport van rolled up under the portico in front of the hotel and Salzman couldn't see anything. The van started to unload passengers and Salzman had a mind to step around so he could keep an eye on Joey.

Then something caught his eye. A pretty young thing in a micro-mini came down the steps of the van, all knees and thighs. To Salzman it was the kind of dress stewardesses used to wear back in the golden age of flight when the boomers were young, before they got sanctimonious and defined everything above the knees as hostile work environment. The driver got her bags. The bellman tried to keep his eyes on his work. Salzman took in the rear view as he drifted toward the back of the van. He watched as she headed up the stairs and into the lobby.

Where the hell was Jenrico? He took a walk around the backside of the van. Joey's truck was still parked there. The other car was gone. The door to the truck was wide open now, but he couldn't see Joey. Salzman headed out into the parking lot. He was getting strong vibes that Jenrico was screwing him around. He threaded his way between cars and made it to the back of the truck. When he stepped around he could see that Jenrico wasn't leaning over into the seat, what he'd thought when he looked from under the portico. He was gone.

Salzman looked inside on the seat. There was nothing. No box, no envelope, just two empty beer cans on the floor on the other side. The fucker had given him a single piece of paper with a dozen words that anybody could have typed on the back on a letterhead that anybody could have gotten. Jenrico had taken his two hundred bucks and stood him up. Salzman slammed the truck door hard, rattling the window in its metal frame. Then he noticed; Joey's keys were in the lock, and dangling from them was a broken piece of chrome chain.

CHAPTER
NINETEEN

A long with his contracts Spencer had Jack sign a power of attorney, listing Morgan as the agent for receipt of money on book advances and royalties. This way Abby maintained control of the money, keeping it out of Jack's hands. Morgan would cut a check paying Jack his share. The rest he would deposit in an account in Abby's name. Spencer was now playing a bigger role, for which he finally accepted a retainer from Abby for his services.

Abby stopped at the cemetery on the way out of town and put fresh flowers on Theresa's grave. She found it hard to believe that only a month before the two of them had clowned over the photographs in the agency's modeling directory. Now Theresa was dead. Of the small circle of friends, intimates that she trusted, only Spencer was left.

She flew out of Seattle on a Wednesday evening and hooked up with Jack at the airport in Chicago. They were destined for the Virgin Islands, to hole up while Abby wrote the sequel. But first Jack's presence was required at the American Booksellers Convention. Jack and the book were now on a fast track, speeding toward an early publishing date. Abby wasn't about to let Jack go alone. She still didn't trust him.

She had never heard of a manuscript brought to publication this quickly. Nor had she ever been to an ABA convention. The event was larger than she had imagined. It had started the day before and took up the entire floor of the Chicago Convention Center.

There were acres of gargantuan booths, many of them opulent, some with two-story columns in faux marble. One of them took on the appearance of a Southern plantation mansion, columns and ivy-covered lattice. The booths dotted the convention center floor, forming broad aisles that were jammed with people. Every major publisher was represented, even some from Europe and Asia. It was the largest gathering of publishers in the world, a part of publishing that most authors never saw. Only the cream were usually invited, and only the biggest names were asked to autograph books.

This year they were expecting thirty thousand people, by invitation only, professional booksellers from around the world, everything from mom-and-pop books stores to the mammoth chains. There was an air of carnival about the place with sales people manning booths like barkers at a county fair. The din of the crowd milling up and down the aisles merged with music from the convention center's speaker system. This occasionally broke from the music with announcements, usually about authors signing their books in a separate wing of the center that had been set up for the purpose. It was an eclectic mix, film stars and other pop celebrities alongside artists who had illustrated children's books. Everywhere there were posters, magical art work from the covers of books from around the world.

At one point, Abby and Jack nearly got trampled by a

crowd fighting for free canvas book bags being given out by one of the publishers. Carla had picked Abby and Jack up in a limo at the airport and was now running interference to the Big-F booth where Jack was expected to make an appearance.

For some reason, people seemed to be looking at him as he fought his way through the crowd. Abby figured it was just his good looks, until several of them began to point and finally a woman broke the ice.

'Would you sign my book.' She pressed her way in. The woman wore a name tag that read 'The Tattered Cover – Denver.'

Jack looked bemused. She handed him the book. Abby had not seen it before. It was an advance reader copy with paper covers, Gable Cooper's name on it, and Abby's title underneath. Jack's picture was on the back.

Jack took the woman's pen and started to sign his name. Abby jammed him in the back with an elbow. He scratched out 'Jack' and instead wrote 'Gable Cooper.'

Before he could give the woman her book back, a line started to form in the aisle.

'Not here.' Carla waved them on. They headed for the Big-F booth, Carla, Abby, and Jack, followed by a growing crowd, an ever-increasing line snaking its way across the convention floor like the Carioca.

By the time they got to the booth, Jack had his work cut out for him. Two of the sales reps took up positions alongside of him, opening covers and marking the place to sign. They could no longer see the end of the line, hundreds, perhaps a thousand, standing with books in their hands. Jack went to work, under a mammoth poster of the bookcover with his picture, a beaming countenance six feet tall smiling out at the convention throngs.

There was a crew with television cameras taking pictures.

'Local news?' asked Abby.

'Part of their marketing,' said Owens. 'T.V. magazine piece to air at the time of the publication. Jack will have to sit for a few interviews.'

They were leaving nothing to chance. Abby marveled at the campaign.

Carla leaned into her ear so she could be heard. 'Alex brought twenty thousand advance reader copies. They put out eighteen thousand of them yesterday morning. On pallets over there.' She pointed to some wooden pallets near the corner of the booth that were now bare.

Abby looked at her.

'They were gone in an hour,' said Carla.

Abby knew that her book had the legs to walk. But she never expected this. She wondered if people had read the advance copies the previous night, or if the mob was simply propelled by Big-F's promotion and Jack's picture on the back cover. Whatever it was, one thing was certain: the tidal wave had begun.

Jack signed books for nearly three hours but the line never ended. Finally Bertoli put a stop to it. They were late for a private reception back at the hotel. Jack and Abby were ushered out through a back service area and into the limo for the mile-and-a-half ride to the Hilton.

When they arrived the reception was already underway, several hundred people in a large banquet room. Bertoli led the way, making introductions as they went and talking to Jack in a seamless stream.

'It's wonderful news,' he told them. 'The film is now green lighted.' After signing their star, the studio had named a top notch director. The script was already into revisions. This would now be an endless task rewriting lines to stroke the egos of the stars until the film was in the can.

Bertoli asked Jack if he wanted to take a cut at the screen play. Jack's eyes lit up, but Abby said no. There wasn't time if Jack was going to finish the next book.

'Good thinking,' said Bertoli. 'Casting for support is proceeding at full pace. They'll be in production within four months. It's timing to die for,' said the publisher. 'The film will be out with the paperback.'

Bertoli had received a half-dozen phone calls from *Variety*, *Entertainment Weekly*, and the trades in a single afternoon following the star signing.

He also knew something else he wasn't sharing until he had what he wanted. The novel had just been sold in a hotly contested auction to one of the book clubs for the highest price ever netted on a first-time novel. It was the kind of outside confirmation that caused the ground to swell. Bertoli was beginning to sense an eruption, and he wanted to move on Jack before it happened.

They popped more corks, poured more champagne. A waiter passed among them with trays of hors d'oeuvres. Most of the executive staff of Big-F was present along with representatives from the chains and many of the independents, owners and managers of large and small book stores from across the country.

For Jack the introductions began to pile up, name overload so that Abby had to whisper in his ear as they mingled. Some of the guests took Abby for Jack's wife until he introduced her as his lawyer.

Bertoli presented him with a crystal champagne glass, bigger than any of the plastic cups the other guests were using. It had a red ribbon around the stem and the title of Abby's novel etched in the glass.

A waiter with a magnum bottle seemed to follow Jack wherever he went, filling his glass. Abby had to wonder how embarrassed and angry Bertoli would be when she went public. He would look like a fool. But if it worked, she didn't care. After seeing the lines forming on the convention floor, mostly doe-eyed women gazing at Jack, Abby was convinced she'd done the right thing. She hadn't made the rules, but she'd learned to bend them.

A few seconds later Bertoli told Abby someone wanted to meet her. He dragged her across the room and introduced her to another lawyer, a woman on their staff. It was ham-handed at best, an excuse to separate Abby from Jack. When she looked back she found herself supplanted by Carla, who'd taken charge shepherding him through the crowd.

Within three minutes the other lawyer drifted off. She'd done her job. This left Abby to sip from a plastic cup quietly in a corner, virtually ignored. She noticed that in one of the small conference rooms off the mammoth reception area everything had been carefully laid out for a meeting. She stuck her head inside and looked. The place had all the signs of a ritual sacrifice, including name plates. The only thing missing was the offering. Abby didn't like it. Across the room Bertoli kept swilling champagne into Jack.

It was all very sociable, but a few minutes later Jack was herded into the little room. Bertoli and Carla and a couple of the other executives from Big-F followed them. When they started to close the door, Abby made her move.

'What's going on?'

One of the minions barred the way. 'Private meeting,' he told her.

'Not without me. I'm his lawyer,' said Abby.

The guy holding the door looked over at his shoulder at Bertoli for direction.

Abby was prepared to make a scene and they knew it.

'Oh sure. She should be in here,' said Bertoli. He scolded one of his subordinates for the oversight and offered Abby a big beefy grin. 'Come on in.'

Like some bouncer in a bar, the man released his iron grip on the door and let her pass. There were knowing glances exchanged between Owens and Bertoli like a quarterback giving audibles on the line, changing the signals. The end run would now have to be a power play up the middle, over Abby's body.

'Get Miss Chandlis a chair.' Bertoli issued the order to one of his associates, a guy at the far end of the table, who immediately rose to offer his chair.

'I'd like that one.' Abby pointed to the man sitting next to Jack. Grudgingly the guy got up and Abby took his place.

'What's this all about?' she asked.

Owens took the lead.

'Alex thought we should have this meeting, that it was essential before we went any further. Everything is moving so fast,' she said.

'Light speed,' said Abby.

'Green-lighted film. Fast track to publication,' said Carla.

'Unscheduled meetings,' said Abby.

'Yes. Well. There is one problem.' Carla broke the ice.

'And what's that?' said Abby.

'The promotional budget on the book is ballooning,' said Bertoli. 'The marketing costs are out of all proportion to the probable return.'

'Oops. Maybe we should put this back in the bottle,'

said Jack. He held up his glass. Jack looked a little drunk.

Nervous chuckles from Bertoli. Maybe they'd gone too far with bottle diplomacy.

'There's no crisis,' said Bertoli. 'It's just that there are formulae in the industry that determine a sound marketing budget. And on this book we've thrown them all out.'

'I appreciate it.' Jack threw his head back and swallowed half a glass of champagne like it was a shot.

'I think what Alex is trying to say is that he can't continue to do this without some assurance that he'll be able to recoup that investment in the future. Isn't that what you're saying, Alex?'

'That's what I'm saying.'

'What kind of assurance?' Abby didn't like the sound of it.

Bertoli cleared his throat. 'Let's say, five books under contract.'

'Five books?' Jack had a look like Bertoli'd lit him up.

'Of course we can negotiate the terms,' said Bertoli.

'Bullshit,' said Jack.

'Surely not that many.' Carla ignored Jack as if he'd sneezed. This was polite New York bullshit. 'Perhaps the sequel you're working on and one or two more.' She looked at Abby, who to this point hadn't said a word.

'That wasn't the deal,' said Abby.

'Everything must be negotiable,' said Bertoli. He was looking at Abby, the mellow one without the drink in her hand. They had played it wrong and Carla and Bertoli now knew it. They'd plied him with booze, but Jack had the signs of a mean drunk.

'Could it be you have a little inside information?' Jack

raised his voice. He was looking at Bertoli through an intimidating alcohol haze.

'Well, I don't think there's anything material that you don't know,' said Bertoli. He looked at Carla. 'I couldn't think what it might be?' he said. 'I'd have to talk to my people. Look at the numbers.' Bertoli started to yammer, all the things that come out of a guilty mouth.

'Perhaps we should continue this at a later time.' Carla stepped in to save him. It wouldn't do to have this turn ugly with three hundred buyers standing outside the door.

'No, I think we should resolve it now,' said Abby. She liked the idea of crazy Jack and the crowd. It gave her leverage. They made a mistake, and now they were going to have to play on her field.

'It's just that Alex loves Jack's work,' said Carla. 'He wants to publish everything he writes. Isn't that right, Alex?'

'Absolutely,' said Bertoli. 'All we're talking about is good faith negotiations.'

Carla was dug in, almost more than Big-F. For Bertoli, it was the price. He wanted to get the books before the cost doubled or tripled. Abby guessed that for Carla it was control. She wanted Jack, Gable Cooper, under her belt for more books. If she had to, she would savage Bertoli later, renegotiate the price upward to keep the author happy. The cost of renegotiation to the author would of course be the perennial demand for still more books. There was a downside to everything in life. For the successful author, it was the agent working both ends.

'You have the one book,' said Abby. 'Publish it. Do it well, and we can talk. That's good faith.'

'But you don't seem to understand. I can't continue to

spend in this fashion,' said Bertoli. 'To, to, how do I put it . . .?'

'Lavish,' said Carla.

'Thank you,' said Bertoli.

As an agent in the trenches, Owens was worse than worthless. She was her own fifth column.

'I can't continue to lavish money,' said Bertoli, 'unless . . .?' He held his hands palms-up and smiled. The message was clear. They were holding hostages in the form of Abby's book.

'So you figure it's a good time to hold us up,' said Jack. He took another drink from his glass, more powder from the keg.

'You're being very unreasonable.' To Carla, all things were made possible by the agent; the deals from heaven. Books were just an incidental bi-product of her power. If she could, she would have skipped the writers completely and allowed the readers to gain their enjoyment from her glow.

'It's extortion.' Jack moved on to other crimes and took another drink.

'Extortion.' Carla smiled and tried to regain her composure. She and Bertoli laughed and tried to dismiss it, the ravings of a drunk who would not remember the next day.

'No one is engaging in extortion,' said Carla. 'This is business.'

'Only if you're Al Capone,' said Jack. He looked at her over the top of his crystal champagne glass.

Jack had driven them into a defensive crouch and now Abby took over.

'What assurance do we have if we give you more books that you'll use your best efforts to market this one?' said Abby.

'What do you mean?' said Bertoli.

'If we give you more books, how do we prevent you from climbing the list on our back, from doing it in marginal increments instead of one big push?'

'Why would he do that?' Carla looked incredulous.

'To conserve his budget. There's only so many dollars. Once we give you more books, we don't exist. You can afford to ignore us.' And Abby knew they would.

'No tours. Your publicity people use their chits with the networks to put other authors on the talk shows. You cut the corners on our print ads. We get the teasers. They get full pages. Squeaky wheel gets oiled,' said Abby. 'And without the ability to negotiate future contracts, we can't squeak. Not so that you'll be able to hear us anyway.'

Bertoli laughed. He looked at Carla. He'd never heard of anything so ridiculous. 'We're in the business of making money,' he said. 'We'd never cut Jack's budget. He's a valued author. We're gonna take him over the top,' said Bertoli. 'Pull out all the stops.'

'But how do we know that?'

'Because I'm telling you.' Bertoli gave her a big grin, something like Boris on Rockey and Bullwinkle.

'There,' said Carla. 'See, you have Alex's word on it.'

'Tell you what,' said Abby. 'You take us over the top, pull out all the stops, and you have my word. We'll give you more books.'

There was a dead beat of stone silence in the room. Bertoli hated lawyers.

'We should hire this woman. Brassy,' he said. 'I like that. You, guy down there. You could take some notes.' Bertoli was talking to his two underlings. 'Still,' he said. 'I have to have something.'

'Or else what?' said Abby.

Bertoli made a face, followed by a long pained silence. It was the kind of expression that left Abby to wonder about the consequences.

'We need to cooperate on this,' said Owens. 'We're a team. We're working together.'

'Oh. We can all see that you're cooperating with him,' said Abby.

Jack actually laughed.

'Tell you what.' She ignored Owens and dealt directly with Bertoli. 'You want security for your investment. We want assurances that you won't squander the book you already have. I think there's an easy answer,' she told him.

Bertoli was all ears.

'We sign a contract,' said Abby.

'You're gonna let these people bulldoze you?' said Jack.

'Hear me out,' said Abby.

'More books?' Bertoli was a smile.

'Not yet,' said Abby. 'We do an agreement to sign a future contract on certain terms and conditions.'

'What do you mean? What terms and conditions?'

'We agree to give you more books in the future, if you carry out your promise to take the current manuscript "over the top." "To pull out all the stops," as you say.'

'How are you going to put something like that in a contract?'

'By defining what you mean by "over the top," and "pulling out all the stops." '

'Just a turn of speech,' said Bertoli.

'So you don't mean it?'

'Oh sure. We're gonna try. But we can't guarantee anything.'

'But you want us to guarantee more books,' said Jack.

'Now that's a double standard if I ever saw one.' He pointed an accusing wobbly finger at the publisher and tried to get up but slumped again into the chair. 'You don't have to do a damn thing, but we have to provide good books. Blood from my veins,' said Jack.

Abby had a hard time keeping a straight face.

'So what do you want?' said Bertoli.

'Two things,' said Abby. 'I want this book to go high on the bestsellers list and I want it to stay there a long time.'

'What? Number one?' said Bertoli.

'For at least ten weeks,' said Abby.

Bertoli actually fell back in his chair.

'That's absurd,' said Owens.

'In addition, you'd have to agree to hold it on the list for an additional five months, inside of number seven.'

Bertoli was flabbergasted. 'That's ridiculous.'

'Fine. Inside of ten. That's the "pull out all the stops" part,' said Abby. If he was going to throw terms around and make idle promises, she was going to nail his feet to the floor.

'Why the hell should I have to do more books?' said Jack.

'Quiet,' said Abby.

Unless Bertoli had a superman complex or was blowing coke on the side, it was a deal he couldn't accept, and Abby knew it. She didn't want him to. It was designed to do one thing: take the wind out of his sails for more books.

'That's outrageous. I can't guarantee placement on the list.'

'I'm not asking you to guarantee anything. I'm offering you a performance incentive. Perform and you get more books,' said Abby.

'It's unheard of,' said Bertoli.

'Not, it's not. You do it to authors all the time,' said Jack. Suddenly he wasn't as drunk as he'd made out.

'What are you talking about?'

'Your bonus clause,' said Jack. 'You put it in my contract. You know the one. Says if we get on the *New York Times* bestsellers list you release the advance a little faster. You aren't paying us any more, you're just paying it out a little quicker.'

Abby was stunned. Jack had actually read the contract.

'That's different,' said Bertoli.

'I know,' said Jack. 'We're offering you something real.'

The silence from Bertoli filled the room.

'What's the problem? Is it that the mark's too high?' said Jack. Now he was taunting Bertoli.

'Where exactly is this "over the top" you've been talking about?' asked Jack.

'It's just a manner of speech,' said Carla.

'Ah, so now we're getting down to it. So it's just a lot of loose talk?' said Jack.

'That's not what we're saying,' said Owens.

'You've got a problem,' said Abby. 'You either have to define it or forget it.'

'I can't do that,' said Bertoli. 'I just can't guarantee a result on the list. You don't understand.'

'Oh, I think I understand.' Jack made it sound like a measure of Bertoli's manhood. What he was afraid of was failure. Reduce the test to writing in a contract and the entire industry would know about it. If Alex failed and lost future books and the author with them, he would be legend. It would follow him to his grave in business hell.

'Do we have a deal or don't we?' said Jack.

'Maybe we should consider the terms?' Carla was pitching Bertoli now, but it was a little late. 'Maybe a few weeks less on the list,' she said. 'How about if he takes you inside of three, instead of one?' She looked at Jack.

'I can't do it. I won't do it.' Bertoli cut her off.

Jack shrugged and looked at her like the sensible drunk that he was. 'You heard him. We're trying to be reasonable,' said Jack. This after Abby had just capped Bertoli's knees.

Jack smiled and stood, looked at his watch. 'Geez, it's getting late. Don't we have the gala dinner tonight?' The producers were flying in the star of the film to meet the author and talk with the book buyers in one of the big ballrooms. The studio had a big stake in the success of the novel, and Abby and Jack knew it. They now had a big stick.

'We'll have to continue this,' said Carla. 'After all, everything in life is negotiable, right?'

'I suppose you would think that,' said Abby. 'Now that we know what you are, all that would be left to discuss is your price.'

Owens shot her a look to kill.

CHAPTER
TWENTY

Lake Washington had the big houses. It was where Bill Gates, the Microsoft magnate, had a mansion. Lake Union, its little sister to the west, had a few apartments and condos, but for the most part it was commercial, boat yards and brokerages, a few restaurants at the south end.

The fire had occurred a few days earlier, but the acrid odor of smoke hung over the water like a guest who wouldn't leave. With the window of his car rolled down, scents of burnt wood and chemicals tickled Sanfillipo's sinuses as he drew closer.

He could hear the constant buzz of tires on the iron spans of I-5 two hundred feet overhead.

He found a place and parked in front of a canvas shop that advertised dodgers and bimini tops for boats, locked the unmarked car, and walked. A dump truck was backed up on the dock being loaded with debris, piles of charred, water-soaked wood. A floating crane, its boom four stories in the sky, drifted in the current off shore. Workmen in hard hats scurried about. Luther saw one of them with a clipboard, symbol of authority, and got directions.

Sanfillipo made his way around equipment and down the paved incline of a driveway toward the water. The breeze suddenly took the smell in another direction. He could see the ridge line of a small building, what was left of it, poking a few feet above the surface of the water about fifty feet out from the docks. There was a small army standing around. Everything had been shut down since they discovered the body two hours earlier. As he approached, they turned and Luther introduced himself.

'Lieutenant Sanfillipo.' He flashed the foreman his badge, and the guy shook his hand. 'I understand they have some business for me?' He saw some uniforms down by the water, but he wanted to talk to the workmen first.

'Coroner's down there right now,' said the foreman. He pointed to a small work barge where several men, some in uniform, were huddled over a dark bundle.

'They're not sure if it was an accident or what,' said the foreman. 'Our drivers found the body at first light. He was tangled in some lines. Looks like maybe something heavy might have fallen on him during the fire.'

'Like half the building,' said one of the other guys.

'How did the fire happen?' asked Sanfillipo.

'We don't know yet. Fire department thinks it could have been arson,' said the foreman. 'With all the paint and other stuff inside, it's hard to tell. We're raising it so the fire marshal can find the point of origin.'

'Guess it burned all the way through the dock,' said the detective.

'No. No. It was an old wooden ammunition barge. Makeshift boat yard,' said the guy. 'Told it dated to World War One. Wonder it floated anymore.'

'Is the owner around?'

The foreman shook his head. 'City's been chasing him around. A lot of complaints filed on the business. Code violations. That sort of stuff.'

Luther nodded like he understood.

'They think he might have started it?'

'I don't think so. Apparently he lost everything, tools, the works. No insurance. Three generations in business down the drain. Just like that. Tough break,' said the guy.

'A tragedy,' said Sanfillipo. 'But not as bad as what happened to the guy in the bag over there. What about him? Didn't anybody miss him when the fire broke out?'

'He wasn't an employee.'

Luther offered up arched eyebrows.

'People from the boat yard don't seem to have any idea what he was doing there.'

'Maybe he set the fire?' said one of the other workmen. 'I suppose it wouldn't be the first time an arsonist got caught up in what he was doing.'

'Yeah. Sort of consumed by his own work, you might say,' one of the other guys chimed in and they all laughed at his joke.

'A lot of gallows humor in this business,' said Luther.

'Yeah, regular Robin Williams,' said the foreman. 'Let's get back to work.' The group sauntered away unhappy that they couldn't stay where the action was.

'It's possible,' said Luther, 'that your arsonist is in the bag out there. Though without insurance you wonder why.'

'Firebug,' said the foreman. 'They don't need a reason.'

'True,' said Luther. 'Any identification?'

'I think they found a wallet. Coroner's got it.'

Luther wandered down toward the work barge, one end of which was tied up against the dock, stepped down into it, and wedged his way into the group. There was a diver in a black wet suit, his mask propped on top of his head, his feet in the water sitting on the edge.

'Harmon.' Luther recognized the deputy coroner.

'Lieutenant.' As soon as he said it, the other men moved aside, giving Luther a little more room and a lot more deference.

'What brings you out here so early?' said the coroner.

'The smell of napalm in the morning.' He looked at the zipped-up body bag on the deck. 'Burned?'

The coroner shook his head. 'Fire burned through the wooden hull pretty quick. Sank like a rock.'

'What can you tell me?'

'May have drowned. It's also possible he may have been dead before it went down. Took a little fluid out of the lungs, but not much. Body's pretty bloated. Been down there over a week. Won't know more 'til I get him on a table.'

'Any name?'

The coroner showed Luther a clipboard with a county form, some notes on it, and pointed. Luther looked at it and thought.

'Did he work in the area?'

'Got me. If he did, you'd think somebody would have noticed that he was missing.'

'You would think so,' said Luther. 'You pretty sure he went down with it at the time of the fire?'

'Oh yeah. He was buried under fire debris. I would say he was there before it started. Also there were some burns. The divers didn't even see him 'til one of them grabbed his foot in the dark.'

'I suppose that might cause a mess in your wet suit,'

said Luther. The diver didn't look at him.

'They tell me you found a wallet?' Luther asked the coroner.

'Yeah.' The man reached for a water-sodden paper bag resting on top of the barge's winch and poured the contents out on top of a flat area on the machinery. There was a ring, some change, and a black wallet. The leather of the wallet was soggy and soft. A piece of green lake weed had worked its way inside the plastic window with the driver's license, but it was still readable. Luther pawed through the contents of the wallet. Inside one of the flaps was the stub from an airline boarding pass showing a flight from LAX, the date and time.

'Lotta possibilities, I suppose,' said the coroner. 'If he wasn't one of the employees, he could have been a customer. Maybe had a boat in the works.'

'Hmm,' said Luther. 'But how did this customer get here?'

'Whadda you mean?'

'Without any keys,' said the detective.

The coroner looked at the items spread out on the rusted metal surface on top of the winch. Luther was right. Among the objects found on the body there were no keys, to a car or anything else.

Luther compared the name on the coroner's notes with the name on the driver's license, then looked at the picture on the laminated license.

'I don't think this man was a customer,' he said. 'I don't think this guy was into yachts.'

They took an early morning flight to Atlanta and from there to Savannah. Abby tried to catch a few winks but the stewardesses kept fraternizing. It was the thing that happened with Jack. He was a magnet for women; even the old lady he helped with luggage in the overhead compartment kept looking at him with eyes of wonderment. To Abby it was getting tiresome. He was good-looking, but he was only flesh and bone. If she was right, the warts were all on the inside; boils of arrogance the size of oranges. Jack didn't seem to mind the gaping looks. She guessed that he'd had a lifetime of it and had grown accustomed to the stares of women.

They landed, grabbed their luggage, picked up the car, and headed for Coffin Point. To Abby, never having seen it, the name conjured ominous thoughts.

As they drove north, in the direction of Hilton Head, the area served up a generous offering of serenity; white clapboard houses against green lawns, towering oaks overgrown with moss, cricketlike sounds, and the smells of the country. It wasn't as lush as western Washington, but it had its own kind of beauty. It reminded her of places in the Delta near San Francisco Bay. Only it seemed much larger. They passed through Beaufort with its stately old homes, picture-card perfect.

They stayed on Highway 21 out of Beaufort, crossed the channel to Lady's Island, and from there to St Helena Island and toward Frogmore. A few miles on they turned off and within minutes the road turned to dirt.

The thought had crossed Abby's mind as they left the state highway and headed down the sandy loam road; she didn't know Jack Jermaine from Adam. She had expected a call from Morgan in Chicago. It never came, and she wondered why. They were supposed to coordinate before she left. Still Morgan had her number at Jack's house. Maybe he'd left a message there.

They rattled along in the Landcruiser on the dirt road, past picket fences and small houses, a few mobile homes.

The inside of Jack's car was clean, meticulous, military, though the outside could have used a wash.

'You took a real chance,' said Jack. 'What if Bertoli had decided to pull the plug when you told him no more books?'

'He wouldn't.'

'Why not?'

'You saw the line on the floor of the convention center.' Abby didn't mention the star-struck gaze of many of the women standing in it. Jack's ego didn't need any feeding. 'They tried and they lost,' said Abby. 'Round one.'

'He seemed pretty angry to me.'

'People in New York like to argue,' said Abby. 'It's all part of the Great Manhattan Mindfuck.'

Jack laughed.

'Look at it this way,' she said. 'Bertoli gave us his best pitch, at least for this inning. We made him eat it. Now he has something more to play for. If I'd given him the books without a fight, Carla and Alex would have had to go home and take depression meds.'

'Then you intend to give them more books?'

'We'll see.' She had no intention of tipping her hand to Jack.

'They didn't just want the books, they wanted bondage. They wanted to own me.'

'They were looking at me,' said Jack.

'You. Me. For now it's all the same.'

'I saved your ass.'

'You saved nothing. My ass was about to walk out of the room.'

'That would have been a mistake,' said Jack.

'Why?'

'Because that would have left me in there alone.'

Abby looked at him and couldn't tell if he was kidding.

'Hey. I wanted to find out what they were willing to offer for four more books,' said Jack. 'Aren't you at least curious?'

'Whatever it is, it's not enough.'

'I saw something recently. An author got twenty-four million,' said Jack.

'That was for three books,' said Abby.

Jack looked over at her. She *was* interested after all.

Abby brushed a string of hair out of her face and then said casually: 'I saw it in the paper last week.'

'Oh right. Next to the stock quotes and obits.' He laughed. 'There's nothing wrong with being interested in money.'

'No. It's just the questionable things it makes you do,' said Abby. She thought, like get in a car with a man I don't know and head down some lonely dirt road.

'Five months on the *New York Times* list,' said Jack.

'I wanted to give him a challenge,' said Abby.

'More like a coronary. Did you catch the look? Like you lit him up. I've seen people touch high tension wires with less effect,' said Jack.

'You're the one got drunk.'

'Putten him on. That's all,' said Jack. 'Who in their right mind argues with an angry drunk. You think I went too far?'

'You were fine. Just your average obsessive author.' She looked at him and they both started to laugh.

'Artsy-fartsy me,' said Jack. 'Make me God or I won't play. The look on his face when you said ten weeks, top of the list, was worth the royalties. Train-struck deer.'

'Carla's probably still peeling him off the ceiling,' said Abby.

'I could have given him the books,' said Jack. 'But then I suppose we would have been in trouble.'

'We wouldn't have been in trouble,' said Abby, 'I would have been in trouble. You forget. You're my alter ego. In the eyes of the law, you stand in my shoes.'

He looked at her feet. 'Now that would hurt.'

'Get serious,' she told him. 'You agree to something and I'm obligated to perform.'

'In that case we should visit the red light district in Atlanta,' said Jack.

'Very funny.'

'I could get you a little bustier, some lace on the thigh. Buy myself a purple fedora.'

'Is that the kind of work you do?' said Abby.

'Do I look like it?'

'Looks are deceiving,' said Abby.

'On a dusty road with a man you don't know. It's a little late to be asking, isn't it?' It was something that her father might have said when she was a teenager about getting into cars with strangers. Jack didn't look at her when he said it. It was also the kind of thing a killer might ask a hitchhiker just before he plunged the knife in or jumped her.

She studied him for a long moment. There was an awkward silence. Abby wasn't sure if she should treat the question seriously. It would only feed her anxieties or, she thought, lead to something worse.

'I was only kidding,' said Jack. 'You're perfectly safe.'

'Right.' Abby didn't look at him.

'Relax.' Jack looked at her and laughed. 'Listen, you want me to stop?'

'No,' said Abby. It was the one thing she was sure of. She didn't want him to stop on a deserted road in the middle of nowhere.

'You never told me how your friend, what was her name?'

'Theresa?'

'Yeah. You never told me what happened. The article in the paper was a little vague. Was it an accident?'

'I don't know. I don't think so.'

'Someone killed her?'

'It looks that way.'

'Her husband?'

Abby looked at him trying to figure how he would put this together so quickly

He caught her glance. 'Well, it makes sense. An angry husband. Bad marriage.'

'The cops don't think he did it.'

'Why not?'

'It's a long story.' Abby didn't want to talk about it. 'Can we discuss something else.'

'Sure. Let's talk about more books. What's your take? You think Bertoli will bury us now that we've turned him down?'

'I don't think he can afford to.'

'Why not?'

'We're into him for three million. He's got to get it back somehow. Plus the film thing. True, we don't get the big bucks there until they get to principal photography. Just the same, the studio's on the hook with the star. They have to keep him happy. Why do you think I got three million for books rights?'

'It's a good book,' said Jack.

'Oh, it's a fine book,' said Abby. 'Marvelous read. But take it from me, the payout wasn't based on my excellent prose. This has all the signs of a deal driven by the stars,' said Abby.

'And you think that gives us leverage?'

'On this book, yes. The only way we lose is if they get more books. Then Bertoli can spread the risk. Make it back over the long haul and let the studio worry about their star. Right now we need to keep Bertoli on a short leash, and keep him hungry. If he makes us big . . .'

'Us?' said Jack.

'Speaking metaphorically,' said Abby. 'Then maybe it's time to talk about more books.'

'So if he brings us to the prom, your theory is why not dance with him,' said Jack.

'As opposed to a sock-hop,' said Abby.

She was right and Jack knew it. The tail wagging the dog. It was the movie deal that had the book on a hot burner.

'There's something else,' said Jack. 'Plain as the nose on your face.'

'My nose is plain?'

'Poor choice of words,' said Jack. 'That's why you're the writer.'

'Not that anyone would notice,' said Abby.

He looked over at her. 'In fact, you have a very nice nose.'

She touched it self-consciously with the tip of her finger like maybe it was running.

'Anyway,' said Abby. She didn't trust him enough to flirt.

'Anyway. There's another dynamic.'

'What do you mean?'

'What I said at the meeting. There's something Bertoli's not telling.'

'What?'

'I don't know,' said Jack. 'Early orders for the book. Something from the big chains.' He shook his head in puzzlement. 'Something's turned the buzz up a notch for him to come after more books that way. Kinda frontal, don't you think? No finesse. I would have figured Carla for finesse. One thing for sure. The books they wanted are worth a lot more than we know.'

Abby thought about this for a moment. 'It does make me angry. The garbage about the forces of the marketplace. That he had to recoup his investment. Couldn't continue to lavish money.'

'Don't get mad. That's business. You gave him a price,' said Jack. 'His house, his soul, and his first born. As soon as Carla rubs his ego down they'll be back. You gotta think there's one rule in the jungle. We come and go. The agents live in the sandbox with the publishers. The writer's always the odd man out. Still, she brought you the deal. You couldn't have gotten here without her.'

'She cut herself a piece of cake,' said Abby. 'Question is, can I trust her now?'

Jack looked at her straight across as he gripped the steering wheel. 'Who ever told you you could trust anybody?'

To say that cops have suspicious minds is like saying cats land on their feet: an article of faith.

When Luther Sanfillipo called Abby's house and discovered that her phone has been disconnected he began to wonder. When he drove over and found a For Sale staked in her front lawn and the house empty he began to worry. And when he called her office and was told that she'd quit her job and left no forwarding address he began to act.

He parked his car in a commercial garage. In this neighborhood Luther figured it was the price of keeping his hub caps. He hiked the two blocks, mostly up hill, to the dilapidated three-story office building. The outside was covered with tattered posters, and a lot of graffiti that would have required decoding by the gang unit.

Downstairs was a video store and a small grocery. In between the two was a single glass door with an address in metal numbers over the top that somehow the neighbors hadn't managed to pry off and steal. Luther entered and made his way to the top of the stairs over the soiled carpet.

At the top a hallway formed a *T* going in two directions, with separate doors at the end of each. 'Marcia's Relaxation Center' was painted on one of them. The other bore the name:

'C. W. CHANDLIS, COUNSELOR
&
ATTORNEY AT LAW'

Luther heard the patter of typing on the other side of the door, opened it, and went in.

'Can I help you?' A man, fairly well dressed, was seated at a desk in an outer office, what passed for reception.

'I'm looking for Mr Charles Chandlis.'

The man continued to hunt-and-peck at the typewriter.

'You found him.'

Luther looked at him sitting at the typewriter. 'You're the attorney?' said Luther.

'My secretary's out for a few minutes,' said Charlie.

It was a bad omen, Luther hadn't even introduced

himself and he was being lied to. He'd done a little checking, including employment records. Chandlis's secretary had filed for unemployment two weeks before, along with a labor claim for unpaid wages. The lawyer was on the financial edge, one more reason why Luther thought he might want to talk to him.

'Who are you?' said Charlie.

'Name's Sanfillipo.' He took out his badge and showed it to the lawyer.

Instant hackles. If Charlie had been a dog, the hair on the back of his neck would have stood up.

'If this is about one of my cases, you can forget it. I only deal with your bosses,' said Charlie.

Luther flexed his eyebrows in question.

'The county prosecutor's office,' said Charlie. Then he looked at the door as if Luther might want to use it again, to leave.

'Oh. No. No. It's not about one of your cases. It's about one of mine.'

The way he said this caused Charlie to pause for a moment and look at him.

'I am looking for your wife,' said Luther.

'I'm not married.' Charlie went back to his typing, and looked at his watch like he was on some deadline. He hit some wrong keys, several letters, and had to back over two of them with the correcting ribbon.

'You should get yourself a computer,' said Luther.

'Yeah, right. And spend six months learning how to use it,' said Charlie.

'Your secretary should be able to do that,' said Luther. He did the kind of Raul Julia smile that so intimidated.

'What do you want?'

'I told you,' said Luther. 'I'm looking for Mrs Chandlis. Abigail Chandlis.'

'My former wife,' said Charlie.

'Yes.'

'As the title implies, we don't live together anymore,' said Charlie. 'You might try her house.'

'I did. It's empty,' said Luther.

For the first time, Charlie stopped typing and swiveled around in his chair to look up at the cop, more questions in his eyes now than on his lips.

'Do you have an interest in it?' said Luther.

'What?'

'Your wife's house.'

'No. Why do you ask?'

'Because it's for sale.'

Chandlis considered this for a moment, and unless Luther had lost his ability to judge body language, the lawyer was hearing it for the first time. He returned to his typing.

'Why are you looking for her?'

'An investigation,' said Luther. 'Just routine.'

'Did she do something wrong?'

'Not that we know of.' Luther made it sound like a question.

Charlie didn't bite.

'We would just like to talk to her,' said Luther.

'Did you call the firm?'

'Hmm.' The cop nodded. 'She quit last week.'

There was no pause in typing, but several mistakes. Luther might have asked him if he knew about this, but he didn't have to.

'I thought you might know where she is?'

'I don't.'

'When was the last time you talked to her?'

'Can't remember. We're not that close,' said Charlie.

'Oh. I was under the impression that you kept in touch.'

'And what gave you that impression?'

'The fact that you received six thousand dollars from her ten days ago,' said Luther.

Charlie didn't say anything but stopped his typing in mid-word and looked at Luther, clearly angry that the police were prying into his financial affairs.

'Do you mind telling me what it was for?' said Luther.

'Why should I? You seem to know everything already.'

'Am I safe in assuming a private debt?' said Luther.

'Not anymore,' said Charlie.

'I can assure you . . .'

'You can fuck your assurances,' said Charlie.

'That would be an interesting trick, but somehow I don't think it would make them any more acceptable to you,' said Luther. He thought Charlie sounded a lot like one of his clients. Perhaps it was contagious.

'How long have you been divorced?' he asked.

'The records are in the courthouse,' said Charlie. 'Why don't you go look?'

It was a possible theory that whoever killed Theresa Jenrico had done so by mistake; that the real target was Abby Chandlis. If so, she might be on the run. Or maybe they'd already gotten her.

'You heard about her friend Mrs Jenrico?' said Luther.

'Yeah. I heard. Tragic,' said Charlie.

'How did you hear about it?'

'The papers,' said Charlie. 'I can read.' He waited for the next question, what he was doing that night, but it didn't come. Luther wasn't that frontal.

'You must admit it's a rather peculiar way to pay a debt?'

'What do you mean?'

'I mean Mrs Chandlis paying it to your credit-card account like that.'

'It's the way she wanted it. For convenience,' said Charlie.

'I see. I'm sure the credit-card company thought it was convenient.' Luther smiled at him. He knew that Charlie was over his limit. The only thing that saved his card was his wife's payment.

'What business is that of yours?'

'Oh none. But I am curious why she would pay you such a large sum of money and then disappear without telling anyone where she was going?'

'You'd have to ask her that.'

'If I could find her I would.'

'Can't help you. Now if you're finished, I've got work to do.'

'Do you know where she got the money? To pay you, I mean?'

'No.'

'That's a lot of money. She isn't a wealthy woman.'

'No.'

Charlie wasn't the only one whose financial life was now under scrutiny.

'And the nature of the debt?' asked Luther.

'It was a loan,' Charlie lied.

'What for?'

'That's private. You wanna know anything more, get a subpoena. And I don't appreciate your fucking around in my financial affairs.'

'Oh, I assure you there was no fucking around,' said Luther. 'We merely called your bank and told them it was a homicide investigation.'

Charlie's eyes lit up.

'They were most anxious to help,' said Luther.

'Wonderful.' Now all the tellers would be looking at Charlie as if he were an ax murderer.

'We have been very discreet,' said Luther.

'I'll bet. Now just you and a few hundred of your asshole friends downtown know my credit rating.'

'I had never considered my colleagues in that light before,' said Luther. 'But I will tell them when I see them.' He headed for the door.

'Do that.'

Luther turned. 'All of this hostility, I assume, comes from your work?'

'I hadn't noticed,' said Charlie.

'That's the problem with job stress,' said Luther. 'It tends to creep up on you and kill you without your noticing.'

CHAPTER
TWENTY-ONE

What was once a grand entrance to a great plantation was now spotted by several houses and a few
mobile homes. In the distance, a half mile off through a
tunnel formed by a tree-lined lane, Abby could make
out the white-washed walls and double staircase of an
old plantation home, its columns reaching skyward.

The long drive leading to the house was overhung by
ancient oaks, their broad branches merging in a canopy
overhead. They nearly shut out the sunlight. To Abby,
the drive looked like the vaulted ceiling of a Gothic
cathedral hung with moss.

The road itself was soft sand, in places puddled with
standing water from the recent rain. The rear end of
Jack's car fish-tailed a little as it hit one of these.

'You own all of this?' said Abby.

'Don't look so impressed,' said Jack. 'You haven't seen
the inside yet.'

As they drew closer she could see that he was right.
Jack's house was like the man, well built, but showing
signs of wear. It could have played well on a movie set;
plantation house sans slaves, fallen on hard times. It
stood three stories if you counted the flood basement set

up on white pillars and shielded behind a mass of shrubbery. Heavy postered beams supported the covered porch that ran the length of the house and the picket-railed balcony at the top level.

Abby guessed that the place dated to the early part of the nineteenth century, something Sherman missed on his march to the sea.

They pulled up in front of the twin staircases and stopped. Jack got out and stretched. Abby joined him and felt the warmth of the dappled sunlight on her face. The smell of early blossoms was in the air. It was a setting as far removed from Seattle or any other big city as was possible; peaceful without a hint of traffic or the bustle of modern life. Without Jack's car parked in front, it could have been a picture from the last century.

'I'll get the luggage later,' he told her. 'Come on inside.'

On the way to the house he took a detour toward a little kiosk under the stairs, went inside, and a second later came out with a stack of letters in one hand, and a red, white, and blue express package in the other, the size of a shirt box.

It seemed the mailman and delivery trucks left mail and packages for Jack in the little building when he was gone. 'An informal agreement,' he told her. 'One of the perks of country life.'

Jack started picking through the envelopes as Abby followed him up the stairs. The front door wasn't locked. Another perk of country life, she assumed.

The entry hall was like something Abby had seen only in museums: broad-planked floors scarred and heavily polished by a century of wear. In one corner was an antique hall-tree, its beveled mirror blotched by missing silver in a few places.

Jack headed into a large central hall and Abby followed.
'Make yourself at home. I'll be right down.' He went
up the stairs, a grand sweeping affair with a carved
railing, the mail in one hand, the box under his other
arm.

Abby wandered toward a large parlor. The interior
was dark. Heavy curtains that looked like velvet with
fringe, dated like the rest of the house, hung from the
windows behind panes of bottle glass and long shades.
The parlor was at the front of the house and was
separated from the dining room by two twelve-foot
pocket doors that rolled back into the walls for enter-
taining. Each of the rooms offered high-coffered ceilings.
An immense crystal chandelier hung over the polished
mahogany dining table and its surrounding high-back
chairs. It looked like a setting for a war counsel.

In the parlor the museum decor continued; cut crystal
dishes and bowls behind curved glass in a French
cabinet. There were open shelves of leather-bound
books, floor-to-ceiling. Some of the titles were in gold
leaf, the histories of great battles and the thoughts of
great minds: Cicero, *On the Republic*, and *Reflections on
the Revolution in France* by Edmund Burke. She took a
book down and looked at it; a first edition. Abby carefully put it back.

There were certificates and diplomas framed on one
wall, something from Annapolis conferred on Joseph
Jermaine, and a glass cabinet filled with trophies, several of them with little bronze men on top pointing
pistols. Three of these had Joseph Jermaine's name on
them. Two more dated thirty years later bore the inscrip-
tion 'Joseph Jermaine, Jr.'

She studied these for a moment, then walked, hands
coupled behind her back, toward the fireplace. The fire

pit itself was the size of a small room, with giant andirons bearing twin bronze horse heads staring out at her. Over the fireplace was an immense mantel carved from a single piece of walnut.

There were military medals in a display case on top of this. Abby recognized one of these, a purple heart. Several others appeared to have inscriptions in foreign languages, one of them in French, and a case of battle ribbons, all the colors of the rainbow.

In a box off to one side, by itself, was another medal. It was not larger than the others but had a distinction. It was set off by the broad blue ribbon from which it hung. The medal itself was a bronze five-pointed star inverted with a single point down. The star was surrounded by a wreath. In this case the pendant was supported by an anchor. It was the Congressional Medal of Honor.

She picked up the box and looked at it, holding its wooden lid with her fingers.

'Most of them belong to my father.' Jack had come into the room behind her and caught her touching things.

'I'm sorry.' Abby put the box back on the mantel.

Jack was carrying a thick sheaf of papers held together by a rubber band in one hand. He came around her, took the box with the medal, and put it in a drawer in a cabinet in the corner.

'What can I get you?' said Jack. 'Are you hungry?'

'No. I'm fine.'

'Something to drink?'

'Anything cold and wet,' said Abby. 'Your dad was in the military?'

'Marines,' said Jack. He drifted toward the kitchen and she followed him.

'Who's Joseph, Jr?'

'I confess,' said Jack.

'You?'

'Jack's my nickname. Joseph Senior was my father.'

'Was?' said Abby.

'He's dead.'

'I'm sorry.'

'Don't be. He had a full life. Lived to be over eighty.'

'Was he a professional soldier?' said Abby.

'You could say that. Others prefer to think of him more as a professional son of a bitch.' He smiled as he said it.

'You make it sound like a term of endearment,' said Abby.

'In these parts? You bet your ass. Camp Perry's right over there.' He pointed casually in the direction of the sound that she could see through the kitchen window. 'Its own kind of hell,' said Jack. 'Among the officer corps, only sons of bitches live there. The rest die or retire early.'

'Besides being a son of a bitch, what did he do?'

'Oh, he wasn't just a son of a bitch. He was *the* son of a bitch of sons of bitches. The Great Son of a Bitch. The Commandant at Perry.'

'You make it sound like a concentration camp.'

'In a word,' said Jack. 'His ghost spends half its time over there, and the other half here in this house.'

She looked at him.

'Oh yeah. He haunts this place. If you hear any salty words at night, it'll be the old man. Any smacking of flesh, you know he's thumping somebody.'

'Sounds like a wonderful guy,' said Abby.

'People who knew him when he was younger tell me we look a lot alike.'

'So are you a professional son of a bitch, too?' she asked.

'Who me? No. I'm a pussycat. Just a little chip off the block. In my case, you could call it more of a splinter.'

Jack rummaged through the refrigerator. 'Cold and wet,' he said.

The kitchen was institutional. The sink was stainless steel as were all the countertops, and a large island in the center of the room. You could have cooked for an army on the commercial gas range, though it looked like it was forty years old.

'Let's see. I've got milk.' He smelled it. 'Scratch the milk.' He put it on the countertop. 'I wouldn't recommend the orange juice. Not exactly USDA,' he said. When he took it out in the clear glass pitcher the orange juice had a brown tinge to it. It looked like maybe it had been there since the previous Christmas. Jack wasn't fastidious about his refrigerator.

'Looks like wine, beer, or soft drinks.'

'Anything diet?' said Abby.

'You got it.' He took out the can and popped the lid, grabbed a glass, and put it under the ice dispenser in the refrigerator door.

'Did you follow in your dad's footsteps?'

'Hmm?'

'Marines, I mean?' said Abby.

'Oh yeah. You heard of the X and Y chromosomes. The things that make little boys and little girls. Well somewhere in my blood is a G chrome.'

'What's that?'

'For grunt,' said Jack. 'My grandfather had it. My great-grandfather had it. You could strop a razor on our necks. Hidebound leather. But it looks like it's gonna end here.'

Abby gave him a questioning look.

'No little Jacks,' he said.

'Ah,' she nodded. 'I thought maybe you'd been married?'

'That's not a good subject,' said Jack.

More questioning looks from Abby.

'Let's just say they weren't fruitful relationships.' He took a swig from a frosted bottle of beer and put the glass, fizzing with soda, in front of her on the stainless-steel island right next to the thick sheaf of papers he'd brought down from upstairs.

'And the house?' said Abby.

'That's inherited,' said Jack. 'Just like the genes. I got the house and nine hundred acres of bottom land, all leased out. Jess. You remember Jess – the leopard-skin flosser?'

Abby nodded and laughed.

'He got most of the family trust. Some stocks and bonds.'

'He must be frugal,' said Abby. 'From the looks of his apartment.'

'Frugal? Jess? Right. Pissed through most of it is more like it,' said Jack. 'Jess likes the fast lane. Life's just a big party. He found L.A. and never stopped.'

'He didn't go into the Marines?'

Now it was Jack's turn to laugh. 'Jess was a throwback. Someone in the wood pile, I think. He and the old man used to come to blows.' He looked at the ceiling and thought, like maybe this brought back memories, not all of them pleasant.

'Lucky for Jess he came along so late in life. If the old man'd been ten years younger, Jess would have never made it out of childhood. But that's another story. Are you tired?' They were leaning on separate sides of the stainless-steel island.

'Wired's more like it,' said Abby. She often got that way after long trips.

'Well, good. Maybe you'd like to sit down, relax, read something,' said Jack. 'We got lots of things here in the house to read.'

'I know. I saw your library.'

'That's not what I meant.' He gave her a coy smile and slid the pile of papers under the rubber band toward her side of the island.

'What's this?'

'Oh. Just something I wrote,' said Jack.

'Is that what was in the box you got outside?' Abby was thinking a rejected manuscript.

'Oh no,' said Jack. 'I stopped making submissions several months ago. The box contained something else.' This was at least good news. Abby had been concerned that Jack might be sending stuff over the transom in his own name, unsolicited manuscripts to publishing houses in New York. If so, and an editor put his name together with Gable Cooper's, it could lead to questions. It could also sully Cooper's name if Jack produced garbage.

She flipped the corners of the pages, a few of them dog-eared, with her thumb. It was a long manuscript. Abby guessed a thousand typed pages. 'You try to sell this by the pound, do you?' she said.

'You think it's too long?'

'Not if you're going to print it in multiple volumes,' said Abby.

They both laughed.

'I can't guarantee I'll read it tonight,' she said.

'Oh, take your time. Take tomorrow. Take it with you when we go. No rush,' he said, though there was a gleam in Jack's eye, like he couldn't wait for her critique.

It was four in the morning and Abby couldn't sleep. She heard noise downstairs and figured Jack was an early riser. He had put her up on the top floor of the house in one of the ornate four-poster beds with a full canopy. There was a porcelain bowl and pitcher for washing in the room, and a bath down the hall. Jack had given her privacy upstairs and taken one of the rooms down on the main floor for the night. Abby's room was bigger than some hotel suites, and filled with antiques.

She had gone to bed about ten, and had slept for nearly three hours when she woke with a start. For a moment she seemed dazed, disoriented, wondering why the window was on the left instead of the right, then suddenly realized that she wasn't in her old room at home.

She rolled over in bed and sat up. Abby didn't know what woke her. Perhaps it was dreams of Theresa. She had thought a lot about it the past several days. She had visions of Theresa's lifeless body on the gurney that morning outside her house. These images haunted her, especially at night. She wondered if the cops had caught up with Joey, and why Morgan hadn't called. There were a lot of things turning over in her mind.

She laid down and tossed restlessly for two more hours, then finally flipped on a light and tried to read. Abby hadn't written a word since going to L.A. with Theresa. She had worked on an outline for a sequel but hadn't actually broken ground on the manuscript. She would do that in the islands. Jack wanted to know the story line, but Abby wasn't talking, not yet anyway. He already had too much control over her life, and she didn't like it. The sequel and its details were her leverage. Publishers were never satisfied with just a single book, especially if what you wrote held the prospect of money. They expected creation on demand, constantly shortening the time between manuscripts. The halcyon days of publishing as part of the arts were over. Books were now just another product, and the people who wrote them were viewed by the industry as an eccentric but necessary evil. Abby knew that sooner or later Carla and Bertoli would be demanding details on the sequel. They would want jacket copy and art for the cover before the manuscript was written. Jack would have to come to her for bits and pieces to keep them happy. It was how she would keep him on a string like a puppet. The sequel was Abby's ultimate source of control.

Lying in bed she read a little Elmore Leonard from a paperback she'd bought at the airport. Leonard was the king of dialogue, and after Jack's manuscript, he was like a dish of sorbet on the heels of a course of raw onions; something to cleanse the reader's palate. If Jack's manuscript contained a message it was that the man couldn't write.

His story was one of those male thumping things, high tech hardware wrapped in a cartoon of global dimensions. It was peopled with an army of evil politicians and bureaucrats, and heroic soldiers. The protagonist was amazingly handsome and had graduated at the top of his class from Pedigree U. All the women were amazingly beautiful but hadn't gone to college. That didn't matter because they all had big tits and long legs. The amazingly beautiful women couldn't keep their hands off the amazingly handsome man. When all of these amazingly beautiful people weren't otherwise occupied humping, they could be found disarming nuclear bombs, and uncovering plots to kill the president. The protagonist was ageless and single, and driven by a purity of duty matched only by Superman.

The only thing faster than a speeding bullet was the hero's dick. All things taken together, Abby guessed that the invention was a lot like Jack himself, unbelievable, except that Jack was the incarnation in the flesh.

There was a degree on the wall downstairs in Junior's name. It didn't come from Annapolis. Jack had taken a degree from Stanford in Latin American studies. She wondered where he'd stood in his class, if he'd ever disarmed a nuclear bomb, or met the president. She had little doubt that he liked long legs and big tits. She wondered how all of this, especially the stint at Stanford, had sat with the old man, as Jack had called him. She could imagine a lot of shouting when Jack stepped out of the military mold.

By now she was reading words, her mind distracted by other thoughts. She heard the sound of gravel under wheels in the driveway, got out of bed and walked to the window just in time to see Jack's car rolling down the lane. By the time the engine started, it was too far away to hear it. The car disappeared into the tunnel of trees. Abby wondered where he could be going at five in the morning.

Wherever he had gone, he would be back. She returned to bed and her book. She read half a page without a single syllable denting her consciousness. She closed her book and got out of bed, considered for a moment the fact that she was now alone in the house.

'No. I shouldn't.' She said it to herself but without much conviction. Then she remembered how he'd bulldozed his way into her life. Without further thought she slipped her jeans on, pulled a sweater over her head, put her running shoes on over bare feet, and slid quietly from the room.

The hall outside was dark, lit only by the dim light of

an early dawn that spilled in through a skylight over the staircase.

She tiptoed down the hall to the door at the far end. She had seen Jack come and go from here, gathering a few things for sleep the night before. She figured it had to be his room. She turned the door handle and it opened. Abby stepped inside and closed the door behind her.

It was a large room, larger than the one she slept in, and cluttered. There were clothes folded neatly on the bed. It was not a postered antique like her own, but a metal frame which, like Jack, had a military hardness to it.

A door on the other side led to a small sitting area. This opened onto a wall of windows, a shed dormer that looked out on the yard, the marsh, and the sound beyond.

Under the small-paned windows was a large antique partners desk inset in leather with a large computer and an array of electronics on top. Crude pine shelves supported on cinder blocks flanked the desk on each side to a height just below the windows. These sagged under the weight of books. Not the uniform leather and gold spines of the library downstairs, but an assortment of cheap covers, many of them stapled instead of bound, what to Abby appeared to be technical monographs.

The surface of the desk was littered with paper, some of it still sprouting from the top of the laser printer.

The bouncing blue globe of an earth careened off the inner edges of the computer's color monitor.

Abby didn't know much about computers. She had purchased a small used notebook just before leaving Seattle. This was to replace her old manual typewriter that had disappeared in Joey's wake. Spencer had turned the basement upside down looking, but there was no sign of it. She could not figure why Joey would have wanted to take it.

Jack's desk-top computer was cutting edge, a million graphical interfaces hooked to the buttons on a mouse; a joystick that looked like it had been ripped from the cockpit of a jet fighter. And games, an entire shelf of games, helicopters and planes, tanks and missiles.

She reached down and without thinking touched the joystick. Instantly the globe on the screen disappeared, replaced by the inside image of a cockpit careening through space at high speed. Abby took her hand away and watched while whatever was flying was shot at by other faster moving things. The pinging sounds of an arcade resonated from speakers somewhere inside the desk. She tried to push the stick away, hoping that the screen would return to the tranquil blue globe. Instead, the horizon on the screen flared up. An instant later there was an orange flash on the monitor and the gargled sound of a crash from the speakers. Large red letters appeared: GAME OVER. Abby could only pray that Jack didn't keep score.

She turned her attention to his collection of books. There were the usual writer's references, dictionaries and an assortment of synonym finders, a volume of famous quotations, and books on how to write novels. Jack had cornered the market on these. *How to Write*; *How to Plot*; *How to Craft Characters*. They were propped up on his desk between a single bookend and the computer as if by osmosis the machine itself could absorb their contents. It was clear that Jack had failed. What he really needed was what he'd found in Abby; a ghost writer. The question now was how she would maintain control until it was time to go public.

She turned her attention to the stack of books next to the desk. These were not the usual reference texts: *Household and Recreational Use of High Explosives; The Anarchist's Armory;* and *The Art of Strangulation.* Some of these were stapled and clearly produced by copying machines, all the signs of an underground press. Abby opened one of them. Inside were explicit recipes for explosives and directions on making bombs, everything from fire jars to road mines. It was a veritable encyclopedia of terror. She had heard of such things but had never seen them. She put it back on the shelf.

A slender trade paperback was open-spined, printed page down on top of a stack of other books; *Making a New Identity.* Underneath the book was a small dark blue note pad. To Abby it looked like a pocket address book. Abby picked it up and turned it over:

Passport

*United States
of America*

She opened the cover and turned it sideways, the way a Customs inspector might to read it. Jack's photo was crystal clear, under plastic laminate on the bottom page. Next to it, typed on the passport form, was the name Kellen Raid.

Jack had an arrangement with the NCO, an old buddy, who ran the commissary at Parris Island. Once a week Jack would drop by in the early morning and leave a list of groceries pinned to the back door of the commissary. An hour later an enlisted man in a jeep would deliver them to the house at Coffin Point. There was nothing particularly wrong with this. Being retired, Jack had commissary privileges and always paid the freight. Besides, he hated to shop.

Dew was still dripping from moss in the trees as Jack drove back toward the big house at the end of the road. He checked his watch. He had been gone only a few minutes and figured she would still be sleeping. A hundred yards from the house he pulled off and parked near a small locked shed, got out, and opened a padlock from the shed door. He went inside. Against one wall was a wooden work bench with two metal presses bolted to it. One was primitive, probably fifty years old. His father had bought it second-hand after the war. The other one was larger, newer, and more sophisticated, what people in the trade called a progressive loader. With brass, primers, and powder it could load a thousand bullets in an hour, any caliber you wanted, depending on the dies that were threaded into the machine.

Against the other wall were four old metal gym lockers each with a combination lock on the door. Jack went to the second locker, worked the dial, and opened the door. Inside, stacked from the bottom nearly to the top, were plastic ammunition boxes with several different calibers of loaded rounds, each box holding a hundred bullets. If he had to guess, there were probably five thousand loaded rounds in the locker. The other lockers contained gun powder, cases of primers and barrels of new brass casings. There were boxes of lead and jacketed bullets. The loaded bullets were mostly copper jacketed, the kind that slide and eject easily from semi-automatic weapons. All of this was stored a good distance from the house. Though Jack's heroes were all invulnerable, he had no desire to become a human skyrocket. What a bullet did in fiction was one thing. What it did to a real body was another. Jack had more potent things besides gun powder in one of the other lockers. The firearms he kept at the house along with a handful of rounds for personal security. In Jack's mind, you could never be too prepared.

He looked for the boxes marked nine millimeter, found one and grabbed it, closed the locker, and spun the dial. He walked outside and locked the door to the shed, then headed toward the house. He left the car parked where it was. There was no sense in taking a chance. He might wake her up. Besides, he would have to drive right up to the house to get the gun that was inside.

Abby was studying the date and place of birth on the passport, scribbling notes on a scrap of paper from Jack's desk, when she heard it; an indistinct creaking somewhere in the distance beyond the door to his room. It sent an adrenaline rush through her body. She stopped the pencil scratching on paper and listened. Maybe it was just the settling of the old house, the creaks and groans of age. She heard it again. This time she dropped the pencil on the desk and literally flew to the window. She looked out on the side of the house. She could see a part of the gravel drive as it disappeared, sweeping in front of the house. But she could not see the area directly in front where Jack had parked his car the day before. Still, she hadn't heard the sound of tires on gravel or the motor. She pressed one eye close to the old bottle glass window but still she couldn't see anything.

Then she heard it again. This time there was no question. Someone was coming up the stairs. Frantic, her eyes scanned the room for a place to hide. First instincts, the closet on the far side of the bed. Then she realized the passport was in her hand. There was no time. She took two steps toward the closet and stopped. It would be the first place he would go if he needed a change of clothes for the day.

Abby hit the floor with an easy motion. A second later she was under the bed, sliding on her stomach on the dusty hardwood floor, just as the door opened and two male feet shod in dark high-top Nikes entered the room. She thought they were Jack's, but she wasn't sure.

Abby held her breath, fearful that the sound might give her away. Her eyes focused on the passport still in her hand. She prayed that he hadn't come looking for it. Until she had seen the passport, getting caught would have been only a major embarrassment. Now she wasn't so sure.

Whoever he was, Jack or Kellen, he strode across the room confidently. He was standing in front of the desk rummaging through papers. Cold sweat dripped down Abby's forehead and mingled with the dust to make mud under the bed.

She wondered if she'd left anything else out of place. Then it hit her; the screen on the computer, the game she had interrupted. If the large red letters were on the screen, he couldn't miss them. He would know instinctively that someone had entered the room.

She craned her neck but still couldn't see the monitor. His body was in front of it. Now he was looking through drawers. Maybe he was looking for the passport. Perhaps he'd forgotten where he'd left it. If so, he might check another room, giving Abby time to drop it someplace and get out, to slink to her own room.

He was in the second drawer at the level of his knees

when his hand disappeared inside. When it came out he was holding something black and hard. It flashed quickly and then disappeared from Abby's view. She'd seen it for only a fleeting instant, but Abby knew what it was; a matt-black pistol. She was breathing in little gasps now. Her hands spread flat, one of them on the floor, the other holding the passport. She heard the sound of metal sliding and clinking. He was doing something to the gun, perhaps loading it. Abby's heart began to pound.

When he finally moved, she could see the monitor on the desk. It was aglow – with the blue bouncing globe. But how long had it been there? She knew it was on a timer. Was it there when he'd entered the room or not? She couldn't be certain. Was he loading the bullets for her?

She took a deep breath and then heard the slam of metal against metal. She didn't have to be told. It was the sound of a clip being jammed into the handle of the gun.

He walked over, closer to the bed now, and stood silent. Abby's body tensed. She slid a few millimeters away toward the other side of the bed. The only advantage was the dust on the floor. It made her body glide. He inched closer. Now the toes of his shoes were actually under the bed with her. Something heavy bounced on the bed and rattled like pebbles in a box. She heard noises but couldn't tell what he was doing. The sound of a spring, but it wasn't coming from the bed. Then he slapped something shut, like the lid on a plastic box. He moved around the bed and a second later he was out the door, closing it behind him.

Her heart pounded. Her temples throbbed. Then she wondered; would he check her room? She listened to his footsteps as they receded from the door. She couldn't be sure which direction he'd gone, whether down the stairs or toward the other bedroom.

Abby lay there for a long time, silent on the cold hard floor, unable to move. When she finally did, she didn't hesitate. She went to the desk first and pushed the passport under a pile of loose papers so that if he came back and looked he might think he'd simply missed it the first time. Then she went to the door, opened it a crack, and peered out. She could see the staircase and down the hall toward her room. He was not there. She listened for sounds. Nothing. She waited a second longer. It was now or never. He might return any moment. She slipped out, closed the door behind her, and tiptoed down the hall. She was four steps from her room when he nailed her from behind.

'Did I wake you?'

Abby gasped and whirled, hand to her breast. Her heart exploded in her chest so that she jumped.

'Sorry. I didn't mean to scare you.'

Jack was standing there ten feet away, in the doorway to another room, the pistol in his hand and what looked like a box of bullets in the other. She couldn't be sure how long he'd been there, whether he'd seen her coming out of his room. Abby was petrified, her eyes focused on the gun that he made no effort to conceal.

'Ah . . . I . . . ah . . . had to go to the bathroom,' she said. She pointed to the door a few steps behind her. 'I got lost,' she said.

'Ah.' He nodded like he understood.

They stood, two adults in the dark hallway, one of them holding a pistol, and the other covered in dust, and said nothing about it. Their own versions of the emperor's clothes.

'Are you feeling alright?' he asked.

'Oh yeah.' Her gaze was monopolized by the pistol in his hand.

'Does this bother you?' He held it out.

'No. No.' But she couldn't take her eyes off of it.

'Good. I was just going to do some targets. Why don't you come with me?'

'I have to take a shower,' said Abby.

He came closer, his eyes on her. Abby wanted to back up, but her feet wouldn't move. Frozen in place.

A step away he stopped, reached out with one hand, and rubbed a smudge of dust from her cheek.

'I can see,' he said.

Nervously she rubbed her face with her hand.

'You can take a shower later. There's plenty of time,' said Jack. It seemed more an order than a suggestion.

'Let's go shoot,' said Jack. He stepped toward her and put his arm around her shoulder so that she felt the weight of the pistol against her breast under the cotton sweater. There was no saying no to Jack.

'Well maybe,' said Abby. She wasn't sure if she was under duress or not. But she wasn't going to press the point. They headed down the stairs. In the service porch he grabbed some targets, orange with a bull's-eye and a cross in the middle. He picked up two sets of ear protectors, the kind of mufflers that ground crews wear at the airport. He handed one of these to Abby.

She started to put it on.

'Not yet,' he said. 'We don't start shooting 'til we get outside.' He laughed a little. 'You've never done this before?'

She shook her head.

'Never fired a pistol?'

'A rifle. Once,' said Abby. 'When I was a kid with my dad.'

'A twenty-two?' said Jack.

'I don't know.' Abby was still shaking. Unless it was an elephant gun fully loaded and pointed at Jack's head, Abby couldn't have cared less what her father's rifle might have been at this moment.

'Relax. It won't hurt,' said Jack.

Abby wasn't sure what he meant: shooting, or getting shot.

They crossed the yard to an area on the far side near the marsh. Here there were several pieces of heavy wire strung between two poles. Jack hung two of the targets from metal clips on the wire.

He then walked to an area near a little wooden table. Abby guessed they were a good fifty feet from the target.

'You want to get a little closer to start?' he asked.

'Whatever,' said Abby. 'Why don't I just watch?'

'Nonsense. You'll enjoy it. Ever written about guns in your books?'

She shook her head.

'Then it'll be a good experience for you. Broaden your horizons. Grist for the mill,' said Jack. 'You can put those on now.' He pointed to the ear protectors. He put his own on and Abby followed suit.

'I'll shoot a couple so you can gauge the sound and see how it works.' He shouted a little so she could hear him. 'Then you can try.'

Jack took aim with two hands, one braced underneath steadying the other, clicked off the safety, aimed, and fired a single round.

It happened so quickly that by the time Abby's body jerked from the shock wave the empty brass casing was on the ground and the slide was back in place with the hammer cocked for the next round. The pistol worked with the speed of light.

He fired again. This time she jerked, but a little less, and she kept her eyes on the target. It didn't seem to move. She was sure he'd missed.

He clicked the safety on, ejected the clip still with bullets in it, pulled the slide to eject the round in the chamber. Without a clip in the handle it stayed open. He put the pistol on the little wooden stand.

'Let's take a look.' Jack walked toward the target. Abby followed along. About twenty feet out they came into focus, two small holes. As she drew closer she could see that they were actually touching, each no more than half an inch from the center of the target.

'What you look for is a pattern,' said Jack. 'Bullet strikes that are close together. You can put a quarter over a good pattern and cover three holes.'

He walked her back to the wooden stand and the gun, coaching her all the way. 'Don't worry right now about hitting the center of the target. Try to keep a tight pattern. Aim for the same place each time.' He picked up the gun, loaded it, and handed it to her.

It felt awkward, too big for her hand. She was still shaking, but she held it out. Abby's hands clasped the pistol between them as if she was in prayer.

'No,' said Jack. 'Like this.' He moved behind her, put his arms around her, and placed his hands over hers. Then he directed them, the left hand underneath, the flat of the palm open so that the heel of the pistol grip rested on it for support while she held the gun with the other hand.

'Don't squint. Keep both eyes open. Line the sights up and aim with your right eye.'

Abby wasn't squinting. She had her eyes closed tight. She opened them for an instant and jerked the trigger. Nothing happened, though the gun waved all over the place.

Jack started laughing.

Abby was starting to calm herself. If she had an emotion stronger than fear, it was anger. She didn't like to be laughed at. If he wasn't careful, the next time he saw the gun it might be pointed at him.

'You have to take the safety off first,' said Jack. 'And don't jerk. Squeeze the trigger. You want to be surprised when it goes off.'

Abby didn't need any more surprises this morning.

He reached up with his thumb, his body braced up against hers, and flipped off the safety, then cocked the hammer with his thumb. Amazingly for a woman whose body had been quaking only moments before, Abby was now stone steady.

'Ready.' Before the words had cleared his lips the gun exploded in her hand. When the recoil stopped, it was aimed somewhere up into a tree out near the marsh.

'It's alright. Try it again,' said Jack.

With the recoil measured from the first shot, she held it down, lined the sights up on the target, and squeezed. It exploded with a sharp crack, only this time she controlled the gun. It didn't jump nearly so much.

'Good. Again,' he said.

She fired four more times before she put the gun down and they checked the target. She had actually hit it three times, twice inside of the big outer circle, each time moving closer in the direction of the bull's eye. She was getting into the challenge of this, competing against herself to improve with each shot.

A few minutes later, she looked at the box of a

hundred rounds and noticed that it was more than half empty. Abby had shot most of them. For many of the shots Jack was standing behind her, holding her steady, giving her pointers.

The fear had drained from her body. His touch up against her wasn't an entirely unpleasant experience. His hard body against her back, the low whisper of his voice in her ear, had a calming, almost mesmerizing effect. She fired four more shots, emptying the clip, when he tapped her on the shoulder and pointed in the other direction.

'We'll take a break. Breakfast is here.'

An old military jeep was rumbling down the road toward the house, a man in fatigues behind the wheel. The jeep pulled up in front of the house, and when the driver got out he gave a lazy salute to Jack.

'Captain. You want me to take it into the house?'

'Appreciate it,' said Jack.

The man carefully handed Jack a big brown paper bag, the wafting warm odors of which escaped and ran under Abby's nose. Suddenly she was famished.

'I hope you like eggs and hash browns,' said Jack.

'Smells delicious,' she told him.

The enlisted man was busy unloading the groceries, lugging them up the stairs.

'So where did this come from?' she asked.

'Officer's mess,' said Jack. 'An old friend who takes pity, especially on my guests. Cooking is not one of my finer arts. You'll appreciate this more if you ever have to eat my cuisine,' he told her.

They headed up into the kitchen, where Jack set two places at the table, and opened a large container of orange juice from one of the bags. He had put up a pot of coffee earlier in the morning, and as Abby sipped she had no complaints with his coffee. She nibbled at her eggs now removed from their plastic container and spread on a china dish.

'Outdid himself today.' Jack dug into what looked like Potatoes O'Brien.

Abby had to admit they were delicious. All the terrible things she had heard about food in the military was a lie if this is how they ate.

She was exhausted. The lack of sleep, and the adrenaline rush of the morning were catching up with her. Though she had to admit she enjoyed the shooting. It had actually taken the edge off of the earlier events, but she still wondered about the books and the passport in Jack's room. Who was he? Had he lied to her about his name?

'Is this how you always get your groceries?' She nodded toward the soldier who had just left the last package on the sink and retrieved a check in payment from Jack.

'Sometimes. Sometimes a lady stops by and leaves things in the fridge for me.'

'Oh.' Now Abby felt like she was prying. A woman in his life.

She tried to change the subject by scanning the little morning paper that lay on the table. There was a lot of country news, but nothing to spark a conversation.

For Jack's part, between scoops of eggs and potatoes, he was writing on a small form with a pen. It looked like an express label. There was a box to match, like the one he'd retrieved the day before when they arrived. The box was on the counter behind him. Again it looked like a manuscript box, and Abby shuddered with the thought.

'Excuse me.' Jack realized that he was ignoring her

and that her eyes were on him.

'It's alright. Finish what you're doing.'

'Be done in a minute. I hope you don't mind if we stop on the way to the airport. I need to drop this off for delivery. I'll just take a minute.'

'That's fine.'

'What did you think of the manuscript?' asked Jack.

'Oh.' She thought for a moment. What could she say? 'I was pretty tired last night.' A lame excuse, but it avoided an awkward subject.

'Well, you can take it with you,' said Jack. 'I don't need it right now.'

'Oh. Great,' said Abby. 'Thanks.' If he kept pushing, sooner or later she would have to tell him that it wasn't only his cooking that sucked.

'Tell me about yourself.' Maybe this would be a more pleasant subject. 'You must have friends?'

'Oh. A few.'

'The lady who drops your groceries off?' Now she was prying. She was also smiling across the table at him.

'Oh yeah. A great woman. We've known each other for a long time. She used to change my diapers.' Jack smiled back. 'An aunt in failing health. Maybe you'd like to meet her?'

'I doubt if we have time,' said Abby. She took another sip of coffee. 'You're going to tell me that there's no one in your life, that writing is a jealous mistress.'

'I don't know if she's jealous or not,' said Jack. 'But she is a bitch.'

Abby laughed. At least he made no bones about it.

'There was somebody. Once,' he said.

Abby gave him a look, like go on.

'Her name was Jenny. She was beautiful. And young. Though not as young as I was.'

'Ah. The older woman,' said Abby. 'Were you in love?'

'Who knows. Never been able to define love,' said Jack. 'But I know I had a fire in the pit of my stomach whenever I was around her. And my heart thumped like a cement mixer. Probably more lust than love.'

'What happened?'

'She caught me looking at another woman.'

'Just looking?'

Jack nodded.

'And?'

'I blinked. Looked a little guilty, I suppose. Started making excuses. What you do when you're young and stupid,' said Jack.

'What did you say?'

'I told her, "What am I supposed to do? I enjoy looking at women." '

'And what did she say?'

'She said, "Gee, that's funny. So do I." ' He gave Abby a kind of smile that made her think this might be the setup to a joke, then sipped his coffee, leaving her to wonder.

'You're pulling my leg?'

He raised his hand with his mouth full of coffee, like honest Injun.

'Swear to God,' said Jack. 'I was eighteen. She was twenty-two. Last I heard she was living in Atlanta with three cats and a woman named Alice.'

'I don't believe you. You're putting me on.'

'Yeah, I am.'

She laughed and gave him a look of exasperation.

'I was exaggerating,' said Jack. 'There were only two cats.'

She looked at him for a moment, waiting for him to laugh again. But he didn't.

'You know, I don't know when you're telling me the truth and when you're lying,' said Abby.

'That's what makes life interesting.' Without missing a beat, he smiled, took a sip of coffee from the mug in front of him, and returned to his address label.

CHAPTER
TWENTY-TWO

'Starl, Hobbs and Carlton, law offices.'

'I'd like to speak to Morgan Spencer,' said Abby.

'Ms Chandlis, how are you?' The receptionist recognized her voice on the phone. There was a totally different attitude toward Abby in the firm now that she was a client and no longer an associate. She had learned from Spencer that even Lewis Cutler, the man who had fired her, was now asking after her welfare. He had discovered that she'd come into a large sum of money and had hired Morgan to handle some business affairs. A well-heeled client was something that every partner in the firm wanted, and Cutler had the audacity to believe that if he played it right, perhaps he could mend things with Abby. Spencer enjoyed tantalizing Cutler while keeping him in the dark. He stored all of Abby's business files at home.

She waited for a moment and Morgan's secretary came on the line.

'Jenny, Abby here. Is Morgan in?'

'He's been trying to reach you for two days. Just a second,' said the secretary.

When Morgan hadn't called her in Chicago, and then

failed to contact her at Jack's house, Abby began to worry that something was wrong. At the airport she slipped away and found a bank of payphones. She looked at her watch. It was almost noon out on the West Coast and she hoped that Morgan hadn't left for lunch. She breathed easier when she heard his voice on the phone. 'Where are you?'

'Atlanta. I have to be on a plane for San Juan in just a few minutes. We'll have to talk fast.'

'I've been trying to reach you for two days,' said Morgan. 'I just missed you in Chicago. The front desk said you checked out fifteen minutes before I called.'

'Jack wanted to get an early start,' she told him.

'Eager beaver,' said Morgan. 'Tell him when you see him that he gave me the wrong phone number to his house. When I tried to call it I got a disconnected number. And he's unlisted.'

'Are you sure you wrote it down right?'

'I didn't have to. He wrote it down for me,' said Morgan.

Abby thought about this for a moment. 'Don't worry about it now. I'll call you when I get into San Juan, and as soon as I get to St Croix. I'll give you the number to the beach house.'

'I don't like it,' said Spencer. 'I don't trust him.'

'Relax,' said Abby. 'Everything's going to be fine.'

'We've got a lot to talk about,' he told her.

'What's up?'

'Good news and bad. Money is starting to pile up.'

'What's the bad news?' said Abby.

'That cop, Sanfillipo, he's been nosing around the law office. In fact, he just left a few minutes ago. His second trip in two days.'

'What's he want?'

'For starters, to know where you are. He wants to talk to you.'

'What about?'

'He's not saying. Only bits and pieces. He's been to see your husband.'

'Why would he want to talk to Charlie?'

'I'm not sure. But he knows you've come into some money. He wants to know where it came from.'

'Damn.' Abby was angry with Charlie. She figured he had a big mouth. That's what she got for being nice, for repaying the money on his credit card when she didn't have to. She was flush with money. She felt bad about stealing his card and knew Charlie was broke. Never again, she thought.

'What did you tell him?' she asked.

'That I didn't know anything about any money.'

She worried now that she was drawing Morgan into some kind of a criminal web, lying to a cop in a murder investigation.

'What else could I tell him?' said Spencer. 'If I told him about the book and where you were, we may as well put it up in neon outside of Bertoli's office.'

He was right. The cops would check it out, and within hours she would be getting calls from Bertoli's lawyers.

'You did what you had to,' said Abby.

'There's more,' said Spencer. 'They found Joey.'

'Great.' Given his penchant for drink, Abby knew Joey couldn't stay ahead of them for long.

'Did they arrest him?'

'Not exactly,' said Spencer.

'Why not?'

'He's dead.'

There was silence on the phone from Abby's end.

'Are you there?' he asked.

'I'm here.'

'I didn't think you'd be that shaken,' said Morgan.

'It doesn't take the edge off my day,' said Abby. 'I'll light a candle when I get around to it. But I am surprised. How did it happen?'

'A fire. The cop didn't give me many details. But from what I gather, the problem is not how he died, but where he was when Theresa was killed.'

'What do you mean?'

'I mean that according to what they've uncovered so far, Joey was in L.A. when Theresa was murdered.'

Now there was silence on the phone and Spencer could smell mental rubber burning on the other end.

'How do they know that?'

'Found a ticket stub in his pocket and checked with the airline. He spent three days down there.'

'He could have wired the box before he left,' said Abby.

'Not according to the police.'

'How would they know?'

'Your telephone answering machine. When the fuses were pulled, the machine quit. Problem is the time and date of the last message. Joey was in L.A. when it was recorded.'

'You're telling me that they've excluded him as a suspect?' said Abby.

'That's what it sounds like to me.'

Her mind was now racing. It threw a whole new light on why the police might want to talk to her.

'Could it have been an accident?'

'I don't know. They aren't sharing that kind of information. At least not yet,' said Spencer. 'But they have a lot of questions. They found his truck abandoned in a hotel parking lot out near the airport, miles from where they found the body. They dusted the truck for prints and they threw a name at me. Hang on, I got it here on a piece of paper someplace.'

Abby could hear the rustle of papers on his desk.

'Here it is. Stanley Salzman. Mean anything to you?'

'No.'

'He's an executive with one of the film studios in L.A. The cops are trying to figure what his prints are doing on Joey's truck.'

'Oh boy.' Abby had one hand to her forehead now as if a migraine had set in.

'Do you want to come back?' said Spencer.

If Abby returned to Seattle, there was no telling when or if she might be able to leave again. The reporter, Thompson, would no doubt be waiting for her. If he found out she was being questioned in a murder investigation, it would only add fuel to the suspicion that he was on a hot story. The cops couldn't seriously consider her a suspect. She had an alibi. She was forty-thousand feet up, on a plane between New York and the coast, when Theresa was killed. She was so sure that Joey had done it.

'Are they certain about Joey? That he was in L.A.?' she asked.

'Sanfillipo didn't seem to be hedging on the issue,' said Morgan. 'He did have a lot of questions about the money you paid to Charlie.'

'What does he think, that the two are related? Theresa's murder and the money?'

'You have to admit, to a suspicious mind it offers a lot of possibilities,' said Morgan. 'Your roommate is killed. Suddenly you have cash to pay off debts and you disappear.'

'If Charlie hadn't told him about the money . . .'

'I don't think he did,' said Morgan.

'Then how did he find out?'

'Probably a subpoena for financial records.'

'If that's the case,' said Abby, 'it won't take him long to find the rest of it.' What she meant was the balance of the six hundred thousand dollars that Spencer had deposited in the account in her name, the signing money for the advance on the book, and whatever else had come in since then.

'If he finds that kind of money it'll fan the flames,' said Abby.

'Yeah. He'll be thinking drugs, and looking for you in Columbia. What else pays that well?' Morgan had a point. 'The check you drew to Charlie was on your old checking account?' he asked.

'Yes.' She had closed out the account the day she left Seattle, after paying for her airline tickets and withdrawing two thousand dollars in cash for expenses.

'Have you used any credit cards?' he asked.

'I don't have any, remember?'

'Right.' Spencer had forgotten.

For the first time in her life it might be an advantage. There was no trail of receipts for the cops to follow.

'It may take them awhile to find the new account,' said Spencer. 'They would have to know where to look, what bank. You haven't drawn any checks on it?'

'Not yet.'

'Good. Don't.'

'I'm going to need money pretty soon,' said Abby. 'Besides, the longer I stay away, the worse it looks.'

'Don't worry about it for now. I can wire some cash to the island. What's the name of the town down there?'

'Christiansted. St Croix.' She could hear his pencil scratching paper on the other end.

'I'll check and see if there's a Western Union Office. If not, I'll figure some other way. That will hold you until I can open something offshore. An account on one of the islands and set you up with an ATM card. In a foreign bank, it'll take them months to find it. By then it won't matter,' said Spencer.

He was right. Once the book was published and Abby came out of the weeds, she would be more than happy to go back to Seattle and answer their questions.

Morgan was rock solid, the kind of person you could depend on in a crisis. Even his enemies in the firm referred to him as the fireman, for his ability to deal with disasters.

'Sooner or later I'm going to have to come back,' she said. 'I'm going to want to come back. I'm starting to feel like an exile.' She had been away less than a week, and she was already getting homesick. Abby was no world traveler. 'I already miss you,' she told him. She might not work at the firm anymore, but in Seattle they could always do lunch.

'I miss you, too,' said Spencer. 'But it's only for awhile. When it's over, once the book is out there, when the paperback's in the works and you go public, it won't matter anymore. You've got an alibi. We can tell the police why you did what you did, where the money came from. They can check it out, and it'll be over.'

He was right. All she needed was time. Abby heard the public address system announce her flight.

'I've got to go.'

'Are you sure you're alright?' he asked.

'I'm fine.'

'Where are you staying tonight?'

'I don't know. Jack made the arrangements.'

'Let's hope he did a better job than with his telephone number,' said Morgan.

'There's one thing,' said Abby. She'd almost forgotten.

'What is it?'

For a moment she hesitated, wondering whether she should tell him. 'I don't want to alarm you,' she said, 'but Jack has a passport in another name.'

'What?'

She could tell by the tone of Morgan's voice that it was a mistake to have said anything.

'I found it when I was wandering around his house the other day. It's a U.S. passport in the name Kellen Raid.'

'You're sure it's his?'

'His picture's in it.'

'Listen, I want you to catch a plane and get back here right now,' said Morgan.

'Why?'

'If he's got a false passport, God knows what else he's into.'

Abby felt almost guilty about mentioning it, prying into a man's private papers. After all, Jack had never threatened her, and he'd had plenty of opportunities. 'It's probably nothing,' said Abby.

'What are you talking about?'

'A lot of people have false IDs,' said Abby.

'Passports?' said Spencer.

'How do I know?' said Abby.

'Precisely,' said Morgan. 'How do you know he's not dealing drugs?'

'I didn't find any paraphernalia,' said Abby.

'You're telling me you searched his house?' Morgan's voice went up an octave.

'Wasn't exactly a search,' said Abby. 'I couldn't sleep. So I took a walk.'

'And the passport was just lying around?'

'It was on his desk. In his bedroom,' said Abby.

'What were you doing in his bedroom?'

'He was someplace else at the time.'

Morgan was already worried about her. Now he had other reasons to be concerned. It was the kind of thing a woman could read in a man, on the jealous edge.

'Are you sure you won't come back?' he said.

'What for?'

'You're traveling with a man who's committed at least one serious violation of federal law. If you don't know I can't tell you,' said Spencer.

'He's not using the passport now.'

'How do you know?'

'Because he used his real one when we boarded the plane, at the counter in Savannah.' While Abby wasn't particularly worried, she wasn't stupid, either. 'Besides,' she said, 'unless you've forgotten, he has another false identity besides the passport. The one we invented.' She was talking about Gable Cooper.

Morgan reminded her that the use of a pen name was not a federal offense.

'How do we know he's ever used the passport?' said Abby.

'Did you look for entry or exit stamps?'

'No. I didn't think to look. I didn't have time.' Abby wasn't used to the formalities of foreign travel. She'd had a passport for five years, but it sat in a drawer; a kind of flight of fancy. She wanted to be ready in case the opportunity for travel ever arose. Until now it never had.

'Check the passport out,' she told him.

'I will.'

'Discreetly.'

'You bet.'

The P.A. system made a second call. Her row was now boarding.

'Listen, I have to go. I'll call you at home tonight from the hotel.'

'Wait a second. We need to talk.'

'From the hotel,' said Abby. 'Wish me luck.'

'Wait . . .'

Abby never heard Spencer's last word. She'd already hung the receiver in the cradle.

CHAPTER
TWENTY-THREE

Jack delivered his package to an office near the airport for express delivery somewhere the next morning. He and Abby flew from Atlanta to Miami and spent the night in a hotel near the airport. The next morning they caught the flight for Puerto Rico.

The 737 coasted in over azure seas, bleached white beaches, and acres of ramshackle tin-roofed huts. In the distance, Abby could see verdant forests and mountains sheathed in tropical jungle. The plane dropped its wheels and two minutes later the tires smoked the runway at Puerto Rico's International Airport.

It was Abby's first time in the Caribbean, and as the door to the plane was opened the humid smells of the tropics ignited her senses.

'We'll get the luggage and go to the hotel,' said Jack. 'You may want to freshen up before we look up Enrique.'

Enrique was a friend of Jack's. He was supposed to help them find a place for Abby to set up, a quiet writer's retreat somewhere further to the south in the islands so that she could work undisturbed on the sequel. According to Jack, Enrique knew the territory.

'Your friend, does he live here in Puerto Rico?'

'You could say that. His family's been here awhile.'

'How long?'

'About three hundred years,' said Jack. He left her standing there looking at him for a moment as he moved on along the concourse.

The terminal reminded Abby of a movie set from the '40s. Casablanca in disguise. She expected to see Bogart in his trench coat and Bergman in her hat around the next corner. While dated and in need of some remodeling, the place dripped of nostalgia and perspiration, not necessarily in that order. The lobby was air-conditioned, but the areas off of it were not.

By the time they hit the sidewalk out front, Abby was bathed in her own sweat. People jostled in the hot humid air heading for cars or taxis. Several school girls in parochial uniforms clustered like flies near one of the windows waiting for friends or relatives to emerge. Security was tight. Except for those with tickets, the public was excluded from the main building by police.

Businessmen in suits with briefcases mingled with tourists trying to read signs and directions, all of which were in Spanish. If life was slower in the tropics, the message hadn't reached this place.

They found a line of taxis, and Abby slid into the back seat of one of them while Jack and the driver loaded the luggage.

'Condado Plaza,' said Jack.

A few seconds later Abby felt the comforting breeze on her face as the taxi sped out along the highway, its windows down to compensate for the lack of air-conditioning in the old Chevy. They rode in silence, Abby taking in the sights as the road wound its way through densely populated San Juan. Abby noted that the most prominent feature on some of the buildings were the security bars over the windows. There were low-slung complexes of apartment buildings, brightly painted in myriad colors behind high cyclone fences; projects, Caribbean-style.

'Some of the best beaches are over there.' Jack pointed beyond the tenements that flanked the highway. 'Condado has some walled villas on the water that are very nice.'

'Is that where we're going?'

'We'll stay at the Condado Plaza. I think you'll like it.'

The snarl of traffic grew thick as they approached the center of the city. The smells of hot food from roadside restaurants invaded the car. They passed over the Puente Esteves and the Puente Dos Hermanos, concrete bridges with sculpted balustrades over the Condado Lagoon. On the left was a strip of sandy white beach. Abby could see brown-skinned girls in thong bikinis lying next to bronze lovers, sunning themselves on towels. A half mile out the open Atlantic crashed on reefs just off shore.

The taxi stopped, made a left turn across traffic, and pulled under the covered entrance of an immense high-rise hotel. Behind walls of glass Abby could see the sprawl of the lobby and beyond that to the other side of the building and the cresting rollers of the Atlantic.

A young man in white livery replete with a spotless pith helmet opened the taxi door.

'Welcome to the Condado Plaza.' He was tall, young, and dark, with a flashing smile to slay any teenage girl. 'Do you have luggage, sir?' His words emitted a thick Castillian trill. He snapped his fingers and a bellman wheeled up with a cart to the trunk of the taxi, and without a word unloaded the bags.

'Will you be staying long?'

'Two nights,' said Jack. He gave the kid a five dollar bill and it disappeared like a flame under water.

'Fernando will take your bags.' The doorman led them to the main entrance and opened the door wide. 'Thank you for staying at the Condado Plaza.'

Inside Abby was beginning to wonder if she had packed the right clothes, or for that matter whether she owned them. Most of the women were dressed elegantly, basic black with tasteful jewels, pearls and diamond necklaces. A young Latin woman, tall and stately, wearing an evening gown that clung to her curvaceous contours, stood with a small group of men each elegantly attired in thousand-dollar suits. The woman was on the arm of an older gentleman six inches shorter than she. He had hair like spun silver. As Abby passed she could hear them speaking in Spanish.

Jack caught her gawking. 'They come up from Rio, and Argentina,' he told her. 'Bring their oil and cattle bucks, sometimes narco dollars. They do a little business. Bring their mistresses along and drop a bundle in the casinos. Then they go home to their wives and ten children. You know,' said Jack. 'Traditional old-world values.'

It was Abby's first look at the upper crust of the Southern Hemisphere, and she was feeling like the ugly American.

'Jesus, you're a cynic,' she told him. 'How do you know it's not his daughter?'

'Because she's too young.'

'Maybe it's his granddaughter,' said Abby.

'Well, there you have me.'

'Maybe you'd like to ask them?' said Abby.

'I'm not the one getting whiplash,' he told her.

'Besides, I don't judge them. As far as I'm concerned, there's nothing wrong with a good mistress. It's why Catholics have fewer divorces. It also makes abstinence easier.'

Abby started to laugh, shook her head, and gave up.

The few U.S. tourists in the lobby stood out like vagabonds, a couple of the men in baseball caps and tourist-trap T-shirts. The women did no better, some in jeans with fanny packs.

Abby nervously rubbed the wrinkles from her own slacks, and adjusted the collar on her blouse, which was soiled and wet with sweat.

'I'm going to need some clothes,' she whispered to Jack as they approached the registration desk.

'Go ahead. Take your time. The shops are down there.' He pointed toward an arcade of boutiques, richly dressed mannequins behind glass and windows of glittering jewelry.

She hesitated while Jack dealt with the woman at the counter. He passed her his credit card.

'Ah yes, Mr Jermaine, we have your reservation. We also have a message for you.' The clerk handed Jack a small envelope.

He opened it and read. 'Henry's found us.'

'Henry?'

'Enrique.'

'Did you tell him we were staying here?'

'No.'

'How did he find us?'

'There is very little that happens on this island that Henry doesn't know about. Seems his limo missed us at the airport. He's sending it by in a few hours to pick us up.'

'Limo,' said Abby. 'Pretty generous of him to rent a limo.'

'Oh, he didn't rent it,' said Jack.

The clerk took an impression from Jack's credit card and a moment later handed him two electronic card keys and hit the bell for their luggage to be rolled upstairs.

'We're on the ninth floor, adjoining rooms.' Jack handed Abby one of the keys in a little envelope with a room number written on the outside. 'Go ahead. Go shopping. I'll take care of the bags and meet you upstairs. Oh, and we'll need to dress for dinner.' He turned and started to leave, but Abby just stood there.

'I . . . ah . . .'

'What's the problem?' he asked.

'I don't have a credit card,' said Abby. Six hundred thousand dollars in the bank and no way to spend it.

'They'll cash a check at the desk,' said Jack.

'I can't do that, either.' Abby remembered the warning from Morgan not to tap her account while the police were trying to find her.

Jack leaned over the counter and whispered something to the clerk on the other side. The woman nodded and pointed to the shops down the way.

'Not a problem,' said Jack. 'You can use that.' He pointed to the key in her hand. 'Charge it to the room.'

'I can do that?'

'It's probably how she got the dress she's wearing.' Jack nodded toward the young Latin woman on the older man's arm. 'Mistressing has its benefits,' said Jack.

'And what's that supposed to mean?'

He smiled and moved quickly toward the elevator before she could grab him.

'It's on your credit card,' she hollered after Jack.

'Don't worry about it.'

'I'll pay you back,' she said.

'We'll figure something out,' said Jack.

'Wait a second.'

Before she could catch him, Jack and his infectious grin disappeared into the elevator and the door closed behind them.

Abby stood alone in the lobby looking at the young woman in the shimmering black evening dress, then down at her own wrinkled slacks. She closed her hand around the card key. It seemed no matter how much money she made, she could never come out on top.

Thrift was a word the shop keepers at the Condado had never heard. Abby hoped Jack had a high limit on his credit card. She bought only two outfits; a casual change of clothes, slacks with a blouse and a light sweater, and a pair of matching navy loafers and handbag. She also found an evening dress. The dress set her back half a month at her former salary. Still it looked better on her than anything she could remember wearing in years. It was a kind of flowing feminine tuxedo. Simple, but with the appearance that it could magically complicate the intrigue of an evening. She purchased a pair of three-inch heels to go with it. It was the most expensive shopping spree she had ever taken. Abby was used to waiting for season-end sales and buying from some of the cut-rate catalogs. People who thought all lawyers were rich were nuts. She would tell Spencer to wire the money immediately, the next time she talked to him. She didn't like the idea of owing Jack money.

Two and a half hours after leaving him in the lobby, the phone in her room rang. The limo was waiting for them downstairs.

Jack was waiting by the elevator when Abby stepped out of her room, dressed in her new evening clothes. He gave a low whistle of appreciation. 'You look great.'

Abby flushed. 'So do you.'

With a genuinely pleased look he took her hand. 'Come on. Let's go see how the other half lives.'

They emerged from the elevator and were greeted by a tall man in a chauffeur's uniform. He was not Hispanic but Anglo.

'Mr Jermaine, good to see you again.' He spoke with a clipped British accent.

'How are you, Zeke? It's been a long time.'

'Too long,' said the driver.

'Zeke, I'd like you meet Abby. Abby, Zeke.'

The chauffeur tipped his hat. 'Ma'am.'

Abby smiled at him. He led them to the car parked at the hotel entrance. It was not the usual stretch limo, but a sleek black Rolls-Royce.

'I see you're still driving the Phantom,' said Jack.

'Wouldn't have it any other way,' said the driver. 'They can keep the stretch Lincolns and Caddys. They just don't have the ride.'

'You ought to talk Henry into buying you the Silver Ghost.'

'He's talked to them about it,' said the driver. 'Rolls won't let it go.'

The driver held the door while Abby and Jack got into the back seat. The driver went around to the other side.

'What's the Silver Ghost?' said Abby.

'The first car Rolls-Royce ever made. Nineteen-oh-eight. They say it's worth forty-four million.'

'Must have been quite a year,' said Abby.

'But as you heard, Rolls won't sell it.'

'And that's the only thing stopping your friend from buying it?'

Jack looked at her and smiled.

'Right.' Abby gave him a skeptical look.

The engine purred softly as the Rolls pulled into traffic.

'I've kept the receipts for the clothes,' she told him. 'I'll pay you in a few days. Just as soon as some financial affairs are straightened out.'

'Don't worry about it,' said Jack.

'But I do worry about it.' Abby didn't like wearing clothes bought for her by a man with whom she had nothing but a business relationship.

'These financial affairs, are they being handled by your friend Spencer?'

Abby looked at him but didn't respond.

'Are you sure you can trust him?'

'I can trust him.'

'As I remember, there were a lot of zeros on that check I endorsed over to you,' said Jack. 'There's an old saying. When you have that much money you should put it all in one basket, and watch that basket very carefully.'

'I'll watch it,' said Abby. 'And I'll pay you as soon as the money is available.'

'No hurry.'

The car breezed along narrow streets, some of the worst slums Abby had seen. These slowly changed to small houses. Another mile and the houses grew walls around them. As they moved on, the buildings inside of the walls got progressively larger, until some of them rivaled the size and stature of art museums, what Jack called Mediterranean villas. The Rolls took a turn toward the coast. Now the traffic was much thinner.

'Where are we headed?'

'Out along the ocean,' said Jack.

'Your friend lives on the beach?'

'Sometimes. He has a couple of different places on the island. Sorta splits his time between them.'

They drove along a rocky shore interspersed with beaches until all of the houses seemed to disappear behind them. A few miles out, the car turned out onto a point of land and a quarter of a mile down the road slowed just a little. An armed guard in uniform stepped out of a stone kiosk, recognized the Rolls, and waved them through a large iron gate that opened and then just as quickly closed behind the car.

They drove further. It seemed like forever to Abby until finally out of the canopy of trees a large house could be seen in the distance across a rolling verdant lawn. Below it swept a broad beach and the azure blue sea. It was evening and the sun was etching the underside of a cloud at the horizon like mother of pearl.

The house itself was unique, unlike anything Abby had ever seen. It was made up of a number of circular pavilions, each with a massive thatched roof. The front door was carved mahogany, and the small-paned windows were framed in teak.

'Henry saw something like it in a village in Bali a few years ago,' said Jack. 'He liked it.'

'I can tell.' Abby stepped out of the Rolls as Zeke held the door open.

'Of course the one in Bali wasn't this big. Still, he had his architect fly over there and take a look. This is the result.'

'I'd hate to have him take a fancy to the Taj Mahal,' said Abby.

'Yeah. It's amazing what a little creativity and five million dollars will do,' said Jack.

Abby was wondering what anyone with that much money would be doing living here, and more to the point, where he got his money. The thought crossed her mind: drugs.

They walked to the front door and Jack pulled a woven silk chord that rang a bell somewhere deep in the interior of the house. A moment later a house-man in a white linen coat opened the door.

He smiled broadly. 'Ah, Mr Jermaine. We have been expecting you. Please come in.'

Abby walked into the entry, a lavishly appointed room with carved and painted native masks hanging from terracotta walls. The furnishings were all Polynesian, dark hardwoods, and heavily carved. It was cool, and Abby wondered how it was possible to air-condition a dwelling with a high-thatched ceiling.

'He is anxious to see you.' The house-man showed them the way. They passed through several large rooms until they came to what appeared to be a library with a heart-stopping view of the ocean. A ship with lighted portholes stood just off shore, a cruise liner that appeared to be anchored in the lee of the bay.

A man was seated at a large carved desk. He looked up as they entered the room.

'Jack, you scoundrel.' He laid his pen down and was immediately out of his chair. 'You did not tell me where you were staying. It was the devil trying to find you.' He was a big man, tall and rangy with dark hair and eyes and an infectious smile, the kind that deceives you. Abby sensed that it could turn cold in an instant if he were displeased. He crossed the room in five easy strides, and his arms embraced Jack in a bear hug.

Jack was clearly uneasy with this display of affection. He patted Henry on the back with one hand while the other hung limp at his side.

'Henry,' he said. 'It's good to see you.'

Abby watched, laughing at Jack and his embarrassment.

'Goddamn, it has been a long time,' said Henry. 'I keep telling you, you must come down and visit more often. What has it been?'

'I've lost track,' said Jack.

'Precisely. It is how you lose track of friends. You know,' he said, 'I would have sent the Gulfstream to pick you up in Atlanta or Savannah. All you had to do was pick up the phone.'

Then Henry realized there was a stranger in the room. 'Where are your manners?' he told Jack.

'Excuse me. Henry, I'd like you to meet Abby Chandlis.'

The man named Henry backed away from Jack and for a moment took in Abby with deep-set dark eyes. Then he extended a hand and a warm smile.

'Abby, meet Enrique Ricardi.'

'Henry's fine,' said the man. 'Everybody on the island calls me Henry, except my mother. She gives me no end of grief. She tells me I'm becoming Anglicized or Anglophiled or some damn thing.'

As he spoke, Abby's jaw hung open. She knew the name. Anyone who had ever entered a bar knew the name. Lamely she took his hand and shook it. The name Ricardi was synonymous with rum, the largest distiller in the world, with plants in the United States and Europe. There were signs with the name on half the roads in America and all over the island. It was no wonder, as Jack said in the hotel lobby, that nothing happened here without Henry knowing about it. For all intents, Enrique Ricardi owned the island. He was one of its wealthiest men, well up on the food chain on the Fortune 500.

'Are you feeling alright?' asked Henry.

'Ah . . . oh, yes,' said Abby. She caught herself staring and diverted her eyes.

'Did you catch the look on her face?' said Jack. 'I've been telling her about my friend Henry for two days, and now you could knock her over with a feather.'

'Well, you didn't tell me,' said Abby.

'Excuse my ill-mannered friend,' said Ricardi. 'May I call you Abby?'

'Sure.' Abby was trying to appear casual in such lofty company.

'Please, have a seat.' Henry called the house-man and ordered drinks, piña colada for Jack, rum punch in honor of her host for Abby.

'You are probably wondering how someone like myself, cultured, and refined, could have ever had the poor judgment to have become involved with someone like this?' He pointed to Jack and shook his head. 'A mean low life.'

'Just a minute,' said Jack.

'Now that you mention it,' said Abby.

'Oh, here we go,' said Jack.

'Well, I had the misfortune, the incalculable poor judgment, to admit him to my fraternity at Stanford.'

'Your fraternity?' said Jack. 'I seem to remember that I was on the membership committee the year you rushed.'

'Goes to show you how clouded your memory becomes with age,' said Henry. 'Ah.'

Before Jack could counter, the house-man came back into the room with a tray of drinks.

'Time for my medicine,' said Jack.

'Yes. To improve your memory,' said Henry.

They laughed and each took a glass as the house-man passed them along. Abby's was tall and frosted, with a small parasol poking from the top, and a slice of pine-apple over the edge. Suddenly it started to make sense; Stanford and a degree in Latin American Studies. Where else would you meet the commercial royalty of the Caribbean?

'You know, you really should be scolded,' said Ricardi. He was talking to Jack. 'You come to my island and reject my hospitality. Of course you will stay here tonight.'

'We have rooms back at the Condado Plaza,' said Jack.

'You *had* rooms at the Condado Plaza,' said Ricardi. 'It seems they have suddenly become overbooked.' A wry smile spread across his face as Henry settled into the couch across from them. 'Zeke has already gone to retrieve your luggage. I have spoken with the hotel manager. There is no charge.'

'What about the charges I put on the room?' Abby said this in a low tone to Jack. She was wearing part of them. Henry picked up on the comment.

'As I said, there was no charge,' said Henry. 'We supply a major staple to the hotel, and their guests imbibe rather generously.'

'What Henry is saying is that he owns a chunk of the Condado,' said Jack. 'Along with every other major hotel on the island.'

'A small family franchise.' Henry grinned, something insidious. She could imagine him owning slaves and giving them away with similar equanimity in another age. It invaded her sense of Yankee independence, which seemed to be eroding like a landslide the further down the road she went with Jack.

'Now we will put you up in rooms in the guest wing,' said Ricardi. 'I understand you are a writer?'

Abby shot Jack a look. She wondered how much he had told Ricardi about their arrangement.

Jack shrugged. Whipped dog. He knew he was going to get a tongue lashing later.

'Yes. Well, Jack has those ambitions,' said Henry. 'I have told him to give it up. To be realistic. That all of that is in the past. But alas, Jack and reality, they are strangers.'

'Really?' said Abby.

'Oh yes. He chases the dream ever since . . .'

'That's enough,' said Jack.

'No, I want to hear more,' said Abby.

'Who am I to interfere with dreams?' said Ricardi. He let it drop. 'I have even offered him a job here, but he will not take it.'

'Nepotism,' said Jack.

'No, nepotism is when you hire your family. God knows I have done enough of that. I think they call it cronyism when it is a friend. Just think, we could travel the world, chase women, and drink.'

'You can do that down the road in your refinery,' said Jack.

'Distillery. Please,' said Henry. 'Anyway. Back to matters at hand. I have a wonderful place selected for you down in St Croix,' he told Abby. 'I think you will like it. Very quiet. Very private. The Kennedy family, Ted, rents the house down the road for Christmas sometimes. But the house I have selected for you is less conspicuous.'

Abby was wondering how much it would cost.

'Now, how long are you going to be on the island?'

'Two days,' said Jack. 'We have a flight out day after tomorrow in the afternoon.'

'Nonsense,' said Henry. 'Certainly you can stay longer than that.'

'I wish we could, but there is a deadline,' said Abby. 'We have to start work immediately.'

'Work,' said Ricardi. 'The nemesis of us all. I myself am off to Europe in the morning. But surely you could stay here. Have the run of the place.'

'Gotta be moving on,' said Jack.

Ricardi understood. 'But you will not fly down to St Croix. Not on that little twin prop job. It is so uncomfortable,' said Ricardi. 'I would give you the Gulfstream, but I need it to fly to London.'

'Not a problem,' said Jack.

'Of course it is not. You will take the *Isabella*.' He pointed to the cruise ship moored in the bay beyond the study window. 'I have already given instructions. Alerted the crew and the captain. And while you are on the island, you will use Zeke and the car.' Henry was the kind who didn't take no for an answer.

Jack made a face, like what could he say.

'I have some last-minute matters to clear away and then we can have dinner. Ah, before I forget,' he said, 'I have the key to the house, and something that arrived for you earlier today,' he told Jack. He reached into a drawer in his desk and removed a small box, an express package that looked remarkably like the box that Jack had dropped off at the office near the airport the day before.

CHAPTER
TWENTY-FOUR

Ever since the cop's visit to his office, Charlie Chandlis had been dying of curiosity. He knew that Abby had come into money. What he didn't know was how much, or where it came from. He thought he knew his former wife, but the episode with his credit card had showed him that he didn't know her as well as he thought. The Abby he was married to would never have had the sand to take his credit card, or to use it.

He didn't show much anger. But underneath he was quietly seething. Abby had made a fool out of him and Charlie didn't like it. Still, there was another aspect to him that was titillated. The thought that Abby had turned over a new leaf, especially one with a slightly shady color, was something strangely intoxicating to Charlie. He didn't know what he would do if he got his hands on her. That was the exciting part.

It had crossed his mind more than once over the past week that perhaps Abby had hidden assets during their marriage, something stashed away that was community property that she had failed to disclose during the divorce. The reason Charlie had a suspicious mind was that he had hidden assets himself, nearly eighteen thousand dollars in retainers, that he had never put on the books of his practice during the months just before they split up. Why she had paid back the six thousand on the credit card Charlie wasn't sure. But if she had that kind of money, maybe there was more.

Abby's law practice wasn't much. For the most part, she was salaried. Still it was possible that she had come into a windfall, maybe a large settlement in a case. It wasn't what lawyers were paid by the hour that made some of them rich. It was the contingent fees when they went to trial or settled a case on the courthouse steps. In a big case, the lawyer's take could be six figures.

Charlie was confronted with the problem of how to find out. There had to be a bank account somewhere. Banks were secretive places. If your name was on the account, they might tell you what was in it. Otherwise you could forget it. If you held a check drawn against the account, they would only tell you whether there were sufficient funds on deposit to cover it. Charlie already knew they were sufficient in the case of Abby's check for the credit-card charges. The card company had cashed it.

It took him a few days to devise a plan to find out more. In Charlie's eyes lawyers were the high priests of society, special people with special powers. They made the laws, so why not use them for their own purposes. Over a two-day period in his spare time, Charlie concocted a civil complaint against Abby, a trumped-up law suit that he filed in the superior court in Seattle. Lawyers did this thousands of times a day all over the country, and no one paid particular attention, unless it was filed against a rock star or some basketball jock.

In the suit he charged Abby with civil fraud, the

failure to disclose assets in connection with their divorce. In fact, he had no evidence at all. But evidence isn't required to file a law suit, only to win one. Charlie had no intention of going to court. In fact, he made no effort to serve a copy of the law suit on Abby either by personal service or publication in a newspaper. Instead, using the court's file number issued by the clerk in the law suit, Charlie then issued a subpoena duces tecum. This was a court order requiring the recipient to produce records. In this case, banking records. Then Charlie started off on a fishing expedition.

The first place he visited was the bank where Abby had written the check to cover the credit-card bill. What he discovered was that she'd closed the account two days after her check had cleared. He wasn't surprised. If she was hiding assets, she would be more cagey than to leave a bundle where Charlie could find it that easily. The fact that the account was closed, however, confirmed in his mind that there was something going on. Abby had something to hide.

He crafted a second subpoena. Calling on the sale of Abby's house and pretending to be an interested buyer, Charlie had gleaned one other vital piece of information. Morgan Spencer, a lawyer with Abby's old firm, was the contact on the sale of her house. If that was the case, it didn't take much to conclude that Spencer might be handling other business matters for her. The question was, where did Spencer and his law firm do their banking?

Charlie combed a back issue of one of the small legal newspapers until he found what he wanted. It was a list of names, young lawyers recently admitted to the practice of law after passing the state bar examination. He ran his finger down the list until he found a likely candidate, then picked up the phone and dialed.

'Starl, Hobbs and Carlton.' It was a woman with a sexy voice on the other end.

'Hello. My name is Daniel Swenson.' Charlie pumped himself up to sound young and naive. 'I'm a new admittee to the bar and I wanted to talk to one of the lawyers at your firm, if I could, about some business advice.'

'What kind of advice?'

'You know. Getting started. Opening an office. Setting up financial records, that sort of thing.'

'How did you get our name?'

As Charlie had suspected, the most difficult part would be getting past the receptionist.

'One of my professors at law school told me that your firm was among the best managed firms in town. A great reputation,' said Charlie. 'So naturally I thought I would start there.'

'Just a moment,' said the woman.

He whistled quietly to himself as he listened to elevator music being piped over the phone.

'Hello. Who am I speaking to?' It was a man's voice, deep and melodious, that came back to him on the line.

'Oh. This is Daniel Swenson. I don't know how much your receptionist told you, but I'm a recent admittee, just getting set up in practice.'

'Yes. How can I help you?'

'I recently attended one of those meetings. You know, sort of bridging the gap between law school and practice. Several of the attorneys who spoke to us mentioned your firm as being particularly well run.' It was the kind of horseshit designed to turn the head of a silk-stocking lawyer.

'They sort of suggested,' said Charlie, 'that more

experienced lawyers wouldn't mind giving a little advice. Just to get us off on the right foot.'

'Absolutely,' said the older lawyer.

'May I ask who I'm speaking to?' said Charlie.

'My name is Lewis Cutler. I'm the managing partner.'

'Oh Jeez, I didn't expect to get the boss,' said Charlie.

'That's alright. What can I help you with?'

'I have to establish some business bank accounts, a client trust fund. You know the sort of thing. I thought maybe you could recommend a local bank that comes highly regarded within the profession?'

'Oh sure. No problem. We've used First National, the downtown branch, for years. Just ask for Jim Hanford. Tell him Lew Cutler sent you.'

'Do all the partners there use the same bank?'

'For business, yes,' said Cutler. 'We use one bank for ease of record keeping. It gets to be a pain when you have accounts spread all over town.'

'Gee, thanks. That's a big help. I'll remember that,' said Charlie.

'Not a problem. Anything else I can do for you?'

'No. I think you've been more than helpful.'

'Listen, I know how it is when you're first setting . . .'

Charlie hung up and left Cutler talking to himself on the phone. He turned to the typewriter and plugged in the name of First National on the form subpoena, then ripped it from the typewriter, signed it, and grabbed his briefcase.

Twenty minutes later he waltzed through the revolving door of First National. He pretended to make notes at the counter in the center of the bank until he found the name plate on the desk he was looking for. He walked up to the bank officer sitting at his desk.

'Can I help you?' The man was middle aged and balding.

'Mr Hanford. My name is Charles Chandlis. I'm an attorney and I have a subpoena for financial records regarding one of your depositors.' He handed the man the subpoena, and the officer looked at it.

'Please have a seat.' He motioned Charlie to one of the chairs on the other side of his desk.

The form was official-looking, bearing the title of the superior court along with the file number of the case.

'It's very specific.' Charlie sat down. 'We seek only information regarding accounts for the named individual. Nothing else. The bank is not named as a party defendant.' He mentioned this in hopes that the banker might see the downside in failing to comply. With Charlie, subtle intimidation was an art form.

'Yes. I see. Our legal department is in another building.' The banker seemed confused as to what to do with the document, whether simply to comply or to have his own lawyers scour the form for awhile.

'You can send it along to them if you like. But I was hoping to get some basic information today. Certainly you can have a reasonable period to produce the records. Ten days. Two weeks. I know you're busy.' First the whip, and now the carrot, thought Charlie.

'I see.' The banker was straining his eyes hoping to find something that might jump off the page at him, some justification for delay. But he didn't find it.

'Your bank comes very highly recommended,' said Charlie.

'Oh really?'

'Oh yes. A good friend. Lew Cutler at Starl, Hobbs and Carlton. Speaks very highly of you.'

'Oh sure. I know Lew.'

'Great guy,' said Charlie. 'Yeah, we go way back. He can't say enough good things about this bank. He keeps telling me I'm going to have to move my business accounts over here. Looks like I'm gonna have to have him up on it,' said Charlie.

There was a budding smile on the banker's face as he looked at Charlie over the top of the subpoena. 'Everything appears to be in order,' he said.

Actually it wasn't. The banker might have asked for a return on service of process. This would have shown that their depositor, the defendant in the law suit, had not been served with a copy of the suit. Without notice of the litigation, Abby had no way to fight the subpoena, to try to quash it. A lawyer in the bank's legal department would have seen this. If Charlie played it right, by the time they did, he would have what he wanted.

'What is it you want to know?' said the banker.

'Very simple,' said Charlie. 'All I need for the moment is whether you have any accounts on deposit for the named individual? And if so, how much is on deposit as of this date? For now, that's all I would need. As I say, you can copy the records at your leisure and send them along later.'

This sounded reasonable to the banker. They didn't have to do anything but look in their computer. 'I think we can do that.'

'Wonderful,' said Charlie. Subpoenas were such wonderful things.

Hanford started punching his computer keys.

'What's the depositor's name?' said Hanford.

'Abigail Chandlis.' He spelled the last name for him. 'It might be under Abby.'

He punched some more keys.

'Yes. We have an account in that name. It's a joint checking account with a Morgan Spencer.' He wrote the account number on a slip of paper and handed it to Charlie.

'May I ask how much is in the account?'

Hanford punched a few more keys and scrolled down on the screen.

He looked at the numbers and had to focus his eyes. He wrote it out on a slip of paper and passed it across to Charlie. It was bank policy when balances got this big, to protect the privacy and the security of their patrons.

Charlie whistled. Abby had a million-two on deposit. He nearly fell out of the chair.

'Can you trace the source?'

'There's only two deposits. But the computer doesn't show where they came from.'

'Is there any way to find out?'

'Just a moment.' Hanford picked up the phone and dialed. 'Yes. I need an account history.' He gave the number of the account and waited a moment. 'Only two items? Could you fax those for me? Great!' He gave the bank's fax number and hung up.

He looked at Charlie. 'It'll be just a moment.'

A couple of minutes later he walked over to the fax machine and collected the pages coming through.

'The most recent check deposited in the account, a little over six hundred thousand, was drawn against the account of Pietros Films, Ltd.'

This meant nothing to Charlie.

The first one, a total of six hundred thousand, was written against a royalty account on a bank in New York. Carla Owens & Associates.

What was strange was that both checks were written to a Jack Jermaine. They were signed over by him and then deposited into Abby's account.

CHAPTER
TWENTY-FIVE

Abby never had the time or the money to travel. Practicing law by day and writing by night left little time for leisure pursuits or for seeing the world. It was the price every part-time writer paid.

She had never seen anything like Old San Juan; buildings that dated to the time of Columbus.

It was early afternoon, the day of their departure from Puerto Rico. Enrique's boat was to pick them up at the docks that evening. Abby and Jack walked through a maze of narrow cobblestone streets and wound past shops whose owners gathered in doorways chatting in Spanish. The historic city was filled with romance and images of an older world. It was rich in color, and Abby considered ways of fitting it into the story for her sequel.

A cruise ship was moored at the docks. Its passengers ambled down the stairs of the terminal building. Like so many fleas they flitted about the streets of the old town, climbing on its monuments and cornering deals on T-shirts. Even Jack looked like a tourist. He wore a tight polo shirt and running shorts and sported a good-sized camera case on his hip.

As they ambled through the plaza, Abby felt strange, almost embarrassed, as Jack fell under the gaze of passing women. Old and young, it didn't seem to matter, his looks were like an aphrodisiac. Even a few men stopped and stared. In a crowd, Jack stood out. Charisma and presence, he should have been a politician. He was taller and tanned with chiseled features. There was something about his thick dark mane of hair and the way he swept it to the side periodically with one hand. And the flashing bright smile, like JFK. Most of the women tried to be cool, subtle glances until they were past. Then they would turn and take a full look, a few of them whispering into cupped ears. For Abby it was a bizarre sensation. She could feel the radiating envy of the passing women like the pings on sonar. It was as if she had somehow cornered the glamour market. The shallow values of the world, she thought. Still she couldn't help enjoying the moment in the sun. Abby was no teenage fashion model, but she was not a bad-looking woman. In a world unpoisoned by the culture of youth, she might have stood out herself. She wondered what it would be like to be dressed to the nines strutting on Jack's arm through some flashy night spot, like the red carpeted walk on Oscar night.

She put away her daydreams as they edged away from the tourists and climbed the steep sidewalks of the town until they found themselves standing on Calle Norzagaray. It flanked the edge of Old San Juan high on a bluff. Jack and Abby stood there looking out at the white capped swells of the Atlantic.

'Over there,' said Jack. He pointed off to the northwest, a mile away. 'That's the fortress of El Morro. It guards the harbor entrance.'

Abby could see the ramparts of the ancient fort,

turreted guard towers and parapets of massive stone, walls that ringed the old city.

'I'd like to see it,' she said.

'Later,' said Jack. 'First let's get something to eat. Do you like Mexican food?'

A block down was a small restaurant with a sign in black letters spanning the second story, 'Amanda's Cafe.' There were two rooms inside, a small triangular bar, and a dining area. Jack and Abby opted for the veranda out front over the street. They ordered margaritas and relaxed, watching the turquoise, white-capped combers blow in off the Atlantic.

The motif of Amanda's was flamingo pink and teal green, the hot colors of the Caribbean. And the food, as Jack had promised, was delicious. They listened to Latin beats, and Jimmy Buffet from the juke box inside, as they labored over sizzling iron skillets of chicken and beef. They built fajitas from flour tortillas the size of Mexican hats, and talked about Abby's book.

Big-F had done a photo shoot for Jack's picture on the back jacket and for publicity. They had also hired a large public relations firm to do screen testing, a kind of briefing for television. Owens and Bertoli wanted Jack well prepped for the talk-show circuit. Abby was nervous about allowing him to go to New York alone. But she had work to do, and sooner or later she would have to trust him.

'What will you talk about in the interview?' she asked him.

'My book.' He gave her a sly grin. 'And how I wrote it.'

'And how was that?'

'With great care. You see, it was a labor of love,' said Jack. 'Every word and comma.'

'And how long did this labor of love take you to create?' she asked him. Questions she anticipated would be asked when they prepped him.

Jack thought for a moment. 'Five months.'

Abby shook her head. 'Longer.'

'Seven months.'

'More.'

'Did you chisel it on stone?' said Jack.

'A good book takes time,' said Abby. 'Like fine wine.' After reading his manuscript, Abby guessed that Jack knocked out a novel a month.

'How long did it take?' he asked.

'Two years.'

He whistled low under his breath.

'It took that long to capture the right voice, to deal with characters and motivation. Even formula fiction takes time,' said Abby. 'If it's going to work.'

'How are you going to have the next one ready in a year?' he asked.

'By working my ass off. Feast or famine,' said Abby. 'Either they don't want you at all, or if you're successful the publishers demand a book every twelve months. Sooner if they could get it.

'The theory,' she told him, 'is that they can addict the reading public like tobacco companies hook smokers.'

'Well, at least the readers don't get cancer,' said Jack.

'I wouldn't be so sure. There's no CAT scan for the intellect,' said Abby.

'So you finished the book in two years,' said Jack.

'Actually I did the first draft in eight months. I spent the next sixteen revising and rewriting.' She could have said dumbing it down, but she didn't.

'Anyone can write,' said Abby. 'The question is, can you rewrite? And when you do, is it better or worse?'

'What do you mean?' said Jack.

'How can I put it? It's like music, only you're not listening for melodies. It's more the cadence of speech and the pattern of prose. Credible writing requires an ear. If you're tone deaf, forget it.'

Jack looked at her as if perhaps she were sending him a message.

'That's a great line,' he said. He reached for a pen in his pocket and wrote it down on a napkin.

'Now what else are you going to tell the vast television audience?' she asked.

'You tell me.'

'You might talk about what you did for a living while you were writing. People are usually interested in that.'

'Ah. The starving author,' said Jack. 'Well, unfortunately I didn't have to work.'

'Independently wealthy, are you?'

'Wealth, no. Independent, you bet.'

'You were in the military.'

'True.'

'Tell 'em about that. What did you do? Remember, you're an instant celebrity. Oprah loves you. The world wants to hear what you eat for breakfast.'

'What does anyone do in the military? Follow orders,' said Jack.

'What kind of a job did you have?'

'Job?' said Jack. 'I was a Marine. Spit and polish, and shining sabers. I trained a lot of boys to become a few good men.'

'A drill sergeant,' said Abby.

'A training officer,' said Jack.

'Better title,' she told him. 'You've got to sell yourself to sell the book. Remember that.'

He saluted with his mouth full of fajitas, like he was taking orders.

'Anything exciting and adventurous?' said Abby. 'What did you do before you were a training officer?'

'What is this, twenty questions?' said Jack.

'No. It's work. It's what you signed on for. Now tell me. What did you do before you were a training officer?'

'I ran a river boat.'

'What, like on the Mississippi? Don't be so mysterious. Inquiring minds want to know,' said Abby.

'Smaller,' said Jack. 'Inflatable.'

'You were the captain of a rubber raft?'

'A twenty-foot Zodiac,' said Jack. 'With a thirty caliber mounted machine gun and a crew of five.'

'Now that sounds interesting.'

'We wore grease paint and black hoods and operated at night.'

'Tell me more.'

'We'd go ashore. Our job was laser painting.'

'What's that?'

'We used a thing called a "mule." It looks like a shotgun on steroids,' said Jack. 'There's a short stock. You aim it just like a gun. It emits a nearly invisible laser beam that illuminates the target for the guys in the sky. You aim at a window or a doorway, sometimes an air duct or an elevator shaft.'

'Like that paint ball stuff?' said Abby. 'For training in war games, right?'

'Like in Panama and Kuwait City,' said Jack. 'We painted targets so that two thousand pound laser-guided bombs could find them.'

Jack stopped talking and looked at her over his tortilla, dripping juice onto his place.

'But you never killed anybody, right?' Abby wanted confirmation of this. Why, she wasn't sure herself.

'I would assume there were people inside those buildings. Besides, you could usually tell.'

She gave him a quizzical look. She didn't want to ask but felt compelled.

'It's the smell of burning flesh,' said Jack. 'There's a real distinctive odor.'

She suddenly lost her appetite, pushed her plate away, and sipped a little of her margarita.

'On second thought,' said Abby, 'maybe mysterious is better.' She had visions of Jack opening his wallet to show pictures of burning babies on the morning shows.

'Hey, you asked, so I told you,' said Jack.

'Why is it so important for you to write?' Abby changed the subject.

'I enjoy it,' said Jack.

Maybe that was the problem, thought Abby. Every good writer she had ever known hated it. What was the line? There's nothing at all to writing. Just sit down and open a vein. She guessed the reason it was so effortless for Jack was that he lacked self-criticism. If you're tone deaf, every click of the keyboard, each scratch of the pen, sounds like Mozart.

'Tell me, does my stuff sound real?' he asked.

'I don't know. I'm not a good judge of what happens in war.' Abby copped out. 'But maybe you're trying too hard.'

He gave her a look. He could tell bad news was coming. 'Here we go,' said Jack. 'Let him down easy. Tell him he has promise, but maybe he should consider another line of work. Ever thought of being an auto mechanic?'

'Did I say that?'

'No, but you're thinking it.'

'Your friend Henry started to say something. That you've had this passion to write ever since, and then you cut him off. What did he mean? Ever since what?'

'Henry talks too much,' said Jack. 'He missed his calling. He should have been a therapist.'

'He seems to think you're obsessed.'

'See what I mean?' said Jack. 'Do I have to have a reason?'

'No.'

'But a little talent would help. Is that it?' Jack finished the thought for her.

'I didn't say that.'

'You don't have to,' said Jack. 'I haven't come all this way without some sense of my own limitations,' he told her. 'Go ahead, say what you're thinking.'

'Maybe you should consider Henry's offer for a job,' she told him.

'Do I look like a charity case? Besides, I don't need the money. Henry doesn't need my help. He's lonely. He wants to buy a friend.'

'So be his friend.'

'I'd rather be a writer.'

'Not everybody can pen a novel,' said Abby. 'Your manuscript needs a lot of work.'

He put his fajita down on the plate and started to sip his margarita. 'That's why I thought we could work on it together.'

'And what gave you that idea?'

'The fact that we're working together on yours.'

'Different definition of working,' said Abby.

'Ah. I see. Flashing a smile and flexing my pecs is not your idea of collaboration. So that I get this straight. You don't want me for my mind, just my body?'

Abby started to laugh. But it was true. It was why she was using him. Men in the field of entertainment always made more money than women. And money was the ultimate measure of success. Of the box-office stars capable of opening a blockbuster film, only two or three were women and they were paid considerably less than their male counterparts. The same was true in the top realms of fiction writing, from legal thrillers to military fantasies. The only place for women was in the genre of romance with a little grudging acceptance in mysteries.

But the heavy guns, the first order, Grisham, Crichton, Clancy, and Stephen King, all were men. Nobody was Chrichtonizing Judith Krantz or Danielle Steele. True, they quietly went about making millions. Still, even with blockbuster sales, they never entered the elite top rung in which every word written was scripted for feature film. The commercial literary coronations were all for men. Abby figured if she couldn't beat them, she would join them – at least until it was time for her grand entrance, out of the shadows to claim what was hers.

'So tell me, in a nutshell, what's the problem with my manuscript?' asked Jack. 'Is the story flawed?'

'It's not the story,' said Abby.

'So it's the writing?'

She made a lot of faces, all of them adding up to yes. Jack was tone deaf.

'We could work on it,' He returned to his meal. 'Like you said, rewriting is the key.'

'If you have a good ear,' she told him.

'We'll use yours. I'm not proud,' said Jack. He had a hide like an alligator. He just smiled and filled his cheeks with food.

'I don't have time,' said Abby.

He ignored her.

'How many of these things have you written?' she asked.

'Manuscripts?'

Applied to Jack's work it was a generous term, but she nodded.

It took him a moment while he counted. The fingers of both hands. 'Eight. So far,' said Jack.

'I would stop there.'

'Quit while I'm ahead?'

Abby waited a beat, smiled, and nodded as gently as she could.

'Actually there's nine, but you don't have to worry about that one.'

'Why not?'

'No reason,' said Jack.

'I don't teach remedial writing, and I'm not a ghost writer,' said Abby. 'I don't do that.'

'Really?' He smiled.

'Don't get the wrong idea. I'm not ghosting my novel for you.'

'Of course not,' said Jack. But he continued to smile.

'Just because you have an unsatisfied obsession,' said Abby.

'And you don't?' said Jack.

'No.'

'I see. You're just a frustrated artist trying to sell her work.'

'That's right.'

'Save it for the depositions if Bertoli sues you,' said Jack.

'I just wanted to improve the book's chances for success,' said Abby.

'Oh, I see. And you aren't interested in the money?'

'Only as a measure of success,' she told him.

'Oh, well. That elevates it to a lofty plane. So if you're not doing all of this – pulling the wool over Bertoli's eyes and the scam with Carla – for the money or for the fame, then what?' said Jack.

Abby looked him dead in the eye. 'For revenge.'

By the time they finished their tour of El Morro, the sun was setting. They didn't notice the two men milling near the gate, looking at tourist maps.

Abby and Jack walked at a brisk pace along the path, more than a quarter of mile across the broad field of grass that separated the fort from Old San Juan.

Jack checked his watch. If they moved they could make it to the docks before Henry's crew began to worry and wonder where they were.

Their luggage had been put on board the yacht that morning from Henry's Balinese palace. The boat then sailed up the coast in the afternoon. Abby and Jack had watched it from the battlements of El Morro as it rounded the point into the harbor. There it would take on fuel and ready itself for the cruise to St Croix.

As they cleared the plaza and began to thread their way through the maze of streets, it became clear to Abby that there was another side to San Juan; the old town after dark. By now the shops were all closed, and the tourists were gone, back to their hotels and cruise ships. In the distance, Abby could see the string of brilliant lights from the superstructure of one of the big boats as it left the harbor with its load of tourists hopping to the strains of mariachi music on their way to the next port of call.

Abby was having trouble keeping up with Jack, whose long legs seemed to devour whole blocks at a stride. He kept asking if she wanted to stop and rest, but

Abby was stubborn. They never noticed the two men walking at a distance behind them.

'How far do we have to go?'

'About ten blocks,' said Jack.

They turned the corner into a street that was too narrow for vehicles. A few children's toys littered the alley. Three figures moving at the far end stepped out of the shadows just as Abby and Jack reached the halfway point along the block. On first glance Abby thought they were just itinerants hanging in the doorways. Then Jack grabbed her elbow and pointed. One of the men, the one in the middle, was carrying something short and stout, like a club in his right hand.

Quickly Jack surveyed the terrain. There were only second-story verandas and doors flush with the street. No doubt these were locked. Even the windows had bars over them. Jack started to pull her back, a tactical retreat.

They'd gone a half-dozen steps when they looked behind them and saw the two men who had been shadowing them ever since they'd left the fortress. The two men entered the alley at the end, sealing off any avenue of escape.

'What do they want?' said Abby.

'Our watches, our wallets, and anything else they feel like taking. Of course that's only a guess,' said Jack.

'They can have them,' said Abby. She started to remove the watch from her wrist.

'Don't be so quick to give away my watch,' he told her.

'You're out of your mind. Give it to them.'

'I paid good money for this. Besides,' said Jack, 'if we give in too easily it may only feed rising expectations. No telling what else they may want.'

The men closed in from the two ends of the alley.

Jack edged toward the shelter of a doorway, and put Abby behind him into the threshold where she was protected on three sides. He put his body in front of her, sealing it off. 'No matter what happens, stay behind me,' he told her.

'Don't be a fool. If we give them what they want, they won't hurt us,' said Abby.

'That's the theory,' said Jack. 'But then I'm not the one they'll probably rape.'

She looked at him, or more accurately at the back of his head, then strapped the watch back on her wrist.

The five men slowly moved in, closing the distance like a pack of jackals until they formed a semicircle ten feet out from their quarry. One of them said something in Spanish and the others all laughed.

Jack forced a smile. 'Do you speak any Spanish?' he asked her.

'Un poco,' said Abby. 'A little.'

'Now's the time,' he told her.

'*Como esta usted?*' Abby looked at the man with the pipe in his hand as she spoke. He was clearly the leader.

'*Oh, muy bien,*' said the man. '*Muy bien.*' He sported a smile like a broken picket fence, a lot of missing teeth.

'*Y usted?*' he asked her.

'*Bien,*' said Abby. She forced a smile as if perhaps she were sufficiently positive it would come true; they would be fine, even though her knees were knocking.

The guy turned to his colleagues. '*Bien.*' They all laughed.

'*No. No. Usted no esta bien. Te voy a robar.*'

'He says we're not fine,' said Abby.

'Why not?' asked Jack.

'Because we're being robbed.'

The man with the pipe motioned with a curling finger, a come-hither gesture. He wanted Abby to step out of the doorway.

Jack told her not to move. 'Fuck you.' He looked the man with the pipe dead in the eye.

By the look on the man's face Abby could tell that it was not the first time he had been told this.

'Oh no, señor, I intend to be fucked, but not by you.' He suddenly dispensed with the Spanish. 'Give me your watch and your wallet and you can go.'

'Let's give it to them and go,' said Abby.

'Who said anything about you?' The man with the pipe gave Abby an appraising look. 'You stay with us for awhile. *Como se dice?*' He struggled for the right words in English. 'We have a party,' he finally said.

'Still want me to give him my watch and wallet?' said Jack.

'Maybe it's not such a good idea,' Abby told him.

'You want it?' said Jack. He pointed to the watch still on his wrist.

The guy smiled, all toothless in front.

'It's all yours. All you have to do is come and get it,' said Jack.

The smile left the guy's face. He swung the pipe in a wide arc and came a step closer. The others fanned out, looking for an opening. One of them pulled a knife from under his shirt, pushed a button, and a four-inch blade snapped out.

They had Jack surrounded in a half circle that began and ended with the wall of the building. Abby huddled in the shadow of the doorway behind him, looking for something she could use as a weapon. Nothing.

Jack took a quick step forward and they all backed up. This left a small gap between Jack and Abby. She stood in the doorway like cheese in a trap.

One of the men on the edge near the wall saw his opening and made a move toward her. In a single fluid motion without even looking Jack lashed out with a foot. Like lightning he caught the man just below the kneecap. Abby heard the crunch of bone. The man shrieked in pain and reached down to grab his knee. As he did, Jack caught him full in the face with the second kick sending the guy sprawling on his back to the ground. His head hit the cobblestones, blood spurted from his mouth. He lay there unconscious. One down.

This seemed to have a mixed effect on the others. One of them backed away. The one with the pipe took another swing but missed. He was now paying a lot of respect to Jack's foot and losing face for it with his comrades.

The man who backed away was talking fast in Spanish, his hands moving quicker than his tongue, a bundle of anxiety. Abby couldn't understand his words, but his body language was clear enough. He wanted to go. This tourista was more than they bargained for.

The man with the pipe shouted something. Orders or encouragement, Abby couldn't tell which. A grim look of resolve came over the others. Reluctantly they closed the circle once more and filled in for their fallen friend.

Suddenly the man with the pipe lunged. Jack caught his forearm on a downward thrust and brought it down over his knee hard.

Abby heard a snap like a branch and realized that Jack had just broken the man's arm. There was a howl of pain and the pipe fell to the ground, sending the echo of metal on stone clanging through the alley.

Using pain for leverage, Jack gripped the broken arm and lifted the man to his full height. Then with a powerful kick he caught him squarely in the groin. With a muffled shriek, the guy crumpled to the ground and lay there motionless, his one good hand groping in his crotch to see what was missing.

One of the others turned tail and ran for the end of the alley.

The other two were of sterner stuff. One of them, the one with the knife, took the lead. He flipped the blade so the point was now between his finger and thumb; in throwing position.

In a reflex, Jack lowered his shoulder and charged. He nailed the man with the knife in the stomach, driving him onto his back in the middle of the street. They grappled and rolled, the knife dropping onto the cobblestones a few feet away. The Puerto Rican lunged for it. Jack's hand closed around his wrist just as the man reached the knife handle and closed his grip. The man had the knife, but Jack had his wrist like a tiger by the tail. They did a deadly dance, rolling to their knees, struggling in a death lock.

All the while Abby and the other Puerto Rican watched. Then suddenly the other man realized there was no one to stop him. He eyed Abby alone in the doorway, then quickly moved on her.

Jack saw it out of the corner of his eye as he fought for his life.

In two steps the man was on her. He grabbed Abby by the throat with both hands and began to press hard.

She scratched at his eyes and got a thumb in one of them. The man merely turned his head and tightened his powerful grip.

Abby felt the pressure building in her head, consciousness waning. She groped in her purse that hung from a strap on her shoulder, frantically feeling in the bottom for the pepper spray she had just remembered.

By now Jack had wrestled the other man to his feet. They struggled for the knife, Jack twirling him, spinning his partner like a top across the alley toward Abby and the man who was choking the life from her body. Like a whirling dervish, Jack and the other man suddenly disappeared behind the human mass in front of her, just as her hand found the tiny canister. She raised it toward his face.

Then suddenly, before she could press the button, the man's eyes went large and round, like two olives floating in mayonnaise. Every aspect of his expression lit up. He stared at Abby like some frozen comic mask. His grip eased, and for some inexplicable reason his hands went soft around her throat. He staggered back a step as if he was about to say something. His mouth moved but nothing came out, nothing but a small trickle of blood that ran down the corner of his lip.

His shoulders seemed locked in a raised position, his hands extended as if he might lung at Abby one more time. She held the pepper spray toward his face just in case.

Instead, he turned, and as he did she saw it. Embedded in his back, near the center of the man's spine, was the handle of the knife now seeping with blood like spigot that ran through his shirt. He took two steps and collapsed in the street.

Abby's hands went to her mouth and she began to shake. For a moment they all stood staring at the body lying in the street, and the growing puddle of blood.

Then suddenly the other Puerto Rican went wild. 'Matò mi hermano.' He grabbed for Jack's throat, scratching him on the neck. The man went ballistic, as if newly charged with adrenaline. He caught Jack by surprise. They rolled on the street a few feet from the bloody body. The man reached for the knife in his friend's back, grabbed the handle, jerking it out. Halfway to Jack with the blade, the man felt cold steel against his temple. When he looked, a sideways glance, he saw a matt-black semiautomatic pistol, its muzzle pressed hard against his temple.

'Enough,' said Jack as he cocked the pistol.

The man's eyes went big, his hand opened, and the knife clattered to the street.

Jack lifted the man to his feet, grabbing him by the collar, and pushed him down the alley.

'Go. Get outta here. Come back and I'll kill you. Muerto.' Jack pointed the pistol so there would be no misunderstanding. Then he kicked the guy in the ass and the man started to run. The other two, the man with the broken arm and his friend, who now needed dental work, had already made it crawling and stumbling to the end of the alley. In less than a minute Jack had filled the street with carnage.

Abby was shaking in the doorway. For a moment, Jack ignored her. Instead he moved to the man lying in the street, placed a finger on the jugular, and searched for a pulse.

'We should call an ambulance,' said Abby.

Jack said nothing for the moment but continued to feel the man's throat. 'He won't be needing one.' He moved away from the body, pulled a handkerchief from his pocket and with it reached down and picked up the knife. 'I don't think I touched it,' he said. 'Still, can't be too careful.' He wiped the handle and the blade with the handkerchief, then stuffed the bloody cloth into the dead man's pocket.

Then he grabbed Abby's hand. 'Let's get out of here before his buddies find some more friends.'

CHAPTER
TWENTY-SIX

'I appreciate your doing this,' said Spencer. 'I know it's not part of your job.' This morning Morgan went to Alvin Cummings's office, a squat single story building out beyond the Lake Union locks near Shilshole on the Sound side of Seattle.

It looked like an insurance office, Venetian blinds with greasy dust on them, and dead flies on the windowsills.

Cummings himself had the looks of an F.B.I. agent, which he had been at one time, before he retired. He had done other things as well for the government, some of which Spencer knew about, and others he could only guess at. His hair was parted in the middle over silver-rimmed glasses, his body lean, flat stomach and butt so that if you saw him at a distance you might not know whether he was coming or going. He was from the old F.B.I., the Hoover days of male WASP agents in gray flannel suits. He still operated with a precision that was quasi-military even if a little worn.

'Listen, it's no trouble,' said Cummings. 'Besides, it didn't take much time. You may be getting exactly what you're paying for.' What Cummings meant was nothing. He had done a freebie for the lawyer who over the years had thrown him a lot of investigative business. Now Spencer had a personal problem and Cummings was eager to help. He handed Morgan a written report, which he'd kicked out of his computer's printer twenty minutes earlier. It contained some information that was confidential, government records that Cummings had acquired from sources better left unidentified. For this reason he did not want to commit the report to a fax, and told Spencer he would have to read it and leave it in the office.

'That's him. South Carolina,' said Spencer.

'Place called Coffin Point. According to the information, old family home,' said Cummings. 'Records show it's been in the family for some generations.'

'Country boy,' said Morgan.

'Except he went to school up north and out west. Degrees from Columbia and Stanford. Then he disappears for awhile, back in the eighties.'

'There oughta be a credit report,' said Spencer.

'Sparse one. Shows income of a few hundred dollars a month. One loan, a car.'

'That's all?'

'Yeah. That's what caused me to look. He was either on welfare during that period or something else.'

'What?'

Cummings handed Spencer another sheet of paper. 'This is confidential. You've never seen it. Understand?'

It was printed on a form with a government department logo and headed 'Department of Defense.'

'His father was deep in the military,' said Cummings. 'Marines. The name Joe Jermaine is synonymous with the Corps. The kid traveled in dad's footsteps. Did a stint as a training officer and then disappeared.'

'Where did he go?'

'Deep cover,' said Cummings. 'Special unit. What they called a "River Rat." He commanded a small boat squadron, riverine vehicles to those in the know. These guys are the first to see action in a conflict. They work with Navy Seals, float up and down rivers in the tules and come ashore at night for reconnaissance. They spot targets for artillery and air sorties, then slither back in the water so you never know what hit you.'

'He did this?'

'Big time,' said Cummings.

'But he's retired now?'

Cummings shrugged a shoulder. 'If the records are to be believed.'

'What do you mean?'

'Shadowy rumors,' said Cummings. 'There was trouble, back a few years.' Cummings settled his butt onto the corner of his desk and talked while Morgan listened.

'Seems your guy Jermaine is the kind who dances to the tune of a different drummer. There had been some scrapes with higher authority along the way, some ruffled feathers, and then trouble.'

'What kind of trouble?' said Morgan.

'One of the men in his squad died under questionable circumstances. There had been bad blood between the deceased and your guy. No charges were brought, but it seems to have put a crimp in his career. Jermaine was passed over for promotion. It was in a period of downsizing in the military and it was either up or out. He was forced into retirement. That's what the papers show,' said Cummings.

'But?'

The P.I. rolled his eyes and made a face that could only be described as a question mark. 'Here's where it gets hazy. There's nothing in writing, nothing anyone would send me, but there's some icy rumors, that he's done some private contracts.'

'What do you mean contracts?'

'I mean hired work for private parties, foreign governments. That from time to time he hires himself out.'

'To do what?'

'Whatever they're paying for. You gotta understand, this guy is heavily trained.'

'No specifics on these jobs?' asked Morgan. He needed something concrete to take to Abby or she would never believe him.

'No specifics. It's the kind of stuff you don't put on a résumé.'

'What about the passport?' said Morgan.

'It's an unusual name,' said Cummings. 'I checked. Passport office has no record of one issued in the name of Kellen Raid.'

'So he made it himself,' said Morgan.

'Or had it done by somebody else,' said Cummings.

'Any record of whether it might have been used to enter or leave the country?'

Cummings shook his head. 'But it's the kind of thing you would do if you had a job outside the country and you didn't want your own government to know you were there.'

Morgan thought for a long time, quietly in the chair, looking off into space.

Cummings got up and headed for the coffee pot, poured himself a cup. 'How about you?'

Morgan shook his head.

'I haven't asked you why you're so interested in this guy,' said Cummings. 'It's none of my business, I suppose.'

Spencer offered him nothing by way of reply. He

wasn't about to tell Cummings about the book and Abby, or Jack Jermaine's part in all of it. Cummings was a P.I. with a good sense of direction. He could keep a secret. Still there was no need to tell him, and Spencer had no intention of doing so.

'Are you thinking that this guy has something to do with the *Cella Largo*?' asked Cummings.

Morgan looked at him, somewhat surprised. The thought had never entered his mind.

'It is his line of work,' said Cummings. 'The kind of thing he would hire out for.'

'I suppose,' said Morgan.

'You sound almost disappointed.'

'No,' said Morgan.

'Do you know this guy?'

'We've met.'

'I understand,' said Cummings. 'You sound like you like him.'

Cummings didn't understand at all.

'It's not that. Just keep it under your hat for awhile. I'll let you know if I need anything more.'

'Sure.'

Morgan got up, grabbed his briefcase, and handed the report back to Cummings.

'What do you want me to do with this?' asked the P.I.

Morgan thought for a moment. 'Hang onto it.'

Cummings nodded. 'Take care,' he said. 'Be careful.'

'I will.'

'Jesus. They could have killed us. There were five of them. Did you count? Did you bother to count? I didn't know what to do. I couldn't think what to use as a weapon. We should go to the police.' Abby was yammering in shock, breathless by the time they reached the sanctuary of Ricardi's yacht.

They got to the cabin and closed the door behind them. Jack took her and held her for a moment while she hyperventilated.

'You're alright. Relax. Take a deep breath. Good. Again.'

'Shouldn't we go to the police?'

'Quit talking and breathe. We would spend the next week answering questions through an interpreter,' said Jack. They were in the master cabin below decks, all teak and mahogany, with a crew to man the boat and an Asian cabin boy.

Jack sat her on the bed and then poured a glass of whisky from the bar while he changed his shirt, which had been ripped in two places and had someone else's blood all over the front of it. Abby was too shaken for alcohol, but Jack insisted. He poured her a shot of brandy and she sipped it.

The crew had just cast off and the yacht made its way slowly down the channel toward the open sea. Their problems, the dead body in the alley, were now behind them.

'Besides,' said Jack. 'If we went to the police, they would want to know about this.' He flipped the semiautomatic pistol from his fanny pack onto the bed, where it bounced twice on the mattress and came to rest.

'They're not the only ones with questions about that,' said Abby. 'I can't believe you carried that through airport security.'

'I didn't,' said Jack.

The way he said it, Abby thought maybe he'd planted it on her. 'Was that in *my* luggage?'

'I had it delivered. I wanted to see if it would work. It did.'

'What are you talking about?'

'If you needed a gun. Just suppose,' said Jack. 'And you had to travel by commercial means. How would you do it?'

'It's not something I stay up nights thinking about,' said Abby. 'Most normal people don't.'

'Most normal people don't write the kind of material I do. If it isn't authentic, if it doesn't work, I don't put it in my books,' he told her.

'Yeah, well, we know how successful that's been.'

'So I thought about it.' He ignored her. 'Do you have any idea how many packages are processed daily by private express delivery companies in the States?'

She shook her head.

'Millions,' said Jack. 'Do you know how long it would take for them to X-ray the contents of every one of those packages?'

'Tell me.'

'I don't know. But I'm guessing it would take more than sixteen hours. And that's the average time they have to deliver an overnight package to most places in the Western Hemisphere.'

'So?'

Jack picked the gun up off the bed. 'So when it absolutely, positively has to be there the next day,' said Jack.

She looked at him dumbstruck. 'You didn't.'

Jack smiled and nodded his head, a proud beaming grin like some college jock who had just pulled off a panty raid. 'I dropped it off when we left my house, remember. The piece was at Henry's before we arrived in San Juan. It traveled through the night. We didn't.'

Abby thought about it for a moment, all the boxes coming and going from Coffin Point. 'And the one that was waiting for you when we got to your house?' said Abby.

'That was the return from Seattle.'

'You had the gun with you out there?'

'I try not to travel without it,' said Jack.

'In Chicago?'

'Especially in Chicago. That's a dangerous city,' said Jack. 'We were there on business.'

'That's what I mean. You're out of your mind.'

'I just believe in thorough research,' he told her. 'Now I know. The express companies don't X-ray their packages.'

'There are other ways of doing research.'

'If I'd called and asked them the question, do you think they would have told me the truth? Not on your life. They would have hemmed and hawed and ultimately they would have lied. They don't want to know what's inside all those packages. But they're not about to tell the public that.'

Abby wasn't sure if he was crazy or merely possessed an eccentric sense of humor. It seemed the longer she stayed around Jack, the more impaired was her judgment. There was a kind of ether that surrounded him. Whether it was his looks or his childlike charm, Abby was losing her critical perspective.

He swept a hand through his dark hair that was now tousled from their street fight and examined his body in the mirror. 'Think about it,' said Jack. 'If you were accepting several million sealed containers from the great unwashed masses and giving them to your employees to deliver all over the world, would you *really* want to know what's inside each one of them?'

'I never thought about it.' Abby studied him.

'I wouldn't. I'd figure ignorance was bliss.'

'What about Customs?' said Abby.

'Ah.' Jack turned toward her with his index finger pointed up like she had stumbled on a subtlety. 'Now that's the interesting part. I figured to be safe I would only send to locations where there's sufficient traffic to keep things humming. Good-sized cities with a lot of parcels coming in. And you always send it priority. Overnight express. That way the delivery companies are pushing Customs to rush things.'

Abby looked at him mystified. In his own inimitable fashion Jack had carefully thought it all through. And he was proud of himself, she thought, like a school boy who had just farted in class. Only in this case he had probably violated a dozen federal laws.

'They probably sniff for drugs,' he told her. 'And X-ray a handful of the packages. Random selection,' said Jack. 'So what are the chances?'

'You took a risk,' said Abby.

'Life's full of risks. You cross the street . . .'

'I know,' said Abby. 'You can get hit by a car.'

'I was gonna say you might get mugged.' He lifted one arm and looked at the back side under his elbow.

'That looks bad.' Abby observed a cut on the underside of his arm. It seemed that not all of the blood on his shirt belonged to other people. 'Let me see what I can find.'

She went into the head, more of a master bathroom, paneled wood and beveled mirrors with gold fixtures. There was a full-sized Roman tub on a platform behind saloon-type swinging doors.

She rummaged through some drawers until she found a roll of gauze and some tape. She grabbed a washcloth and wet it. By the time she came out Jack was bare to the waist, rippled abs and tanned. He was now

345

dressed only in his running shorts and was checking an abrasion on his knee.

It was a hard body, rugged with a few scars on it. Abby remembered how it pressed up against her own that morning when they shot at targets near the marsh at Coffin Point. His touch that day lingered with her, hard body and soft hands and the deep whisper of his voice up close in her ear. Jack's tones carried just a hint of slow Southern drawl almost imperceptible unless you listened closely. It was an exotic cadence.

She remembered how his fingers closed around her own as she held the pistol. Jack steadying her. There was something about him. For all of the bluster and cynicism, there was an edge of softness under it all, a sort of school-boy charm. It was in the twinkle of his eye, and the angle of his head when he smiled, and the flashing white of his teeth against the bronze tan.

While she was attracted, Abby was scared. Of what she wasn't quite sure. To this point, Jack had been every inch the gentleman. He had never hit on her. In this moment, as they looked at one another, it was as if he was waiting for her to give him some signal, to say 'yes.'

Abby started to clean the wound on his arm. In a flash, the moment passed.

'Since we're sharing such intimacies, when are you going to tell me about the outline for the sequel?' said Jack.

'When it's time.'

'When will that be?'

'When I decide.'

'How far along is it?'

'It's coming.'

'When will it be finished?'

'When it's done.' Abby looked at him, a kind of

motherly expression of exasperation.

'It's what I like about you,' said Jack. 'Your candor and openness.'

'Then why do you ask?'

'Because we both know they're gonna press me on it.'

'Who?'

'Carla and Bertoli. When I get to New York. They're gonna want to know how it's coming.'

'They don't own the rights.'

'They have an option.'

'Tell 'em it's going well,' said Abby.

'They may want a little more than that.'

'Tell them it's going very well.' She smiled and Jack laughed.

'I'm sure Carla will accept that.'

'Take my word. The sequel is not a subject you want to get into,' said Abby.

'Why not?'

'For the same reason delivery companies don't look inside their packages.' She offered a sly grin. 'I'm sure you can hold them off. Besides, if we were to tell them anything, they'd only want to know more. Then they'd insist on plotting the story probably over dinner. By the time you finish dessert, they'll change the title three times, invent four new characters, and suggest that you include a dinner fork in the plot because they already have a nice drawing of one for the cover art. And when they're finished they'll claim they have proprietary rights on the book because they've contributed to it.'

'Whatever you want. It's your story,' said Jack.

'Don't tell them that.'

'I forgot. It's my story.'

'And that's exactly what you should tell them. And nothing more.'

Owens and Bertoli weren't the only ones Abby didn't trust. The less Jack knew about the sequel, the better. It was one of those pressure points of control she could use if he became difficult.

'So what do you suggest for small talk?' said Jack.

'Tell them you knifed a guy in an alley in San Juan. That should get things going.'

'It was an accident.'

'Right,' said Abby. 'This Puerto Rican just fell on his own sword. Bertoli should understand that, the corporate jungle being what it is.'

'Ow.' Jack flinched and pulled his arm away. 'What are you doing?'

'Cleaning the wound.'

'Yeah, but you're enjoying yourself a little too much,' said Jack. As he said it, he lifted his forearm to check the wound. As he did, he peeked at her from underneath, their faces less than a foot apart.

Abby's was a smile. 'If you don't like it, you should stay out of street fights.'

'Like I had a choice.' His words were slow as their eyes met.

'You could have given them what they wanted,' said Abby.

'As I recall they wanted you.'

There was something in her look at this moment that told Jack it had suddenly dawned on Abby. He had saved her life.

'I suppose I should thank you.' His gaze was on her lips, moist and parted as she uttered the words. Their thoughts converged like psychic energy, the snap of electricity spanning the distance.

'It was nothing. Besides, they wanted my watch.' Their eyes locked. Somewhere in the ionized atmosphere

Abby's eyes said yes. Their lips met.

He settled back onto the bed and tugged her by the arms down on top of him. The running shorts rode high on his thigh, exposing flesh and a tan line.

Her head went on his chest to the side, her eyes cast down. 'They got you there, too,' She said. She touched him on the thigh, a wound high on the outside.

His fingers covered hers, tugging, pulling her hand to the center of his body, to his stomach that quivered with the touch of her fingernails, to the band of his shorts.

'That's an old one,' said Jack. He shifted, lifted his knee until it wedged between her thighs, lifting her at the vortex. With his hand he tilted her chin until their lips met, gently nibbling.

'Old one,' Abby repeated his words in an erotic daze.

'Hmm. Diving accident.' Teeth closing gently on her lips, his tongue touched the tip of her own, his words the last intelligible sound as they descended into sensuous seas, the gentle motion of the ship, silk sheets, and satin comforters.

CHAPTER
TWENTY-SEVEN

He checked a local bookstore first, where he cruised through *Books in Print* on their computer. It listed nearly every book written in the last five years, cross-referenced by title as well as author. Morgan had the clerk look under two different names; Jack Jermaine, and Kellen Raid, the name Abby had found on Jack's passport. There was nothing.

Morgan was worried. He was in love with Abby and she didn't seem to notice. Now she was off to the ends of the earth with a man she didn't know, a man who, if Alvin Cummings was to be believed, spent his time in the military, slithering out of rivers like a snake to kill people.

Morgan trekked to the county library next. He could be dogged when something bothered him, and this did. It was nothing but a hunch, one of those nagging points that pick at the subconscious in your sleep.

Ever since Abby had told him about Jack's passport in the name of Kellen Raid, it had been turning over in Morgan's mind. Jack's seemingly boundless desire to be published, almost compulsive, and the way he'd inflicted himself on Abby caused Morgan to wonder;

had he used the name for something else?

In the library, Spencer located a volume that defined the origin and meaning of names. The name 'Kellen' was Gaelic. It meant warrior. Raid was only a guess on Spencer's part. But together the first and last name looked suspiciously like an action-oriented pen name, something an author might use who fancied himself a writer of military fiction.

He tried the library's computer catalog next, and struck out. There was nothing under either name. But the librarian pointed him in one last direction. Public lending libraries, even large ones, didn't possess copies of every book printed, especially when it came to popular fiction. Except for the classics there was a short shelf life.

He went back to his office and called the phone number the librarian had given him. Several days passed before they called back. It had taken that long, but they found something. Morgan wasn't sure exactly what it was. But it was enough to cause him to skip lunch and hoof it eight blocks through the noonday traffic.

The shop was small, squeezed in between a café on the corner, and an art studio. It specialized mostly in collector's items, rare editions, and other obscure works. What they didn't have on their shelves they could locate. The store belonged to a national network of used book shops. If a customer wanted something, he could place an order and put out the word. It might take a week, or a month, or a year, but if it existed, sooner or later they would find it.

It was a long shot, but Morgan was a gambler at heart. He knew that while the odds of finding anything might be slim, the payoff, if he did, could be huge. It was the kind of thing you prayed for in the closing days of a trial, that last-minute piece of evidence that showed your opponent was a convicted child molester. It was the kind of dirt you could shovel in front of a jury to tilt the entire case. Only in this case Abby was the jury.

Morgan was worried. For a hard-bitten lawyer, somebody on the jaded side when it came to publishing, Abby had become far too trusting of Jack. To Spencer it was beginning to look as if Jermaine had cast a spell over her. There was something about the man that Spencer didn't like. Maybe it was his good looks, or his quick tongue, a little too quick for Morgan. As far as he was concerned, Jack was the wrong kind of man for Abby. When Spencer's antenna was up, it was unfailing. At the moment he didn't like the signal he was getting. Several times in their telephone conversations Abby had let slip that she was talking to Jack about her work. Increasingly she was turning to Jermaine. Sooner or later she would take him into her confidence. To Morgan that spelled trouble. He should never have allowed her to go off to the islands, especially with Jack.

He breezed through the door of the small shop, setting chimes ringing over his head, shades of Dickens. The place was musty, and crammed with crude wooden bookcases to the ceiling, and as far as Morgan could see to the back of the building. There were narrow dark aisles and an old wooden ladder against one wall for reaching books on the upper shelves.

A young man sat on a stool behind the counter. He didn't look up when Spencer entered but continued pricing a stack of books with a pencil on the inside covers. The kid's hair was dyed a shade of chartreuse and shaved on the sides, the kind of stuff that you saw all over town these days. He wore the single obligatory earring, like a medal of defiance. Spencer wondered why anyone would hire somebody who looked like this.

'Can I help you?' The kid was polite and businesslike, but Morgan had a hard time seeing past the appearance.

'My name's Morgan Spencer. You're holding a book for me.'

The clerk spun around on his stool and thumbed through a stack behind him against the wall. 'Did they call you?'

'This morning,' said Morgan.

'Spencer. Spencer. Ah. Here it is.'

The clerk plucked the volume from the shelf. The title was printed in gold letters on the cloth spine. *Shadow War*. The clerk opened the cover and looked for the price in pencil on the inside. He punched a few numbers into a calculator on the counter next to him.

'With shipping that comes to nineteen dollars.' That didn't include the search fee that Morgan had already paid on a credit card over the phone.

'Can I look first?'

'Sure.'

Morgan checked the copyright for the date of publication. The book had been published nine years earlier by one of the large publishing houses in New York. This alone caused Spencer to suspect that he was barking up a wrong tree. If Jack was as talentless as Abby had said over the phone, how could he ever get published, let alone by a major publisher? Still, nine years. That was enough time for the book to have been forgotten in the perpetual tidal surge of fiction.

'There's no paper cover,' said Morgan.

'The dust jacket,' said the clerk. 'Probably came in without one. We get a lot of them like that. Jackets get tattered over the years, people toss 'em out.'

'Is there any way I could get one? The dust jacket?'

The clerk gave a big sigh, and checked a card catalog behind the counter. 'It's the only copy we found. If you want, I can take it back and try again.'

'No. No.'

Morgan's interest in the dustcover had nothing to do with the book's value. It was purely informational. The dustcover was where the author's picture would be if there was one, along with any biographical note. Without it, all he had was a title, and a name, the author's name: Kellen Raid.

'Have you ever heard of this guy before?' said Morgan.

The clerk shook his head.

'So there's no way for me to find out if he's ever published anything else?'

'If he'd published anything before this they would usually list those titles in the front of the book, right after the title page.' The clerk looked. There was nothing.

'Do you know where I could get a biography, anything at all on the author?'

'There are some literary source books. But I can tell you, he's not going to be there.'

'Why not?'

'They mostly cover classics and maybe some commercial authors,' said the clerk.

Morgan was up against the proverbial rock. It was a unique name. Still, it left Jack enough wiggle room. He could claim it was a coincidence. Maybe Jermaine had read the book and liked it. He could have used the author's name on the passport for that reason. He might even say it was subconscious. Morgan was a cynic. He was sure he had something. But Abby wasn't likely to buy it unless he had proof. She would want to give Jack the benefit of the doubt. Innocent until proven guilty.

'Would the publisher have anything on him?'

'You could try.'

Morgan feathered the pages of the novel. There were more than five hundred. He felt the cloth cover with his fingers and wondered if Jack was capable of writing such a thing.

'Can I have a minute?'

'Take your time.' The clerk turned to other duties. He rolled a cart out from behind the counter to an area a few feet away, climbed a foot stool, and began stacking some new arrivals.

Morgan opened the book and began to read. The writing was O.K., a little clunky in places, but the book opened with a gripper, an action sequence set deep in the jungle, according to a headnote somewhere in Southeast Asia. He read the prologue, eight pages. The story had a good hook, but Morgan was looking for something else. When he finished he was no closer to proving the identity of the author.

He turned back to the title page, flipped to the next page. There was a lot of small print, the name of the publishing company and its address. This was followed by a disclaimer that the characters in the story were all fictional. There was something about the Library of Congress. And after that was the author's name, Kellen Raid, and the designation of copyright in that name. Underneath, at the bottom of the page, were a line of numbers, what looked like three through ten, but printed in a peculiar order, odd numbers to the left, even to the right, with the number ten in the middle.

'Do you know what this is?' said Spencer.

The clerk turned to him from the stool and then down for a closer look.

Morgan pointed to the numbers at the bottom of the page.

'That's the press count. It tells you how many times the publisher went back to press for further editions. This is not a first edition.' If there had been any doubt, the clerk now knew that Spencer was no book collector.

'If it were a first edition, the number one would appear there on the left-hand side,' said the clerk. He checked the numbers. 'This is the third edition. There were two earlier printings. That's why the numbers one and two are missing.'

'What does that mean?'

'What it says,' said the clerk. 'It affects the value of the book as far as collectors are concerned. First editions are usually worth more.'

'Is it unusual that a book would go back to press that many times?'

The kid gave him an expression like he wasn't sure. 'Most books probably only get one printing. They get a small initial run. Unless there's demand for the book, that's it.'

'So this book would have been in demand?'

'Enough for three runs.'

'Could it have been a big book?' said Spencer. 'Commercially successful?'

'Depends what you mean by big. If it had been huge, I think I would have remembered the author. If somebody writes one that hot, they usually do another. Law of the marketplace,' said the clerk.

'But it could have been successful?'

'Possibly. It would depend on the size of the press runs. There's no way to tell that from the information here.'

Again Morgan had nothing to show for his efforts. He

offered the clerk a deep sigh and reached for his wallet. He paid with a credit card, and while the clerk was processing the slip, Morgan continued to scan the page, over to the other side, to the acknowledgments. There were only five paragraphs. Morgan didn't find what he was looking for until he got to the last one. There, buried in a single line, was what he'd been looking for all along.

> '*Mostly I thank my father, Joseph Jermaine, for an inquisitive mind and the questions that inspired this story.*'

St Croix rests on a shallow shelf at the edge of the Atlantic Ocean. It is separated from its sisters of the Virgin Islands, St John and St Martin, by a rift in the ocean's floor more than four miles deep, a canyon known as the Puerto Rican Trench. The chasm divides a chain of islands that define the outer edge of the Caribbean Sea.

But for Abby it was as if somehow a barrier had been bridged. Their time on the ship, the embrace of his arms, the sharing of intimacy, brought her to know Jack in ways she never thought she would. The combination of power and gentleness that was Jack overwhelmed her. For the first time in her life she felt safe. They made love and they talked about things they had not discussed before: Jack's time in the military, his relationship with his father. He wanted to know about her marriage. There was a time when she actually thought she loved Charlie. But now Abby was certain that she had never really fallen in love. She had just stepped in it.

For the first time since Theresa's death, Abby opened up with another human being. In bed, Jack was tender and warm, as warm as the afternoon sun that cascaded down upon them as they stepped off onto the dock at King's Wharf in Christiansted.

Jack had ditched the shorts and fanny pack, in favour of a pair of pleated khaki pants that draped his long legs, and a safari vest with a million pockets. Abby wondered if one of them held the semiautomatic pistol. She was still uncomfortable about this, traveling with a man who thought nothing of being armed.

Up on the docks the first thing that caught Abby's eye was the bright yellow walls of the little Dutch Colonial fort, and the villagelike atmosphere of the town. She heard people on the docks, visitors speaking French and German.

Jack had told her that tourists from Europe spilled over from the British Virgin Islands to the American side for a day of shopping and sightseeing. The place reminded Abby of some exotic port of call, Java in the last century. The calm water of the little harbor was azure blue illuminated by the white sand on its bottom. There was a small island a quarter-mile off the docks, with what looked like a hotel perched over its sandy beach: Protestant Cay.

'We'll have to clear Customs,' said Jack. 'Shouldn't be a problem.' The captain of Enrique's yacht had greased it for them on the ship-to-shore radio coming in. A Customs agent met them at the dock, asked two or three questions while their luggage remained on board unopened. He stamped their passports and left. Being friends with the largest rum dealer in the world had its advantages.

Jack hailed a taxi and they headed out of town, east past Gallows Bay along what was called the East End Road. The taxi driver drove on the left, British style.

They passed lush fields and old stone towers. The island was dotted with the remnants of ancient windmills, their wind-catching apparatus snatched by hurricanes whose names had long since been forgotten. They passed ruins of eighteenth-century sugar plantations where the windmills had been used to crush cane, and drove through a rain squall that seemed to be the width of a cloud so that the hood of the car was awash in water and the trunk was bone-dry.

It was a short drive, less than ten minutes, when they pulled between a pair of pink and white pillars and onto a private drive. It wound a half a mile off the highway, past tamarind trees, some of which Jack told her were more than a hundred and fifty years old. They came to a stop at an old stone building, two stories, with a guard and barrier gate.

'Another of your friend's estates?' said Abby.

'A resort,' said Jack. 'You should get to know it. It's close to where you'll be. We'll just spend the night. We can get groceries in the morning and you can move into the house. It's just down the road, off the grounds.'

In locating the house Jack had thought of everything. 'The resort has a good bar and a restaurant,' he told her. 'A well-stocked wine cellar, all the comforts of home. If you don't want to cook, you can just come over here. It's a little walk, but not that far.'

The resort was gorgeous and private. On the land side were acres of manicured grass, a golf course. The buildings were all flamingo pink and old mortared stone. Most of them looked like they were at least three hundred years old. The place had once been a sugar plantation. The main building of the hotel sat on a promontory overlooking a deep bay of Caribbean blue water.

The taxi pulled up to the entrance and an attendant

got their luggage. Jack headed for the front desk just beyond a pink-and-white-covered portico. Over the entrance was a sign, black letters on old marble:

1653 THE 1947
BUCCANEER

Abby stayed with the luggage. She had no intention of losing her little computer. The outline to the sequel, now nearly completed, was in it. This was becoming an increasingly important document. With the first book presumably worth millions, the outline to the second was like gold, and Abby treated it like a state secret for good reason. She kept one paper copy and a backup on a disc. The notebook computer was quickly becoming her lifeline if she was going to finish the next book on time.

By the time she caught up with Jack at the desk he had a message for her from the clerk.

'Seems your friend Spencer's caught up with us.'

'How?'

'I told him to leave any messages here before we left,' said Jack. 'He's sent you a gift.'

'What is it?'

'It's out in the parking lot, right in front of the building.' Before Jack could speak, the woman behind the counter answered the question with a broad smile. She was convinced they had some luminary staying with them. Gifts like this were unusual.

Abby looked at Jack quizzically.

'Don't ask me.' He shrugged.

She stepped outside to the end of the walkway. There at the curb was a sporty little convertible, a Z-3, with its top down, parked in the shade.

Abby went back inside. 'Did he rent it?'

'Seems he bought it,' said Jack, 'with your money.' He dangled the keys from their ring on his little finger while he read a note from an envelope and then passed them to Abby.

'Greetings from the Home Front.

Knew you were going to need wheels so had this shipped from a dealer in Miami. Don't get mad. You can afford it. Besides, you need to celebrate. Trust me.

Morgan.'

Abby wasn't just angry, she was steaming. It was an act of extravagance, something that brought attention to her on the island, the precise thing that she didn't want. The woman behind the counter was smiling at her. She knew the car had to cost at least thirty thousand dollars. Now it marked her as a rich tourist, making it that much more difficult for her to blend in with the locals. Morgan had no right. He had overstepped the bounds of friendship.

Inside the envelope was another smaller one, this one very stiff and sealed. She opened it. There were two small plastic cards inside with the name of a bank in French, and another note. They were debit cards on a bank in Martinique, two separate accounts, a place where Abby could now draw funds without being found. He would give her the PIN numbers over the phone.

It was like Spencer. With one hand he infuriated you, and with the other he saved your bacon.

Abby and Jack checked into separate rooms in a part of the resort down on the water. The place was dated, just enough to be comfortable, blue tile floors in some kind of Dutch print with a king-sized bed and a large bath. Each room had a private patio overlooking the water. The beach was off to the right a hundred yards away, where it formed an arc and disappeared into a cove.

'Give me your passport and any credit cards you're not gonna use regularly,' said Jack. 'Got any jewelry?'

'What is this, a robbery?'

'Henry told me there's no safe at the house. You have to be careful down here. A U.S. passport is worth a lot of money.'

Abby looked at him wondering whether she should. Then she handed over her passport and one of the debit cards.

'Come in here and I'll show you.' He led the way. 'We'll use the one in my room since I'm gonna keep the room.' They went into the closet in his room through the adjoining door. Inside on a wooden platform was an electronic ElSafe, the size of a large microwave oven.

'What's your birthday?'

'You don't know me well enough for that,' said Abby.

'Lie,' said Jack.

She gave him six digits that would have made her thirty-four. Jack punched them into the electronic combination and removed a metal pin from the inside of the door. 'Now it's set. Unless somebody puts the pin back in and changes it, that's the combination that will open it everytime.'

He closed the door and pushed the lock button. The steel door hummed and sealed itself tight. He punched in the combination. It hummed again and opened. Jack put Abby's passport and one of the debit cards into the safe, closed the door, and pushed the lock button.

'You can put your outline in there, the manuscript, whatever you want. Feel free to use it.' Jack helped her with her luggage, then told her they could get lunch at the bungalow out near the beach.

She looked at her watch. 'I have a phone call to make first. Give me fifteen minutes.'

Jack smiled. He knew she was going to call Spencer and chew his ass. Abby wore her anger on her sleeve, and at the moment she was still steaming over the little car.

'It's beautiful,' said Jack. 'Wish I had a friend like that. You should thank him.' He wanted to stay and listen.

'See you in a few minutes,' said Abby.

'Can I take it for a spin?'

Abby gave him a look that pointed to the door.

'Just kidding.' He left and closed the door behind him.

It was nearly noon. Four hours difference. It was not yet eight o'clock out on the coast. If she was quick, she could catch Morgan before he left for the office.

She tried to dial direct, but it didn't work. The phone system on the island was primitive. She had to go through the hotel operator, who in turn connected her to a long-distance operator who placed the call. The phone line kept crackling. Water in some of the underground lines on the island from the last hurricane according to the operator. Abby listened as the phone rang on the other end, a lot of static. She was hoping she wouldn't lose him.

'Hello.'

She heard Morgan's familiar voice.

'What in the world do you think you're doing?'

'Abby.' Spencer's voice was elevated, almost euphoric. 'It sounds like you're in a tunnel. Where are you?'

'St Croix. I didn't order a car, Morgan. What are you thinking?'

'I know. But I thought you could use it. Besides, I got a sweet deal. Don't be mad at me. Please.'

The pleading tone of his voice and the familiarity of it from thousands of miles away instantly cut her anger by half. It was the thing about Abby. She would flash fury, but she could never stay mad for long, especially with those she liked. The phone crackled again.

'Are you there?' he said.

'I'm here. Everybody in the place knows my name,' she told him. 'The woman with the flashy little car.'

'Have you driven it?'

'Not yet.'

'They're a kick in the ass,' said Spencer. 'I tried one at a dealership here in town before I ordered yours. Stop on a dime, turn on a nickel,' said Spencer.

She could see him, his mane of graying hair streaming in the wind. It was the kind of thing that Morgan lived for, the staid attorney acting like a child.

'You shouldn't have done it.'

'You have to learn to enjoy your success,' he told her. 'I knew it was something you would never do for yourself.'

He was right and Abby knew it. She could never slow down enough to enjoy what she'd achieved in life, whether it was graduating from law school or authoring a novel. She was always too busy working, trying to find the seam of opportunity or to make one; moving on. And now she had managed to cut herself off from any public acclamation on her own book, by putting Jack and his picture up front. She was beginning to wonder if she would be able to reclaim her property. Maybe Jack was right. Maybe the public would never accept her.

'Do you want me to see if they'll take it back?' Spencer was talking about the car.

It would be a graceless thing to do. Besides, the dealer would never take it back and the damage was already done. It wasn't the money. It was the fact that Spencer was asserting control that angered Abby.

'No. I should thank you. But I want you to promise that you won't do anything like this ever again.'

'I promise.'

'Do I have your word?'

'Hope to die,' said Spencer.

She didn't want to humiliate him.

'Then you're not mad at me any longer?'

'I'm not mad at you.'

There was a deep sigh on the other end.

'Then let me give you the good news. First, the car is a business expense, at least part of it is. Think of it as a gift from the tax man,' said Morgan. 'And you're going to need more of them.'

'What? Cars?

'Business expenses,' said Morgan. 'You better start thinking about setting the next book someplace expensive. Maybe in the South of France, a private villa.'

'Why?'

'Because I'm going to be depositing a lot more money than we thought into the account. Hold your breath,' said Morgan. 'Nearly' – there was a crackle on the line – 'million dollars.'

'Say again?'

'I said three million dollars.'

'We weren't supposed to see that kind of money for almost a year.'

'I know,' said Spencer, 'but the foreign sales are way beyond Carla's original estimate. She says it's the dynamic of the film sale. She didn't have the numbers when you guys met at the convention. There's a feeding frenzy going on in Europe over the book. And she wants to talk to Jack, to give him the good news. You know, agent to author,' said Morgan. 'She's been bugging me for days trying to figure out where you guys went. You'd better prep him. Tell him to act surprised and to kiss her ass when she calls. She'll figure she deserves it.'

Three million dollars. Abby's knees folded like a tent with the news. She sank onto the edge of the bed. She had no idea what to do with that kind of money, how to spend it or invest it. She wasn't sure she wanted to know. She was sure of one thing. It would change her life, perhaps in ways she didn't like.

'What do I do?'

'What do you mean?'

'With all that money,' said Abby.

Morgan told her not to worry. He had it parked in a safe place, growing interest. 'I wish I had that kind of problem,' he told her. 'Cutler and his pals are circling like vultures at the firm. They want my blood. Everyday it's a new move. Always watching my backside, and it's more difficult now that you're gone.'

'If we keep doing this, you won't have to worry about it. You can quit and go to work for me, full time,' said Abby.

It was what Morgan wanted to hear; that he was back in her good graces.

'Did you get the bank card?' he asked.

'Yes.'

He gave her the PIN number and she wrote it down. 'You don't have to worry. There's plenty in the account, and the authorities won't be able to trace you when you use it. They might look in the Caymans, but Martinique, I don't think so. It's a little too far. Besides, it's French and you know the French,' said Morgan. 'They are notoriously difficult to deal with. If the cops go poking around, they'll find themselves in diplomatic hell.'

'Good,' said Abby. 'That should give us the time we need.' In a way Abby wanted to talk to Sanfillipo, to find out what was happening in Theresa's murder. But she knew that if she did, she would be trapped in Seattle, facing questions not only from the detective but from the press. And it wasn't just Thompson anymore. As buzz around the book grew, others were circling, trying to track down Jack and anybody who knew him.

'There's one more thing,' said Morgan. The phone began to break up again.

'I can't hear you,' said Abby.

'Be careful with Jermaine. Don't trust him Abby.' Morgan was shouting into the phone to make himself heard. It was a terrible connection, like talking through a tube underwater. 'Is he there with you right now?'

'No.'

'We have to talk, but not on the phone. I'm taking a few days and coming down there.'

'Why?' More crackling on the line. Abby sensed that she was about to lose the connection.

'I have a briefcase full of foreign contracts to be signed by his majesty,' said Spencer. 'And something else we need to talk about. Very important.'

'Tell me now.'

'I can't. Not over the phone. I'll try to clear my calendar and come down there.' He didn't know how he was going to do it with Cutler on his back, but somehow he would have to figure a way.

'Tell me now,' said Abby.

'Not on the phone.' He didn't know if she'd heard him or not. The line had gone dead. It was just as good. Spencer was a firm believer. Bad news, especially when it was this good, had to be delivered in person.

CHAPTER
TWENTY-EIGHT

Luther hadn't had a break in the case of Theresa and Joey Jenrico in nearly a month. Sanfillipo had to wait in line in the D.A.'s office along with other law enforcement agencies waiting for them to process warrants and subpoenas. It always took longer for the cops than for those with private lawyers. In this case, the wait took its toll. After getting a subpoena, he ran into a stone wall tracing the financial records of Abby Chandlis. After some banking sleight of hand, she'd disappeared. Luther found evidence of large sums deposited into a bank account, but the account was closed.

The lawyer Spencer was uncooperative. He now claimed an attorney-client privilege with Abby Chandlis and refused to answer more questions, challenging the cops to arrest her if they had grounds. To Luther, lawyers were all assholes. They weren't interested in the truth. That wasn't their job. For the time being, he lacked sufficient evidence to bring charges against Chandlis, and Spencer knew it. Even so, Luther was sure that she was either involved in the murders or knew much more than she was saying.

In the weeks of picking through the evidence, forensics

did come up with one piece of information that Luther found intriguing. After finding his body in the lake, authorities sealed Joey Jenrico's apartment for a period of time and combed it for whatever they could find. What they found was a mess. Mr Jenrico was a disgraceful housekeeper. Among other things, they found a lot of fingerprints. It seemed he never dusted.

The police were still running down leads that the prints provided, a veritable who's-who from local topless joints and roadside bars. Joey had a penchant for picking up things late at night, mostly strippers, and if the coroner was to be believed, an early case of herpes simplex B. Whoever killed him did the public health department a favor.

In some cases, forensics was unable to match the prints they found in the apartment with known samples on record. One such set came from Joey's refrigerator door. The state's biggest bank of prints, motor vehicle as well as their department of justice, turned up nothing. But there was something else in the prints that caught the technician's attention. These prints were particularly well formed due to an oily substance left on the enamel of the door. This was not your ordinary set of greasy fingerprints. After lifting them from the door, technicians took trace evidence and had it analyzed. This particular brand was a light machine oil, and not just any kind. It was manufactured by a company known as Hopps. It was gun oil, the type used to lubricate light arms.

Luther suddenly took a keen interest in the unidentified prints. He had them sent to the F.B.I., something local authorities didn't always do. It was expensive and time consuming. But this time it paid off. The prints belonged to one Jack Jermaine and were on record with the military. Luther had to wonder what a man who lived in South Carolina was doing with his fingerprints on Joey Jenrico's refrigerator door in Seattle.

What was even more interesting to Luther was that Jermaine's name showed up on bank records as having endorsed two large checks over to Abby Chandlis before her accounts were closed. Jermaine, it seemed, was the link between Chandlis and Joey Jenrico's death. Maybe she had hired him to do it. The question was why?

Luther considered the possibilities as he pushed the button in the elevator for the ninth floor. It was ten o'clock in the morning, and he was taking a chance that Morgan Spencer would be in his office. Sanfillipo wanted to hit him unannounced. Spencer may have been able to claim an attorney-client relationship with Chandlis, but what about the man Jermaine? Besides, Luther now had what was looking very much like a continuing criminal conspiracy, something that the attorney-client privilege did not embrace. He wanted to see if the lawyer jumped with the mention of Jermaine's name.

The reception area was empty when Luther entered the office. One secretary sat behind a long counter.

'Can I help you?'

'I'm here to see Morgan Spencer.'

'Do you have an appointment?'

'No. But I think he will see me.' Luther fished his badge from a leather case in his coat pocket and flashed it at the secretary.

'Just a moment.' She punched a few numbers on her telephone key pad and spoke with someone in the back of the office.

'Your name?' she asked Luther.

'Lieutenant Sanfillipo.'

A few moments later another secretary came out from the back. 'Lieutenant, if you'll follow me.'

They did a short parade past the rabbit warren of little cubicles to more palatial digs where the partners hung out, offices with views out onto Elliot Bay.

'Mr Spencer's in conference right now, but I'm sure he'll see you when he's finished. Can I get you a cup of coffee?'

'That would be very nice,' said Luther. The woman disappeared and Luther took a seat in one of the two chairs arranged for clients in the small area just outside of Spencer's door. He could hear voices inside, but nothing as distinct as words. It sounded like two men, but he couldn't be sure.

Coffee came and the secretary left him and went to her work station a few feet away. Luther picked up a newspaper from a side table and started to read. The Mariners were on a roll again, maybe headed for the playoffs. Luther scanned the headlines. The voices inside the room were now up a notch. He could now tell it was definitely two men. And things were getting heated. The secretary looked at him to see if he'd noticed, but Luther continued to read the newspaper as if nothing had happened. They were going at it fast and furious behind the closed door. He could now make out words.

'No more time off. Enough is enough.'

'This is business.' Luther recognized the second voice as Spencer's. He didn't know the other one.

'Right. Three days in St Croix is business. Forget it.'

'What is this? I have to ask you for permission to go out of town on business?'

The secretary was now clearly concerned that she had brought a stranger close enough to hear all of this.

'The meeting could last a long while,' she told Luther. 'Are you sure you want to wait? I could have Mr Spencer call you immediately when he is finished.'

'No. No. That's fine. I'll wait,' said Luther. She couldn't have moved Luther with a crane. He went back to listening.

'You're not going. Not on the firm's nickel and not on company time.' It was the other voice in the room. 'And we're not going to cover your court calls while you're gone, either. Look at the calendar,' said the other. 'You've got three appearances on pending cases during that time. Who's supposed to do your work while you're gone? You've been taking nothing but trips and you want to know why the partners are upset. Look at your calendar. You've been out of town four times for a total of more than three weeks in the last four months. That doesn't include vacations.'

'That was business.'

'I didn't see any billable hours.'

'Flat fee,' said Spencer.

'Right.'

'You can assign somebody. One of the junior associates to cover my cases,' said Spencer.

'No. It's not going to happen.' This last must have been intended as the final word because it got much louder as the door opened. Luther glued his eyes to the newspaper that was now held fully open in front of his face so that he assumed the identity of a news rack in the outer office.

'So you want me to tell her that the firm doesn't want her business? Seven figures and growing,' said Spencer.

The other man who was leaving came to an abrupt stop in the doorway. He was now facing Luther but couldn't see him behind the paper. He must have been another lawyer, thought Luther. The only thing that moved him was the sound of money.

The guy turned in the doorway. 'Where did Ms Chandlis come into all of this? And what is she doing in St Croix?' He filled the frame of the door with his back as Luther peeked over the top of the paper. He was doing Luther's work for him. The cop was all ears. Then he walked back into Spencer's office and closed the door.

Luther strained his ears but was unable to pick out anything. Now that it was money, they'd returned to civil discourse, just the mercenary hum of male voices through the solid door. Still Luther had one big piece of the puzzle he didn't have when he'd arrived. He knew where Abby Chandlis was.

Luther got up and folded the newspaper, put it back on the table, and started to go.

'Are you leaving?' said the secretary.

'I think I will come back at a more convenient time,' said Luther.

'Can I show you out?'

'No. No. I know the way.' Luther headed down the corridor. It was not a good time to talk to Spencer. He was hoping that the secretary might even forget to tell the lawyer that Luther was sitting there listening. If he moved quickly he might be able to find Chandlis before she moved on to someplace else. What Sanfillipo wanted was to check with the authorities in St Croix. He would save the information regarding Jermaine for another meeting. For the moment, Luther figured, why reveal anything more than he had to?

In what seemed like no time at all the house on the beach felt like home to Abby. Shoy Beach Road started on the grounds of the Buccaneer and paralleled the ocean for more than a mile where it ended in front of the gates of an estate at a point overlooking the sea.

Abby's house was not nearly as large as the estate at the end of the road. It was a small yellow single-story bungalow about a half mile from the resort.

The house was set back from the road behind a driveway lined with young palm trees. It was surrounded by a sea of Bermuda grass that ran to the sand dunes above the ocean. The beach itself was a tropical dream, deep and crescent-shaped. It lined a cove that was ringed by heavy vegetation and palms leaning toward the ocean. A white froth of waves surged endlessly up out of the blue green sea to spend itself on the powdery fine sand.

Abby had dreamed of such a place all of her life; the smells of the sea and the sound of the surf, black frigate birds with their split tails dancing on currents of the trades, gliding motionless in the sky over a verdant bluff on the coast. At dusk she would walk the beach feeling the breath of the sea upon her face and watch as the fading sun turned the clouds on the horizon from pink to purple. It was as if time had not touched the place. By night, as she worked at the small computer in her room, she could hear the rhythms of reggae as they erupted from the bar at the Buccaneer just one cove away. Jack maintained a room there, but spent most of his time with Abby at the house. It was a liaison that at times and with increasing frequency had its softer moments. For the first time in her life, everything seemed to be going right for Abby. That she was now here, doing what she wanted most in life, writing, and with a book about to explode upon the bestsellers list, seemed too good to be true.

Within two days she was into her schedule, rising

early with the sun to work at the little computer that she'd set up on a table in the living room looking out at the sea. Like clockwork, she broke for breakfast by nine. Jack would return with fruit and yoghurt from the market in town. Then she would return to work.

Abby could usually crank four or five good pages before noon. During these hours, except for breakfast which they shared, Jack kept his distance, a kind of unwritten rule. Abby was disciplined in her work and did not like to be disturbed. Like many writers, she required total concentration. She induced a sort of mental state, a kind of psychic transport that ferried her mind to the fictional world of her creation. Like a camera lens, unless she could see it in her mind's eye, she couldn't write about it.

The islands seemed to favor Abby. In two weeks she had added five more chapters to the new manuscript. She was flying and was now nearly a third of the way into the sequel. The book seemed to be writing itself. It was almost too easy.

In the early afternoon, she and Jack would roam the beach. To a casual observer it might look like two lovers at play. It was actually part of their schedule. Jack required intensive briefing on the details of the book he was going to have to sell. If he was going to New York to stand up to the scrutiny of the press and the glare of cameras, Jack would have to speak with authority.

Commercial fiction might only be a part of the entertainment world, but to people who covered it, wrote about it, and reported on it, it was serious business. They played the game for keeps. Those who followed pop culture still remembered Milli-Vanilli and the scandal that brought them down. One slip by Jack and the entire scheme could collapse. Whatever he said about the book would have to sound real, as if he had written it himself.

They talked about the mechanics of writing, the daily schedule that Abby employed, and the process of creation. She reminded him that she'd written the manuscript on a typewriter.

'You never know what Carla or Bertoli might get into over dinner,' she told him. She knew that the manuscript would speak for itself with X'ed out words and typeovers that could not have come from a computer printer. It was a minor point, but the kind of thing that could trip him up in a conversation over cocktails.

'If they ask, tell them you lost the typewriter in the move to the islands. The next manuscript will be written using WordPerfect, an old DOS-driven version. They'll probably want discs if we sell them the book. Most publishers do. Tell them that if we come to terms we'll supply them.'

Jack wanted to know why she didn't use Windows for her writing.

Abby didn't like all the bells and whistles. They slowed her down and got in the way.

'You have to decide whether you want to write, or play computer games.' She winked at Jack and he smiled sheepishly.

'If they ask, tell them that you keep it simple,' said Abby.

In the afternoons, Abby and Jack would swim in the ocean, Abby thinking of things and talking as they bobbed in the surf. She was increasingly anxious as the time drew short. Jack was scheduled to be in New York in ten days. The lay-down date for her novel, the time when the book would start appearing on store shelves across the country, was rapidly approaching.

'Are you sure you can handle it?'

'You worry too much.' He gave her one of his beefy school-boy grins. Jack was made for the lens of a camera.

'I'm trying to think of anything we might have forgotten,' said Abby. 'Remember the characters are all composites.'

'I know,' said Jack. 'We already went over that. There's no one in the book I've ever actually known. My characters are just bits and pieces, mostly fictional, sometimes little fragments of people I've rubbed up against in life. I'll call it a fictional gene pool,' said Jack.

'Good,' said Abby. 'That's a nice touch.'

She danced over the top of a wave and Jack reached out to grab her. He threw an arm around her from behind, and as the wave passed he rubbed his body seductively against her backside.

'There. Now you can be one of my characters,' said Jack.

'Not now.' Abby tried not to smile. 'This is business. And unless you pay attention, you're gonna get us both in a lot of trouble. These people are not fools.'

He tried to ignore her. Jack was getting bored.

'Where did the idea for the story come from?' said Abby.

'Another pop quiz,' said Jack. He continued to hold onto her tightly from behind. 'Let's talk about something else.'

'What?'

'I don't know.' He thought for a second. 'The sequel,' said Jack. 'Is there a seduction scene in it?'

'No.'

'Why not?'

'I don't talk about work in progress.' She gave him a sideways glance. 'It's bad luck.'

'You don't trust me.' He spun her around in his arms.

She looked at him for a moment, the square jaw and broad shoulders, locks of dark hair glistening under the bright sun.

'That's not true,' said Abby.

'Tell me, does Morgan know about the sequel?'

'Morgan has to know about certain things for reasons of business.'

'Like the copyright on the book,' said Jack.

'Like the copyright,' said Abby.

'But you haven't copyrighted the outline.'

'True,' said Abby.

'So then why does he know and I don't?'

'You'll have to trust me,' said Abby.

'When are you going to learn to trust me?'

She looked into the pools of his eyes.

He smiled that kind of juvenile grin that melts most women, then buried his face in her shoulder and started to nibble. 'I need to know what's going on if I'm going to pull this off. At least give me the story line. Some of the details.'

'No.'

He went back to work on her shoulder and Abby started to giggle. 'Cut it out. Come on, Jack. You can't eat my shoulder.'

'Why not? It tastes so good. A little salty maybe.' He sank his teeth into the soft flesh at the side of her neck, not enough to hurt, but enough to ignite erotic fires.

'Quit it.' She was laughing as his tongue made its way along the side of her neck and up under the lobe of her ear.

'All I want is a little peek,' said Jack. 'Just a peek.' He was talking about the outline, but his fingers toyed with the strings of her bathing suit.

'Stop it.' She tried to sound serious but couldn't. She could feel the warmth of his lower body against her own. Even in the cool water Jack radiated heat like a nuclear reactor. A wave washed over them, and one of Jack's legs found its way between her thighs so that it supported her body, and she rode on it. They floated and bobbed in the sea as one.

He nibbled on her ear, catching the lobe gently between his teeth and she quieted, her arms around his neck.

'That tickles,' said Abby.

'It tastes good. You should try it.'

'I can't reach them,' she told him.

'Not yours, mine.'

'Oh.' She laughed and rested her chin on his shoulder. 'Why is it so important for you to know about the sequel?'

'What if they ask questions in New York?' said Jack. 'Carla may be pretty persuasive.' As he said it, Jack slipped a hand into the bottom of her bathing suit. 'She may have techniques of torture we can only imagine.'

'Cut it out.' She reached for his hand and tried to remove it, but his grip was firm. She wiggled in his grasp, but her movements only spurred him on. Abby looked toward the beach. It was deserted. There was no one there to see them. Jack's hand was soon joined by a second, where they met inside the bottom of her bathing suit. Gently he gripped the cheeks of her buttocks, lifting her until her legs were locked about his midsection.

'She may have ways of getting information that cannot be resisted,' said Jack.

'Steel yourself,' said Abby. Their eyes met.

'What if she forces me to tell her a lie?'

'Make it a good one,' said Abby.

Their bodies were gently raised and rocked by another passing wave as Abby's eyes closed, and their lips met.

'I forgot to tell you. Morgan's coming down next week.' It was Saturday, mid-morning, and Abby and Jack had slept in. Abby was drying herself with a towel after her shower.

'What for? Anything he needs to do he can do over the phone.'

'What's your problem with Morgan?' she asked.

'He's a hard-ass lawyer,' said Jack. He had never forgiven Spencer for his tactics that day when he forced Jack to sign the contract and to play by his rules.

'So what? I'm a lawyer, too,' said Abby.

'Yes, but your ass is much softer,' said Jack. He pinched her as she walked by as if to prove the point, and Abby scampered to the foot of the bed with a towel wrapped around her. She rummaged through the closet for something to wear.

Jack admired the view as he propped himself against the headboard of the bed with a pillow behind his back. 'So what does he want?'

'It's something important, but he won't tell me what.'

'You should tell him no. He's just gonna be in the way. Another distraction,' said Jack.

'God knows I don't need any more of those,' said Abby.

She looked at him with a smirk. Jack had a single sheet covering his body and an erection that was now at half-mast.

Abby selected a pair of pants and a matching top and

headed back toward the bathroom. He grabbed her towel on the way by, and she had to fight him for it.

'Stop it. We've got to get ready.' Abby finally gave up and retreated into the bathroom, covering herself with the clothes in her other hand. Quickly she slipped on her panties and bra and started to fix her hair.

'You better get out of bed. The photographer will be here in twenty minutes. *Entertainment Weekly*,' said Abby. Like Jack had forgotten.

'Let 'em wait,' said Jack. 'I'm an artist.'

The crew from one of the network magazine shows was coming down later in the day to do candid shots of the writer at work at his island home. The piece was scheduled to air the week of publication. Jack the author was about to earn his money.

He got out of bed and didn't bother to cover himself. There wasn't a modest bone in the man's body. He stood naked next to Abby, peering into the mirror over the bathroom sink and plucked a gray hair from his temple.

'Little devils keep showing up,' said Jack.

'Keep pulling them out, you're going to be bald,' said Abby. 'Something tells me you're not going to age gracefully.'

'I'm not going to age at all.' He smiled at her.

Somehow Abby sensed that he might be right. Whoever said that life was fair?

Jack smiled for the mirror and checked his perfectly spaced teeth as if he was looking to see if they might have shifted on him during the night.

'He didn't give you any hint of what he wants to talk about?' said Jack.

'Who?'

'Spencer.'

'No. He said he couldn't discuss it over the phone.'

'Something about the book?' said Jack.

'Possibly. Or Theresa's death.'

Jack suddenly looked over at her. 'What's happening on that front?'

They hadn't talked about it in weeks. It was not a subject that Abby wanted to discuss.

'The police want to talk to me,' she told him. 'Routine. Nothing unusual.'

Jack shot her a look.

'They traced the bank account.' She shrugged like what could she do. 'The advance on the book.'

'Spencer hasn't told them where you are?'

'No. And he moved the funds to where they couldn't find them.'

'That should be giving them food for thought,' said Jack. 'A woman is murdered and her roommate disappears with a shit load of money that keeps vanishing. Yeah, I'd say they might have a few questions.'

'We'll find out when Morgan gets here,' said Abby.

'Let's hope the surprise isn't a warrant for your arrest.'

'There's no arrest warrant. I had no reason to kill her. I wasn't even in town when it happened. I have an alibi.'

'You don't have to convince me,' said Jack. 'I'm not the one with the questions. Personally, I think Spencer's just looking for an excuse to come down here.'

'Why would he do that?'

'Because he wants to check and make sure you're alright. He doesn't trust me.'

'Maybe he has good reason.'

When Jack looked over at her he couldn't tell whether she was serious or not.

Then Abby cracked a smile. 'Morgan thinks he's my father.'

'Be careful he doesn't have his mind set on a little incest,' said Jack.

Abby looked at him. 'Morgan and me?'

Jack nodded.

'You gotta be kidding.' He was Jack's age but a generation older. It was not so much a matter of age as it was a state of mind. It was the reason Spencer was a father figure and Jack was a lover. 'We're friends. Nothing more.'

'Have you told him that?'

'I never had to. Unlike some people he's never put his hands inside my bathing suit.'

'Lacks confidence, does he?'

'He's a gentleman.'

'That's what I mean,' said Jack.

The afternoon was taken up doing photo shoots and staging pieces for the network magazine program. First *Entertainment Weekly* showed up with their photographer and took pictures of Jack dressed entirely in black, set off against the stark white sand of the beach. They seemed to like artsy shots.

An hour later the television crew showed up and began setting up their equipment. Jack did a quick change of clothes, and they did a long distance telephoto shot of him walking on the beach with the female interviewer, and talking about the sacrifices made by the novelist for his craft.

'Of course it's a lonely life. But I wouldn't trade it for any other.' Chatter and prattle.

'How do you write such a good story?'

Jack gave her a thoughtful moment before he spoke.

'Michener probably said it best. He said he was actually one of the worst writers in the world. But one of the best rewriters who ever lived. I'm a great rewriter,' said Jack.

With bullshit like that Jack should have been working in the White House rewriting history, thought Abby.

'Is that where it's at, the revisions?'

'Absolutely. It's like music,' said Jack. 'You have to have an ear. If you're tone deaf, you'll never make it as a writer.'

Abby huddled with the television crew under the shade of a palm tree and listened to the feed-through sound equipment, to the echo of her own words emitting from Jack's lips. She tried to convince herself that she had done the right thing. It was, after all, everything that Abby detested, the glitz and buzz of commercial fiction. It was a world in which the contour of Jack's face and the form of his body took precedence over the content of Abby's book.

But as she watched him on the beach, Abby could not deny the pangs of regret and resentment. She knew that the book was hers, but millions of viewers watching Jack on the tube would not. Would they ever accept her? Maybe Jack was right. She had created a mirage so alluring that it now threatened to consume its own maker.

She had bared her soul to Jack during weeks of preparation. Now as her own words came streaming back through the headset propelled by Jack's voice, there was a sense of loss that she could not explain. She had given up not only the credit and recognition for her work but a part of herself. Listening to him talk as he walked on the beach, Abby realized for the first time that she had surrendered a large chunk of her own identity.

They moved inside to take some shots of Jack sitting at the table over Abby's little computer.

They talked about his childhood as a military brat, and how it felt to be on the cusp of literary fame.

'A fleeting thing,' said Jack. 'It doesn't feel real. It won't,' said Jack, 'until I can see the title of my book squarely on the bestsellers list. Maybe not even then.'

'It takes a lot to convince you,' said the interviewer.

'Only because I know it can slip away. Until the book is firmly established, I know it can always slip away.'

He thought for a moment, one of those wistful expressions that the anchors on the networks do so well. Then Jack looked directly into the camera, nothing shifty-eyed or shy. 'It's like a dream,' said Jack. 'You always know that you can wake up at any moment to discover that it wasn't real.'

He allowed a short beat to pass in silence. Jack's timing was a gift that could not be learned. Then he spoke. 'I wake up every night with the same bad dream, the nightmare that this, all of this, is just an illusion.'

The interviewer sat dazed, enveloped by his gaze. As the echo of Jack's words died in the room, she came back to reality and turned to her cameraman.

'Harry. Tell me you got that?'

'Got it,' said the cameraman. He had just faded out to black on Jack.

'I'll do a voice-over just after he says that last line, the part about illusion, and we'll use it for the close. Maybe catch the setting sun, the green spark as it flashes on the horizon. Do we have any of that footage left over from Hawaii?'

'I think so,' said the cameraman.

'Good. We'll use it. They'll never know the difference.'

'Then you liked it?' said Jack.

'I loved it.' Jack and the interviewer stood in the center of the room and she took his hand. 'What's more, the audience is gonna eat it up.'

It was at that moment that Abby realized Jack was dangerous. He lied with a smile that paralyzed reason.

CHAPTER
TWENTY-NINE

Jack was due in the office in less than an hour and Carla was scrambling to get ready. With her assistant she was pulling together all of the last-minute bits of information that Bertoli had given her on marketing for the book.

Owens wanted to be the first to give Jack the good news. Agents always wanted to be bearers of glad tidings on the theory that the client would equate the news with the messenger.

'Do we have the figures on the television ad campaign?' asked Owens.

'In your folder,' said the secretary.

'And the "dumps"? The stuff on the up-front floor displays at the chains?' said Carla. 'Do we have the figures on that?'

'In your folder with everything else.' Jadra, Carla's assistant, was getting perturbed. Owens was always a basket case before meetings with important clients.

This time it seemed to be worse. For some strange reason, Carla was intimidated by Jack. She hoped he wasn't bringing the lawyer-consort this time. At their last meeting Abby seemed to be able to read Carla's mind, and Owens didn't like it. She was still working on ways to separate Jack from this troublesome woman. Give her time and she would figure it out. It was Abby Chandlis who had blocked her from selling more books to Bertoli, books that could have meant millions in commissions for the agency and put Jack in book bondage for at least five years. Control was the name of the game and right now Jack had it and Carla wanted it.

'Tell me about the dumps?' she asked the secretary. 'How many did Bertoli do?'

The assistant fished for a paper in one of the files. 'Five thousand.'

Carla whistled. She had never heard of a book with such a large purchase of up-front store space.

'Dumps' were shorthand in the industry for cardboard racks that the publishers provided to the book-stores. Each of these held twelve to fifteen books in a portable stand-up display, with a colorful riser showing the title and the author at the top, with all the hype that the publicity department could muster. Publishers had to pay to rent space in the front of the stores for their dumps. Space in a single chain of stores could cost a publisher thirty thousand dollars for a single week. For Jack's book, Bertoli would be spending nearly two hundred thousand dollars for space in the first sixty days. Without this, a book seldom, if ever, had a chance to become a bestseller. For this reason there was hot competition among publishers to get dump space.

It was only one of the things that publishers did to get an edge in the market. On the paperback side they actually rented the numbered racks in supermarkets across the country, numbers that had no real correlation to placement on any bestsellers list. For the right price you could buy number one. In commercial publishing, if you had enough money, you could create your own version of reality.

Bertoli had also purchased expensive print ads, full-page spreads in the *L.A. Times, Washington Post, New York Times*, and the *Chicago Tribune* as well as several high-circulation national magazines.

One of the chic tabloid magazines had named Gable Cooper among its fifty most beautiful people in America, right next to Mel Gibson and Antonio Banderas. Inside rumors were already circulating that Big-F had managed to influence this decision through its pricey print advertising buys.

In three days ads would go up inside all the New York subway cars with the title of the book, some appropriate hype, and best of all, Jack's picture. New York was a pressure point to establish buzz within the industry. Sample chapters of the book as a teaser were being delivered with selected copies of the morning newspaper on the day of publication. These would go to more than a thousand opinion makers in New York and Los Angeles, the A-list of the entertainment and publishing worlds. It was the biggest promotional push for a book in nearly ten years.

If Bertoli was successful, it would launch a career that most writers couldn't even dream of. The name Gable Cooper would be synonymous with hot books and even hotter movies. Anything penned under the name for the next twenty years would be gobbled up in Hollywood and New York. Carla knew this, so today she had a single objective in her meeting with Jack. Somehow she had to convince him that additional contracts now for more books were in his own best interest.

The com-line rang on Carla's phone.

'Oh shit.' Carla looked at the clock on the wall. 'He's

early. Jadra, finish up there quickly.'

Her assistant went into hyperdrive, slipping last-minute papers into folders, two sets of which sat on the conference table in Carla's office.

'And make sure we get coffee,' said Owens. 'And lunch. Call Da Umberto's and have them prepare something nice and have it delivered.' Carla had no intention of letting Jack get into a public restaurant where other agents might be courting introductions. His picture was already all over town.

The com-line buzzed again and Carla picked up the phone.

'There's a Mr Chandlis here to see you.'

'Who?'

'Mr Chandlis. Says he's related to an Abby Chandlis.' The receptionist sounded like she was about to hang up and throw him out the door. Strange people, some of whom wrote with crayons from institutions, often showed up unannounced at literary agencies. 'Do you want me to tell him you're busy?'

Carla thought for a moment. 'No.' She put her hand over the mouthpiece. 'Jadra.'

The secretary turned just as she was heading out the door.

'If Mr Jermaine shows up, entertain him for a couple of minutes. Tell him I'll be with him as soon as I can. Take him to the conference room.'

Jadra nodded, left, and closed the door.

Carla went back to the phone. 'Show Mr Chandlis in.'

Two minutes later there was a tap on Owens's door and another secretary opened it. 'Mr Chandlis.'

An instant later Carla got her first glimpse. Charlie had a head start on a five-o'clock shadow. His suit was wrinkled. He'd slept in it on the plane and had come directly by taxi from the airport to the office. He was carrying an attaché case. He looked like a salesman.

Carla rose from her chair and greeted him from on high, up on the pedestal behind her desk. She had no idea what the man wanted and figured a posture of authority was always safe.

'Mr Chandlis. Carla Owens. Please come in.'

Charlie seemed to look around a lot as he made his way between the door and Carla's desk. He had never seen an office as large as this or as elaborately decorated; purple plush carpets and smoked glass, a desk like a crystal altar. Charlie thought he'd died and gone to pimp heaven.

'Good to meet you,' he told her. When he finally arrived at the desk he handed Carla a business card. Charlie always did this with people he met. You could never tell when one of them might need a good criminal lawyer.

She looked at the card. 'What can I do for you?'

'It's about my wife,' said Charlie. 'Abby Chandlis.'

Carla nodded slowly but didn't say a word.

'You do know her?'

'I'm acquainted with an Abby Chandlis,' said Owens. 'She's your wife?' Carla didn't show it, but she was suffering a major adrenaline rush, visions of a peccadillo on the eve of publication with an angry husband who was a lawyer. Some authors drank. Some found other diversions. Maybe Jermaine's vice was married women.

'Actually we're not married any longer,' said Charlie.

'Ah.' Carla's heart dropped twenty beats a minute. 'Please have a seat,' she told him.

Charlie ascended, one giant step for mankind, and flopped into one of the tufted chairs across from Carla's desk.

'So what is this about Ms Chandlis?'

'I'd like to know where she is.'

'And why do you think I can help you with that?'

'You paid her a lot of money,' said Charlie.

Carla gave him big eyes, this was news to her.

'Well not exactly,' said Charlie. 'You wrote a sizable check to a mister –' he took a note from his shirt breast pocket and looked at it – 'a Mr Jermaine.'

He looked at Carla. Her expression at the moment was a stone idol. She was giving up nothing.

'This Jermaine endorsed the check over to my wife. A very large sum of money. This money was commingled with other funds and then the entire amount was withdrawn and the account was closed.'

The first crack in granite. Carla tried to hide it, but the news came as a major blow. Abby Chandlis had a stronger hold on her client than Carla realized. If she could get him to sign over a seven-figure check, getting rid of the woman might be more difficult than Carla thought.

'And what is your interest in all of this?'

'You can call me Charlie.' He smiled at her. Charlie sensed that she was hearing some of this for the first time. So was Charlie. He was making it up as he went. If he played his cards right, he might not have to tell her everything, especially the parts he guessed at.

'It's about community property,' said Charlie.

'I don't understand.'

'We have reason to believe,' said Charlie, 'that a portion of this money was in fact earned during the course of my marriage to Abby, Ms Chandlis. We have evidence that the funds were diverted to avoid a fair distribution at the time of the divorce.'

'We?' said Carla.

'I have a team of lawyers looking into this right now.'
It was Charlie at his bull-shitting best.

'I see. But you didn't have your lawyers call me. You came here yourself.' Carla had a well-trained nose for bullshit.

'I figured you're an innocent third party. No sense getting you involved in a messy law suit.' Charlie looked at her to see if he was making a dent. 'Unless it's necessary of course.'

Carla just smiled at him. Her lawyers could eat him for lunch. That is, if she didn't do the job first. Still, if this awful man knew Abby, maybe there was a silver lining here. Why be hasty?

'So you think your wife was hiding things from you during your marriage?'

Charlie made a face like this was a definite possibility.

Wait until he gets a gander at Jack, thought Carla. 'We would have a certain interest in this. Actually Mr Jermaine is our client. Our only contact with your former wife was through him.'

'I see. And you don't know where she is?'

'We might have some information,' said Carla. She knew of course that Charlie's story was gold-plated garbage. Publishers were up to their hips in friends, lovers, and former spouses, people who knew people, who were related to somebody who had a friend who wrote a big book. They came out of the woodwork with every hot novel. Charlie Chandlis had the classic look. His ex had gotten her claws into somebody who'd hit it big and Charlie now wanted a taste. He was probably jealous to boot. The whole thing smacked of sleaze, not the kind of publicity you wanted on a break-out book. She figured that's what this Charlie was gambling on.

'I'd have to check our records. I'd want to talk to Mr

Jermaine first. And of course we could not cooperate in any way if it meant trouble for him. You understand that?' said Carla.

'Of course,' said Charlie. 'I appreciate your position.' Charlie's own position at the moment was on his hands and knees. He was willing to agree to anything. Abby had disappeared like a puff of smoke. He had no idea how to find her. Without help from the literary agent he was up the proverbial creek with a broken paddle. He had a theory as to what was going on, but he wasn't willing to share it with Owens, not until he knew more. She might tell her client and Charlie would get zip. If nothing else, his theory had good nuisance value. And what was nuisance worth when you had a few mill in the bank, and a giant pain in the ass? Charlie didn't know, but he wanted to find out.

'What exactly is your relationship with this Mr Jermaine? I assume he's an author?' said Charlie.

He measured Carla's silence as assent.

'I suppose you wouldn't be paying that kind of money to someone who wasn't,' said Charlie. 'What did he write?'

'That's confidential,' said Carla. The use of a pen name made it awkward. If Chandlis really intended to make trouble and ended up suing Jack, it could look very bad; allegations of concealed money and an alias used on the book. There was probably nothing to it, but Carla wasn't willing to take the chance.

'Are you staying in town long?' she asked him.

'Just long enough to find out where my wife is.'

The phone rang on Carla's desk. Instinctively she knew what it was. She measured in her mind the next move.

'One moment,' she told Charlie. Carla picked up the receiver.

It was Jadra. 'Mr Jermaine is here. I've got him in the conference room. Do you need more time?'

'Ah. Yes. Hold him out there for a moment. I'll be right out.' She hung up the phone and smiled at Charlie. 'A matter I have to attend to. But if you can wait a moment, I'd like to talk to you further.'

'No problem,' said Charlie.

Carla quickly left the office and closed the door behind her. She headed down the hall. On the way she mussed her hair a little and took on a frantic appearance so that by the time she reached the conference room out front she looked like someone had raped her, at least mentally. She opened the door and rushed through.

Jack was drinking a cup of coffee, one cheek up on the conference table talking to Jadra, who didn't seem to mind the duty.

'Jack! Jack! God, I'm glad you're here. Jadra, could you excuse us for a minute.'

The secretary stepped outside, and as soon as the door closed Carla returned her full attention to Jack.

'We've got a major problem,' said Owens.

'What's the matter?' Carla's panic was becoming contagious. Jack's eyes took on an anxious look.

'There's a guy in my office. A lawyer. He says he's married or was married to Abby.'

Jack studied Owens's face.

'He says he's looking for her. That he has a team of lawyers ready to bring legal action. That she's been concealing community property from their marriage. He says his lawyers are looking at the present time to find out if you're involved. He's got some bank records. I don't know what it's all about, but it sounds serious. I shudder to think what Bertoli would do if he found out. This kind of scandal on the eve of publication. I don't have to tell you.'

'Where is he? This guy?'

'He's in my office right now.'

Before she could stop him Jack was out of the door. Carla was behind him like a shadow. 'Where are you going?'

'To talk to him.'

'Wait.'

Jack turned and stopped.

'Let's discuss this before we just blunder in there,' said Carla.

Maybe she was right. Jack listened.

'I don't know exactly what your relationship is with Ms Chandlis. And believe me, it's none of my business. But we're at a critical point. For the next several weeks we don't need any problems, especially problems like this. My advice,' said Carla, 'is to distance yourself. If there's a problem between the two of them, don't get in the middle of it. If you have to, stay in New York. We'll arrange accommodations. Alex and I can provide cover. Think of your career,' she told him. 'Let them sort it out. It's their mess.'

'Right,' said Jack. 'Good advice.' He turned and headed down the hall again like he hadn't heard her.

For Carla it gave her the excuse she needed to drive a wedge between Jack and Abby. 'I know what you're thinking,' she told him. 'You're thinking he's probably out to get whatever he can. He found out about your good fortune with the book and he's using Abby to shake you down. You're probably right. But there's no reason for you to get involved. If you do, you could end up flushing the entire deal.'

'I want to talk to him.' Jack had a problem. He'd never met Charlie. Abby had talked about him a few times, but he had no idea if Charlie might know something. Maybe Abby had said something about the book, or worse, about her plan to market it under a pen name from deep cover. If the truth about the book were leaked to Carla or Bertoli before publication, the book could be dead on arrival at the bookstores. Big-F might get nervous and pull the plug.

'What are you going to say to him?' said Carla.

'I don't know. But I want to talk to him alone. Find out what the hell's going on,' said Jack.

'You're not going to hit him or do anything stupid?'

Jack looked at her over his shoulder like who, me?

'Jack, use your head. Don't do anything foolish.'

By the time they got to the door to her office, Carla was beginning to think that maybe she'd made a mistake. She managed to wiggle around him and get in front before they reached the door. Carla took the lead into her office. They caught Charlie standing up on the pedestal behind Carla's desk reading her private papers.

'What are you doing?' said Owens.

'I thought maybe you might have an address for my wife,' said Charlie.

Carla started thinking that maybe it wasn't such a bad idea if Jack was to hit him.

'Mr Chandlis, this is Mr Jermaine. I talked to him about your problem and he agrees that the questions that you raise are matters between your former wife and yourself. He's willing to put you in touch with your wife so that you can obtain whatever information is required and this matter can be resolved. Now I think that's reasonable.' She turned and looked up at Jack to see if this would be alright.

Jack let it stand.

'Fine by me,' said Charlie.

'First I want to talk to him alone,' said Jack.

'Listen, anything said here is in the strictest confidence,' said Carla.

'Alone,' said Jack.

Owens gave him a look like maybe she should pat him down first before agreeing to this. Jack seemed to calm down a little too quickly.

'You can talk right here. I'll just step outside,' said Carla. 'I'll be right outside the door.' She made a point of it. 'Call me if you need anything.'

'We'll call.' Jack smiled at her. As soon as she closed the door behind her Jack turned and smiled at Charlie, a big blustery grin.

'It's good to finally meet you,' said Jack. 'Abby's told me a lot about you.'

'She has?'

'Oh yeah.' Jack extended a hand behind his broad smile and quickly closed the distance, climbing up onto Carla's platform. The move made a handshake a measure of manhood, so that Charlie had no choice but to step around the desk. As soon as their hands met, it was like lightning. Charlie wondered where his arm went, what it was doing up behind his back, and why his nose was suddenly pressed into the In basket on Carla's desk.

'Now let's talk.' Jack was up close in his ear, whispering so that Carla couldn't hear. 'What do you want?'

'I want to talk to Abby.'

'She's busy.'

'What the fuck is this? Ahh!'

Jack used a little leverage on the arm.

'Keep your voice down or I'll unscrew it and you can carry it home in a case.'

'Ahh.' Charlie whispered in pain.

'Now what is this about community property?'

'I had to say something,' said Charlie.

'So there's no team of lawyers hatching a law suit?'

'No.'

'What else did you tell Owens?'

'Nothing.'

Jack pressed on the arm a little more.

'Ahh! Ahh!' Charlie sounded like he'd stepped on hot coals.

'I swear I didn't tell her anything. I don't know anything.'

'But you've got some educated guesses, right?'

Charlie didn't say anything.

'Right?' Jack now had the back of Charlie's right hand up against the nape of his neck, a move that only the double-jointed could make without severe pain.

'Right! Right!' said Charlie.

'Well? Tell me.'

'I figure either you wrote a book together or you stole the book from her. That Abby's got a piece of it.'

'And what led you to that conclusion?'

'She's always writing.'

'So?'

'I figure it's a big book. Worth some money. That's how she got all that money in the account.'

'What if I told you I wrote the book?'

'Then why did you give her the money?' said Charlie. 'I know my wife,' said Chandlis. He was now breathing heavily. 'She suffers insecurity. She might have you stand in. You know. To do all the public stuff.'

Charlie was right. He knew Abby. Jack had a problem.

'You sure you didn't share any of this with Ms Owens?' Jack pressed on the truth lever a little more.

'No. No. I wouldn't do that. Why would I do that?'

'So what do you want?'

'I just want to talk to my wife.'

'You want to ask her for a little money, right? Shake her down?'

Charlie's head went sideways on the desk, just a little. It was the kind of shrug you might do if your face was pressed into the top of a desk and somebody was kneeing you in the ass.

'The thought had crossed your mind?'

'She had a lot in the bank. I thought I might talk to her.'

'And if she doesn't want to give you any, what then?'

'Nothing,' said Charlie. 'I just want to talk to her.'

'For old times' sake?' said Jack.

'Yeah. Yeah. For old times' sake.'

Jack slowly let him up. He thought about his options. He couldn't allow Charlie to stay in New York. Carla and Bertoli would pump him for information.

As soon as his arm was released, Charlie swung it around like an empty sleeve and grabbed it with his other hand. He cradled it like it was broken.

Jack turned him around and straightened the lapel on his suit coat while he talked in his face.

'What are we gonna do with you?' said Jack.

Charlie looked at him. For the first time there was real fear in Charlie's eyes. It was almost easier when he was in pain, looking the other way.

'Let me ask you,' said Jack. 'Why do you think I would endorse all the money over to Abby if we co-wrote this book?'

Charlie hesitated, but he had a theory on this, too.

'I don't know. Maybe you were hiding money from an ex. So you transferred it all to Abby?' Charlie looked at him, a question mark.

Jack didn't say a word but just looked back.

Charlie figured he wasn't far off the mark. It was precisely what Charlie would have done if he was in similar circumstances. As far as Charlie was concerned, it was a badge of honor. A male bonding thing, another way of cheating on your wife. All he wanted was a little piece of the action.

'I'll tell you where you can find her,' said Jack. It was the only safe course open to him; send Charlie down to the islands and let Abby deal with him. Maybe she could keep him quiet, or at least give them time to figure out what to do. In any case, Charlie would be out of New York, away from Bertoli and Carla. Jack would have to call Abby and give her a heads-up, that Charlie was on his way down.

He scrawled an address on a slip of paper from Carla's desk and handed it to Charlie.

'Do you know where this is?'

Charlie looked at the paper and shook his head.

'The Caribbean. You fly through Miami. Do you have a passport?'

'Back at my office.'

'Have 'em send it overnight express to this hotel, make a reservation there for tonight.' Jack scribbled the name of a cheap hotel near the Miami airport. 'In the morning you get your passport and you get your ass down there and you talk to her. You don't bother her. You don't make a pest out of yourself. Do you understand? And you wait there until I get back. Then we can all talk. There's a place called the Buccaneer. You present yourself at the desk and give them my name. The manager's a friend. He'll get you a room. And if you're smart, you won't say anything to Ms Owens or anybody else on the way out of the office.'

405

Charlie gave him a look like maybe he would and maybe he wouldn't. He was still massaging his arm to get circulation flowing again, flexing his hand to see if he could get the feeling back into it.

'If you say anything you're going to kill the goose,' said Jack. 'There won't be any more money for anybody.'

Charlie understood this.

Jack grabbed him by the ear like a school boy and led him to the door.

'Open it slowly,' said Jack. 'We wouldn't want Ms Owens to topple over and break her nose.' He guessed Carla had her ear pressed to the door.

'No, I think we can work this thing out.' Jack's tone was suddenly warm and loud very amicable, so Carla would have time to get up off her knees before the door opened.

'You go on down and talk to Abby, and I'm sure she'll explain how the whole thing happened.'

As the door opened Carla was framed in it, trying to look casual. Jack made a play of harmony and took Charlie's hand, shaking it while he looked at Owens. 'All a big mistake,' said Jack. 'Damn banks, they screw everything up. We'll have to sort it out. I'm sure Abby will be able to get to the bottom of it.'

Charlie even smiled, something sinister. His game was never physical. Jack was a Neanderthal. Charlie would use his brain. With Carla in the picture, he now had leverage. Jack couldn't afford to beat on him anymore, not in front of Owens anyway. There was something Abby and Jack didn't want her to know. All Charlie had to do was figure out what it was.

'You're not going to leave us so soon?' said Carla.

'He's got a plane to catch,' said Jack.

'Can I show you the way out?' Owens wanted to get Charlie alone for a couple more minutes.

Jack gave him a look to kill and Charlie declined her offer.

'I can find my way,' he said. 'But it was nice to meet you. Maybe we can get together again sometime.'

'Absolutely,' said Carla. 'Give me a call.'

'I'll do that.'

Charlie would have the last laugh. He had found the point of control.

CHAPTER
THIRTY

The phone rang but he finished typing the sentence into the word processor before he picked up the line.

'News room.'

'Is this Robert Thompson?'

'Yes. Who is this?' Thompson was the reporter for *The Intruder* and at the moment he was on a deadline.

'Nevermind who this is. Are you still interested in that piece involving the lawyer Abby Chandlis?'

'It's you again.' It was the second phone call that Thompson had received concerning Chandlis. 'Who is this?'

'Someone who is willing to give you information if you're smart enough to listen.'

Thompson shut up and listened.

'You were on a hot story. You shouldn't have quit so easily. It's much bigger than you could have guessed. One of the giant publishing houses in New York is about to publish a major blockbuster, a novel, except there's a scam going on with the book and they don't know it.'

'What's it all about?' said Thompson. 'I'm tired chasing shadows.'

'The book's going to be huge. The agent who handled

it doesn't know about the scam, either.'

'What's the title?'

'Later,' said the voice on the phone.

'At least tell me the publisher or the agent.'

'Not now. For now, all you need to know is that the lawyer Chandlis knows what's going on.'

'Listen, unless I have more information . . .'

'Film rights have already been sold on the book for three million dollars.'

Thompson stopped asking questions and started penning notes.

'The producers of the film don't know, either. Everybody's in the dark except Chandlis and a couple of people she's working with.'

'Why are they doing it?'

'That's for you to find out.'

'This sounds like a publicity stunt,' said Thompson.

'The police don't get involved in publicity stunts.'

'What are you talking about?'

'The Seattle police are trying to find Chandlis to question her.'

'Why?'

There was a brief silence on the phone as if the caller was trying to collect thoughts, wondering exactly how far to go.

'There have been two murders. Her roommate and her roommate's husband. There's a lot of unanswered questions.'

'They think Chandlis had something to do with this?'

'They want to talk to her.'

'What does this have to do with the book?'

'Talk to Chandlis.'

'I'd like to. I don't know where she is.'

'Try St Croix, the Virgin Islands. A house on Shoy

Beach Road just outside of Christiansted.'

'What's she doing there?'

'Avoiding you. And if my information is correct, hiding from the police back in Seattle.'

Thompson began to salivate. A scam on a book was one thing, murder was another.

'Give me something I can check, something I can confirm with another source besides Chandlis.'

'Why?'

'Because my editor's not going to let me waste any more time on this unless I can show him something concrete.'

There was another pause, breathing as if the voice on the phone was measuring how far to go.

'The victims' names were Jenrico. Theresa and Joseph Jenrico.'

'And these deaths are connected to the book?'

'The cops are looking for Chandlis. That's all I can say.'

'How do I confirm any of this?'

'That's your job.' The voice on the phone provided a number with an area code for the Virgin Islands. Thompson was told that the number would ring at the house on Shoy Beach Road.

'Who are you?'

'Nevermind that.'

'Just a second,' said Thompson. He fished in the drawer of his desk for the micro-cassette recorder and the little suction cup microphone that he used on the phone. It was highly illegal, but every reporter in the world had one. Thompson wanted something on tape that he could take to his editor.

'That's all I can tell you.'

'Hold on just a second. I'm making notes.' Thompson

licked the suction cup and stuck it on the outside of the earpiece of the phone.

'When did this murder happen?'

'A few months ago.'

'And Chandlis is involved.'

'I told you the police are looking for her.'

'And she's hiding in the Virgin islands?'

'What is this, are you hard of hearing? Enough. Check it out if you don't believe me.'

'Just one more question.'

The line went dead.

Thompson quickly played back what he had on the tape. It wasn't much, but it did mention murder and the fact that Chandlis was hiding from the police.

He punched out his piece for deadline and five minutes later dropped downstairs to a payphone in the lobby of a building a half-block away. He checked the phone book, the area code for Seattle: two-oh-six. Then he dialed long distance information.

'Can you give me the number for the Seattle Police Department? No, it's not an emergency.' He wrote the number down and dialed it.

A second later a female voice answered. There was a periodic beep on the line so that Thompson knew that he was being recorded.

'Hello, I'd like to have the name of the officer who's handling the Jenrico murder investigation? My name? My name is Bill Robinson. I'm a reporter for the *New York Daily News*.'

It took less than a minute before Thompson had the name and telephone extension of Lieutenant Luther Sanfillipo.

'Can you tell me, is he doing both murder investigations, Theresa and Joseph Jenrico? He is. Thank you.'

Thompson hung up. He didn't like dealing with the police. He never knew whether they had caller I.D. on their lines to trace the number of incoming calls. For this reason whenever he had to call them he always used payphones in one of the busy Manhattan office buildings, where there were a gazillion people roaming in the lobby.

In less than two minutes he had confirmed one part of the anonymous caller's information. The Jenricos were both murdered. But the caller could have gotten that information from anywhere.

He picked up the phone and dialed again, reading the number off the note he had just taken.

A man answered the phone. 'Homicide.'

'I'm calling for Lieutenant Sanfillipo.'

'I don't know if he's here. Let me check.'

Thompson heard what sounded like a hand being cupped over the mouthpiece. 'Anybody seen Luther?' He couldn't hear what came back by way of an answer.

'Think he's out to lunch.'

'I'm calling in regard to the Jenrico investigation.'

'Yes?'

'Do you know whether Lieutenant Sanfillipo is still interested in talking to Abigail Chandlis in regard to that matter?'

The hand went back over the phone and there was a lot of hushed conversation. Thompson couldn't make out what was being said.

When the voice came back on the line it was more subdued. 'Who's calling?'

'I'd rather not give that information. Can you tell me whether your office is still looking for Ms Chandlis, in connection with the Jenrico murder investigations?'

'We have some questions we'd like to ask her.'

It was all Thompson heard because an instant later he hung up the phone. It was all he needed. Chandlis was wanted in a murder investigation involving a book worth 'boo-koo' bucks.

For three days Abby juggled Charlie and kept him occupied with an open tab at the Buccaneer and a cover story that she couldn't agree to anything financial until Jack, her partner, returned from New York.

The ante to keep Charlie quiet seemed to go up when he saw the sporty little Bimmer, the Z-3, parked in the driveway under the palm trees in front of Abby's house with its top down. As far as Charlie was concerned, Abby was living the good life and he wanted a piece of it.

He spent his time partying at the Buccaneer on Jack's open tab, hitting on 'babes' at the beach as Charlie referred to them, and zipping around the island in Abby's little car.

Charlie didn't seem to pay much attention to the fact that Abby was working feverishly on another book. To Charlie all that mattered was that money was flowing freely. For him there was no correlation between hard work and its reward. He didn't believe in personal responsibility and knew that somewhere embedded in the Constitution was the absolute right to a free ride. Charlie was a life-long Democrat.

His first night in Christiansted he tried hitting on Abby. He wanted to spend the night, but she was having none of it. Their conversation was civil and short. Her mission was to not piss him off but to keep him in the islands until she could figure out what to do.

Spencer was due in St Croix that afternoon. He might have some ideas. She couldn't wait to see Morgan, somebody with a level head. She liked Jack, but he was like a whirling dervish moving in a dozen directions at once. He was a bundle of energy she couldn't seem to control. She'd watched him on the morning talk shows. He'd hit two of the networks in a single morning and did the third one the next day. According to plan, Jack lit up the screen, flashing teeth, sparkling blue eyes, and timing that was meticulous.

The magazine show they'd filmed on the beach aired the night before so that you couldn't turn on your tube without seeing Jack's picture. Even *Entertainment Tonight* had picked up on the buzz surrounding the book, a dividend they hadn't counted on. There was a synergy to this stuff. It seemed to feed upon itself like an atomic pile.

Abby was mid-paragraph and rolling at the little computer in front of the window facing the sea when the phone rang. Still typing with her left hand she reached for the receiver with her right.

'Hello.'

'Abby.' It was Jack. 'I don't have much time, but I wanted to call you.' There was an edge to his voice.

'What's wrong?'

'Not a thing. I'm a little tired. Bertoli called and got me out of bed this morning, early.'

'What did he want?'

'He wanted to tell me that we hit the *New York Times* bestsellers list.'

Abby didn't say a word. She was numb. She had conditioned herself to wait at least two weeks before asking when they might hit, if at all. It had been almost three years of hard work, writing, plotting, and planning. Now the news came like a thunderbolt. Her eyes began to water, and when she finally did speak, her voice broke. 'Jack, you'd better not be putting me on.'

'I'm not. It's true.'

'But we've only been on sale for three days.'

'I know,' said Jack. 'The book's flying off the shelves all over the country. Bertoli says it's on after-burner, incredible sales velocity. The hottest thing he's ever seen from a first-time novelist. His words. It'll appear on the list a week from Sunday.'

It was the practice in New York to provide publishers with a heads-up when one of their authors hit the list. The news was given out ten days before the list actually appeared in the paper.

'That's the good news,' said Jack. 'Now do you want the great news?'

Abby was trying to collect her thoughts, still recovering from the fact that her book had now made it. 'What, there's more?'

'You're number four,' said Jack.

'You're kidding.' Abby had always had a hard time celebrating. But at the moment she couldn't restrain herself. There was a whoop like a war cry from Abby's end of the phone. It almost pierced Jack's eardrum. Half a week of sales and they had catapulted inside of five.

'We won't know for another week, but they're pretty sure we'll go higher. With that kind of velocity, we can't help but climb. Bertoli says he might want to reconsider our offer, more books based on time and placement on the list.'

'I'll bet he would,' said Abby. Like placing a bet after the horses were out of the gate.

'They're making a lot of noise, both he and Carla. They want to see the outline for the sequel,' said Jack. 'The quick success has made both of them real antsy.'

'Tell them they can wait.'

'I have. But you should see the claw marks on my body. I can't hold 'em off much longer.'

'The answer's no. Tell them not 'til the manuscript is finished.' Abby was adamant. There were a lot of reasons, some of them having to do with film. Abby didn't want the storyline shopped around Hollywood before the book was finished. She knew the outline would wind up out on the coast the minute it landed on a desk in New York. When it came to feature film and hundred-million-dollar movie budgets, promises to keep a secret were worthless. If Jack thought he had scratches now, he would be flayed to the bone if the film people got their hands on the story and started lobbying for changes while Abby was writing.

'We'll talk about it when I get back,' said Jack. 'There's so much I need to tell you. Things breaking every minute.'

'Fill me in.'

'I can't,' said Jack. 'I'm off to another studio for an interview. I've only got a minute. Besides, I want to know what's happening with your husband.'

'Charlie's off somewhere in the car. I can handle him,' she said. 'Besides, Morgan's due in sometime this afternoon. He'll have some ideas on what to do.'

'I should be there when he arrives.'

'What for?' said Abby.

'To protect myself.'

'Give him a break. Morgan's only doing what he thinks is in my best interest.'

'Yeah, bad-mouthing me,' said Jack.

'He doesn't bad-mouth you. He gives me advice.'

'Yes but why does all of it involve taking my name in vain?'

'You're paranoid.'

'You know what they say about every paranoid's delusions possessing a kernel of truth. With Morgan I think I could make popcorn,' said Jack.

'He's coming down for business. Besides, I told him Charlie was here, that I've got a problem. I'm hoping Morgan will take him back in tow and deal with him in Seattle until this is over.'

She could hear Jack fuming on the other end.

'I saw you on *Good Morning America* yesterday. You were great.'

'You liked it?'

'It was wonderful. I thought of going out and buying the book myself.'

'Why didn't you?'

'I'll wait for the paperback,' said Abby.

Jack laughed. 'Still, it's easy to sell a great book.' They were getting into bilateral back-slapping now. Kudos all around.

'It's good of you to say,' said Abby.

'I mean it. I only wish I'd written it,' said Jack.

'Don't tell Charlie that.'

Jack laughed. 'It would light up his day. He thinks he has his teeth into you now. How did you ever pick such a loser?'

'He wasn't always this way. There was a time,' said Abby. Then she stopped herself. 'It's a long story. I'll tell you about it sometime.'

'Listen, there's other information I should be passing on to you. Bertoli's given me a ton of stuff on sales. I've taken notes but I can't remember all the details.'

'Where are you now?'

'Carla's office. They're waving to me from outside. I'm gonna have to go in a second,' said Jack. 'But I'll be back down there in two days,' he told her. There was a break in his schedule before he headed out on the fourteen-city tour. 'We'll crack a bottle when I get down there,' he said. 'I'll bring the champagne. We'll bodysurf in the buff, and get drunk. How does that sound?'

'Like shark bait,' said Abby.

'We'll be numb. Won't feel a thing. Gotta run.' They were waving at him again. 'The car's double parked downstairs. See you in a few days. Love ya,' said Jack.

Before she could say another word she heard the click on the line as he hung up. For a moment Abby dwelled on his last words.

Jack was at the top of his form. She could envision him running with the celebrity set in New York, flashing infectious smiles at camera lenses, and dashing through packed bookstores at autograph parties. He was a natural, show-boating in a stretch limo, doing the night spots of Manhattan after a busy day writing the name of Gable Cooper inside the covers of a thousand books.

At the moment even Abby, the soul of reserve, was caught up in the rush of a natural high. She picked up her can of Diet Coke from the desk and tapped it against the edge of her computer screen, then took a drink as if in toast of her own accomplishment. She had come from nowhere to write a novel that had fought its way onto the toughest bestsellers list in the world, a rocket that had landed inside of number five. It was no mean feat. For Abby only one thing took the edge off of absolute euphoria: the knowledge that her success had required so much deception. Bertoli and his pack in New York would never have allowed it had they known the truth; that Abby was the author. To anyone who cared, she was still a writer with a failed track record. Men still looked at her with a lustful gaze when she walked past, but that was not good enough for Bertoli. As far as he was concerned, she was over the hill.

Her gaze returned to the small computer screen, seven and a half inches of blue iridescence. For the next four months it would define the entire cosmos of her universe. It was a painful reality, but if her plan was to work she would have to stay the course and live with it.

The phone rang. Abby reached for it. Jack must have remembered something else.

She picked up the receiver. 'Don't tell me we climbed to number one already.'

'Excuse me?' It wasn't Jack's voice on the other end.

There was a cold moment of silence on the phone before she spoke. 'Who is this?'

'I'm looking for Morgan Spencer.'

'He's not here yet.'

'Can you give him a message?'

'Sure.' Abby reached for a scrap of paper and a pencil. 'Tell him the ship is the *Cuesta Verde*, in San Juan.'

Abby wrote it down. 'That's all?'

'Yeah.'

'May I ask who's calling?'

'He'll understand the message.' Whoever it was hung up.

Abby put the phone down for only a second before it rang again. It was driving her nuts. She thought about unplugging it, but it was her only lifeline to the outside world.

'Hello.'

'Am I speaking to Abby Chandlis?' It was a deep male voice, but she didn't recognize it.

All of a sudden everybody had her number. She had gone to great lengths to make sure the phone was unlisted. 'Who is this?'

'We talked once before, my name's Robert Thompson,

The Intruder. You didn't tell me you were moving.'

A chill ran down Abby's spine. How could he have found her? Her mind raced. 'How did you get this number?'

'It wasn't from information,' said Thompson. 'You're a difficult person to find.'

'I don't have time to talk right now.' Abby tried to figure some way to get off the phone gracefully.

'I'd give you my number, but somehow I don't think you'd call me back,' said Thompson.

'I have to go,' said Abby.

'I think you might want to talk to me. I'm much more pleasant than the police in Seattle.'

Abby's mind now went into hyperdrive.

'If I wanted to make trouble I would simply have told them where to find you. But I didn't do that.' He made it sound like he deserved a medal.

'What do you want?'

'I'm not trying to cause you any problems.'

'You said that already. How did you get my number?'

'We have our sources. They seem to have provided some accurate information.'

'What do you mean?'

'The phone number was right.'

Abby didn't say anything.

'And the police are looking for you.'

'How do you know that?'

'They told me so.'

'You talked to them?'

'Relax. I didn't tell them anything. They don't even know who called. I protect my sources.' He was cultivating Abby, trying to turn her into one. He guessed that she was a fringe player, a lawyer with information. If there was something scandalous happening, it was probably with a client, or somebody her client dealt with.

'We have a pretty good idea what's going on. It would be to your interest to make sure that we have your side of the story before we go to press.' Thompson didn't have shit and he knew it. But he was hoping that Abby would panic and start talking.

At the moment she was scared. She was also smart enough to know that scared people make mistakes. One of them is to talk too much.

'Some of our sources.' Suddenly they were multiplying, thought Abby. 'Some of our sources are telling us that you're involved in some rather strange dealings on a big book.'

'I don't know what you're talking about,' said Abby.

'Why don't you tell us what's going on? We don't think you're involved in anything criminal,' said Thompson.

'I'm glad to hear it,' said Abby.

'Who was Theresa Jenrico and why was she killed?'

There was a long breathless pause from Abby's end. She wondered for a moment if she should just hang up. But Thompson had already talked to the cops once. What if he got angry and called them back with an anonymous tip? They'd nail her at Immigration trying to get through the airport.

'She was a friend,' said Abby. 'And I don't know who killed her or why. I wish I did.'

'Why do the police want to talk to you about it?'

'I don't know.'

'Why aren't you talking to them if you're not involved?'

'Because right now it's not convenient.'

'I'm told that her death has something to do with the

422

book,' said Thomspon. It was a guess, but not a far stretch. The voice on the phone had mentioned the murder and the book in the same breath.

'Then you've been given misinformation,' said Abby.

'Then there is a book?' Thompson was sly.

'Why don't you ask your sources?'

'Why did you run from Seattle?'

'I got squeamish about staying in a house where my best friend was murdered.'

'And that's the only reason?'

Abby thought about answering him with a lie, but figured why bother. 'This conversation is going to end,' she told him. 'I have work to do.'

'What kind of work? What are you doing down there?'

'It's been nice talking,' said Abby.

'Can I call you again? At a more convenient time?' He sounded like a suitor, someone desperate for something. Abby was hoping it was information. Maybe he didn't have anything. Maybe he was just bluffing.

But Abby didn't want to take the chance. 'I can't tell you anything. But if you want to call I can't stop you.' She left him a glimmer of hope. It would at least buy her time.

'Is it something that's protected by attorney-client privilege?' asked Thompson.

Abby imagined a mental buzzer in her mind – *Wrong*. 'I can't discuss it.' She allowed him to form his own conclusions. If they were the wrong ones that was fine with her.

'When's a good time to call?' he asked.

'Early afternoon. Before two.' This was when she walked on the beach. Abby figured she'd get his message on her tape. At least she'd have some warning before she talked to him again. He wouldn't catch her flat-footed. 'But I'm telling you there's nothing to talk about.'

'The police think there is,' said Thompson.

Abby couldn't tell if he was trying to extort information or just keeping her like a bird on a wire in hopes that sooner or later she would tell him what he wanted to know.

'Somebody's getting you into a lot of trouble.' He made it sound very ominous, but then he would if he didn't know anything.

'I've got to go.' Without another word Abby hung up.

At the other end Thompson listened to dead air as it hissed on the line before he hung up. He toyed with copies of several clipped newspaper articles in front of him on his desk as he moved them around to see how they fit. They'd been sent from a clipping service earlier in the day. One of them showed a three-column photograph, a picture of a large green zippered bag on a barge, a bag containing the body of Joey Jenrico.

CHAPTER
THIRTY-ONE

Two main streets run through the center of Christiansted; King Street going east, and Company Street going west. These are flanked by Government House and a myriad of colonial buildings, most of them Dutch in their design. When tour ships are in, these streets are body-to-body with shoppers all looking for bargains in clothing, jewelry, and liquor, even Cuban cigars on the underground market.

Abby noticed that there were very few street signs and virtually no street lights left in the town. These had fallen victim to a hurricane a year before, and had not yet been replaced.

A few days earlier she had tried to take pictures of the damage done to Government House, mostly windows blown out, but a guard had chased her off. There was a virtual conspiracy to keep the outside world from learning of the damage, that the phones didn't work and that accommodations in some places were marginal at best. If you called from the States they wouldn't tell you. Tourism was too important to the island's economy.

As Abby walked past the old scale house toward King's Wharf, she could hear the drone of the motors, the twin engine Seaborne Vista Liner. It taxied over the choppy harbor toward its mooring station on the docks. The plane carried nineteen passengers and formed a transportation link with St Thomas and the other islands. Morgan had managed to catch a flight to Charlotte Amalie on St Thomas that morning and was now on the last leg of his trip to hook up with Abby.

She saw him getting off the plane, the perennial briefcase in hand. For Morgan this was like an extra appendage, what a pouch is to a kangaroo. He was holding a wide-brimmed straw hat on his head with the other hand, keeping it on as it flapped in the prop wash from the plane.

She smiled at him and waved. Abby had long since forgiven him for his indiscretion in spending her money on the little sports car. It had served a purpose, if nothing else to occupy Charlie.

'How was the trip?' She hollered over the drone of the engines as the plane revved up and prepared to depart with another load of passengers.

Abby's shoulder-length hair, which was now bleached by the sun, blew in the wind as Spencer looked at her and then gave her a peck on the cheek. He was dressed in a white linen suit, something comfortable for the tropics that she would not have guessed Morgan had in his closet. She wondered if he bought it for the trip. 'All you need is the whip and the gun,' she told him.

'I could have used those with Cutler. He didn't want to let me come. I told him I had a meeting with an old maritime client in San Juan.'

'He bought it?'

'It's true. Hey, listen, any lawyer who can't come up with a reason for business someplace in the world in fifteen minutes has no business practicing.' Morgan smiled at her.

'Besides, the guy's file's been on my desk for two years. It's about time I got around to it. Of course I could have done it by mail. I called him, set up a meeting for next week. We'll do some business, go to a bar and have a few drinks, and I'll send the bill to Cutler.'

Abby laughed, then led him away from the noise and hustle of the docks toward Company street, past the white wood-framed church with its tall steeple. They talked as they strolled along the covered sidewalk.

'So how much does he know?' Morgan looked tired and drawn after flying all day. He was talking about Charlie, who was off on a frolic somewhere on the island in Abby's car.

'He's making noises about staying down here,' said Abby. 'That's all I need. And he knows enough to make trouble if he decides to.' But Abby was worried about more than Charlie.

Around the corner and a block up from the old apothecary was Indies, one of the better restaurants and watering holes in Christiansted. It served exotic cuisine to the strains of music that owed its tempo to West Africa and its lyrics to Latin America, all spiced by the hot beat of steel drums. It was a good place to talk because people couldn't hear you, and Charlie wouldn't waltz in on them.

The entrance was a wrought-iron gate that led into a bricked courtyard. There were hanging carriage lanterns and a kitchen behind an arched stone doorway. Built in the 1700s as a carriage house, the courtyard was covered with a series of translucent roofs under which were tables and a bar against one wall.

The maître d' led them to one of the tables and a

waiter took orders for drinks, a mai-tai for Abby, and a beer in a tall frosted pilsner glass for Spencer.

There were tanned tourists all around, a lot of young women on bar stools, so that Spencer had a hard time keeping his eyes and his attention on business.

'I will say Jack found you a gorgeous spot.' Apparently he approved of St Croix. 'But it's awfully damn hot.'

'Thick blood,' said Abby. She tapped her drink to his. 'Take off your tie and drink some of that. It'll thin it out.'

Spencer was a fan of the Northwest. He was used to rain that was cold. Still, the bodies on the stools were a definite attraction and Abby smiled as she watched him stealing glances. It seemed as if Spencer never got away for much fun. Even with her problems she planned to show him a good time while he was down here.

'Before I forget,' said Abby. 'Somebody called for you the other day. Left a message.' She pulled the note from her purse, the one with the name of the ship, the *Cuesta Verde* – San Juan. 'He didn't tell me who he was. He said you'd know what this meant.'

Morgan read the note and laughed. 'Cummings. You'd think he still worked for the F.B.I. He's an investigator. Never wants to leave a name. Just tell 'em only what they need to know. Loves to be mysterious,' said Morgan.

'He succeeds,' said Abby.

Morgan pocketed the note.

'Now tell me about Jermaine. What's he up to?'

'Jack's still in New York. He'll be down in a couple of days.'

'Good. Then we can talk. Is he living at the house with you?' Morgan's eyes darted and he took a sip as if to cover the question.

Abby didn't like it, but she answered. 'He has a place at the Buccaneer. It's a resort down the road.'

'He's staying there?'

'That's what I said,' said Abby.

Morgan looked at the bubbles rising in his glass before he spoke. 'He's wrong for you. You know that.'

'How is it that everybody else knows what's right and wrong for me,' said Abby, 'when I don't even know myself.'

'There's just something wrong about him,' said Morgan. 'Call it intuition.'

'Yeah. He says the same thing about you.'

'What does he say?'

'He says you're a humorless tight-ass. And if you keep asking questions like this I'm inclined to agree with him.'

Morgan smiled. 'O.K. But he is trouble.' He raised his hand before she could respond as if to say it was the last word on the subject.

'Listen to me. You're getting deeper and deeper into trouble here,' said Morgan.

'I'll tell you what trouble is. Trouble is all of these distractions. Until two days ago I was flying through the manuscript on the sequel. Then Thompson calls and I haven't written a word since. He's given me a terminal case of writer's block. You'd think the man has nothing better to do in life but to track me down. You'd think it was Watergate,' said Abby. 'What I can't figure out is how he found me. What do we do about him?'

'A problem,' said Spencer.

'Tell me about it.'

'No. I mean bigger than you know.' Morgan was trying to figure some way to break it to her so that she would believe him.

Abby looked across the table at him.

'I think I know how he found you.'

'How?'

'Listen, I know what you're thinking. I'm jealous. Vindictive, whatever. But I think Jack told him.'

'Give it a break,' said Abby. She reached for her hair and pulled it, shaking her head at the same time. She was getting angry at their constant backbiting. If they didn't quit, Abby was of a mind to disappear where neither of them could find her until the book was finished.

'Think about it,' said Morgan. 'Who else knew where to find you? Who had your phone number? I mean, besides you and me.'

'For one, there's Charlie,' said Abby.

Morgan made a face of dismissal. 'Why would he call the reporter? He wouldn't even know the guy's name. How would he have found him?'

Morgan was right. Charlie didn't know that Thompson was chasing Abby on a story. Jack did.

'Admit it,' said Morgan. 'He's gotten to you. He's playing you like a piano, and the tune right now is not sounding good.'

'Stop it.' Abby didn't want to hear it. 'I'm starting to feel like a scrap of meat being fought over by two dogs.' She turned sideways in her chair so that she didn't have to look at him anymore and sipped from the drink that she now held in her hand. There were icy drips off the bottom of the glass onto her legs that were now darkly tanned. They contrasted nicely with the tight white shorts that she wore.

'I'm sorry you feel that way,' said Spencer. 'But somebody has to tell you. I think you're in danger.'

When she glanced over her shoulder at him, Spencer

had a look of seriousness that Abby could not ignore.

'Think about it,' he said. 'Think about your conversation with Thompson and what he said when he called.'

'What do you mean?'

'Did he say anything about Jack or Gable Cooper not being the author?'

Abby thought for a moment. 'He didn't seem to know the title of the book or the author.'

'Precisely. Because it wouldn't serve Jack's purposes to give him that information. What were the questions he asked?'

'He talked about the murders, Theresa and Joey. He linked them to the book. And he knew the police were looking for me.'

'Someone had given him that information along with the implication that maybe you were involved.' Morgan thumped the table with two fingers to make the point. 'It's just the kind of stuff someone might like to see in print if they wanted to discredit you. Now think, who would have a motive to discredit you? Who would gain if you were linked with some scandal just as you were trying to go public on the book?'

'What are you saying?'

'I'm saying look at the facts. Open your eyes.'

'Are you trying to say that Jack killed Theresa?' Abby now turned and looked at him across the table squarely.

Morgan's silence answered the question.

'I don't believe that. No. He wouldn't do that.'

For a moment she said nothing. Morgan allowed the silence to erode her convictions.

'What would he gain by her death?' said Abby. They were back to logic, Morgan's court.

'Theresa knew about the book,' he said. 'She knew you were the author. That would be a threat if he were making a move on the book. Don't you see it?'

'And Joey?' said Abby.

'He screwed with the movie rights, remember. Put himself in the middle. And Jack knew that, too. Remember? He was blind but he still covered it in New York with Carla. That cock-and-bull story about his old drug-induced friend who was passing himself off as Gable Cooper.'

Abby thought for a moment. 'No. I can't accept that. He wouldn't kill two people. Not over something like this.'

'What, over seven million dollars in advances and royalties. I've got relatives who would kill *me* for that. People who actually like me,' said Morgan.

'So what are you saying? He's going to steal the book?'

'We've tied it up in a nice package for him already,' said Morgan.

'But you've got him nailed seven ways from Sunday,' said Abby. 'Signed contracts and copyrights.' She looked at him, but Morgan didn't say anything.

'Well, you do, don't you?'

'Yes we've got contracts. We have a copyright. But the publicity has a life of its own. I've never seen anything like it. It's huge. Jack's face is all over the airwaves. Every twenty minutes I'm seeing ads on T.V. You've been down here. I don't think you realize . . .'

'That was the plan,' said Abby.

'Yes, but you don't understand. Jack and the book have become the same thing. I don't know how to explain it.' Morgan started talking with his hands, for once at a loss for words. 'Celebrity has a dynamic all of its own. Once it's out there, it's like the genie out of the bottle. The atom out of the bomb. How do you corral it?

Control it for your own purposes?'

Abby listened to him. She didn't like it, but she had to admit that he was right.

'It's gonna give Jack a big stick to use on us,' said Morgan. 'It puts the publisher in a hell of a position to scream fraud if they don't like it when you tell them the truth, especially if you're being questioned by the cops in a murder investigation at the time . . . Well. Jack's got extra leverage, doesn't he?'

'But I have an alibi. I was on a plane.'

'Tell it to the cops. He doesn't care. Besides, people have been known to hire other people to kill,' said Morgan.

'But why? Why would I kill Theresa? She was my friend.'

'Friends kill friends all the time. That isn't going to sway the police. We made a tactical blunder,' said Spencer. 'We should never have allowed him to bring you down here. It made it look like you were running. Evidence of flight. Guilty conscience,' said Morgan.

'I had to get away, you know that. The police would have been all over me, asking questions about the book.'

Still Abby knew he was right. Her plan had succeeded at a level far beyond her wildest dreams. She had underestimated the buzz on the book and the public's ready acceptance of Jack. She had started a small fire to warm her career, and now it was threatening to burn her alive.

What they couldn't control was the spin when Abby came clean. When she went public with the truth about the book. Was fame transferable like a children's game of tag? Or would the spin take a darker turn toward scandal? Neither of them had any answers.

Morgan took another swallow of beer before he spoke.

'I have something here that may change your mind. I didn't want to tell you over the phone. Jack is not the innocent you think he is.'

'I never said he was innocent.' Abby could have said innocents don't carry guns, but why throw fuel on Morgan's fire.

'I mean in the literary sense,' said Spencer. 'He's written a book.'

'I know. He's got a trunk full of unpublished manuscripts. He's shown them to me.'

'Did he show you this one?' Morgan fished in his briefcase and pulled out the book from the used book store. He passed it over to Abby.

She was now stone silent. She read the name of the author on the spine, Kellen Raid, the same name Jack had used on the false passport at his house.

She gave Morgan an incredulous look like she didn't believe this.

'How do you know it's his?'

'Look at the dedication,' said Morgan.

She opened it and read. The look on Abby's face when she finished was one of sheer pain, the realization of betrayal.

'Why?' she said. 'Why didn't he tell me?'

'If he had, would you have used him?'

'I don't know.' At the moment, it was the only honest answer she could give. The fact that Jack was published would have spelled trouble. If Bertoli had known, he would never have agreed to the big book budget. In publishing circles, with its idiotic rules, the sheen would have been off the package if he couldn't present Jack, his major find, as a virgin author.

'That's why he didn't tell us,' said Morgan. 'And it gets worse.' He disappeared back into his briefcase and a moment later came up with some folded pages. He passed them to Abby.

'Read and weep,' he told her.

Abby didn't know if she wanted to. Everything was coming apart.

'I stopped in South Carolina on the way down.' Morgan talked without looking at her, his head cast down at the table as if muses were speaking to him from his glass of beer.

'I went to Beaufort. It was a long shot, but I figured it was a small town with a newspaper. I thought maybe the fact that a local resident had published a book might be big news in a small town. I was right. I found this in the paper's morgue. The piece was done almost nine years ago. Jack was a lot younger.' He pointed to the picture on the first folded page. It was a photocopy, but still it was clear enough for Abby to recognize Jack's beaming smile as he sat at a desk and held up a copy of the book. The title and his name were in the cutline underneath.

'Apparently his editor did a lot of work on it. Cleaned it up,' said Morgan. 'But their timing was off. It was a military thriller published a little more than a year before military thrillers hit it big. They talk in there about military stories having no future. Even so,' said Morgan, 'it hit the regional bestsellers list in Atlanta. That was the hook for the news story.'

Abby felt like she'd been sucker-punched. She picked up the pages and read while the sharp timbre of steel drums and the hum of human voices blended in the open courtyard.

The portrait drawn by the article was of a young

writer obsessed by the bestsellers list. When the book hit the regional list, Jack had taken a mortgage on his house and had spent all his savings trying to promote the book onto the national lists. He bought advertising space in newspapers around the country and went on tour. He even tried selling the book out of the trunk of his car. But he had failed. It was a testament to the dynamics of distribution and marketing. Without a push from a big publisher and their network of contacts, he had wasted his money, and lost his dream.

When she finished reading she dropped the pages on the table and stared off into the distance, right through Morgan as if he wasn't there. She was in a state of shock, her stomach turning over. She didn't know whether to be angry or to cry. She couldn't believe that Jack hadn't told her about this. They had talked about his manuscripts. He wanted her to help him get them published; eight of them, and one other that he had mentioned but declined to discuss. Now she knew why.

'How could he?' Abby thought she loved him. She had trusted Jack, told him things she had never told anyone, not even Morgan. The sense of betrayal was overwhelming.

'Listen to me.' Morgan tried to get her to focus. 'We can deal with Charlie. We can even deal with this reporter. You can move again if you have to. Find another location. There's a million islands. We can lose him again. Right now our biggest problem is what to do with Jermaine.'

Abby's first reaction was to call him in New York and scream at him over the phone. Morgan talked her out of it.

'We know he's lied to us,' said Spencer. 'What else

he's done or planning on doing we don't know. We still have leverage.'

'What?'

'You haven't shown him the outline for the sequel?'

She shook her head.

'Or any of the manuscript?'

'No.'

'Smart girl. From everything we know the guy's landlocked when it comes to a keyboard. He can't write and he knows it. That's our trump card.'

'He could find a ghost writer,' said Abby.

'Not if he doesn't know what the story's about.' They were both confident that Jack would never be able to come up with a story line that would track well on the first book. Not something that would satisfy Bertoli or Carla. For the moment they still had a leash on Jack.

But Abby was troubled by something else. 'Do you really think he killed Theresa?'

Spencer looked at her but didn't speak. His eyes said it all.

'Don't tell him anything. Keep him in the dark. Don't say anything about this.' Morgan tapped the cover of the book on the table. 'At least until we can figure some way to move him out of the picture. To take control.'

'How?'

'I don't know. Give me some time and I'll figure it out. I've been thinking,' said Morgan, 'about leaving the firm. We could go someplace. Get away from all of this. Jermaine. These games. Live a real life. Maybe go to Europe. You and I.'

Abby was stunned. She had known for years that he was attracted, but she never thought he would actually bring himself to say 'Let's go away.'

'I can't.'

'Why not?'

'What are you suggesting?'

'I'm not suggesting anything,' said Morgan. He was silent, just looking at her for a moment, and then popped it. 'I'm asking you to marry me.'

Abby didn't say a word, not with her lips. Her answer was conveyed more by the look she didn't give him. Eyes off to the side, she refused to make contact, looking for a graceful way to say it. The man Abby loved had betrayed her. The man who loved her was a friend. Friends and lovers were two different things, like night and day.

'I know you've had a bad marriage,' said Morgan.

'It's not that.'

'Then what?'

'I value your friendship. Enjoy being around you,' said Abby.

'But?' said Morgan.

'But there has to be something more than that.'

'There could be if you give it a chance.'

'We've known each other a long time,' said Abby.

'But not in the way that I mean.' He was pleading, and it made it all the more difficult.

'I can't marry you, Morgan.'

'Why?'

'Because I don't love you.' She finally said it.

Morgan looked at her across the table, eyes that were filled with hurt. It almost brought tears to her own so that she ended up looking away. He was saying nothing. Abby finally turned to him, reached across and touched his hand. 'Friends?' she said.

For an instant, it looked as if he would pull his hand away. Then he left it, lifted his eyes, and said: 'Friends.'

CHAPTER
THIRTY-TWO

The dance floor overflowed with couples moving to the beat of steel drums, as Abby, Jack, and Morgan arrived at the terrace bar of the Buccaneer for dinner.

Jack had flown in a few hours earlier, expecting them to be throwing parties over the book. Instead, Abby was cool and withdrawn. Morgan had set up in the guest room at the beach house with Abby. Jack's things were back in his room at the Buccaneer.

Jack had whispered in her ear that he wanted a moment with her alone. She told him that anything he had to say he could say in front of Morgan. She said it loud enough that Spencer could hear. At that moment, Jack knew something had happened. He was in trouble.

He ordered drinks from the bar and waited as the bartender mixed them. Maybe a little alcohol would ease the tensions and loosen tongues.

Back at the table, Spencer tried to keep Abby from saying too much. 'When he comes back, let me do the talking. Whatever you do, don't mention his book.'

She nodded. For a woman with a novel high on the bestsellers list and an audience that was growing from thousands towards millions, Abby was remarkably subdued. Suddenly none of it seemed to matter. Abby's mind was occupied by a single thought: whether Jack had anything to do with Theresa Jenrico's death.

She kept trying to convince herself that it wasn't possible. She wanted to believe that her instincts weren't that flawed, that she could never feel the way she did about a man who would do such a thing. But the questions kept coming, the kind that lawyers deal with when they have a client they don't trust; mostly motive and opportunity.

Abby tried to remember where Jack was when Theresa was killed. She tried to piece it together. He had left New York ahead of her. Business at Coffin Point, he'd told her. But Jack had turned up in Seattle, unannounced. Abby's mind was working overtime, tortured by the possibilities.

She watched as Jack leaned on one of the brass elephant heads that graced the bar railing, waiting on the bartender.

A young woman with long dark hair and curvaceous moves boogied to the edge of the dance floor, gyrating to the sounds of the music. She took a good look at Jack. She seemed to undress him with her eyes as she did the bump and grind. Jack offered one of his enigmatic smiles in return. Connery as Bond. The girl displayed the pouting look of erotic arrogance that pretty young women seem to own.

Jack raised a glass in toast to her as he headed back to their table with two drinks. Abby was abstaining. Morgan had ordered scotch and soda.

The soft breezes of the eastern trade winds wafted through the open air of the dining room under the barrel-vaulted ceiling with its fans like wounded birds.

Some of the paddles were missing, victims of last season's hurricanes. The pungent odor of Cruzan rum filled the place along with strains of music.

Without asking, Jack took Abby's hand, and before she knew what was happening she found herself on the dance floor in his arms. They went cheek to cheek. She was stiff and uneasy.

Jack had lied to her. He never told her about the book he published. Now she was left to wonder what else he might have done, about Joey Jenrico, and whether Jack had killed him. The vocalist tortured lyrics, *'knock, knock, knockin on devil's door.'* The words of the song echoed in her ears, and Abby wondered whether she had not made a deal with her own kind of devil.

'Why don't you pitch it in for the night and join us with a drink?' said Jack. As the music ended, he ran his hand up Abby's arm and rested it on her shoulder, a gesture of intimacy. She froze.

'I have a book to write, remember?' She forced a smile and took her seat at the table.

Jack pulled up a chair. 'Where's Charlie tonight?' He looked at Abby, but Spencer answered.

'We don't know.'

'Putting mileage on my car and his body,' said Abby.

'Shacked up somewhere,' said Morgan. 'Maybe he'll catch the clap.'

'Now there's poetic justice,' said Abby. Charlie hadn't returned the car in three days. The last time she drove it, there was a pair of woman's panties in the glove box.

'Well, I hate to throw hot water on a cold party,' said Jack. 'But assuming he doesn't drive off a cliff of contract a quick social disease, has anybody considered an alternate plan for dealing with him?'

'We have,' said Morgan.

'Well, is somebody gonna tell me?'

'We're providing him with a financial incentive to cooperate,' said Spencer.

'Is that lawyer-speak for buying him off?' said Jack.

'If you like.'

Jack raised an eyebrow and looked at Abby. 'You do what you want,' he told her, 'but I think you're making a big mistake.'

'We've already discussed it,' said Spencer. 'We made a decision and it's done.'

Morgan had drawn a line in the sand that was hard for Jack to miss even though he'd only been back on the island for two hours. Spencer was in charge, and it didn't seem like there was much Jack could do to reach Abby.

'I take it you've already told Charlie you're gonna pay him?'

'Not yet, but we have every reason to believe he'll accept,' said Spencer.

'Oh yeah. Like Dracula taking in a bleeder,' said Jack. 'How much are you going to offer?'

'That's not for you to know,' said Spencer.

'Does he know you wrote the book?' Jack was trying to draw Abby out, but Morgan answered.

'Not unless you told him.'

'I didn't tell him a thing.'

'He doesn't know,' said Abby. 'He thinks we wrote it together. If he knew it was mine, the price would go up. He figures he has no claim on your part of it.'

'That's decent of him,' said Jack.

'Decency doesn't enter into it. You'd know that if you knew Charlie.'

'And you've agreed to all of this? Paying to keep him quiet even though he's stumbling around and doesn't know squat?'

She nodded.

'Stumbling around he could cause a lot of trouble,' said Morgan.

'If it were my money, I wouldn't pay him a dime.'

'It's not your money,' said Abby.

'You're right,' said Jack. 'Your money. Your mistake.'

'Jeez, you're a hot shot, aren't you?' said Spencer.

'Morgan, don't!' Abby tried to stop him.

'No. No. I want to hear what he has to say. How he'd handle it. Tell me. I want to know. What would you do?'

'I'd talk to him.'

'Just like that.'

'Yeah.' Jack shrugged. 'Just like that.'

'And what would you say to him? What magic words would you use?'

'I'd reason with him.'

Morgan smiled, then he laughed. 'You'd reason with him.'

'Yeah. He's a very intelligent guy. We reasoned in New York,' said Jack.

'You make logic sound like a four-letter word,' said Spencer.

'Jack can be very persuasive,' said Abby. 'I saw him reason with some people in San Juan.'

Jack looked at her. 'They aren't asking you for money anymore.'

'One of them isn't asking for anything anymore,' said Abby.

'What the hell happened in San Juan?' said Morgan.

'Nevermind. I'd rather pay the money.' Abby'd had enough of the conversation.

'And what's to stop him from coming back for more?' said Jack.

'There won't be any more, because by the time he gets

around to spending what we give him, it'll be over,' said Abby.

'What are you gonna do, give him your bank card?'

'No. We're moving the schedule forward,' she told him.

'What are you talking about?' Jack looked at her.

'I mean we're not waiting for paperback publication to tell Bertoli that I wrote the book.'

Jack looked dazed. He had expected a lot of things, but not this. 'But it's going great in New York.'

'Charlie brings a new dimension,' said Abby. 'We can't keep him quiet forever.'

'Besides, some other things have come up,' said Morgan.

'What things?'

'You don't have to worry,' said Morgan. 'You're going to get your share. That's all you need to know,' he told Jack.

'No. What I need to know is what's going on. When are you going to tell Bertoli?'

'We're going to give it a month on the list,' said Abby. 'By then the hook should be set.'

Jack shook his head like he couldn't believe it. 'When you start something, you should finish it.' This was aimed at Abby. 'I didn't mind playing your games. Going to New York and doing the Alex and Carla show. In fact, for a while diddling corporate America was sorta fun. But these people are playing real business with real money,' said Jack. 'They made promises and they've lived up to them. You can say what you want but they delivered, which is a hell of a lot more than you've done.'

'They got what they bargained for,' said Abby. 'They got you.'

'Yes, and now you want to screw with their hardcover campaign,' said Jack. 'In the middle of it you want to jerk the carpet out from under all of us.'

'What's wrong,' said Morgan. 'You don't think the book will continue to succeed without you?'

'I put myself on the line,' said Jack. 'That's what wrong.'

Abby looked at him. 'What are you talking about?'

'You sent me up there alone and told me to wing it. So I did. I made a promise.'

'What kind of promise?' said Abby.

Jack hesitated for a moment. Then he spoke. 'I told Bertoli that from what I could see he'd delivered on his part of the deal. I told him we'd deliver the outline so he could see where the sequel was going. I thought that was fair.'

'You thought it was fair?' said Abby.

'You're on the list inside of five. When's the last time that happened?'

'You had no right,' said Abby. 'I told you on the phone . . .'

'And I told you we'd talk about it when I got back,' said Jack. 'I come back to find that you're getting ready to pitch me out onto the street.'

'There's nothing to talk about.' Abby was furious. She had visions of the outline landing in Hollywood before she could finish the manuscript. Morgan was right. Without her realizing, Jack was taking control.

The maître d' came over. Their table in the dining room was ready. Abby was angry. Her face was flushed.

Jack was the first one out of his chair. 'I gave them my word.'

'I guess you're just going to have to tell him you made a mistake,' said Abby.

445

'A mistake?' said Jack.

'Fine. Tell them you lied. I don't care what you tell them. They're not seeing the outline.'

'Well. I guess you've made your decision.' Jack froze Abby with a look and then turned a hard gaze on Morgan.

'Enjoy your dinner.' Without another word he turned and headed off in the other direction, toward the stairs and the path that led to his room down on the water.

A few tables away in a dark corner of the bar, an African American dressed in a sport coat and tie sipped what looked like bourbon as he read a newspaper. The drink was iced tea and the newspaper was three days old.

His eyes kept wandering over the top of the paper, looking at the three people at the table thirty feet away. They were engaged in a heated argument, but Logano couldn't hear a word. The music was too loud.

What the people at the table couldn't see was that on the table behind the newspaper was a photograph. It was a picture of Abby, mildly distorted by the electronic transmission that had sent it from Seattle to the Patrick Sweeny Police Headquarters in St Croix.

It had taken Sergeant Logano four days to locate the woman. The island was not large by U.S. standards, with only two sizable towns, but there were a thousand secluded houses along the shore and more up in the hills. She could have been staying in any one of them. Logano felt fortunate to have found her at all.

If you knew the island, there were only three or four places where you went to look for tourists. The bartender at the Buccaneer was one of them. He recognized Abby's photograph. Logano staked the place out for three nights running. Tonight he got lucky.

He continued to watch them while he wiped the sweat from his forehead with a handkerchief.

He pocketed the handkerchief and studied the two men with her. One of them had to be the lawyer. Which one Logano wasn't sure. He didn't know who the other one was. The Seattle homicide detective who gave them the information said nothing about a second man. But they had tailed the lawyer to the airport. After he boarded his plane, the Seattle police had talked to the airline clerk and discovered that he was headed for St Croix via South Carolina. What he was doing in the Carolinas they didn't know.

For Logano it was a sensitive assignment, one that required discretion. Seattle didn't have a warrant for the woman's arrest, though they were working on it. Right now they wanted to talk to her. Logano and his department were performing a professional courtesy. His job was to find her and call Seattle.

Logano was no fool. He knew that the woman was as good as cuffed and on her way to the States. When the Americans got their teeth into something, they were relentless. They might pick her up on a technical violation, Customs or Immigrations, but they would get her, of that he was sure.

He lowered the paper onto the table and covered the photograph. He felt the bulge under his left arm, the Smith & Wesson three-fifty-seven magnum with its four-inch barrel. Logano was of the old school. No semiautomatic spray and pray for him. He didn't want to shoot anybody, but if he had to, he believed that doing people should be like elephants; one shot with something that would bring them down.

He lifted a copy of the faxed report from Seattle out of

the inside pocket of his coat and glanced at it while he watched them.

According to the report, they didn't think she was armed, but they couldn't be sure. They wanted to talk to her regarding a double homicide. Logano wasn't going to get his ass shot off performing a professional courtesy for anybody.

As he put the report back in his pocket, the maître d' approached the woman's table. He couldn't hear, but Logano assumed that they were being told that their table in the dining room was ready. It seemed the maître d' had interrupted their argument.

One of the men, good-looking and tall, stood. They had some words, then he turned and headed for the stairs and the parking lot. The woman and the other man got up and headed for the dining room.

For a moment, Logano thought about following the man down the stairs, then settled back in his chair. Right now his job was the woman walking to dinner with her companion. Lose her and he might not be so lucky again. He had to find out where she was living and call the information to the police in Seattle. There was no hurry. He could always pick up other threads later, after he had the place where she lived under surveillance.

Cheeseburgers in Paradise was an open-air restaurant with live music on weekends and a bar that served anything you wanted to drink. It was a hangout for the young set, and lately Charlie was feeling particularly young.

He hit on a sweet little thing sitting on a bar stool. She was wearing a short skirt like a cheerleader, a tight pull-over top that showed her tits. Charlie was big on tits. He bought her dinner, a burger and fries, while he was busy throwing back shots of Grand Marnier with tequila chasers.

The girl was talkative, tanned, and vivacious. She was living on a small boat with a friend who had sailed to another island for a few days, and now she had no place to stay. Charlie couldn't believe his good luck. She was freckled and athletic. Charlie figured she could screw like a bunny.

About eleven-thirty he took her to his car to impress her and found her boyfriend waiting for them. They rolled him in the dirt of the parking lot, took his wallet and watch, and left Charlie in some tall grass to sleep it off. They were too smart to take his car. Where do you go on an island with a stolen car?

He woke up in the weeds a little before four in the morning, staring up at a sky full of stars that all seemed to have twins. Charlie's head felt like a balloon. Slowly he sat up.

The lights from Cheeseburgers in Paradise were out, and the parking lot was empty, except for Abby's little blue sports car. Charlie couldn't remember what happened. He had only vague recollections of his face being pressed between two breasts when the lights went out. The girl's face was a hazy memory.

He got to his knees, and found his keys in his pocket, then stumbled to the car. When he looked at his hand he found there was blood on it. Charlie felt the back of his head. There was a knot the size of a baseball and when he touched it everything above his shoulders throbbed. He wondered what they'd hit him with.

He went to check the time and realized for the first time that his watch was gone. 'Shit.' He patted the seat of his pants and realized they'd gotten his wallet, too. 'Son of a bitch.'

He hoped he wouldn't get stopped by a cop on his way back to the Buccaneer. It took him twenty minutes weaving all over the two-lane road. He was lucky there was no traffic.

Even the guard at the gate had gone home. The barricade was up so Charlie didn't have to pass muster. He drove up the hill past the main building and down toward the bungalows on the water, then parked the car in front of his room. For a few minutes he thought about sleeping right there, behind the wheel, then finally cleared his head enough to fish for the room key in his pocket. They had left this and a little pocket change.

He didn't bother to lock the car but made his way to the short path leading to his room. Nothing was going right tonight. The light over the door had burned out and Charlie couldn't seem to find the keyhole in the door. It was probably just as good he hadn't gotten her home. He probably couldn't have found that hole, either.

He missed three times with the key when he heard something thrashing in the brush behind him and started to turn.

'What the fu . . .' Charlie didn't feel anything, but he couldn't understand why his words no longer had sound.

CHAPTER
THIRTY-THREE

It was early morning, just a little after six, when Abby burst into Morgan's room. She threw open the door so hard that it slammed against the wall and came back at her.

'Get up. Get out of bed!' she yelled. 'Jack's left the island.'

Spencer rolled over in the bed and lifted his head, sleep still apparent in his eyes.

'What?'

'He's gone.' She grabbed his feet at the bottom of the bed with both hands. 'And he's taken my outline with him.'

'What are you talking about?'

'I left it on the table next to the computer last night and this morning it's gone. I called Jack's room at the Buccaneer. They told me he left for the airport early this morning.'

'Where's he gone?'

'They didn't know, but if I had to guess I'd say New York.'

Morgan wiped sleep from his eyes sat up and shook his head. 'He checked out of the room?'

'No.'

'You said he wasn't scheduled to go back to New York for three more days,' said Morgan.

'I know. It looks like you were right. He's making a move on the book.'

Morgan got out of bed and started looking for his clothes, stepped into the bathroom, and they talked through the closed door while he changed from his pajamas.

Abby had turned the house upside down, but there was no sign of the outline to the sequel. Apart from the copyright, it was her only remaining point of control. She remembered leaving the outline on the table by her computer before going to dinner the night before. Now it was gone.

'You heard him last night. Something's going on in New York. He's cut some kind of a deal with them. He intends to deliver the outline. So what do we do?' she asked.

'We don't panic,' said Morgan.

'He'll deliver the outline. Maybe he already has. He could have faxed it this morning for all we know,' said Abby.

'We need to think. The important thing now is how to deal with the publisher,' said Morgan.

'That's going to be tough with Jack in the middle,' said Abby. Morgan came out of the bathroom with his clothes on, looking for his socks and shoes.

'That's why we took precautions,' said Morgan.

She looked at him.

'The documents. The registration of copyright and the contracts we had him sign. It's time for plan B,' said Morgan.

'What are you talking about?'

'I guess it's O.K. to tell you now. You promise you won't kill me?'

'Kill you for what?' said Abby.

'I never trusted him from the beginning,' said Morgan. 'I was worried he had too much control. So I contacted another lawyer in New York, with a major firm that specializes in publishing matters, First Amendment, copyright infringement, that kind of stuff. I knew sooner or later there would be a problem with Jack. So I wanted to flank him.'

Abby gave him a look. 'What about this firm?'

'I figured they would give us credibility if we got into a showing match with Jermaine. It's a large firm, one that publishers deal with all the time. I put them on retainer about two months ago and made arrangements with one of the partners. Kept 'em in my hip pocket,' said Morgan. 'I hope you don't mind. I used your money.'

Abby smiled at him. Morgan was always two jumps ahead. It was the reason she valued him. His mind was like a taxi meter, running twenty-four hours a day. If his billings had kept pace, he would have retired as a millionaire ten years earlier.

'How much have you told these lawyers in New York?'

'They know Jack didn't write the book. At least they have my word for it. The trick now is to get to them with the documents, the copyright, and the contracts that Jack signed. To have them finesse it with the publisher so as to minimize damage.'

'Minimize damage hell,' said Abby. 'I want to kick his ass.'

'Trust me,' said Morgan. 'Damage control. That's the key right now. Otherwise we run the risk of scaring

Bertoli. If he sees a protracted court battle with all of its bad press, he's gonna pull the plug on the book. That leaves you and Jack fighting over a bag of bones. This is business. We'll get even later.'

Morgan was hopeful that they could keep the ball rolling on the book without missing a beat. Simply have the publisher make Jack disappear. That would be much easier with a powerful New York law firm that talked the publishing language. Their lawyers could nail Jack's feet to the floor with one hand while they finessed Bertoli with the other.

'We can forget about waiting thirty days to tell Bertoli the truth,' said Abby. 'Jack made that impossible. Everyday we wait gives him more time to erode our position.'

'So what now?'

'First we've got to get the documents, the contracts, and the copyright, and then we've got to get to New York.' Abby's brain was in hyperdrive. 'If we're lucky, we might be able to do that by tomorrow morning.' It was now Sunday.

'They're in a safe deposit box at the bank. I didn't trust Cutler. He's probably been going through my files at night. No. I'll have to get them myself.'

He laced up his shoes. 'I'll call the airline and make reservations.'

'What do we do about the outline?' she asked.

'Do you have an extra copy?'

'In my computer.'

'Print it out. In the meantime, you package up your computer and your printer. See if you can find a box for shipping, we'll send them directly to the firm in New York.'

'What for?'

'Evidence,' said Morgan. 'You produced the outline

with that equipment, didn't you?'

Abby nodded.

'A good expert can probably prove it. One more piece of evidence for our side,' said Morgan.

It hit Abby like a thunderbolt. 'Oh my God!' The missing typewriter from her house. She looked at Morgan sitting on the bed lacing his shoes.

From her expression Morgan knew that she'd finally figured it out.

'That's why it was missing. Jack took it. How long have you known?'

'I didn't want to say anything,' said Morgan. 'I had no proof. But when we couldn't find it, you had to figure whoever demolished your house also took the typewriter. Ask yourself one question: why take an old manual typewriter and leave a perfectly good television set behind?'

'Because the manuscript had been typed on it,' said Abby.

'Precisely.'

A sober look came over Abby as she stood at the edge of the bed. 'And the accident with the electrical box.'

'It was intended for you,' said Morgan. 'Theresa just showed up at the wrong time.'

'And he killed Joey,' said Abby.

'One more loose end.'

'Aw God! I'm gonna lose it,' she told him. Abby felt sick, nauseous. She turned away and nearly retched thinking about it. She had made love to the man and all the while she was sleeping with Theresa's murderer.

'I never loved him. Never.' As if by saying it she could erase the intimate moments they'd spent together. Abby also knew it was a lie. She started to tear up.

Morgan reached out for her, but Abby was too angry

to be held. She wanted to lash out. 'I'm sorry,' she told him. 'I'm going to the police.'

'With what?' said Morgan. 'There's no evidence. What are you going to tell them, that Jack stole your outline?' He was right. She had nothing.

'I don't know. But I have to tell them something. At least point them in the right direction.'

'That's what he wants you to do. While we're trying to explain to the police, he's going to be selling the outline to Bertoli. He's probably already making plans to revoke the power of attorney.'

She looked up at him. She had forgotten about the power of attorney, the document that directed Bertoli and the film producers to send the royalties and advances to Morgan's office. Now that he'd broken from them, Jack, with a single stroke of a pen, could divert the stream of money to himself.

'He's going to have problems when he tries to write the book. I've seen his writing,' said Abby.

'For a quarter of million he can find somebody to ghost it. That leaves him with four or five million and change,' said Morgan. 'Not bad for a day's work. And right now he's got the only commodity that counts.'

Abby looked at him, a question mark.

'The name you gave him, Gable Cooper,' said Morgan. He was right. Bertoli's ad campaign had turned it into gold.

'I wanted a commercial book. I guess I got it,' said Abby.

'The question is how to keep it. If he cuts off our stream of cash, starts getting his hands on the advances and royalties, he'll be using your money to fight you in court. Where do you think Bertoli will come down if Jack gets his own army of lawyers?'

'I don't know,' said Abby.

'I don't want to find out,' said Morgan. 'We got to move fast. Oh, shit I forgot!'

When she looked over, Morgan was looking at the ceiling.

'What's the matter?'

'I'm supposed to meet with the client in San Juan tomorrow. The maritime case I told Cutler about.' He made a face at Abby, a lot of consternation.

'Break the appointment,' said Abby.

'Don't worry. I'll find some way to get out of it,' said Morgan.

He headed for the kitchen and the telephone. Morgan called the airlines, looking for reservations while Abby packed a bag, and boxed up the computer and the printer. Fortunately she'd kept the boxes she'd bought them in.

When she came into the kitchen Morgan had his hand over the mouthpiece of the phone and a dour look on his face. Things were not going well.

'Next flight doesn't leave until seven tonight.'

'Book it,' said Abby.

'Problem is they've only one seat available.'

Abby thought for a moment. 'You take it. You've got to get to Seattle and then back. I can catch a flight in the morning and go directly to New York. We can meet there. Is there anything open on the morning flights?'

Morgan went back on the line.

'They've got open seats tomorrow. Early morning flight.'

'No problem,' said Abby.

Morgan hesitated. 'I don't like it.'

'Why not?'

'What if Jack comes back?'

'Why would he come back?' Abby shook her head. 'By tonight he'll be having dinner with Carla and Bertoli. They'll be working changes into my outline and suggesting casting for the film. He's not coming back.'

'I don't know,' said Morgan. 'I don't feel comfortable.'

'What choice do we have?'

Morgan had no answer for that. He got back on the phone and ordered the tickets using his credit card, then hung up.

'We can pick them up at the airport tonight. Deliver the computer and printer for shipping at the same time.'

'I wish I knew where Charlie was,' said Abby.

'Yeah. Then we'd have your car.'

'Not that,' said Abby. 'I just don't want to leave him here alone. I know he doesn't deserve it, but I'd like to give him a heads-up. Tell him to get off the island.' While she was telling Morgan that Jack wouldn't be back, Abby was worried. She remembered Joey. He knew very little about the book, but if Morgan was right, he was killed because of that knowledge. Charlie was in danger and he didn't know it. She remembered Jack's comments about reasoning with him and the fight in San Juan. True, it may have been self-defense, but Jack thought nothing about leaving a bleeding body in the street.

'Leave a message for him at the Buccaneer,' said Morgan. 'Something discreet. Tell him to get back to Seattle. Tell him there's a pile of money waiting there for him. He'll know what to do.'

They spent the rest of the morning and the afternoon planning their moves in New York. Spencer called and left a message on voice mail with the lawyers in New York, telling them that things were now on a fast track and that a meeting was necessary Tuesday. Then he made reservations for two rooms at the Hilton in Manhattan for Monday night. Morgan, if he was on time, would come in Monday afternoon. He checked the flights between Seattle and New York and made another set of reservations. He would be flying through the night.

About six o'clock Abby called the cab while Morgan made a note with the law firm's name and address on it and taped it to the outside of the boxes with the computer and printer inside.

Ten minutes later they were on their way to the airport. Morgan gave the driver twenty bucks to forget all the speed limits. They raced through Christiansted and out toward the north end of the island. They headed west and got to the airport with only a few minutes to spare.

Morgan got the tickets at the counter, separated them, and handed Abby hers.

'I don't like this at all,' he told her. Morgan didn't want to get on the plane without her.

'There's nothing to worry about. He's in New York. I'll be out of here first thing in the morning.' She checked her ticket. 'Seven-fifteen sharp,' she told him.

'Transfer in San Juan, then to Miami, hold over for an hour and to JFK.' He repeated her itinerary as if it wasn't on the tickets.

'Now listen to me.' Morgan had a stern look on his face, all business. 'After I leave, take the package to air express and as soon as you're finished, go back to the house, go inside, and lock the doors. Don't let anybody in. Catch a cab in the morning and come right back here. No other stops, do you understand?'

She nodded dutifully and gave him a mock salute.

'I'm not kidding.'

'I know. I'll be fine.'

'I'll call you tonight, from San Juan.' He looked at his watch. 'I should be there in about an hour and a half. Stay by the phone.'

'I will.'

'Then I'll see you in New York Monday night.' He paused. 'When I asked you to come away with me, this isn't exactly what I had in mind.'

Abby smiled. 'I know. I have no right to ask this of you.'

'You didn't. I offered. Friends, remember?'

He kissed her on the forehead, then the cheek, then disappeared through the gate.

Abby went back to the taxi and told the driver to take her to air freight. There was a line, and by the time she finished, it had taken almost forty minutes to process the packages, and more than a hundred dollars to send them. She put it on her debit card.

On the drive back in the taxi she actually fell asleep so that the motion of the car stopping in front of her house woke her. When Abby opened her eyes the driver was waiting with his hand over the front seat for the fare. She collected herself, looked at the meter, then fished in her purse and came up with the money.

The cab drove away and left her standing out on Shoy Beach Road. She turned and started down the dirt driveway. It wasn't until she was halfway down that she saw it. The little blue BMW with its top down was parked in the carport next to the house. Charlie was back. At least she wouldn't be alone. She moved quickly down the driveway to the house. The front door was unlocked. She thought Morgan had locked it, but she couldn't remember.

'Charlie.' She called his name. There was no answer.

She checked the kitchen, then walked through the hall to the bedrooms. He wasn't there. She opened the sliding glass door and looked out on the beach. It was getting dark and the sand was deserted. Stars had begun to emerge in the night sky. A fingernail moon was riding a ridge of clouds on the horizon.

Abby closed the sliding door and locked it, then looked at the clock on the wall in the kitchen. Morgan's plane would be approaching San Juan. He would be calling in half an hour.

'Charlie. Don't play games with me.' Her tone was now that of a mother giving a final warning to a child. She had visions of Charlie drunk, hiding in the house, getting ready to jump her bones as she got ready for bed. It was the kind of thing Charlie would do, especially with a few drinks under his belt. Tonight he would get all he was looking for. Abby was already on edge.

His fingers moved deftly to sever the line at one of the fittings. He used two adjustable wrenches, one to hold the pipe and the other to turn the fitting. He covered both on the inside with cloth to dampen any noise and avoid scratches on the fitting. Scratches on an old pipe might be something investigators would key on.

He loosened the pressure fitting until he heard the hiss of gas. It would look better that way, something that worked its way loose. It would also give him more time to finish the job before the air in the crawl space became unbreathable.

He made his way to another junction in the line. This one led to the kitchen and up through the floor to the propane stove.

He had already smothered the pilot light for the furnace and disconnected the electronic ignition for the stove. He didn't want any unintentional accidents.

There was an open chase four feet away that led from the crawl space under the floor along an outside wall to the attic above. This was used as a passage for plumbing and electrical lines.

He fed a plastic tube he'd brought with him up into the chase measuring off twelve feet. The polyurethane tube would begin to melt at three hundred degrees. It would vaporize at the temperatures ignited by a large propane fire. They would find none of it when it was over. He opened the other fitting, and using duct tape fastened the open end of the tube to the leak in the line. It wasn't a hundred percent efficient, but it would work. Gas began to move through the tube into the attic where it would lie like a deadly fog until it was time.

Abby checked the two bathrooms. There was no sign of Charlie. Finally she went outside to the carport. The keys to her car were in the ignition. They were still on the ring with a little piece of red ribbon around it, just as they had been when Jack took them out of the envelope at the front desk of the Buccaneer the day they arrived. So much had happened since then. It seemed like another lifetime.

She removed the keys from the ignition and put them in her pocket. Abby looked around to see if maybe Charlie had taken a walk, perhaps to have a cigarette outside, but there was no sign of him.

Maybe he'd gone back to the Buccaneer. Knowing Charlie, that was it. To get a drink or carouse on the dance floor until they closed up. Half of her wanted him to stay there, to work off his horny attitude on somebody else. Half of her wanted him to come back to the house, if for no other reason than to give her someone to talk to.

Still her mind kept picking at something that didn't fit. If he wasn't here, what was the BMW doing in the carport? Maybe Charlie'd had a sudden pang of conscience? She thought about it. Not Charlie.

Abby went back inside and remembered Morgan's advice. She locked the front door and put the chain on. Then she went around the house and checked all the doors and windows. She felt paranoid, but she did it anyway.

Trade winds and open windows were the only air-conditioning the house had. The night was warm and muggy, and within a few minutes the house began to feel uncomfortable. Abby felt dizzy. She didn't know why. The accumulation of the day's heat trapped in the attic was now finding its way out down through the ceiling. There was a cool breeze outside on the beach. But tonight Abby would have to try to sleep with the windows closed.

She stepped into the bathroom, dropped her clothes on the floor, and climbed into the shower. She allowed cool water to run over her body for ten minutes, keeping track of the time on her waterproof sports watch. She didn't want to miss Morgan's call. If she failed to answer, he would panic and think something had gone wrong. He would be back on the next flight. Abby knew Spencer.

With five minutes to spare before his plane was scheduled to land in San Juan she turned off the water, toweled herself dry, and threw on a robe. She continued to towel her hair and grabbed a diet Coke from the refrigerator. Then she picked up around the house. The place was a mess. Abby had no idea when or if she would be back. She thought about arrangements to have the car shipped to Seattle and how much it might cost. She hoped Charlie had enjoyed it. Between Charlie and Jack she had only been behind the wheel twice. Men were such pricks.

It would take only a slight spark, the completed synapse of an electrical circuit to ignite the gas. He pulled himself through the small hole at the side of the house and out from under the crawl space, then took his first deep breath in several minutes.

Quickly he moved to the little metal box nailed to the siding. He lifted the cover and attached two fine lead wires to the copper terminals inside, then looked at the wire going from the box along the side of the house. It joined the power lines at the corner near the front and from there disappeared into a plastic conduit for the journey underground.

In the islands burying utility lines was the least of two bad options. Hurricanes blew down power poles and surge tides flooded underground lines.

He wired one of the fine lead wires to the end of a small spark plug and wrapped the other around the metal tip near the gap. Then he tossed the spark plug as far as he could through the hole into the crawl space.

He sniffed the fumes of gas that were now surging under the house. With every cycle a new spark would bridge the gap in the plug. He couldn't imagine that it would take more than one or two.

Abby had laid her airline tickets on the kitchen table when she entered the house, and now she picked them up to place them in her briefcase so she wouldn't forget them.

It was getting too hot. Advice or no advice, she needed some air. She opened the sliding door and stood there facing the ocean. Cool currents washed over her, blowing open the folds of her robe and bracing her naked body in the crisp salt air of the sea.

She drank her Coke and remembered the first nights on the island when ignorance was bliss, before she knew about Jack and all of his lies. Thoughts flooded her mind, all the things she had to do before morning. She remembered her manuscript, the hard copy of which was printed and piled on her work table in the bedroom. Without her computer she was out of business, at least until she got to New York.

She took another sip of Coke and looked down at the tickets in her other hand and suddenly, as if the drink had done something for the mental synapse of her brain, it hit her like a lead weight. Her passport! Abby didn't have it. It was locked in the ElSafe in Jack's room at the Buccaneer. She had forgotten about it. Where was her mind? Without it she couldn't get off the island.

She headed for the bedroom. A cold sweat broke out on her forehead. Somewhere she had a key to Jack's room, one of those plastic coded cards with holes drilled in them. But where was it? Abby hadn't used it in weeks. She couldn't remember the combination for the safe. Jack had asked her for her birth date that day she put the passport and the second debit card in the safe, and Abby had lied. She couldn't remember what she'd told him, the year. What if he'd changed the combination, or destroyed the passport? She would be trapped on the island with no way off, not before filling out a flood of forms and the bureaucracy. A million worries flooded her brain.

She headed down the hall to the bedroom. The first

thing she needed was clothes. She opened the closet and as she did, something caught her eye in the corner of the room. It was a jacket, one she had seen before, Charlie's jacket. When Abby turned her head to look for her slacks her heart nearly stopped.

'Oh shit!' It was fright on the edge of pain, like ice in her veins.

'Damn it. Jesus, Charlie.' She turned and walked away. She was gasping for air, deep breathing and feeling dizzy.

'The next you do something like this so help me!' She felt her pulse pounding in her chest. Her hand, still clutching the airline tickets, was in the opening of her robe above her breast. For a moment she thought she was actually going to pass out.

'Damn you, Charlie.' She struggled to catch her breath. She was doubled over, one hand on her knee. Charlie wasn't saying a word.

'If you ever...' It took a couple of seconds for her pulse to steady, and then anger started to take hold. She stood up straight, stretched the muscles of her rib cage, and took a deep breath. As she did this, Abby stared directly into the mirror over the dresser drawers.

Charlie was still in the shadows of the closet. He hadn't moved. He was wearing some artsy tie-die shirt, white with a brown-red blaze from shoulder to waist. No doubt some hot threads for the clubs, she thought.

She looked in the glass without turning around and suddenly realized that Charlie seemed to have legs of rubber. His knees were splayed akimbo like some puppet, his shoes lost in the hanging garments at the rear of her closet. It was a posture that defied gravity.

His expression was of the queerest smile, and when Abby turned she saw the reason. The black wire of a coat hanger was coiled around his neck and wound over the clothes rod that held up his body. The rust-colored hue of Charlie's shirt took on new meaning.

Abby's hands went to her mouth, but the scream never came out. She ran headlong down the hall. Two strides and a piercing screech that she hardly recognized as her own echoed off the walls. Like water finding the course of least resistance, she erupted into the living room and saw only one thing – the open sliding door to the deck. In an instant she was though it into the darkness beyond, bare feet over rocks and marsh grass, not feeling the broken conch shells like knives cutting her flesh.

She was twenty feet from the house, breathless, and frantic, out of her mind when she heard it. The ringing of a telephone somewhere in the distance behind her. It stopped her dead in her tracks like she'd been hit by a bullet from a rifle. Morgan! He was calling. She turned and took one step back.

The next chime of the phone was seared in her mind by the heat of the blast. It lifted her off of her feet, and toasted the front of her body as the concussion of the shock wave threw her ten feet onto her back in the sand. It was like a surreal dream. The fiery mushroom jumped a hundred feet into the night sky, its brilliant orange and yellow flare obliterating the stars. The roof of the house actually lifted skyward and buckled in mid-air. An instant later it disintegrated into a million flaming pieces.

Abby scrambled to her feet and ran, then dove for the sand as burning embers and fiery shards of wood descended around her. There was a secondary blast and the remains of a water heater bounced with a dull thud on the ground twenty feet from where she lay. One hand went to her face and she felt the warmth of blood. A tiny piece of glass was embedded in her cheek just below her right eye. She plucked it out and lay there dazed. A corner of her robe was on fire, still burning. She finally gathered enough sense to sit, and managed to pound out the flames on her clothing in the sand.

Then she crawled toward the beach under the shelter of a young tamarind tree. She pulled the robe tight around her naked body and looked back toward the house. The walls and roof were gone. All that remained were the flaming innards fueled by the night air, and flickering embers on the dark ground like stars as far as she could see.

In the glow of the burning house a solitary figure was silhouetted on a bluff above the house near the road. For an instant, Abby started to get up to run toward it. Then she froze, trained her eyes to the night sky, took a closer look and realized – it was Jack.

CHAPTER
THIRTY-FOUR

A bby was naked except for the short terrycloth robe. Everything she owned on the island was now either cinders or burning. The remnants of the small sports car, its fuel tank blazing, was a burned-out hulk in the carport.

On the hill, silhouetted in the headlights of a vehicle, Jack stood looking at the devastation. At this moment the only advantage that Abby possessed was the fact that he thought she was dead.

She lay huddled in the darkness under the tamarind tree, waves crashing on the beach behind her. The white water lapping at the shore took on a fluorescent quality in the dark crescent shape of the cove. It was a rising tide and the foam washed up on the sand just a few yards from her feet. In the distance, she could see the indistinct outline of dark cliffs at the point near the Buccaneer. Abby could hear the loud music from the bar, but the building was around the point. There was no way they could have seen the blast. It was more of a whoosh than an explosion. She doubted if they heard it.

She had no money, no clothes. Her purse with the debit card now lay in the burning ashes of the house.

Jack had been thorough. His only mistake was one of timing. Charlie had saved her life. The last act of a dead man.

She wondered if Jack had used some kind of a clock or watch to set it off, or if he had detonated the explosion by remote control. This sent a shudder through Abby. The flash that singed her body seemed to come from the back side of the house toward the beach. She guessed he had wired the large propane tank near the kitchen. There was nothing left to indicate that the tank even existed. The police would think it was an accident.

When she looked back at the bluff, Jack was gone. She sank further into the shadows, wondering if he'd left, or was he searching? Maybe he had seen her running from the house. She looked for a path of escape. The only way out was the beach behind her.

She heard footsteps in the grass. Abby pressed herself against the trunk of the tree. When she peered between two branches he was standing less than fifty feet away. He had one arm extended out in front of his face to ward off the heat. Still, Abby could see every crease and shadow, the face that launched a million books. He edged around the flaming ruins closer to where she was hiding, then stepped on something. He looked down, stooped, and picked it up.

Abby couldn't tell what it was.

She looked at the road. Someone had to see or hear the blast. Even so it would take time before the authorities responded. They were miles from Christiansted and the nearest fire station. There was no one staying in the large estate house at the end of the road, and the other small houses were vacation spots mostly empty this time of year. The Buccaneer might send security, but by then, if Jack found her, it would be too late. For all intents the house on Shoy Beach Road was the perfect place for an accident, and Jack had picked it.

He turned and looked toward the water. Abby clung to the base of the tree, motionless and perspiring. He was holding something in his hand, a piece of singed paper that he'd picked up. He looked alternately between this and the beach. Suddenly Abby realized, it was the folder with her airline tickets. She had been holding them in her hand when she found Charlie's body. With the shock of the explosion, the blast that threw her to the ground, she'd dropped them.

Like radar, Jack's eyes scanned the distance to the beach, looking first in one direction and then the other. He looked back at the flames as if he couldn't quite piece it together.

It was Abby's last chance. Any second he would come up with a theory and start looking for footprints in the sand.

She slid down the incline to the water. The robe was now soaked as well as singed. She stripped it from her body, balled it up, and carried it under one arm so that Jack wouldn't pick up on the white terrycloth against the dark water and the night sky. She ran through knee-deep water and thanked God for the clouds that covered the moon.

The surf washed away her footprints, and the sound of the waves swallowed the noise from the patter of her feet. She ran more than a hundred yards down the beach, then darted up toward the marsh grass still carrying the robe under one arm. Abby huddled behind a bush long enough to don the robe and catch her breath. She was still stunned. It all seemed like a nightmare, as if at any moment she would rouse herself from a fitful sleep. But the pain, the cuts on her face and feet, and the blood on her cheek were real. She would not wake up from this dream and she knew it.

She climbed up onto the bank above the beach and looked back toward the burning house. She could see Jack's car still parked with its headlights on. She ran across the broad expanse of grass toward the road. There was a small vacation house set back on its own driveway, deserted and locked. Abby huddled near the deck at the back of the house behind a lattice grille work with a gate in it. The lattice concealed a storage area under the deck. She opened it and slipped inside. She hid there in the darkness for several minutes, listening for sounds, trying to catch her breath and stop her heart from pounding.

The space under the deck was cluttered with cast-off lawn furniture, and children's toys, and infested with spider webs. Abby hated spiders.

There were rubber rafts and paddles, and a small canoe. Inside the canoe she found a pair of water shoes. She shook these out to make sure there was nothing making a home inside. They weren't much. Abby managed to stretch them onto her feet. It was better than being barefoot.

Suddenly she heard sirens off in the distance, slow, lumbering, more than one. Fire trucks. Someone had called it in.

She crawled out from under the deck and ran as fast as her feet would carry her. It was a long way to the road, and it took her more than two minutes to get there, dodging around boulders and bushes, scrambling up a steep incline.

The first engine came barreling over a rise and nearly ran over her. She waved but on the dark dusty road they never saw her. Another pumper truck followed. Abby was left choking in its dust.

She started to run after them, then realized there were lights coming on behind her. She turned, this time in the center of the road, and waved one arm while the other held the bathrobe closed around her body.

It was a police cruiser, a white sedan with a light bar flashing red and blue overhead and siren screaming. It came to a screeching stop and the driver tried to wave her out of the way. Abby refused to move, and instead launched herself at the hood of the vehicle, and then stepped around to the driver's window.

He didn't look much like a cop. He was heavy-set and wore a faded black T-shirt soiled by sweat and a pair of black chinos. Around his chest was a black nylon shoulder holster with a chrome revolver the size of a bazooka.

'What's you doin', lady? You gonna git yourself killed. Get the hell outta da road.' He waved at her like some angry midwife.

Abby stammered for words, then finally found them. 'Someone's trying to kill me. Please help me.'

'What you been drinkin', lady?'

'Listen to me. Someone fire-bombed my house.'

For the first time the driver looked at her as if she might be telling the truth.

Abby couldn't see the man in the passenger seat, but he appeared to be better dressed, a sport coat and slacks. The passenger door opened and the other man got out. He was a tall, slender African American, and he seemed to take a close look at Abby over the top of the vehicle when he stood.

'What's your name?' he asked her.

She had soot on her face and dried blood under one eye. Her hair was a tangled web of wet ringlets.

Abby didn't answer him. It was the look in his eye that troubled her, as if the cop recognized her.

Sergeant Logano reached for a flashlight in the car and shined it in Abby's eyes.

She shied away and held up a hand.

He reached back inside the vehicle and opened a large folder that lay on the seat next to the driver. As he did, a four-by-five photograph of Abby spilled out of the folder onto the floor of the car. In that instant, their eyes met over the top of the vehicle and Logano blinked.

Another pumper truck pulled up behind the squad car and Logano told his driver to pull over to the side of the road so that the fire truck could get by. For a fleeting instant he reverted to traffic cop directing the truck around the car on the narrow road. The car pulled over, the truck roared through, and when Logano looked back, Abby was gone.

She had no idea why the police would have her photograph, but she wasn't waiting to find out. If they had her picture, it was for a reason. The police would never buy her story. She had no evidence that Jack blew up the house. It was her word against his, and there was a dead man in her closet.

In the passing dust and confusion of the truck, Abby lost herself in the brush and shadows at the side of the road. Then quickly she retreated from the road, putting distance between herself and the squad car. She could see the two cops with flashlights beating the brush and hear their voices. She listened to them talking for sometime until the tall one in the sport coat pitched it in.

'Nevermind. She can't get far. Dressed like that she stands out like a sore thumb. Put out an APB. If we don't get her tonight they'll pick her up in the morning.' They got back in the car and drove toward the ebbing glow that had been Abby's house.

She watched as the taillights disappeared over a rise and then she moved, parallel to the road, as fast as she could. It took her several minutes to make it to the security gate at the Buccaneer. There were two men talking downstairs inside the stone tower.

Abby watched for some time and a third man joined them, part of the maintenance crew. They were gossiping about all the excitement, loud voices and animated gestures.

Abby shielded herself behind a couple of small utility vehicles on her side of the road and headed up the hill toward the main building. She didn't go inside but stayed on the road, passed the parking lot at the rear and the second-story veranda where the bar and restaurant were located.

With all of the excitement, explosions and sirens, the band at the bar hadn't missed a beat. She could hear the crowd clapping their hands and shouting to the hypnotic beat of steel drums and guitars.

Abby hustled down the road toward the sea and the bungalows on the beach. She kept a wary eye on the road, any sign of Jack returning, but it was dark, and except for the music on the knoll she was alone.

Toward the bottom of the hill was a paved parking lot with spaces marked in front of the rooms. Most of the rooms were dark. Abby knew some of these were vacant. Other tenants, she figured, were either out partying or asleep.

Jack's room was the second from the end near the beach. She had no idea how she was going to get inside. All the room doors locked automatically and used punched card keys. She had one of Jack's keys, but by now it was melted plastic in the ashes of her purse.

There was a small building across the parking lot from the bungalow set into the side of the hill and lights were on inside. It was some kind of a utility building. Abby had seen maids coming and going from this the day she and Jack checked in. A door was open on the side of the building and a light was on inside. She made her way to it and looked in.

There was a woman ironing what looked like uniforms. A large industrial dryer was tumbling sheets and pillow cases. The woman was listening to her own music being pumped into her ears by a headset from a CD player strapped to her waist. She had her back to Abby, who could have fired a cannon and not been heard.

Against the wall just inside the door were a set of lockers, maybe a dozen in all. These each had padlocks on them, except for one that was open. Abby watched from the open door as the woman finished ironing one of the uniforms, placed it on a hanger, and hung it on a bar against the far wall with others. She returned to the ironing board, took another from a hamper, and started again.

Abby looked down at her terrycloth robe. It was burned and had blood on it in two places. By daylight she would be a walking neon sign saying 'Arrest Me.' She had to find something to wear. She looked at the open locker, and the woman ironing, her rear end gyrating to the rhythm of the music in her ears.

Abby slipped through the door, across the concrete floor to the open locker. Inside were two maid's uniforms, a pair of jeans, and a top. The jeans and top were too small. The pants would have been four inches too short. She grabbed one of the uniform dresses. It should have been mid-calf but went almost to her knees. She took it anyway. There were no shoes.

Abby looked back at the woman. She was wearing white running shoes. They wouldn't have fit Abby in any event. She was stuck with the swimming shoes. The woman finished ironing half of the uniform and flipped it over on the board.

Abby saw a purse on the shelf of the locker. She grabbed it and looked inside. There was a wallet with two dollars in cash, some cigarettes and keys. She didn't want to do it, but she took the money. If nothing else she could get change and make a collect call to Morgan. She was putting the purse back when she saw it, a card key, probably a master for maid service. It was sitting on the shelf under where the purse had been. She grabbed it and put it in the pocket of her robe, then moved quickly across the room and out the door.

In the shadows outside she changed, took the key from the pocket, and threw the robe in a trashbin. She still had no underwear, but the dress would draw less attention than the burned and bloodied robe.

Now she moved quickly across the parking lot to Jack's room. The outside light was on over the door, but the bathroom window was dark, and there was no car parked in front. She took a chance, held her breath, and used the key. She was inside in a matter of seconds, closed the door behind her, and stood quietly in the darkness. She listened for any sounds but could hear only the clicking of the clock, its luminous dial visible on the dresser drawer in the bedroom.

The room was empty, but Jack's suitcase, still packed from his trip, lay at the foot of the bed. She hesitated to turn on a light, but she needed to see. She flipped on the lamp at the bedside table and quickly moved to the hall that separated the bathroom from the sleeping area.

Here there was a closet with louvered folding doors. She opened one side. The ElSafe was mounted on a wooden platform on the floor.

Abby kneeled down on the floor and tried to remember the combination. Jack had asked her for her birth date and she had lied to him. But she couldn't remember what year she'd used. It was part of the combination he had punched in. She prayed that he hadn't changed it. She did trial and error on the safe, punching in the month and day and then trying several different years. Finally she heard the hum of the motor and saw the word 'Open' in red letters appear in the window on the door. She pulled the latch with her fingers and it opened.

There were a number of items inside, envelopes and papers, a set of car keys that must have belonged to Jack. Then she saw it in the back. The dark blue cover of a passport. She picked it up and opened it. It was Jack's. She dropped it on the floor and frantically tore through the safe. Under a stack of papers on the bottom Abby saw another blue cover. She opened it and her pulse quickened. Inside was Abby's picture. She breathed a sigh of relief. She picked up Jack's off the floor and dropped them both into the large patch pocket of the uniform dress. Jack would have trouble following her off the island without a passport.

There was some loose cash inside. She grabbed it and counted: one hundred and seventeen dollars. This joined the passports in her pocket. Then she found the second debit card with her name on it. She took that too, then closed the safe door and pushed the lock button. The motor hummed again.

Abby went into the bathroom but didn't turn on the light. This would been seen from the parking lot outside.

478

She washed the soot and blood off of her hands and face, found a brush on the sink and brushed her hair so that she at least looked human again.

Then she went back to the closet. She opened the other side and surveyed the hanging clothes for anything she might use. Jack's pants and shirts were all far too big. She was better off in the maid's dress. She would use the automatic teller machine in Christiansted for cash as soon as she got there, and in the morning she would hit one of the many shops in town for the clothes she needed. Then somehow she would get off the island as quickly as she could.

On a hook in the corner of the closet she saw the blue fanny pack, the one Jack used to carry the pistol. The flap was unzipped. She lifted it. The pack was empty. The gun was gone.

She went back out into the sleeping area to the dresser and rummaged through the drawers. There was nothing she could use. She found a white pair of sports socks and wondered if she could fit them on under the swim shoes. She dropped them into her pocket.

She had just finished and was closing the drawer when she heard tires moving slowly on the gravel out front and saw the glare of headlights as they streamed through the window of the bathroom. Abby dove for the light on the night stand and turned it off just as she heard the motor die and the *thunk* of a car door being closed out front. An instant later there was the sound of a card key slipping into the lock of the door.

Abby dashed across the room in the dark toward the patio door, but it was too late. A shaft of light penetrated the room from outside and Jack came through the door.

Abby darted back, to the other side of the bed, scrambling on her hands and knees and lay on the floor. She lifted the bed covers. The mattress was on a platform. There was no place to hide underneath.

She lay stone still.

He came in and turned on the light next to the bed, then slumped onto the edge of the mattress. The springs groaned and Abby nearly screamed. She could hear his breathing, things being emptied from his pockets onto the nightstand on the other side. She prayed he would take a shower, comb his hair, anything to give her two seconds to get to the patio door.

He flipped a shoe onto the other side of the bed and it almost hit her. She held her breath for fear that he might try to retrieve it. He didn't. The other one followed, and then his socks.

He got up off the bed and she could hear the bottoms of his feet making suction on the tile floor as he walked to the bathroom.

Abby got up and dashed to the door. There was a simple turn-key lock under the handle. She turned it gently to avoid making any sound, then looked back toward the bathroom.

It was then that she saw it. On the floor behind her was one of the passports. It must have slipped from her pocket when she was crawling across the floor.

Suddenly she heard the flush of the toilet, Jack coming back. She looked at the passport, and the shaft of light from the bathroom door, Jack's shadow on the wall as he approached down the short hall.

Abby took the only option open. She stepped out onto the dark patio and eased the door closed. It was still moving when Jack turned the corner, but he didn't see it. She could see him moving in the bedroom ten feet away and prayed he wouldn't see the passport on the floor.

The urge to run was overwhelming, but she kept her head and checked the pocket of her dress, opened the single passport that remained and saw Jack's picture. There was nothing she could do. She was trapped on the patio. She would run if he found it. Otherwise she would have to wait and hope that he would go back in the bathroom or leave. It was her only ticket off the island.

Fortunately the passport was out of Jack's line of sight, around the corner of the bed. If he went there he would step on it, but there was no reason to go.

He picked up the phone and dialed. She heard him talk to the overseas operator, then wait on the line. He sat on the edge of the bed. He looked tired and worn. Killing people must be hard work, thought Abby. She couldn't see a spot of blood on his clothes. He must have showered and changed after slaughtering Charlie. If she had his pistol, Abby thought she could have shot him at this moment as he sat on the bed.

'Jess. Jack here. Listen, I need your help.' Jack stood, turned his back, and lowered his voice. Abby couldn't hear what he was saying now. They talked for several moments and all she could pick up was the hum of Jack's voice without the words. Then he turned toward her.

'No, I think she's still alive. I can't be sure. I'm looking.'

He listened while Jess said something on the other end.

'No. No. Don't give me any crap. I gotta nail Spencer. First I gotta find him. And I need help to find her before she gets off the island.'

Jess said something.

'Get out of it. I don't care what you do, but get down here.'

Jess was now doing all the listening. 'I'll call and have a ticket waiting for you at the airport, at LAX. I'll try for a flight tonight.' It was four hours earlier out on the coast.

Jess was arguing. He was probably getting ready to hump some starlet.

'Sleep on the goddamned plane,' said Jack. 'You gotta hit the ground running when you get here.'

Jess said something.

'Good. Listen, I owe you. See you in the morning.' Jack hung up. He wandered aimlessly in the room for a moment as if he was thinking. Then he glanced down at his suitcase still unopened on the floor at the foot of the bed.

Abby looked at the passport. Jack would see it if he grabbed the suitcase. In a moment she would run. Her heart was pounding. They were planning to kill Spencer. If she couldn't get off the island, she could at least call and warn him.

Halfway to the suitcase, Jack stopped as if he remembered something, thought for a second, turned, and headed for the bathroom. Like that he was gone. She could still see the shaft of light. The door to the bathroom was open, but she had to take the chance.

Quickly she slipped back in through the patio door, four steps across the room. Abby picked up the passport, turned, and in an instant was gone.

The door to Jack's room clicked shut as it closed. He heard it and stepped out of the bathroom. Instantly he knew what it was. He ran to the patio, threw open the door. There was no one there. He looked at the two-foot stone wall leading to the patio next door and the sea of bushes beyond.

CHAPTER
THIRTY-FIVE

The only thing she possessed of her own was the watch on her wrist. Abby had worn it into the shower before finding Charlie's body. She looked at it nervously several times as she sat in the back of the cab and wondered how she was going to get off the island and how long it would take.

Jack had her ticket for the morning flight. He would be watching the airport as would the police if they were looking for her.

It was a ten-minute drive to Christiansted. She told the driver to let her out near the shopping district at Gallows Bay and paid him with some of the cash taken from the safe in Jack's room. After seeing her on the road, the cops would question every cab driver who was anywhere near the Buccaneer. This way the driver wouldn't know where she went.

She walked the distance into town. It took her almost a half-hour. There she rented a room in a small hotel near King's Wharf. The clerk looked at her strangely, swim shoes and a wrinkled maid's uniform. But he took her money and didn't ask any questions.

She went up to the room and immediately made a

long-distance call to Morgan's house in Seattle. She knew he wouldn't be there, not yet anyway, but she left a message on his answering machine. She tried to mask the panic in her voice. There was nothing Morgan could do from Seattle, but she wanted to warn him. Jack and now Jess were after him. Morgan had suspicions, but he had no idea of the danger he was in.

It was nearly three in the morning by the time she peeled off the swim shoes, set the alarm, and collapsed on the bed. She didn't bother to take off the dress. She thought she would sleep immediately, but she didn't. Instead her mind turned over with thoughts of Theresa and Jack. The man she loved had murdered her best friend. The man who she thought loved her had just tried to end her life. She hugged a pillow to her chest, wrapped her arms around it, and began to sob. She cried herself to sleep.

It was light streaming through the window and not the alarm that woke her three hours later. Abby rolled over and rubbed her eyes, got up and looked out the window. Her mouth had a taste like she'd swallowed a rhinoceros. And she was hungry.

A few merchants were stirring on the wharf. Trucks were parked in the lot next to the hotel, their drivers already making the rounds delivering goods and groceries to the shops and restaurants that honeycombed the area around the docks.

In a few hours the place would be teeming with tourists, the first flood of the day from the cruise ships, and Abby would lose herself in the crowd.

She took a shower, tried to fix her hair as best she could, and slipped down the back stairs of the hotel so that she wouldn't be seen in the lobby. She was glad of one thing. When the police questioned her on the road, she was still wearing the soiled terrycloth robe. This would likely be included in any description of her. They wouldn't be looking for a maid's uniform, not for a few hours anyway, and once they figured it out, the dress, too, would be in a trash bin in Christiansted.

She scurried four blocks through alleys, staying close to buildings and watching out for the police. In five minutes she made her way to one of the banks on King Street and used the debit card to withdraw a thousand dollars in cash, all in twenty-dollar bills. She folded it and put it in her pocket, then crossed the street. She ordered coffee and a pastry from a small vendor and disappeared like a mouse under one of the trees in the public market a few blocks away. The market was only open on Saturdays so the stalls were all empty. Dressed as she was in the maid's uniform, Abby blended in with the few locals who wandered through the area on their way to work.

She killed an hour while she continued to watch the streets at the south end of town. Slowly they started to fill with shoppers. The covered veranda of the sidewalks started to crowd up, and people began to jostle for position in the doors of the shops.

Abby joined the human tide. First she went to Java Wraps. She bought underwear, two pairs of slacks, a pair of boat shoes and four tops, a light jacket, and a canvas bag to put it all in. On a coat-tree display she found a large straw hat with a broad brim and a polka-dot red ribbon for a band. She paid cash for everything. This way she didn't have to sign her name using the debit card. If the police questioned the clerks, at least they wouldn't have a name they could check.

Next she hit one of the perfume shops where she purchased makeup, a brush for her hair, and other toiletries. She walked two blocks through the crowded streets to Little Switzerland, where she found a pair of designer sunglasses.

Abby disappeared into a ladies' room in the lobby of one of the hotels near the wharf and by the time she emerged half an hour later, she looked as if she'd walked off the pages of a woman's fashion magazine.

Her hair was pulled back and piled on top of her head underneath the straw hat set off by its broad red-ribboned band. The white slacks were well creased and the blue sleeveless top was casual and cool.

The white boating shoes made it look as if she was headed for her yacht anchored off shore. Over her arm was the stylish canvas bag with her other purchases, the debit card, all the cash that was left, and the passports. She would dump Jack's in a trashcan once she got off the island and let him think up some stories to tell Immigration. She looked the part of the rich tourist. The only panic was in her eyes, and these were hidden behind the large oval dark glasses.

She melded with the tourists in King's Alley and went into one of the open-air restaurants, where she ordered a Long Island iced tea and took a table. It was a place where she could sit, collect her thoughts, and survey her options.

In the hotel lobby Abby had grabbed some tourist literature, folders on charter boat rentals and private air excursions. She looked through these trying to figure if any of them might get her to San Juan. Most of them only ventured as far as a few of the smaller off-shore islands.

One of the brochures caught her eye. It featured a sleek twin engine float plane, the Seaborne Vista Liner. It was the one Morgan had taken to get to St Croix from

St Thomas. She wondered if the police would be looking for her there. It all depended how wide they had thrown their net, how badly they wanted her. On that score Abby didn't have a clue, though with the discovery of Charlie's burned body in her closet their interest would no doubt be heightened.

She couldn't go to the airport. They were sure to be laying for her there. A small charter boat would take days to get to San Juan and by then they would be waiting at the docks. She had to move quickly. Abby figured at most she had a brief window of opportunity, a few hours, before the cops got their act together, or worse, Jack found her. In three or four hours the tour ships would pull out, leaving Abby alone on the streets of Christiansted looking like Audrey Hepburn in *Breakfast at Tiffany's*.

She sipped the last of her tea and merged with the sea of bodies on the street again.

Tickets for the float plane to Charlotte Amalie on St Thomas were sold through the window of a little building on the dock. The next flight departed just before one in the afternoon. There were a few seats open. She checked her watch, a little over an hour. Abby didn't like it, but she had no choice. She bought a single one-way ticket, then she headed for a payphone that she'd staked out earlier in the lobby of one of the hotels. It was one of those English telephone booths you might see in pictures of London, red with a door and little pane windows all around, a lot of privacy.

She stepped inside and dialed the overseas operator. Abby gave her the area code for Seattle and the number for Morgan's house. After four rings she got his message machine again. She didn't leave another message. Abby wondered if he hadn't arrived there yet, or if he'd come and gone. Maybe he was already on his way to New York. She called the law office. It was just after eight in the morning on the West Coast and Abby was hoping one of the receptionists would be answering the phone.

On the second ring they picked up. 'Starl, Hobbs & Carlton.'

'Hello. I wonder if Mr Spencer is in?'

'I'm afraid he's out of town.'

Abby hesitated for a moment, then figured she had nothing to lose. 'This is Abby. Abby Chandlis.' She thought she recognized the voice on reception, Janice, a girl she'd gone to lunch with a few times.

There was a momentary pause on the other end.

'Abby. Where are you?'

The question sent a shiver up Abby's spine. It was a little too pointed. No 'How are you?' – 'What are you doing these days?' – The woman only wanted to know one thing: where she was. Abby wondered if the police might have paid them another visit after Spencer left to come to the islands. With Morgan away from the office, the cops might have talked to Cutler. If that was the case, Abby was not on friendly ground. She could envision the frantic snapping of fingers by the receptionist as she tried to get the attention of a co-worker, perhaps to call the police, not that it would do them any good.

'Do you know where Morgan is?'

'Let me see. I think we have a message here. He called in over the weekend. Just a moment. I'll see if I can find it.'

Abby thought about hanging up. She wondered if the police might have put some kind of a tap or a trace on the line. Maybe they were taping her words as she spoke. She looked at her wrist watch. Fifteen seconds, twenty seconds, half a minute. The woman was still looking.

'Ah. Here it is. He called from San Juan, Puerto Rico. Says he's going to be a few more dàys. Some business down there. Where are you?'

Abby ignored the question. 'When did he call?'

'Let's see. The message was left on our machine early this morning. About six o'clock.'

Morgan was closer than she thought. But why hadn't he gone on to Seattle to get the documents? Maybe he couldn't get out of his meeting in San Juan? No. It didn't make any sense. He knew what was at stake.

'Are you sure it was Morgan's voice on the tape?'

'I didn't listen to it. Someone else cleared the machine. But who else would it be?'

'Did he leave a phone number?'

'No.

'Any address where's staying?'

'Not that I see on the slip. Where are you, Abby?' The perennial question.

'Nevermind. I'll call later.' She hung up. She actually wiped the telephone receiver clean with one of the new tops from the canvas bag and rubbed across the buttons on the phone. She wasn't sure why, whether it was a nervous gesture or something she'd seen in a movie. As she walked away from the booth, Abby tried to make sense of Janice's information. Why hadn't Morgan left San Juan? Maybe his office wasn't telling her the truth? But why would they make up something like that? Maybe Jack had already gotten to Spencer. Just like he'd gotten Charlie. If that was the case, Abby was now all alone.

She racked her mind trying to remember the name of the ship in San Juan that the caller had given her over the phone the day he called for Morgan. She'd written it down and delivered it to him at Indies over lunch, and now she couldn't remember. *Cuesta, Cuesta, Cuesta* what? Her mind was a blank. It was the only lead she had for Morgan in San Juan. Whatever his business was, she guessed it had to do with this ship. They should know where he was.

She headed toward the dock. Abby's mind was lost in thought and she was looking down at the ground. She let her guard down for an instant and it cost her.

From across the open pavilion near the old Customs House Jack zeroed in on a large straw hat. It wasn't the face, because he couldn't see it. The woman was hidden behind a pair of oversized dark glasses. Instead it was the way the woman carried herself, straight and tall. She stood out among the mostly elderly cruise passengers milling around the shops.

Abby didn't see him until he was within a hundred feet. By that time Jack was on the run, coming right at her. Abby panicked, adrenaline flooded her body, fight-or-flight. She turned and ran, pushing her way through the crowd. She clutched the canvas bag like it was a life line. She drew the ire of several tourists, nearly knocking down an old man. They hollered at her, but Abby didn't stop. She headed down King's Alley and went left on King Street. Jack was right behind her. She went around the corner of Church Street, and a half-block down darted into Little Switzerland.

There was a mob scene inside. People jostling in front of display cases, looking at watches and rings, comparing prices. The store was on two levels, jewelry and pens out front, and other gifts and sundries up two steps in a larger area of the store at the rear.

Abby managed to maneuver her way through the

crowd without drawing too much attention. She removed the straw hat and put it in her bag, hoping that Jack would be keying on the hat. She slumped down several inches and merged with a group of women ogling a necklace of Columbian emeralds. She kept one eye on the two doors at the front of the shop, the only way out onto the street.

A few seconds later she saw Jack push his way through the sea of humanity outside, past one door and then the other. She almost darted for the door, but before she could he was back, looking in one of the doors.

Abby slumped down further and looked at her watch. If it was on schedule the plane would be taking off in less than ten minutes. She would have gotten down on the floor and crawled if she could. But it would have drawn attention.

She peeked over the shoulder of one of the shoppers. He was still standing in the door scanning the crowd inside, looking off in another direction at the moment. He was wearing the little blue fanny pack off to the side on his hip, and Abby knew what was inside. Sooner or later he would see her.

From where he was standing he had both doors covered. If she made a move, he would grab her.

She thought for a moment, looked down into the canvas bag, and had an idea.

There was an Asian couple looking at the display case containing watches.

Abby moved over to them and spoke to the woman. 'Excuse me.'

They looked at her.

'I'm trying to decide whether to buy this hat, but I can't tell what it looks like from a distance.' Abby was holding the straw hat in her hand now.

'I wonder if you'd mind just for a moment walking up onto the stairs over there and putting it on?' Abby wasn't sure if they understood English, but the man seemed to. He explained to his wife, and she gave Abby a broad grin, bowed a little, then took the hat.

She walked twenty feet through the crowd with her back to Abby and her husband before she put the hat on her head. Then she climbed the two steps so that Abby could get a better look. When the woman turned, she was surprised to see her husband standing there alone. She was more surprised to see a tall man wearing a blue pack on his side pushing through the crowd, knocking people over, coming on like a locomotive, almost on top of her.

He didn't stop until an instant after she turned and he saw her face. It registered like a jolt of electricity, as if she'd lit him up. Then his eyes got big. He turned and looked at the door, but it was too late.

Abby made it past the crowds and to the corner by running down the middle of the street. She dodged two cars. One of the drivers leaned on his horn and came to a screeching stop.

Abby brushed by his fender and kept going. People were now looking at her. She ran down King's Alley towards the docks. She could hear the drone of the motors. The twin-engine sea plane was revving up. She ran as fast as her legs could carry her past tourists and carts with vendors selling their wares on the street. As she reached the end of the alley, Abby saw the plane still tied to the dock. But a crewman was starting to remove the gang plank leading to the door.

Abby shouted and waved her arms. The man looked at her, then lowered the plank back into place.

She fumbled in her bag for the ticket, handed it to

him, and stepped aboard. She found a seat by one of the windows on the dockside just behind the wing and one of the rumbling motors. She sat down and strapped herself in. If she could have she would have helped them close the door.

Abby turned to the window and searched the dock for signs of Jack. He couldn't be far behind. She looked back down the aisle of the plane. What was taking so long? There was a conversation going on at the door. The guy at the gang plank was now talking to one of the plane's crew, slapping him on the back and laughing.

She turned the other way, looked out the window again, and saw him. Jack had tracked her to the end of the alley where it met the dock. Now he saw the plane. It registered instantly. He started running. The door finally closed. The engines roared, and the plane started to drift away from the dock. As Abby looked out the window, Jack was standing screaming in her face less than twenty feet away. His hands were cupped to his mouth and he was shouting something that she couldn't hear. She couldn't read his lips, either, and she didn't want to. She turned her head away and his words were swallowed by the roar of the engines. One of the dock crew was trying to pull him back away from the prop-wash of the propellers and the tail of the plane as it turned and headed for open water. The engines revved higher and Abby finally caught her breath as the window next to her was covered by spray off the surface of the bay.

On the dock, Jack tried to ignore the crewman pulling on his arm while he shouted at the top of his lungs. 'Spencer did it! Abby, listen to me. It was Spencer!'

CHAPTER
THIRTY-SIX

'We don't have time to talk right now,' said Jack. 'Maybe on the plane.'

'But I just landed.' Jess looked tired and confused.

Jack took him by the arm and led him toward another gate. They passed through the metal detector and had their bags checked. The clerk asked if they had passports. Jess started to reach for his, but Jack stopped him and merely said 'yes.' Immigration wouldn't check them here departing from St Croix, but in San Juan when they landed. Jack would worry about it then.

'Where are we going?'

'I'll tell you on the plane,' said Jack. 'Did you get the bag I asked you for?'

Jess had made a detour to Coffin Point on the way down. He pointed to one of the pieces of luggage he was hauling toward the tarmac.

'Let me give you a hand.' Jack took the one piece and felt around inside the bag as they walked quickly across the taxiway.

The plane was fueled and waiting, Enrique Ricardi's sleek Gulfstream. The swept-wing executive jet sat whining like a cougar in heat. The words 'Ricardi

Spirits' in script were over the door.

'Hurry up.' Henry was waving them on from the top of the stairs. 'They've just given us clearance. We must take off.' If they moved they might be able to get to San Juan ahead of Abby. The unscheduled private jet gave them an edge.

They raced up the stairs and into the cabin, stowed their luggage, and took seats in plush swivel chairs. Henry went into the cockpit and told the pilot to take off.

'Now tell me what's going on,' said Jess.

'Spencer tried to kill Abby. She doesn't know it, and she's running right to him.'

They felt the wheels roll and a couple of minutes later the acceleration pressed them back into their seats. Twenty seconds and they were airborne. Cruising at five hundred and twenty miles an hour, it would take them less than one hour to get to San Juan. Henry had already given instructions to have the plane taxi to the American Airlines concourse. He was guessing. It was the major carrier between Puerto Rico and the Virgin Islands. The odds were with him that Abby would be coming in that way.

He also called ahead and alerted authorities to try to stop her at the gate if she got there ahead of them. To hold her if necessary. If they missed her there, Customs or Immigration would get her when she showed her passport.

'Sounds like you got it covered,' said Jess.

'I thought I had her covered in Christiansted,' said Jack. 'She ran my ass ragged and stood me up on the dock for a salt-spray shower.'

'How did you find about the lawyer?'

'There was a note under my door when I got back

496

from my trip,' said Jack. 'Saturday evening. It said Abby wanted to see me at the house at eight-thirty that night. Something about an explanation and a big mistake. Fortunately for me I was running late. The note didn't tell me it was a barbecue.'

Jess gave him a questioning look.

'He tried to get us both when he torched the house. She thinks I did it. It's a long story.' Jack reached into an inside coat pocket, pulled out an envelope, and handed it to his brother. 'It's where I went when I left the island on Saturday morning. Washington, D.C. To do a little research.'

The copyright office was closed on Saturdays, but the Library of Congress had a computer system. If you had the title of a manuscript, or the author's name, you could pull up the copyright registration on the screen and print it out.

'I was looking for the copyright on Abby's book. The one she had Spencer file for her months ago. The problem was I didn't have the title. I tried the one it was published under, but I only found the second registration, the one filed by Bertoli's lawyers. So I figured Abby must have used a working title for the earlier registration, something Bertoli wouldn't trip over when he went to file his. So I tried Abby's name.'

'And you found this?' Jess held up the envelope.

Jack shook his head. 'I found nothing. Oh. I found her earlier books alright, but not this one.'

Jess opened the envelope and removed a single sheet of paper. It was a dot-matrix copy, the registration of copyright for a novel entitled *Every Dangerous Dream*. It was stamped with the date of receipt, and at the top it listed the owner of the copyright: Morgan Robert Spencer.

'It was a hunch. I searched the computer under Spencer's name.' Jack shook his head. 'She never asked him for a copy. She trusted him.'

Jack wanted to get out and push the plane. Moving at the speed of a bullet it wasn't going fast enough for him.

'My guess is his name is all over those contracts I signed.' He was talking about the ones Morgan had him sign at his house that day.

'I never read them. Never got copies. Not that it would have done any good. Unless I miss my bet, he structured the signature pages so they could be removed and added to another set of agreements later. Ones that had his name on them. We were fools, both of us, Abby and I. He had total control, over the money, over the documents. Abby was busy writing. I was busy pretending. And Spencer was busy minding the store. The only thing wrong, he had his own name in the window.'

'How do you know he's in San Juan?' said Jess.

'I don't. If she gets away from us at the airport, we're screwed.' Jack sat shaking his head, powerless to do anything about it at the moment. They flew on in silence for twenty minutes.

There were so many signs, and Jack and Abby had missed them all. The typewriter they couldn't find, the one Abby used to write the book. Who but a lawyer would think of that? Possession of the writing instrument if a dispute arose could be used as evidence. An expert could match the keys on the typewriter to the manuscript pages.

Joey may have been the initial source for Thompson the reporter, but Jack guessed that Spencer had picked up this ball and run with it after Joey's death. How else would Thompson have found Abby in the islands?

'My guess is he's getting ready to tell Bertoli that Abby was his lawyer,' said Jack. 'That she died in a tragic accident along with yours truly. That we were just friends who agreed to help in the promotion of his book. He will apologize for the charade, and in the face of tragedy he'll come clean, or at least look like he is. He'll tell the agent and the publisher that he wrote the book. And who's gonna question him,' said Jack, 'when he's got everything – including Bertoli by the balls?'

It was true. With Jack and Abby dead, Bertoli had a winning horse and nobody to ride it. That gave Spencer all the leverage he needed. Nobody was going to rock a boat when it had that much money in it. In terms of commercial fiction, Gable Cooper was a name that was now made. Armed with that and Abby's outline, Spencer would find a ghost writer for the sequel. The publisher could help him with other stories later. They called it editing, and for the next ten years people would be reading books by Gable Cooper without a picture on the cover, and Morgan owned the franchise.

Henry came back into the cabin.

'We'll be starting our descent into San Juan in about five minutes. How are you feeling?' He looked at Jack.

'I'm fine.'

'My people will be there to help,' said Henry. He possessed a small army of security to protect his business as well as a personal body guard.

'I owe you,' said Jack.

'For nothing.'

'Can I ask you for one more favor?'

'What is it?'

'I had to leave my pack back in St Croix.' It was a code word and Henry understood.

'There was no time to send a package,' said Jack.

Henry smiled. 'And too many metal detectors at the airport?'

'You always understand,' said Jack.

'My security people will get you something when we land.' Henry spoke as if they were going to mix him a casual drink instead of delivering a deadly weapon.

'Besides myself, you're the only two people who know her on sight. If she gets loose in San Juan and finds Spencer, well . . .' Jack didn't have to finish the thought.

'How did you know Abby was alive after the explosion?' asked Jess.

'I wasn't sure, not until this morning, when I went into the safe to get my passport. She took it while I was getting ready to shower last night.'

Jess looked at him, a kind of wise-ass smile. 'She's got your passport?'

Jack nodded.

'Who's gonna vouch for you at Immigration when we land?'

'Not to worry.' Jack reached into his coat pocket and pulled out a blue passport cover and opened it toward his brother. 'Meet Kellen Raid.'

It was like the origami paper bomb. Jack never wrote about anything unless he tried it at least once. A kind of literary license.

When she saw Jack's face looking up at her from the shadows, Abby's heart skipped two beats. The drone of the jet engines had put her to sleep. When she opened her eyes he was staring at her, from the seat next to her, and the chair across the aisle where the woman had laid the book down and gone to the restroom.

Jack's ever-present dark and brooding face was everywhere, staring back from the cover of Abby's novel, the name Gable Cooper emblazoned on the front. She had seen at least half a dozen of them being plucked from knapsacks and book bags as she boarded the plane. It was surreal. He was stalking her, trying to kill her, and his picture was everywhere. She couldn't tell a soul, not without sounding crazy. Who would believe her? The only one was Morgan.

It was dark by the time the wheels hit the runway at Luis Munoz Marin International Airport. The shock of the tires on hard ground jolted Abby back to her senses. She blinked several times as the lights in the cabin came on and people started reaching for their luggage underneath seats. Abby was busy looking out the window, praying that Jack wouldn't be able to get off of St Croix without his passport. Abby had bought time.

In her mind she kept playing with the name of the ship: *Cuesta Cuesta, Cuesta* what? What was the rest of it? The name in Spanish that the man had given her over the phone. The message left for Morgan.

Once she found him she would be safe. They would go to Seattle, gather what they needed, and lay it on Bertoli's desk in New York. There would be nothing Jack could do at that point. In two days, the nightmare of the last twenty-four hours would be over. They would arrest Jack and it would all end.

Henry assembled his employees near the lounge by the gates. Most were engaged in security work for Ricardi's rum distillery. Together with Jack and Jess they fanned out to cover the incoming flights. Jack was worried they might have already missed her. There was one in-coming flight that had already landed. The passengers had cleared Customs and were gone. Jack prayed she wasn't on that flight. They searched the lounges in case she was waiting for a connecting flight.

He gave Henry's men a description of Abby, and hoped she hadn't changed her clothes or colored her hair while she was waiting for her flight in St Thomas. She would be nervous. He told them this and instructed them not to chase her. If they saw her, they were to follow and observe, and call Jack on walkie-talkies that the security people had provided.

If Jack approached her in a group, in a public place, maybe she would stop long enough to listen. All he had to do was get close enough to hand her the copyright. Once she saw it, she would understand. The pieces would fit like a puzzle. Jack was sure of it. His biggest worry now was that she had already slipped the net, that somehow she was on her way into San Juan to meet up with Morgan.

The plane pulled up to the gate, the jetway rolled out, and a moment later the door opened. Abby had no luggage, just the canvas bag. But she didn't want to be the first one off the plane.

She waited, then merged with the army of people jamming the aisle. Abby's only zone of comfort came from crowds. She immersed herself in them, submerged in anonymity. If Jack couldn't see her, he couldn't kill her.

They did the duck waddle down the aisle, carrying suitcases and packages, inching their way toward the door of the plane.

Abby was all darting eyes and wary looks from behind her sunglasses. No one seemed to notice, even though it was dark outside.

'Please watch your step.' A flight attendant was at the door. A tall, good-looking blond man with epaulets on his shoulders stood in the open door to the cockpit behind her.

'You coming to the party at *Isla Verde* tonight?' He was talking to the stewardess.

Abby thought about going to a party. It sounded good. Anything that hinted of a normal life sounded good. Then somehow the words clicked – *Isla Verde*. That was it. *Verde*. The rest of the message from the man on the phone. The name of the ship was the *Cuesta Verde*. Now all she had to do was find it.

Abby stepped through the door and out onto the jetway. She was halfway home. She could almost reach out and touch Morgan. Maybe she would call and try to find the ship. The harbor master would know where it was. She could call from a payphone.

She started to make the turn to go up the ramp, and she saw him.

Jack was at the top by the door leading into the lounge like a gatekeeper. He was looking the other way. She recognized Jess standing next to him. They were waiting for her.

Abby tried to go back, but she couldn't. She was being washed along by the sea of people coming off the plane.

She looked up the ramp again, and this time Jack saw her. He grabbed Jess and they started coming. A clerk tried to stop them, but they pushed their way through the door and waded into passengers exiting the plane.

There was a door that led from the jetway down some stairs to the tarmac. It was open. There was a man with a headset on and yellow overalls standing in the way.

Abby ran for the door, and the guy grabbed her.

'Not that way, lady.'

She kicked him as hard as she could in the leg and he let go. Before he could recover, she was out the door and down the stairs.

She ran under the wings of planes in front of giant tires that stood nearly as tall as she did. She was clutching the canvas bag.

Jack threw open the door at the top of the jetway and Abby saw him. He was down the stairs in less than three seconds, one of the flight crew yelling at him.

Abby saw an opening in the building and headed for it. It was a service area with vehicles coming and going. Little tractors towing trailers filled with luggage.

Abby got behind one of these and kept pace, running alongside until she was in the building.

This left Jack looking underneath and jumping to see over the top. One second he saw a pair of feet under the luggage cart on the other side, and the next they were gone. He ran the gauntlet of vehicles, and by the time he crossed the threshold under the terminal and inside the service building she was gone.

Jess caught up with him. 'Did you see which way she went?'

The police were coming with one of Henry's security people.

'In there somewhere. Take some of Henry's people. Cover the exits.'

They fanned out. Henry told the cops in Spanish so they would understand that Abby was neither armed nor dangerous. He told them she was a material witness so they wouldn't shoot her if she ran.

The people inside the service area wore various uniforms, from the bright yellow reflective overalls of the ground crew, to khaki work pants and shirts.

The cops covered the exits from the maintenance area.

There were only two doors, but once through them a person could move directly to the main lobby, bypassing Customs and Immigration. The doors were not locked from the maintenance side but secured by coded push-button locks from the public concourse inside. Jack combed baggage handling, while Jess searched the maintenance area.

There was no sign of Abby.

Jack checked the conveyor belt that carried bags to the level above where they were collected by passengers. It was possible that she could have jumped on the belt and gone up with the bags. But she would have caused a stir when she arrived, drawn a lot of attention. Airport security would have nailed her. Besides, she would still have to clear Customs and Immigration from that point.

He turned his attention to the baggage itself, big boxes and crates, anything she could hide behind or in.

In the meantime, Jess and two cops worked their way to the locker rooms, where several employees were changing their clothes, either coming on or going off shift. They did a careful search and found nothing. They were three minutes too late.

She was sweating under two layers of clothing in the tropical climate. Perspiration ran down her face. Her hair was piled up inside the construction hard hat as Abby made her way up the stairs and found the ladies' room near the ticket area in the terminal. No one except a little boy with big brown eyes seemed to pay much attention to the woman dressed in the bright yellow jumpsuit.

Abby hung the hard hat on the hook inside the bathroom stall, stepped out of the jump suit, and retrieved the canvas bag that she'd hidden inside one leg in order to get past the cop at the door. Then she straightened her clothes, and a minute later was headed through the front doors to the terminal.

Jack had given up on the crates and boxes. If Abby was there, she wasn't going any place. He left the cops to check them and headed out one of the exits with Jess right behind him. They climbed the stairs up to the terminal. Jack's fear now was that she had somehow slipped away. They moved quickly down the concourse to the public area out front.

Jack wanted to get his people onto the street in front of the terminal where they could watch for her. The net was widening and Jack was worried.

Out on the street Abby saw a string of cabs and made a beeline. A group of drivers were standing and talking twenty feet from the first cab in line. They seemed in no particular hurry, though one of them eyed Abby and gave her a lascivious smile.

She motioned to the taxi, and he held up a hand as if to say 'just a moment.' The drivers weren't quite through with their conversation.

Abby was looking over her shoulder, standing by the door to the cab. She wasn't certain which one belonged to the driver who waved at her. He was still trying to tear himself away, talking with his hands as much as his mouth, laughing and arguing.

Jack came out of the terminal door a hundred feet away. Abby saw him instantly. She opened the door to the first cab in line, an old blue Fairlane, and nearly dove onto the floor in the back seat, closing the door behind her. She pushed the button and locked it, then slumped down so that she couldn't be seen through the window.

She could hear the drivers talking in Spanish, one voice getting louder and laughing as he came closer. Finally the driver came around to his door, climbed in behind the wheel, and looked over the seat. At first he couldn't see her.

Abby was lying on the back floor.

'Are you alright?'

'I'm fine.'

'Where you want to go?'

'Old San Juan, near the docks.' Abby looked up at him from the floor.

The driver turned around, shrugged his shoulders, and the cab pulled out away from the curb.

Jack quickly keyed on the cabs. If you were throwing a net, this was the outer perimeter. He saw one pull out of line and he ran for it. He tried to stop it but couldn't. The driver didn't see him. In that instant, Abby sat up in the seat and looked out the back window. Their eyes met, and Jack shouted.

The taxi merged with traffic and headed for the highway.

'Fifty dollars extra if you take me by the scenic route,' said Abby. 'By way of the back streets past the El Condado.' She didn't dare tell him she was running from someone. He might stop the car and tell her to get out. If Jack followed her, she wanted to get off the highway as quickly as possible. They could lose him in the traffic of the downtown streets.

The driver looked in the mirror at her like she was crazy.

'And do it quickly.' The contradiction of taking back

roads and getting there quickly didn't seem to bother Abby. She was busy looking out the window behind. A second later she passed a twenty-dollar bill over the seat as an incentive.

'Sí, señora.'

Abby's car was out of sight by the time Jack flagged a cab. Jess was right behind him.

'Talk to the drivers over there,' said Jack. 'Find out if you can get the number of the cab or the driver's name.'

Jess took off and Jack climbed into the front seat of the taxi next to the driver.

'Out to the highway, fast!' Jack started peeling off bills and told the driver to step on it. He was using fives and tens, dropping them on the seat like an accelerator. He told the driver he'd take care of any tickets. The guy was doing eighty out the airport parkway, until he hit traffic backed up on the highway.

Jack figured Abby had to be caught in it as well. They started weaving around cars. More money on the seat. The taxi had two wheels in the median, going around cars in the fast lane, while Jack leaned out the window trying to look over the top of other vehicles to find Abby's cab.

He was just about to tell the driver to forget it when he saw the blue Fairlane. It was eight or ten cars ahead, stalled in traffic.

'Go around!' Jack almost grabbed the wheel from the driver, pushing toward the center of the highway, squeaking between cars in the fast lane and the concrete median barrier. You couldn't slip a finger between the side of the taxi and the wall that separated them from oncoming traffic.

They were now only four cars back behind Abby. Jack

could see her through the back window.

Abby's car was crawling at twenty miles an hour.

Through the rear window she saw him coming on in the outside lane. Abby looked ahead. There was an off-ramp.

'Get off here.' She screamed at the driver and he nearly jumped out of his seat.

'El Condado is two miles up.'

'I don't care. Get off here.'

The guy shrugged his shoulders and pulled to the right without signaling. There was a blare of horns as they dropped off the highway into the squalor of one of the outer districts of San Juan.

Jack was trapped in the fast lane. He grabbed the wheel and tried to pull to the right. Horns blared. The fender of the taxi caught the bumper of another car as they passed. The driver of the other vehicle threw his brakes on. The car went sideways in the lane, crossed over, and two other cars hit it. The chain that followed was like a train going off the rails, cars everywhere. Jack's taxi rolled past the off-ramp as a mass of vehicles piled up behind them. There was no way back.

Jack threw open the door and raced toward the cyclone fence that flanked the highway. In one leap he threw himself halfway up the fence for a view. Abby's taxi took a left-hand turn at a crossing intersection and disappeared.

CHAPTER
THIRTY-SEVEN

In the dust of headlights and the rantings of angry Puerto Rican drivers, Jack hopped the cyclone fence that bounded the highway and ran two blocks to the intersection where Abby's car had disappeared. There was no sign of her.

He used the VHF walkie-talkie and called Henry. Ten minutes later a large dark Mercedes pulled up at the intersection. Henry was in the passenger seat. One of his security men was driving, and Jess was in the back.

Jack climbed into the back seat next to his brother and the car sped off.

He had taken more lives than some serial killers; six people in all. Still Morgan didn't see himself in that way. One was an accident; the crewman on the *Cella Largo*. Two others were the moral equivalent of crushing cockroaches; Joey Jenrico and that leach of a husband Abby had married. Jack and Theresa were necessary. They knew too much.

The only real regret was Abby. He couldn't deny it. He loved her, bared his soul to her, and she had rejected him. He tried not to think about it and instead busied himself with the task at hand.

The secret was to use the minimum of materials. In this case, that meant two eight-foot lengths of detonating cord. The det-cord looked like heavy poly-plastic clothesline. But instead of nylon strands inside, it contained a seam of high explosives. It was flexible, extremely fast, and powerful. Wrapped around the base of a small tree and set off, it would sever the trunk in the flash of an eye without much noise.

Morgan used a linoleum knife, a wicked instrument with a short scimitarlike blade that was razor sharp. Carefully he cut a length of the cord and examined the water intake line that ran along the ship's plates.

The *Cuesta Verde* was old and rusted out. That she hadn't been delivered to the scrap yard years before was a testament to the owner's patience and the unusually high limits of their insurance policy.

He had agreed to perform this last job months earlier, before Abby's book shot through the roof on the list. Morgan no longer needed the money. He would have sidestepped the job if he could. But the owners of the *Cuesta Verde* were not the kind of people you crossed. They would become suspicious, start to wonder if maybe he was setting them up, perhaps working a sting with the insurance company. Morgan looked at the job as a kind of sending-off party, his final fling before retirement. The owners would make a killing on the insurance, and Spencer would quietly slip away to a new life of luxury, preferably in some cooler northern climate. Morgan mopped sweat from his brow as he considered Ireland. They had no income tax on writers, and with the money from the books he could probably afford a castle.

He wiped his gloved hand along the pipe looking for

lettering that indicated 'water.' The ship was so badly maintained that most of the markings on the pipes had long since worn off. Still there should be some indication. He grabbed a rag and wiped oil and dust from the surface of the metal. There was nothing. He was sure it was a raw water line for cooling the steam turbine. He had traced it to a point in the boiler room where it disappeared between the boilers and the inside of the hull.

He wrapped a single strand of det-cord around the large pipe three times. When it blew, the sea would flood the boiler room and the bilges below. There was fifty feet of water beneath the ship.

He looped the ends of the det-cord in a loose knot, then slipped an electrical detonating cap between the cord and the pipe.

He moved to the other side of the ship and repeated this process. This time the pipe was clearly marked as a water line by white lettering, chipped and faded but still visible. If it was done right, the two blasts would occur simultaneously. All that would be heard above decks was a sharp crack, nothing that could be described as an explosion.

Morgan took the drop wires, a hundred feet of number fourteen electrical wire. He attached the ends to the two detonators and retreated through a door in the bulkhead into another compartment near the boiler room.

Henry's driver took a circuitous route doing sixty down alleys and back streets. Jack could see the amber luminescence of old San Juan against the night sky as they approached. They took a wide, sweeping arc on two wheels around the plaza and stopped on Calle

Marina, directly in front of the cruise ship terminal.

There were two police cars parked at the curb, and between them was the blue Fairlane cab – but Abby wasn't in it.

Henry's car pulled up alongside and Ricardi got out. 'Let me handle it.'

The taxi driver was standing beside his vehicle being questioned by the cops. Henry approached them and identified himself.

The driver and Henry talked for a couple of minutes, then Henry returned to the Mercedes. He got in and looked over the back seat at Jack, knitted eyebrows and serious expressions.

'He says he dropped her off back by the warehouses on Fernandez Juncos. About a mile from here.'

'Did he see where she went?'

Henry shook his head. 'But he says she stopped to make a phone call before they got down here. He doesn't know who she called, but he heard her say something over the phone. Does the name *Cuesta Verde* mean anything to you?'

Jack shook his head.

'Nor to me,' said Henry. 'But it's what she was looking for. She asked the driver to take her to the warehouse district near the docks. He let her out and that's the last time he saw her.'

'A cargo ship?' said Jack.

'That would be my guess.'

Henry said something in Spanish to his driver and the Mercedes left rubber on the road. It took them less than two minutes.

The commercial waterfront area of San Juan was not large or sprawling. It covered only a few blocks and was dingy and poorly lit, with dilapidated metal buildings and no sidewalks. It was bounded by alleys with a lot of potholes and gravel.

Henry had his driver prowl these with their headlights on high beam looking for any sign of Abby. All they saw was a mangy dog, its eyes illuminated like amber in the headlights, and its ribs showing like washboards.

Most of the buildings sat behind cyclone fences with barbed wire or coils of razor wire on top.

They wound through alleys and up dead-end streets, but there was no sign of Abby. In fact, there was no one walking on the streets at all. At night this was no-man's-land.

Henry got on the car's cellular phone and made a call. A few seconds later he hung up and turned around to Jack in the backseat.

'There is a ship,' he said. 'The *Cuesta Verde*. It's waiting for repairs near the dry dock. Just over there.' He pointed down one of the dark alleys. Henry had called the harbor master's office.

Jack turned to Jess. 'Where's the bag?'

His brother handed it to him, and Jack looked inside. There was an old starlight scope and some tools inside.

'You keep looking,' he told Henry. 'Check all the streets.' Jack started to get out of the car.

'Not without me.' Jess followed him.

'One more thing,' said Henry.

Jack stood near the passenger window at the front of the car.

'Here, take this.' Henry handed him a matt-black semiautomatic pistol, a nine millimeter Beretta just like the one Jack was forced to leave in St Croix.

In Jack's grip it felt like an old friend.

'Thanks.' Then he and Jess disappeared down the dark alley toward the docks.

It had taken her almost a half hour, but Abby finally found a gate that was loosely chained. She threw the canvas bag over the top, then managed to squeeze her head and shoulders through the gate. She was struggling with the rest of her body when she saw headlights approaching the intersection a half-block away. Abby prayed that the car wouldn't turn into the alley. It didn't. Instead it stopped at the intersection.

Two men got out of the back seat and a chill raced up Abby's spine. One of them was Jack.

Abby pushed at the gate and strained to get through. They were talking to someone in the car. At any moment they would turn. She had time in the darkness, but only if she moved.

Abby caught her arm on a sharp piece of wire, flinched, and the gate rattled. She stopped for an instant, hoping they didn't hear her. Then she struggled, tore flesh, and finally pushed her way through.

The car was turning, its headlights making an arc toward the alley.

Abby got to her feet and ran. She literally dove into the shadows next to some pallets. She rolled onto her side and lay motionless on the ground. The lights surged over her like a cresting wave, then swept the area as the car continued its turn. In the inky darkness she got to her feet and ran.

She was forty feet from the gate behind some containers when she finally stopped and looked back. She pulled one of the blouses from the canvas bag, tore a portion of it, and wrapped the frayed cloth around her arm.

She was busy doing this when Abby heard the hollow wail of feet against cyclone fencing. She moved for position and saw them. Jack and the other man, bare

516

outlines in silhouette, scaled to the top of the fence. She heard metal snipping and a second later the four strands of barbed wire on top coiled away. Jack slipped silently over the fence and dropped down on the inside. He was joined a few seconds later by the other man. She had no idea how they'd found her. Maybe they were looking for Morgan.

They were close enough now that Abby could see their faces. It was Jess. Jack pulled something from the back of his pants and examined it in dull light. It was a pistol. He checked the clip, sliding it from the handle, then jammed it back in and pulled the slide, chambering a round.

Abby didn't need to see anything more. She disappeared into the shadows and huddled in the dark among pallets and metal containers. As they moved closer, she retreated to the other side of the pallets, out closer to the edge of the dock. She was running out of ground.

In the distance she could see the large concrete dry dock floating next to the pier. Just this side of it was a ship, and on the stern was the name *Cuesta Verde*. The paint was chipped and rusted. Abby watched as they approached from the fence. If they got between her and the vessel, she would be trapped on the dock.

She ran for the ship. Giving up cover she raced for the stairs leading from the dock up the side to the top deck. She hit the first step and her feet clattered on the expandable metal. Abby was afraid to look back. She had to find Morgan now, before they did.

Jack heard footfalls on metal and followed the sound. He cleared the corner of one of the large green steel containers, and for a fleeting instant he saw her. Abby was climbing the stairs. She ran across the scaffold at the top and disappeared through the gunnel and into the shadows on the deck.

Jess was behind him. He started to give chase and Jack grabbed him by the arm, held him still, and listened for footfalls on the deck above.

Jack knew that by the time they got there she could lose herself in a million places on the ship. They would have no idea where to look.

Now unless he missed his bet, Abby was getting close to Spencer. Jack could smell him, the acrid odor of death.

There was nothing but silence from the deck above.

Jack found a ladder propped against a stack of containers and silently climbed to the top. He crawled to a place where he had a vantage point down onto the deck of the ship, then fished in the bag and pulled out the cylindrical black tube. He removed the old starlight scope and began searching for thermal images on the deck.

Minutes passed in silence as Abby huddled in the dark. She was scared and alone, stalked by two armed men. She couldn't be sure that Morgan was even on the ship. For all she knew, she was there alone, facing death. If she showed herself, she knew that Jack and Jess would kill her in an instant, just like Jack had killed Theresa and Charlie.

Then she heard a whisper, raspy and harsh, like someone trying to shout but under his breath.

'Abby. Come out where I can see you.' It was Jack's voice.

'Listen, Abby. It was Spencer. He set fire to the house. Can you hear me?'

Several seconds passed in silence, Abby motionless in the dark.

'If you don't want to say anything, just give me a signal.' His voice was coming from out in the shadows, somewhere above her, looking down on the deck.

'Just give me a signal, Abby. Something I can see or hear. I can prove what I'm telling you is the truth. Give me a chance.'

He was lying. Abby knew it. Jack would tell her anything to get his hands on her. Then he would find Spencer and kill them both.

'Throw something. Toss something out. Anything. Just so that I know you can hear me.' His voice sounded so plaintive, so familiar, the same tones he had used when he told her that he loved her.

She thought about that warm day, the beach on St Croix, as they floated in the surf, Jack's arms around her, the feel of his lips on her neck and shoulders. How he could always make her laugh. Dancing with him on the terrace at the Buccaneer, the intimate moments they had spent, the things they had said to each other. Then she remembered Theresa's lifeless body on the gurney.

She saw something flash, the glint of light on glass. It came from the top of one of the giant steel containers on the dock. Abby retreated deeper into the shadows and the thought dawned: Jack had a scoped rifle. She would be dead in an instant if she stepped into the light. Abby would never hear the bullet that killed her.

She watched and listened, straining her ears for the slightest sound. There was only the rasping of her own breath. She remained huddled in the dark as minutes ticked away.

Abby fought the conflicting emotions of rage and fear. She was scared and shaking, but she was also furious, at herself for being so foolish to fall in love with Jack. He had murdered her best friend, and butchered Charlie. While she didn't have much use for Charlie, he didn't deserve to die that way. If Abby had a gun at that moment, she wouldn't have asked a single question or said a single word. She would simply have fired at the reflection of the glass on the container. She would have killed Jack without a second's hesitation, because he deserved to die. Rage boiled over in her and fed an adrenaline rush.

Suddenly there was clatter on the stairs, not footsteps but something else. Abby froze, listened for a moment, heard it again, and ran. She ran like the devil was after her. Any instant a bullet could rip through her body. She raced toward the front of the ship, toward the superstructure looming three stories above, and into the companionway that passed beneath it on the port side.

She tried several of the steel doors. They were locked and the latches bolted tight.

She heard muted footfalls behind her, turned and looked. They were coming, already at the top of the stairs, running. Suddenly she realized they were shoeless on the steel deck and much closer than she thought.

Abby raced down the companionway. Twenty feet on she found another door. This one was open. She stepped across the threshold and tried to close it but couldn't. She looked and saw the hook on the back, released it, and slammed the steel door shut an instant before Jack's hand reached the opening.

He would have yelled but Jack was afraid Spencer would hear him. They pounded with their hands against the hard steel and kicked at the door with bare feet.

Abby had managed to turn the friction handles on the

inside, sealing it tight. They fought with the latches and Jess managed to open the bottom two. Jack was having more trouble with the ones up top. It was as if they were spring loaded. Every time he got one open it would snap back to a locked position. He could feel her hanging on the metal latches from the inside, pulling down with every ounce of strength she could muster, leveraging the force of gravity to her advantage.

He tried to whisper through the door, a half-inch of steel, but it was useless. Either she couldn't hear, or didn't want to.

They fought with the handles and finally they got three of them open. They pushed on the door, but it wouldn't give, not with the last latch in place. Jack fought a losing battle. Somehow she had managed to jam it from the inside. The latch wouldn't budge. Jack gave up. 'Come on. Let's find another way in.' They headed down the companionway.

Spencer attached a set of the wires to one of the terminals on the battery and looked around for a good place to shield himself. Tempered steel was like glass. It could fracture into a million pieces and fly in as many directions.

He found an old mattress in one of the compartments and carried it to the area by the boiler room. He propped it against the bulkhead near the open door.

There was one last chore. Morgan was four levels deep in the ship, inside a dozen watertight doors. He wanted to make sure these were open not only to flood the ship but to secure a path of escape.

He climbed three levels and checked each door. He had worked his way to the outside, one level below the main deck, when he heard footsteps running along the companionway overhead. There wasn't supposed to be anyone on that level. They had assured him – only a skeleton crew on the bridge. Someone had screwed up. Quickly he headed back down.

Morgan had to move. He slid down the ladder, ran for the opening in the deck, and dropped quickly two more levels into the boiler room. He raced past the cold boilers, through the bulkhead door and the machine room, and into the small compartment where the mattress blocked the door.

There was no time to connect the detonating switch. He could hear someone descending from the ladder above. He grabbed the loose drop wires and touched them to the empty battery post. A spark arced from the battery, and an instant later a blast roared through the compartment, a flash of light, fire and smoke.

The explosion threw Morgan halfway across the room onto his back on the steel deck. For an instant he lay there dazed. The only thing that shielded him from the blast and flames was the mattress. It had saved his life. Instinct told him immediately what had happened.

Spencer had severed a fuel line. Barrels of bunker oil were blazing, mixing with sea water rushing into the forward compartment. He got to his feet, shielded his face from the flames that licked through the open doorway. He tried to close the steel door but couldn't. The pressure of incoming water and the heat from the burning oil forced him back. Flames floated on water over the threshold. Morgan retreated to the ladder and climbed for his life.

Abby lay sprawled on the hard steel deck. It was dark with the acrid odor of smoke. A klaxon echoed in her ears, its cadence in time with the flashing red light over the door, the one she had just jammed shut with the broom handle.

She was stunned, her senses paralyzed, mind numbed, as sensations of heat from the metal deck embraced her in the folds of its comforting warmth.

Slowly, in a daze, she dragged herself to her feet and stumbled to the door. She removed the broom handle and tried to turn the latch. It wouldn't move. The explosion had twisted the bulkhead and sprung the steel door in its frame. Abby was trapped.

There was only one way out: toward the smoke and the heat. She covered her face with her arm and headed into the darkness.

The blast caught Jess on the ladder and sent him sprawling to the bottom. He landed fifteen feet down on a steel catwalk and gripped his leg in agony. Excrutiating pain shot through his calf below the knee, and when he looked down he could see the jagged end of bone protruding through the flesh. It had ripped through his pant leg and blood was spurting.

Jack scrambled back along the catwalk to his brother and made a quick assessment. Jess was going into shock. Jack removed the belt from his pants and fashioned a tourniquet above the knee using the case from the starlight scope to turn it. He tied it off and raced back up the ladder.

On the outside deck he found a fire hose in a glass cabinet, smashed the glass, unreeled the hose, and dropped it back down the ladder. He flew down the rungs to his brother, lashed the hose under Jess's arms, and tied it off like a safety harness. It took him nearly three minutes to hoist his brother to the outside deck. All the while the ship was settling in the water. Flames

billowed from one of the stacks overhead. He propped
Jess against the railing, then lowered his head for shock.

'I've got to go back down to find Abby.'

'Go.' Jess waved him off. 'I'll be alright.' He was
breathing heavily but conscious.

Jack turned and headed back down the ladder.

Spencer entered an open metal bridge-work that
spanned the area over the boilers. Flames floated on
water and had risen halfway up the boilers. He started
across the bridge.

'Morgan.' The voice seemed almost etherial. It came
from somewhere above, surreal, something from the
grave.

For an instant Spencer actually thought he might be
dead. Heat waves wafted off the plates of the giant ship.
Maybe this was hell.

He turned and looked up. There on the ladder,
descending, was Abby. He rubbed his eyes and fear took
hold. Apparitions from beyond the veil. She was coming
to claim retribution. Her face was covered with soot.
Her hands were bleeding and her clothes were singed.
She dropped from the ladder and he grabbed her,
almost as if in a reflex. Morgan was stunned. She was
flesh and bone.

She hung on him, her arms draped around his neck as
she tried to catch her breath. The air over the boilers was
filling with smoke. It was stiffling and fouled with the
odor of burning oil.

'How did you find me?' It was all Morgan could think
to say.

'I found the ship. The message on the phone.
Remember?'

The look on Morgan's face said that he did. The

question now was what to do with her. He looked over the edge of the railing at the burning cauldron below and considered the possibilities.

'We've got to get out of here,' said Abby. 'He's up there.'

'Who?'

'Jack. He must have done something to the ship.'

Morgan quickly forgot the raging flames below. 'Right.' He tried to take it all in. More mistakes in a week than he'd made in a lifetime; missing Abby and Jack at the house and now a fire.

'He's armed,' said Abby. 'He has a pistol. I saw it. Maybe a rifle, I don't know.' Morgan had a faraway look. She wasn't sure he was hearing any of this.

'You think he did the explosions?' said Abby.

'Must have.' It was as if Morgan was trying to figure things out. 'Right now we've got to move.' He grabbed her hand roughly and dragged her across the steel bridge that spanned the boiler room two levels up.

There was a burning inferno at the bottom of the ship and the flames were rising, a floating hell. The heat was nearly unendurable. Torrid waves of air coursed up from the boiler room as the searing temperatures penetrated the layers of Abby's clothing. The rubber soles of her shoes went soft as gum starting to melt. It was like running on a griddle.

They raced across the bridge and through an open door. Morgan stopped and closed it behind them to seal off the heat. He swung one of the latches closed.

Abby screamed.

When Spencer turned he saw Jack. He was standing six feet away at the foot of a ladder, the only way out. Jack reached for the Beretta and pulled it from the back of his pants. He aimed it at Morgan.

'Abby, step over here.' He was watching Morgan's hands every second. Taking a double-hand hold on the pistol, his eye aligning the sights on Morgan's chest.

Spencer moved behind Abby until a part of her head was framed in the front sight.

Jack moved a few inches, searching for an angle of fire if he needed it. They did a deadly minuet.

'Listen to me. Get away from him.'

Abby froze.

'Don't move.' Morgan was behind her, his hands on her shoulders as if for support.

'You don't understand. He tried to kill you on the island,' said Jack. 'It was Spencer who blew up the house.'

'Put the gun down, Jack. There's no need for this.' Abby tried to reason with him.

'If I put it down, he'll kill us both,' said Jack.

'You're sick, Jack. You need help. The police will understand.'

Morgan got up in her ear and whispered, 'You're right. He's out of his mind.'

'What's he saying?' Jack waved the point of the pistol as if he was trying to move them apart.

'I'm telling her to stay calm. Don't you think we should all get out of here?' Morgan looked over the edge of the railing. So far the flames had been confined to the forward area behind the bulkhead. But the metal plates were creaking, expanding. Morgan knew that any second the ship could explode. His grip became firmer on Abby's shoulders until they began to hurt.

'Abby, listen to me. I have proof.' Jack took one hand off the gun and tried to unfold the piece of paper from the envelope, but it wouldn't come. Heat from the ship's bulkhead was turning the area on the catwalk into an oven.

'Help me.' Jack held out the paper, but she wouldn't move toward him.

'Don't go. Stay still,' said Morgan.

'Don't listen to him. He tried to kill both of us at the house,' said Jack.

'He's sick.' Morgan was feeling the heat as it radiated off the plates of steel. 'He would tell you anything, Abby, anything to get you over there. Then he would kill you. He murdered Theresa and Joey, slashed Charlie's throat. You can't believe anything he says.'

In that instant as Jack's gaze met hers, Abby knew. It was in the aspect of his eye and the crooked angle of his head as if Jack were saying, 'See, there it is.' He held out the paper, but Abby didn't need it. How would Morgan know Charlie's throat was cut – unless he did it himself?

She tensed and he felt it. Suddenly Morgan realized what he'd said. In a single fluid movement he brought the glint of steel from the inside of his boot to Abby's throat. The razor-sharp blade of the linoleum knife, its needlelike point drew a pimple of blood from her neck.

'Move and I'll kill her. I mean it,' said Morgan. 'I didn't want to do this, but you forced it.' He was talking to Abby, a scolding father, the blade to her throat. 'You wouldn't listen to me. I tried to warn you. I told you he was no good. But you wouldn't believe me.'

Imperceptibly, leaning, Jack edged a few inches sideways on the catwalk, angling for a shot.

Morgan saw him and adjusted. He pulled Abby into Jack's line of sight. 'I swear I'll kill her.'

'Is that how you did it with Charlie?' she said.

'It was more than he deserved. He never knew what hit him. He didn't feel a thing,' said Morgan. 'There was no pain. No suffering. He would have bled you dry. You're a lovely woman, Abby, but you have lousy taste in men.'

'Almost as bad as my taste in friends.' She tried to pull away from him, but Morgan pushed the blade tighter to the flesh of her neck and she stopped.

'Throw the gun over here.'

'Not a chance,' said Jack.

'I'll kill her if you don't.'

'You'll kill her if I do. This way I get the pleasure of blowing your ass over the railing the second you move,' said Jack.

Morgan knew he meant it. Mexican stand-off. The heat was rising.

'If we stay here we're all gonna fry,' said Morgan.

'Throw the knife over and let her go,' said Jack.

The steel around them creaked.

It came from the bowels of the ship, the deep roar of an explosion that shook the vessel to its keel. One of the main fuel tanks. It lifted the three of them off their feet and dropped them onto the expanded steel of the catwalk like sacks of cement. Morgan hit the metal first.

Jack landed on one shoulder and the pistol bounced on the catwalk and slid. A second explosion racked the ship and Abby slipped over. She dangled by fingers on the edge of the catwalk, hand slipping.

Jack clung to the grating of the catwalk and lashed out with one arm reaching for her. Caught her by a wrist, sliding to hands, sweaty palms, he held tight.

The steel walls below them buckled. Flames and water poured into the level below as Jack struggled to get another hand on Abby's arm. He swung her like a pendulum once, twice. Her leg hooked the edge of catwalk and Jack pulled her up onto the grating, her bare arms hitting the searing steel.

'You should have let her go.' Morgan was standing there, looking at them, holding the pistol trained on Jack.

Abby rolled a few inches over onto something hard on the expanded metal, and buried it under her side.

'Get up. On your feet.' Morgan started to wheel around, toward the ladder where Jack had come down.

They looked at the pistol. The safety was off. One shudder from the ship and it would go off.

'Move,' said Morgan. 'Or I'll kill you both right where you are.'

Jack got to his knees and stood. He helped Abby to her feet. She held one wrist to her chest as if there was something wrong with it. Together they inched their way around toward the closed bulkhead door. The one Morgan had secured with a single latch.

Abby could hear the steel around them expand with heat, creaking under the pressure of water and fire. She heard the hiss of hot metal and the vibrations of the ship as it came apart. The *Cuesta Verde* was going down.

'Move,' said Morgan. 'Now.'

Jack and Abby took a few more steps until they were in the corner, near the hinges of the iron door.

Morgan looked up. There was another watertight door on the level above. He could leave them, close it, and they would die in a blazing tomb, a solution to all of his problems.

Spencer got to the foot of the ladder, one hand up.

'If he gets there, we're dead,' Jack whispered in Abby's ear.

'I know.' She looked down at her chest and Jack saw it, the shiny glint of steel concealed between her wrist and the tattered cloth over her breast. She followed

Jack's eye to the sealed latch on the door.

'It didn't have to be this way.' Morgan looked at her, and with the pistol in one hand he started to climb.

Jack made a move. Morgan pointed the pistol right at him and Jack froze.

Morgan looked back for the next rung on the ladder and began to reach for it. Just as he did, Abby grabbed the blade of the linoleum knife between two fingers and flung it at him.

It was a reflexive action. Morgan moved a hand off the ladder to ward off the flashing blade of the knife, and for an instant he was suspended in midair.

Jack grabbed Abby with one arm, pulled her into the corner behind the steel door, and with the other he jerked the searing steel of the latch.

The superheated air of the boiler room expanded with an explosive force. The door shot open like a cannon. A dragon's tongue of fire lashed the catwalk incinerating everything in sight, catching Morgan in mid-flight and turning him into a human torch.

Screaming, in flames, he fell from the ladder, pulling off rounds from the pistol. They ricocheted off steel as Jack embraced Abby in his arms behind the shield of the iron door.

Morgan raced toward the railing of the catwalk, his body fully engulfed in flames, his brain ablaze. He plunged over the edge and into the swirling flame-filled water pouring into the ship.

Jack kicked the door closed, then tearing strips from his shirt he wrapped his hands and sealed the latch. He gave Abby strips of cloth to wrap her hands and they climbed the ladder.

Water was rising fast behind them. By the time they reached the open deck it was lapping at the bottom of the railing near Jess. Jack grabbed him by one arm. Abby took the other and they eased him over the side.

As they cleared the ship they could see the lights of the Mercedes on the dock, and police cars around it. Henry and one of his security men were running toward a wooden ladder that ran down from the wharf.

The salt water burned as it found every cut and burn on Abby's body. They floated among the debris and watched the flames as they raged beneath the surface of the harbor fed by air trapped in the compartments of the *Cuesta Verde*.

EPILOGUE

A bby and Jack sat quietly, relaxing at a sidewalk table in Fairhaven a block from Village Books. They were far enough away that no one seemed to notice, just two tourists sitting and talking. Today there was a lot of excitement in the village. Fairhaven was the historic section of Bellingham, not far from the Canadian border in western Washington.

Portions of Abby's big book were set here, and now scenes for the film were being shot just a few blocks away. There were cameras and trucks, and most of the people were busy gawking.

The producers had hired Abby as a consultant. They now knew the truth, and so did Bertoli. It didn't seem to matter.

Today she had come to autograph books. Lines were wrapped around the block. Abby's sequel was out in hardcover.

She and Jack were the hottest story in America, but not for the reasons that she'd planned. It was Morgan's effort to claim the book, the calculated murders, and his attempt on their lives that made it front-page news from coast to coast. No doubt audiences warmed to Jack's good looks, but their attention was riveted by the age-old forces that invariably weld curiosity to any story: a fascination with the tempest of violence and the forces that drive it. With all of Abby's meticulous planning, fate still played the trump card.

For the first time in her life Abby walked in the publishing sunlight, acknowledged as the author of her own work, Jack the rugged face on the dustcover standing beside her. The story of how they did it now assumed mythic proportions in the press, boosting sales to record highs, levels beyond Bertoli's wildest dreams. The book showed no signs of coming off the list. It swept the globe. Foreign sales were soaring. The novel had been translated into seventeen languages, and the numbers were growing. *Gable Cooper* was a brand-name.

Bertoli, in a master stroke of marketing, delayed publication of the paperback for Abby's first book and instead brought out the hardcover of the sequel. The two novels would now duel toe-to-toe for the top spot on the hardcover bestsellers list.

And yet with all of her success, it was a bitter-sweet moment. Morgan was right about one thing. Theresa had died because of the manuscript. She was in the way. She knew too much. Morgan had to get rid of her.

Jack lifted his cup and sipped. After nine months his hands still showed some signs of scarring from the white hot metal of the bulkhead door. His thick mane of dark hair floated in the breeze. It was one of those bucolic days on the Sound, what the natives had called the Salish Sea; wafting currents of salt-tinged air.

'I don't know if I told you. Sanfillipo called,' said Jack. 'They found your typewriter.'

Abby lifted her gaze from the surface of the table where she was lost in thought.

'It was in a small storage shed,' said Jack. 'Morgan rented it under a false name. They found everything. The forged contracts, certified copies of the copyright.'

The police actually found it two months earlier but had sealed the evidence until their investigation was complete. They also discovered the outline, the one Abby was sure Jack had taken from her desk that night in the islands. They found it in a hotel room in San Juan, along with Morgan's briefcase and a suitcase filled with his clothes.

'Why did he do it?'

'Seven million dollars is a strong incentive,' said Jack.

Abby shook her head. She could never bring herself to accept the obvious answer.

She wondered if Morgan had made the decision that very first day, when he discovered *she* was Gable Cooper. Sitting in his office looking at her across that vast gulf that separated them, did Spencer somehow realize what she did not; that the book was more than a dream, that it had a destiny. Perhaps he was grasping for the last straw of the desperate soul, a man beyond the pale of his career. For all of the violence, Abby knew in her heart that Morgan loved her. She was sure that he had pitched into that fiery grave knowing it himself.

Abby could not help but dwell on the chain of fury that she'd set in motion. It was a violence born of unrequited love, a senseless lashing out at the things that hurt him. At Charlie who had once possessed her and Jack who now did, but most of all at Abby, because she never understood his need.

There was evidence that Morgan had been burning his clients' own ships for some time to keep the wolf from his door, pyrotechnic skills he employed on Abby's beach house. This was something the police had now confirmed.

The registration of copyright, the document that Morgan made out in his own name, now languished, as Abby had originally intended, in the bureaucratic dustbin of the copyright office. It was not likely anyone would ever look for it again.

In the flush of excitement, Bertoli never noticed when Abby scrapped the outline to her sequel, and instead crafted a substitute.

Jack left a tip on the table and they headed down the street toward the crowds milling in front of the bookstore. As they drew closer, scores of curious eyes took a bead. Then there were hushed whispers, and a subtle motion rippled through the line like a Chinese dragon. People further back stepped out of line to get a glimpse. It was like a crafts fair for the famous; the star of the movie on one street, Jack and Abby on the other.

There were whispers and a few screams as the two of them came into view. Then quickly they were escorted past the crowd and through the door.

Inside there were stacks of books, windows piled high, everything Abby had ever written. On the table in front of her was the sequel. It bore the name Gable Cooper on the cover, and Abby's picture on the back, Jack's rugged countenance beside her, a partnership bound by love.

It was the story of a down-and-out writer, a woman approaching her middle years who crafted the novel of a lifetime, a terror-ridden tale in which she used a handsome and dangerous male face to sell her novel, a book entitled – *The List*.